BUILDING JERUSALEM

Thomas Wood

"I will not cease from Mental Fight,
Nor shall my sword sleep in my hand:
Till we have built Jerusalem,
In England's green and pleasant Land."

From "*Jerusalem*" by William Blake.

In loving memory of Morag

South Yorkshire Late 1984

'*What the fuck got into 'em today?'*

Alan looked up. It was the balding guy speaking, one of the pickets who'd come down from Shirebrook he thought, and now with the beginnings of a massive black eye, Tony maybe, but in the van he'd been too focussed on the pain in his own head to pay that much attention to what was going on around him.

'*Fuckin' cunts.*' A younger lad. No visible injuries but the awkward way he shifted his position on the bench suggested he'd taken a battering too. '*The bastards smashed my windscreen. One of them just walked up to my car and ...*'

'*At least they stopped beating us once they'd got us in the station.*' Someone to Alan's right but it was too painful to turn and look.

'*Aye. Those bastards from the Met are going to kill somebody someday soon.*'

Alan pressed the palm of his hand gently against the wound above his right ear then held it out in front of him. That bleeding seemed to have stopped at least. Fuck. This was the worst day yet for him, and these were Yorkshire police; he didn't want to think how he'd cope with the Londoners' attentions.

The man who might have been Tony broke the silence again.

'*I could murder a pint.*' Someone had the decency to laugh.

'*I could murder a fucking copper,*' said the younger one. Somehow Alan didn't think that was going to happen. Despite everything, the revolution was a long way off yet, but the lad was getting an education.

'Where you from?' Alan asked. It turned out he was local and one of the strike breakers was a neighbour of his.

'He was in my house last week. Thursday. Sitting across the table from me with a cup of tea. This far apart. As far as you are from me now.'

'What makes someone turn like that, give up on ... How...' But he had no more words. Another time Alan would have known what to say by way of reassurance, but not today, not in this battered state.

Outside the cell someone started shouting, 'He needs a fucking doctor. Get him a fucking...' The voice died, cut off in an instant by a blow they could only imagine. Eyes met but what was there to say?

Alan looked down between his knees at the blood, some of it his, some of it other people's, smeared across the floor at his feet. There had been something very different about today. The usual pushing and shoving before the bus had gone through with the half dozen or so scabs, and some said most of them weren't really miners, just people brought in to sit on the bus and make it look like the strike was crumbling. Certainly not enough men to bring up any coal. A few bricks thrown for sure. But this wasn't Nottingham anymore. This was Yorkshire. This was their own now. Then some sort of commotion had started right by the gates. No one around him had paid much attention to begin with, people were chatting about this and that, one or two had started heading back to their cars, but the shouting had got louder and suddenly there were people running. Moments later the police were everywhere, lashing out left and right without any apparent reason. People were going down, then being hit again as they tried to get up. He'd fled down an alley only to meet two policemen coming the other way and that had been that. He'd

2

put his hands up in front of him, part surrender, part defence, and from that point on it was, so far as he could recall, a succession of beatings, of greater or lesser intensity, accompanied by shouts of 'Commie bastard,' and so on until he was thrown into a police van with a dozen other, equally bewildered, pickets.

'How about you mate?'

Alan looked up.

'Where are you from?' It was Tony.

'Thurcroft. I'm an electrician.'

'Still solid there?'

'Pretty much. There's been a few from out of the village gone back and one with a mortgage to pay. We'll hold the line.'

The thick, grey metal door of the cell swung open and a policeman in shirtsleeves, who must have been six foot four, stepped in. He pointed at Alan.

'You. Get out here.'

Immediately half a dozen voices started up. 'How long... 'What time do we ...' 'I need to speak ...' The man paid no attention, not to the questions, and not to the evident difficulty Alan was having getting up from the bench. When he saw Alan was on the move he simply looked at the wall above their heads and waited till Alan got himself out into the corridor before locking the door behind them. Sealed off from the voices of his fellow pickets by the thickness of the cell door Alan felt suddenly alone. Still without speaking the policeman indicated the direction and Alan stumbled towards the stairway, resting his arm against the wall from time to time when the dizziness got too much. But at the staircase the officer relented and gave Alan an arm. And from the top of the stairs he continued to help him the short distance along

3

the corridor to an empty interview room where, almost gently now, he helped Alan take his seat at a bare metal table. Alan heard the door close behind him and a key turn in the lock.

Minutes passed. He guessed they were trying to unnerve him. That wasn't going to work. It had been a long time since he'd found himself in this situation but he was still too much of an old hand to let a bit of waiting trouble him. Even so when they finally came for him he was a little unsettled by the fact that neither of them were uniform. As he watched them walk past him round the table and take their seats he tried to size them up. One was a well-built figure with dark sunken eyes and a world weary air. When he spoke his accent was local. Probably special branch.

'This doesn't look too good for you son. You've got previous. And now resisting arrest. The mood the magistrates are in right now that's six months easy. Don't even think about bail.'

'I want a lawyer. Now.' He was mildly curious to know how they'd got his file so quickly but it didn't surprise him. So many phones were bugged now. He wondered whether his own phone was tapped. Had they listened to everything he had said, to his wife, to his children? Would he be sitting round the table with them tonight, would ...

He tried to bring his focus back to the present. The second man was speaking now. Older, with a hint of grey in his brownish hair. Posh too. Or trying to sound posh. And not like a policeman. Instead he adopted the tone of someone so assured of their own reasonableness they are almost embarrassed by the need to explain themselves.

'Alan. You'll understand the pressure we're under in the present political climate. The powers that be see this strike as

4

the work of left-wing wreckers and anything we can do to help create that impression is going to go down very well with our... political masters. You and I know it's much more complicated than that. But the fact is you are precisely the sort of person they want in the dock and right now. However, if you can help us...' He paused, as if to let the unfortunate truth sink in. 'You see...'

Alan was hardly listening but he got the gist of what he was being offered. And his mind went back to the young man in the cell, sold out by his neighbour, and he thought of all other bloodied men down there he was being asked to betray and he was overcome by a sudden, unfocussed rage.

'Fuck you. You know I never punched anyone that day. And you know I never resisted arrest. And you can take whatever filthy deal you're thinking of and shove it up your collective fucking arses.' This was a war. And they were going to win it, whatever the cost.

The younger man bristled but his colleague remained entirely calm.

'Take your time to think it over Alan. And I'm afraid you will have plenty of that. But we can be very helpful. In the right circumstances.' Then he looked at his colleague, nodded very slightly and the two of them got up and left without another word.

After another minute or two the same policeman as before came in to collect him and together they made their way down the corridor until they had to move to one side to allow a group of four men to pass. The first two were senior officers of some sort listening to a smaller man in a suit talking too fast for him to follow in his current state, and behind them a taller figure, not in uniform... Alan looked again. He knew that face... Where did he know it from? His mind was clouded

5

by pain and by the stress of the interview. He knew he wasn't thinking clearly but he knew that face should not have been there.

CHAPTER ONE

London 2007

David was just bored now. Almost sixty but capable of passing for fifty perhaps. A full head of hair, still mostly black but greying around the temples, an averagely handsome face, a little jowly but lived in, not ruined. And, for someone of his age, still powerfully built. He got up from his desk, the desk he had occupied for the last four years now, walked over to the window and looked out across the river. He'd miss this view. The stately, timeless ebb and flow of the tide, the double decker busses crossing Lambeth Bridge, the medieval brickwork of Lambeth Palace half concealed behind the plane trees; not much you wouldn't see in a World War II movie; if you half closed your eyes. The most significant blot on this landscape, and so far off to the right you could almost ignore it, was the hideous rectangular yellow headquarters of SIS squatting on the opposite bank by Vauxhall Bridge. "The Swindon Office"; though that was what they called MI5 too apparently. His boss Nigel loved going over there for meetings, loved having them round, but David didn't share his enthusiasm. Too many supercilious public school boys indulging their imperial fantasies by cosying up to the Americans, blundering round the Middle East like it was a game of Risk and leaving MI5 to pick up the pieces.

'Don't complain David, it keeps us in work,' Nigel had said on one occasion. Work. You haven't picked your way through the inside of a crowded pub after a bomb has gone off, David didn't reply. Looking for someone you knew. And finding bits of them.

His thoughts were interrupted by a mocking voice from the other side of the room. 'Truly the end of an era,' Manjit called out, prompted by the emailed reminder for David's leaving drinks. Turbaned and neatly bearded but speaking accentless English. Only David knew he gave a significant slice of his income to his Gurdwara, a confidence Manjit had only shared after five, or maybe six pints of Kronenbourg. David had worked with him for three years now and was still surprised by how young he looked.

'Who'll be left to tell us about the old days now?' Manjit looked across the room at David.

'There's one or two others left.'

'Not on this floor,' said Manjit.

'That's a bit below the belt.' David smiled. His few remaining contemporaries in the building had long since risen to grades far more senior than his and now occupied offices several floors above. And with the influx of recruits after 9/11 there were so many faces he didn't recognise it no longer felt like the organisation he had joined so many years ago. It was time to go.

'You know I've always respected your willingness to speak truth to power.' Manjit continued, pushing his chair back from his desk. 'No one has ever articulated the fatuousness of forward job plans in our line of business more convincingly than you. Or more publicly. No David. You can leave this building with your integrity intact and your head held high. Albeit as a humble deputy assistant director.'

'You're still young. You can get out. Go and do corporate security for some multi-national corporation at three times the salary.'

'But I still have my ideals.'

'Have I taught you nothing these last three years.'

Manjit grinned. 'From 4.30?'

'Yeah. And come early. I don't want to be stuck there with just Peter Finchley and that nob he hangs out with from IT security for the first hour and a half.'

'Derek Stephens. I'll spare you that. And there'll be a good crowd. Like I say, it's the end of an era. Big day. There might even be a Deputy Director or two.'

'Fuck off.'

There was nothing to do now except wait. The paperwork surrounding his "early retirement" had finally been signed off. He was leaving only two months early but a juggling of budgets meant that while he didn't lose out the team could somehow afford another Arabic translator till the end of the financial year. And the casework handover procedures had all been completed yesterday. Access to all his files had been now granted to the case officers taking them over, with the result that since noon he had been locked out of the system. And nine times out of ten the new caseworker was the already overworked Manjit. He trusted Manjit; to work out which leads to follow up, to deflect the panicked priorities of management and, as near as possible in this imperfect world, to squeeze a little justice out of the material they had to work with. Catch some villains, save some lives and minimise the collateral damage. These last few years minimising the collateral damage was often as much as he had hoped for.

He'd even contemplated including it on his forward job plan the year before, but Manjit had dissuaded him. 'Not if you hold out any hope of picking up a bit of consultancy work after you're gone.' So he'd bitten his tongue, dreamt up another "challenging objective" and allowed the process to wash over him.

His thoughts were interrupted by the arrival of Nigel. Ten years his junior, and his boss for the last four. A slight, dapper man with a very shiny, very bald head ringed by a band of neatly oiled brown hair. Undeniably efficient. Undeniably ambitious. Occasionally human.

'David, I just want to check a few dates with you. Make sure I get the facts right.' Oh Jesus, he was going to make a speech.

'When exactly were you in Northern Ireland?'

'April 1974 to September 1979.'

'And how long were you in F Branch?'

''72 to '74, then the mid '80's, I forget the exact dates.'

'And now you're on the front line in the War on Terror. What a career. Listen, if you can think of any amusing anecdotes email them to me and I'll see if I can work them in. I'll hope to get there at around 6.00 but there's a meeting with the FCO at 5.00 about … well, not your problem any more… so I might be a little late. Don't get too plastered before then,' and he laughed uncomfortably. 'It won't be the same…'

'I thought we'd stopped calling it the War on Terror,' said Manjit after he had gone.

David didn't respond. They hadn't had these sorts of vacuous slogans when he'd started. None of these "Values." He looked at the wording on his mouse mat.

"Teamwork.

10

Working as one as MI5, bringing together in common purpose the best that everyone can give, supporting colleagues and treating each other with respect, and forging close partnerships and teams with others we depend upon."

It wasn't even a fucking sentence. No. They'd had... Scruffy offices with walls made of bricks. People had smoked at work, there had been ashtrays everywhere, tweed jackets, an older generation who'd paid their dues in North Africa and Normandy. Or Burma. Ex-colonial policemen with their tales of chasing communists in locations so much more exotic than the docks of Liverpool or Cardiff. The Sudan Souls. The Malay Mafia. There had been Provo's, the Soviets, revolutionary socialists. A tolerance of eccentricity. Not to mention long, boozy lunches. That was all gone now. And in its place was management-speak, shiny glass offices and computers. 'Our coloured cousins', as Paddy McClintock used to call them, doing casework. Less racism certainly. And a whole new generation who acted like this was an episode of Spooks and who looked far, far too young for this kind of world. And it was a long time too since he had felt fear. Real, gut-wrenching, am I going to die a slow and messy death, stomach crushing fear. He turned to the window again and looked back down at the river. The tide was nearly out now and a handful of gulls, crows and pigeons were shuffling about to little apparent purpose on the stony shoals each side of the retreating waters.

Manjit was right. A lot of people had made the effort and the upstairs room at the Marquis of Granby was becoming uncomfortably full. Noisy too, with the echoes of a dozen conversations bouncing off the dark, wood-panelled walls.

11

Pretty much the whole of his team, except Ned, whose wife had just had a baby, and he'd come over specially to apologise before disappearing to catch his train. Characters from across the office plus several recent and even not so recent retirees. Tony, who'd been in Northern Ireland with him for three years and a couple of the old lags from F Section. David was touched and found himself, to his surprise, looking forward to the rest of the evening. For now he was chatting to Nick Simmons, the sole representative from SIS and one of the few spooks he actually liked. David wondered if he had been sent to fly the flag or whether he had actually chosen to be there.

'I know we had our differences but ... you were never less than professional,' Nick offered. Nick fitted the SIS mould. A well fitting suit, a plain maroon tie, smartly polished brogues. His receding hair, small nose and rounded features were superficially unremarkable but beneath the upper middle class sheen there was a toughness and a realism born of several years bitter field work in West Africa.

'I don't think that's true,' David replied and Nick laughed.

'Maybe not,' Nick conceded. 'But ...'

'If you lot had had the balls to say there was no good evidence of WMD...' It was on the subject of terrorism that their paths had crossed and David had crossed swords with some of Nick's colleagues.

'Some of us tried. Who do you think was briefing Gilligan?'

'Yeah. That worked... or if that tit Goldsmith had had the balls to say the invasion wasn't legal we wouldn't be in this mess,' David continued, and they both looked down in silence for a moment or two.

'Dark times,' said Nick. 'And I don't think it's going to get better any time soon. You're probably doing well to get out. Got any plans?'

'Bird watching.'

'I didn't know you were a twitcher.'

'A recent convert.' He paused for a moment. 'There's a bird reserve down the road from me. I've driven past it thousands of times without going in but they had an open day a couple of months ago and I went and had a look round. A really interesting young man showed us round and I thought I'm going to need something to keep me out of mischief. And it's like most things, the more you look into it the more interesting it gets.' David could feel himself losing conviction but he persevered. 'Did you know that female cuckoos will only lay eggs in the nests of the species they were raised in, but male cuckoos can mate with any female, regardless of which species raised them?'

'I have to confess I didn't.' Nick didn't pursue the subject. Instead he asked, 'Any work lined up?'

'Nigel hinted at the possibility. I could use the money really. What with...' A divorce, a misjudged house sale ... 'Would your lot have anything?'

'I'm afraid David that even if they did...' They both knew David was mostly joking. 'Any idea what Nigel had in mind?'

'Not really.' He did actually but the habit of not giving anything away, particularly to SIS, was too deeply ingrained. Yesterday morning Nigel had called him into one of the glass walled meeting rooms which lined the open plan area they worked in and asked if he would be willing to come back for a few weeks. 'It's probably nothing but our American cousins have some concerns they want looked at.' He'd said no more and because Nigel was always so keen to please the higher powers David had been unable to tell whether the nervousness he picked up on was simply the man's eagerness to impress US intelligence or whether there was something deeper in play.

Rather than share any of these concerns he asked Nick how much longer he thought he'd stay in the game, but before Nick had a chance to answer their conversation was interrupted by the arrival of Nigel.

'Good to see you Nick. Just you tonight?'

'Yes, just me. Everyone else was too scared of what David might say on a night he had nothing left to lose.'

'I'm not sure David ever lets what he has to lose influence what he says. Not in my experience anyway. Well David, I've got a short speech prepared, but nothing too fulsome. I wouldn't want to embarrass you. When would be a good moment?'

'The sooner the better I guess,' said David, trying to hide his lack of enthusiasm. 'The drunker people get the harder it'll be to get them to keep quiet.'

'You're probably right.' Nigel hesitated for a moment then looked around for some means of getting people's attention. Finally he took his mobile phone out of his jacket pocket and started to bang its metal rim against the side of an empty pint glass.

'Good evening everyone,' he said loudly, and the volume of chatter started to fade. 'We're here to mark a very, very special occasion.' He waited until the remaining conversations had subsided. 'We're here to mark the departure, after many years of dedicated service, of one of our longest serving officers, David Nixon. It's been my pleasure to manage David for the last four years, if you can

14

call it "manage". But he built his reputation many years before that, when I was still in short trousers. More or less. It's hard to imagine now, thank goodness, but there was a time in the early 1970s when the stability of this country was seriously threatened by extremists on the hard left and we needed people like David to step up to the plate and confront some of these organisations, to carry out, well I don't have to tell you... to carry out the sort of operations necessary to ensure the hard left did not prevail and that this country was not dragged down into some sort of Orwellian socialist quagmire...'

That took him back. To the mid seventies. To long months in northern towns living on baked beans and potatoes and not much else, the endless meetings. Power cuts, marches, and slogans, the constant sense of menace...

'But that isn't where David really made his reputation. That was later on in Ulster, in the darkest times, when Paddy looked like he was going to keep going for ever; even I remember that sense that the killing was never going to stop. And it was people like David who stood firm, who did what had to be done to put Paddy firmly back in his box and give us the peace that, touch wood,' he tapped the table next to him, 'seems finally to have arrived.'

Did what had to be done. Jesus. Like blackmailing a terrified kid into informing on his neighbours, even his family. Like fetching Jimmy Doyle's body out of a ditch in Armagh and trying not to think how many hours of unspeakable agony lay behind the burn marks on his body. God ...

By the time David started listening again Nigel had moved on to wishing him a long and happy retirement. The room echoed to the noise of drunken applause and then, from behind the tables which had been pushed to one end of the

15

room, there emerged a succession of boxes and cards. The presents were mostly bird themed, a couple of books and a CD of birdsong. And then, as the crowd hushed, Ginny, the team's long standing administrative assistant, brought out a rectangular package wrapped in striped yellow and pink paper.

'Thank you Ginny.' She smiled. She was an only child, now in her early fifties, with a mother in serious decline and no one to share the burden with. He was one of the few team members who bothered to really talk to her and he reckoned she would miss him when he was gone.

With the eyes of the whole room upon him he tried to get the paper off carefully but still managed to rip it enough to make it unusable. And inside, as he had more or less guessed, was a spotting scope, and one that he knew from his own researches was far from cheap. He looked up at the faces ringed around him and smiled.

'Thank you very much. This is very generous of you all.' He paused and somebody shouted 'Speech!'

'You wouldn't want that. I'll just say. Thank you all for coming. And thanks for your kind words Nigel. Keep up the good work.' Everyone applauded. 'And don't let the bastards grind you down.' There were one or two cheers before people settled back into their conversations.

Terry came over to him, one of the F section veterans, three years into retirement and looking good on it. Clasped in his hands were three or four empty glasses, all due for a refill. 'Not a bad speech as these things go. Covered all the bases. You've certainly earned your rest.'

'God, it all seems so long ago now. A different world. When you look back do you sometimes find it hard to believe it all happened?'

'I wrote so many reports in those days I think it's etched into my soul David. No, I don't think I'll ever write my memoirs but,' and he tapped his head, 'it's all pretty clear up here. For the time being.' And he tapped his head again. 'Touch wood. Can I get you a beer?'

David eyed his half pint and hesitated for a moment. 'No, I'm fine for now thanks. Maybe later.'

As Terry continued on his way towards the bar David caught Manjit's eye and made his way over to where he was standing with a slim, dark haired woman David knew by sight.

'David, this is Esther. I worked with her on operation CREVICE before I joined your team.'

'How do you do.' There was a sparkle in her eyes but he tried to put out of his mind any thoughts of sexual interest. At his age it was ridiculous.

'Hi. I hope you don't mind my coming along. Manjit has talked a lot about you.'

'Not a lot,' Manjit said. 'But we were discussing the appraisal system and it was sort of inevitable.'

'Manjit told us a bit about your time in Ireland too,' Esther said. 'The boys all think that stuff is really cool, but it sounds pretty grim to be honest.'

'Grim is about right. I wouldn't want to go through all that again.'

'So you're not going to spend your retirement writing your memoirs?'

'I don't think so. Even if they'd let me.'

'Too many dark secrets?'

He knew he shouldn't be reading the teasing as flirtation. 'One or two.' He paused a moment. 'The biggest difference between now and then is that… the people we are after now, don't have any widespread support. Back then half the population of Ulster would have happily seen you dead. Well. Not quite half, that was why we were there but... Back then there were whole areas of Belfast ... Londonderry where you risked your life just walking down the street.' He paused again but Manjit and Esther made no effort to hurry him. He thought to himself, I'm droning on like an old fart but, fuck it, it's my leaving drinks. 'Today half the time it's the suspects' parents that call the police.'

'Are you saying that kids today don't know they're born?' said Manjit.

David laughed. 'I am. Do you want another drink?'

'I'll get these,' said Manjit and headed off towards the bar.

After a moment Esther said, 'We've got one or two dark secrets even now.'

David waited.

'How badly did they treat the prisoners in Northern Ireland?'

'They? You mean "you"?'

'I just mean generally.'

'It got better. But in the early days, when we knew next to nothing about who we were up against, I think sometimes it got pretty bad.'

'Do you worry about it now? I mean does it keep you awake at night?'

'The worst of it was before my time.' "Sometimes" would have been a more honest answer.

She looked him in the eye for a moment and he sensed she was looking in some way for reassurance.

'You see, when I got back from maternity leave just before Christmas they put me onto background research. Predictable hours and all that. But about a month ago I was updating our records on a suspect. Who his contacts were, his movements, cross referencing with Special Branch files, highlighting the stuff we still needed to nail down. All that sort of thing. And I passed it on to my line manager. Two days later he came back in a flap with half the blanks filled in. They'd arrested the subject in Pakistan and they must have used my notes as a basis for questioning him and now my boss wanted to know what else we should be asking him for. And he wanted to know right then. And my first reaction was I had to get home to collect Liza from nursery. You get fined some ridiculous amount if you're 5 minutes late. I mean... that's why I was doing background research.'

Jesus, thought David, childcare interfering with operational efficiency. But he realised that even to question this arrangement meant he was overdue for retirement.

'Thanks,' said Esther.

Manjit had reappeared with a glass of red wine, a pint for David and an orange juice for himself. As David watched Esther take the glass of wine he realised that Manjit had set this meeting up.

'But once we'd sorted out who was going to pick up Liza, there was that excitement at being back at the sharp end. It was all that like... Would people know he's been lifted? What was the time critical intelligence he might have? And we worked through it all and came up with a line of questioning and we sent it off to Lahore and I thought, great. And then my boss leant back in his chair and said, "Well this shouldn't take long."'

She stopped and both she and Manjit looked at David. After a moment she said, 'I thought we didn't do that any more.'

'Did you say anything?' he asked.

Esther looked almost lost. 'No. I just sort of froze. After a moment or two he asked if I wanted a cup of tea. Which I really didn't. And then he walked off to the tea point. I didn't see him again till some answers came back over the wire about two hours later. And that was it.'

'No more questions?'

'No. My boss just said "That's it. Well done. You can go home now." I haven't dared look at the file since. It's crossed my mind he might be dead.'

'I doubt it. You'd probably have heard.' There would have had to be some half arsed, back-covering investigation if he had actually died. 'Have you reported it to your line manager?'

'What's she going to do?'

What could he say? What more did she want? This was what they did now.

Manjit broke the silence. 'Have you heard the rumours about Steve Knight's surveillance team?'

'Not yet,' said David, pleased to see the conversation deflected.

'The story is they've bugged an upmarket brothel in Fitzrovia somewhere and that on Tuesday they came away with rather more than they bargained for.'

'What exactly?'

'They're acting really coy but it's obviously something good.'

'Stop teasing us,' said Esther. 'What have you heard?'

'The best one is that Nigel Farage was in there demanding an older woman dressed up as Margaret Thatcher.'

Esther pulled a face. 'Can you imagine having sex with Nigel Farage?'

'Can you imagine having sex with an ageing whore dressed up as Maggie?' David asked.

'I'm not sure, given that choice, I wouldn't go for Nigel,' said Manjit, thoughtfully.

'I think I'd go for the Maggie look-alike,' said Esther. 'What about you David?'

'I think I'd shut my eyes and go for Maggie. But you're right Manjit, it's a tough call. I suppose we can only hope the story's true?'

'Unfortunately no. I checked and he was in Chesterfield, addressing a poorly attended meeting on the subject of the threat to British values posed by European integration.'

'I'd definitely rather have sex with an ancient prostitute dressed as Margaret Thatcher than sit through that,' said David. 'I suppose it would have to be the missionary position rather than doggy style though.'

'Why?' asked Esther, looking slightly alarmed.

'The lady's not for turning.'

'That,' said Manjit, 'is unforgivable. Even on your last day in the office.'

'What's he done now?' Nigel appeared at David's side.

'Manjit was just filling us in on the latest from Steve Knight's team,' David explained.

'Is this the story about the shadow Minister for Defence and the My Little Pony T shirt?' Nigel asked.

'No,' said David. 'Tell us more.'

Nigel gave Esther a brief, embarrassed look. 'I wouldn't recommend it, if I'm honest.' Then more breezily, 'Listen Terence Drake is leaving in a few minutes. I said I'd see if I could track you down.'

'I told you there'd be a Deputy Director,' said Manjit. David pulled a face and Manjit grinned.

'Play nice, just for once will you David,' said Nigel. 'It'll make it easier for me to get you back for this consultancy work.'

They found Terence propped against a pillar chatting to a couple of eager young case officers who worked on David's floor and who he hardly knew but had included in the general invitation. Nigel interrupted without ceremony.

'The man himself,' he declared.

'David. This is a momentous day.' As Terence turned to greet them he pulled back his shoulders and leant backwards a little in a gesture that was meant to be read as open and welcoming. He was a well-built man, a little overweight with thinning sandy hair. To David's eyes the undone top button behind his tie and the fact that he was still wearing his pale, belted mac gave him a slightly seedy air. But Terence himself was free from any such doubts. 'The department is about to be become the poorer by forty years of hard won experience. A real loss.' The tone of voice was warm, but it was a practiced warmth.

The two case officers looked on, anxious to enjoy a few more seconds in proximity to power, but their moment in the sun was plainly over and they sidled off towards the bar.

'Thanks,' said David. He still resented the way he was expected to be grateful for the brief attention of someone so senior. But he was mindful too of Nigel's request that he play nice, and of the benefits of another couple of months' money, so he continued. 'This has been a great place to work. All things considered. I wouldn't have missed it for the world.'

'Loyalty's a vanishing quality,' Terence continued. 'You look at all these young ones and you think, give them ten years and half of them will have jumped ship and be working in corporate security. Mind you, for the money they're offered…' and David wondered what plans Terence was making for life after MI5. 'You weren't tempted?' Terence asked.

'With the references I'd get?' Or, I'll put up with patronising dickheads like you for Queen and country, but I won't eat that shit just for the cash.

'But I gather we might not have quite seen the last of you?'

'Nigel said there was something he might want me to have a look at.'

'So I gather. I don't think it's a big deal but we need to keep the Americans happy. Shouldn't take you long to wrap up from what I hear. Beer money only I'm afraid. Listen, I've got to shoot. Promised the wife I'd get home in time for a late supper. But all the best, and… hope to see you soon.'

As Terence departed David wondered what exactly he was hearing. Was he being warned not to dig too deep into whatever it was, or was the job genuinely no more than a bit of tidying up they didn't want to waste a permanent member of staff on?

With Terence gone Nigel relaxed a little.

'He could at least have bought you a drink,' he laughed and David thought he'd probe a little further. 'How long should I block my diary out for?'

But Nigel it seemed wasn't giving anything more away this evening.

'There's still a bit of an argument about whose budget this comes out of so until that's resolved nothing's definite I'm afraid. But I think we can be 90% confident it'll happen. As Terence says, we've got to keep the Americans happy. I'm sure we'll find a way. Let me get you another drink.' David looked down at his nearly empty glass. Playing confessor to Esther had proved thirsty work.

'Thanks. I'll have another pint.'

The discussion went no further and at the bar they parted company. Nigel was waylaid by another team member with a shared interest in opera and, as he turned away to discuss a recent production of Rigoletto, David was hailed by a group of three older figures who had, now numbers were dwindling, managed to find themselves a table. There was Terry seated with his back to the wall, and on his left another former colleague from the F section days, Eric Hanley. Time did not seem to have been as kind to Eric as it had to the others. David remembered him as quiet and occasionally prickly but undoubtedly dedicated. There was something shrunken about him now, like a schoolboy in clothes his mother had bought for him to grow into, and his crinkly grey hair was brushed into something near a comb-over. But when he leaned over to shake hands his grip was as firm as ever and his voice remained strong.

'Long time no see.'

'Yes. Good to see you. Glad you could make it.'

On Terry's right the third member of the group was another old hand, Gavin Hughes, a Welshman who had joined straight from university. His father had worked as a manager in the mining industry in South Wales where the communist party had been a force to reckon with and Gavin had initially been disappointed to be assigned to Ulster rather than to dealing with the Soviets. But he had soon come to regard the Provisional IRA as an equally worthy enemy and he and David had worked alongside each other for four hectic years in the mid-seventies. Of the three, he had put on the most weight, but his hair was still so black David wondered if he dyed it. His teeth seemed straighter than they'd been in the old days and his open-necked shirt looked tailored to his substantial form. He's done well for himself, thought David. But it wasn't greed that had taken Gavin into the private sector, it was boredom. With the end of the cold war and the first on-off ceasefires in Northern Ireland Gavin had lost interest and gone to work in security for an international mining company. David had heard him speak at a conference he'd been sent to during the lull between the Good Friday agreement and 9/11 when people were scratching around for things to do. Afterwards Gavin had been whisked off before David managed to speak to him but reading between the lines of his somewhat anodyne talk, salted with occasional references to his time in Ulster, David had fleshed out a system of union informers and occasional cooperation with local and unscrupulous police forces which had guaranteed his employers cheap and uninterrupted production. And Gavin, it would seem, had been well rewarded.

It was Gavin who reached over and dragged another chair to their table.

'Sit down old man. It's good to see you. It's almost like old times.'

David looked around the table. Someone had just bought a round so there was no need to move for a while and, for the first time that day, he felt fully relaxed.

'The last of us to shake off the harness,' said Terry. 'How does it feel to be free?'

'I'll let you know in a few weeks. But good so far. Good.'

'Good speech I thought. Got all the main points in there. The major feathers in your cap.'

What wasn't in there was quite significant too, David thought.

'Overall, looking back... I think we can be pretty satisfied,' Terry continued, 'We saw off the Provos, we saw off the communists...'

'And the miners,' Eric added.

'Same thing,' Gavin said, to general agreement. 'Did you ever listen to any of those tapes of Mick McGahey's phone calls during the strike? Pissed out of his skull on union funds and, to the untrained ear, completely incomprehensible. Once that poor transcriber, what was her name ... admitted she could understand what the bastard was saying that was all she did for the entire strike. Mind you, she said it was better than having to write up his missus' phone calls. Hours and hours of blathering on about nothing at all apparently with only the occasional nugget of usable intelligence thrown in. In deepest Scottish. No. Between us we've earned the undying gratitude of a miserable nation and all they want to talk about is our gold-plated pensions. Gold plated or not, we've earned them.'

'Those days in F section seem a world away,' said Eric. 'When was the last time anyone said "Communist threat" in earnest?' He smiled at the thought.

'Maggie saw to all that thank God,' said Gavin. 'Sorting that bastard Scargill out was ... that was Alamein and Stalingrad rolled in to one.'

'Yes,' said Terry. 'But somehow, right from the Falklands it was our time. What a turnaround that was. In every way.' It seemed to David that everyone accepted this statement without reservation. He looked round the table at the cheerful, satisfied faces and wondered, was he the only one who remembered the burnt, blackened figures stumbling ashore from the Sir Galahad, or the mass grave of the Paras' dead at Goose Green? Terry continued, 'She started to get a grip even before that though. Remember Red Robbo? The British

26

Leyland shop steward? She fixed that bastard pretty much as soon as she arrived. She was...' He shook his head as if still in awe of her achievements. 'I'd love to have seen the look on his face when he found out management had the minutes of his meeting with the ...'

'With Mick Costello?' Gavin interrupted. 'That must have been a picture. Do you remember who got hold of them? Who was running agents in the Midlands Communist Party then?'

'Garry Spence,' said Eric. 'I think he got a personal letter of thanks from the lady herself.'

'That's right,' said Terry. 'Acted like the sun shone out of his behind for the next six months.'

'And how did you find the "War on Terror"?' Gavin asked. 'We missed out on all that.'

David detected the same mocking attitude to the phrase that Manjit had expressed earlier that day.

'MI6 really landed us in the hole with that one. You lot did well to get out before then.'

'Spared you a trip to C section though. Or whatever they call it now.'

'I suppose I've got that to thank Bin Laden for.' Working out his final years vetting blameless recruits and poking around other department's compliance with document handling procedures might well have been worse, but he wasn't sure.

At that moment he felt a hand on his shoulder. He looked up to see Manjit in his coat and obviously ready to depart.

'Manjit, meet some people who are even older than me.' To the others, 'This is Manjit. I've taught him all I know.'

'How long did that take?' Gavin asked, addressing himself to Manjit. 'About twenty minutes?'

27

'Maybe twenty five,' said Manjit. 'David, it's been an honour. I won't break up the party but when you're up in London give us a call. It would be good to meet up. Give me a chance to seek some more of your invaluable guidance.'

In the confined space David struggled to get to his feet. The beer was not helping. 'It's been great,' he said, taking Manjit's hand. He was going to miss Manjit but he could not say so. 'Definitely on for a beer.'

The four of them carried on drinking for another hour or so, filling the time with a mixture of war stories and the exchange of information about their lives after MI5. The combination of shared history and the warm glow of the alcohol created a companionable haze David had not enjoyed in a long time. There was only one moment which jarred. Following a good natured disagreement about who should get the next round, a number of people moved off in the direction of the bar and David took the opportunity to take a leak. When he pushed open the door he was greeted by the sound of raised voices, muffled somewhat by the sound of the hand dryer. They tailed off immediately but not before David heard the words "stupid bastard" spoken with some force. It sounded like Terry and when he turned the corner he found Eric and Terry, doing their inadequate best to look like nothing was happening. Terry almost pushed his way past David, then turned to Eric and said, 'A whiskey?'

'Yes please,' said Eric, who then turned on a tap and started to wash his hands. He was still there, poised to use the dryer, when David joined him at the sinks.

He remembered that Eric's wife had had a stroke and, partly to dispel the awkwardness, he asked how she was doing.

'The old girl's bearing up. And we've come into a bit of money recently which has helped. It's an awful thing to say but … she had an unmarried sister and we've … we've been waiting for her to die really. She'd been very ill.' He finally managed to make eye contact with David. 'She didn't leave a lot but it makes a difference.'

David followed him back to their table.

'I've had to get a professional carer to look after her tonight,' Eric continued, 'and that's £20 an hour.'

Terry rejoined them a minute or two later, bearing Eric's whiskey but David noticed Eric didn't touch it once.

Eventually there came a point when people started thinking about last trains.

'We must do this again before too long,' said Gavin.

Everyone seemed to agree and a lunch sometime during the following month was more or less settled on before they went their separate ways. David had booked himself into a hotel for the night. There was no one to drive him home from the station and a taxi would have cost little less than a room. Alone now, he walked the short distance through the quiet, neon-lit streets to the hotel where he was staying. This, he thought with uncertainty, was the beginning of the rest of his life.

'Frampton.' It was an announcement rather than a greeting.

'Good morning Alex,' Lord Frampton's demeanour softened, relaxed a little.

'Peter. Good to hear you.'

'Up to a point Alex. Up to a point.'

'Something wrong?'

'It's all in hand Alex but I thought I'd put you in the picture.'

Frampton waited as the speaker on the other end of the line drew breath.

'Seems you've upset the Americans.'

'Again?' Frampton laughed but of the two it seemed he was the only one who saw the funny side.

'It's your Iraq "investments" Alex. The Americans seem to think they look more like a bribe.'

'Well of course they were a ...'

'The Americans have asked for an investigation. The matter's going to be handled in MI5. But they've got someone reliable. An old hand, just coming up to retirement. Name's David Nixon. Looks like you may have overlapped in Ireland.'

Lord Frampton cycled through his memory of faces, names, sensations...

'Rather tedious ex-policeman. Yes, I remember him vaguely.'

'Tedious maybe Alex but you need to be on your best behaviour. They can kick this one into the long grass so don't make it harder for them than necessary.'

'I'll be charm itself Peter.'

Lord Frampton waited for Peter to make some bland concluding remark.

But when he next spoke Peter's tone had changed. It had become less definite, more probing. 'Is everything all right otherwise?'

'Yes thanks. The Rumalia contract is working out almost as well as expected, which is very well indeed.'

'Good.' Another pause. 'Alex we can handle most things. We've still got the ear of the people who really count. But we don't like surprises.'

'Understood. And thanks for taking care of this for me.'

When he had replaced the receiver Lord Frampton leant back in his chair and stared at nothing in particular.

"Is everything all right otherwise?" "We don't like surprises." How could Peter know anything? They must just have been throwaway comments. But the remote possibility that Peter might know something more still cast a shadow over the rest of his day.

CHAPTER TWO

David was cleaning his teeth when the phone rang, his mouth full of minty froth and his gaze fixed vacantly on his own reflection. He let it ring.

Whoever it was, it wasn't urgent; nothing in his new life was urgent, but it was surprisingly early. He pondered the relative silence of his retirement. Maybe he'd ring a couple of people. See about a beer. He wondered if Manjit would like to meet up or whether that was just one of those office friendships that couldn't survive outside the workplace. He could always send a text, say he was just passing and see what response he got. Momentarily he contemplated the possibility of not shaving.

Around nine o'clock, half way through a second piece of toast and an article on an Egyptian police crack down on militants, he remembered the call. He reached over and checked his phone. There was a message.

'Hello David. Hope this isn't too early. It's Nigel here. Give us a call. It's about the possibility we discussed before you left.'

David noticed his heart didn't immediately leap with joy. For all that he was eager for the money, to go running back so soon seemed like defeat. He gazed out the window. A small bird flew past and he realised he had no idea what it was and probably never would. Fuck it. He finished a mouthful of toast and called Nigel. And got his answer machine. 'Nigel, it's David here. Thanks for your message. Speak later.'

Nigel's message hadn't suggested any urgency, which rather pointed towards something tedious. Still, a couple of weeks on the sort of money he imagined consultants got would be a useful sum to stash away. He picked up the paper again and carried on reading. He knew enough about the treatment of "militants" in Egypt to fill in the details that the journalist, perhaps out of respect for his readers' appetites, had chosen to gloss over.

He was making a second cup of coffee when Nigel called back. It was strange to hear the man's voice here in his kitchen. And it turned out there was a bit of a flap on. 'This isn't a secure line so all I can say is that we have credible but … irritatingly… imprecise intelligence of an attack in the near future so it's all hands to the pumps at the moment. And of course that means that a lot of other things that need to get done aren't being taken care of. So the job I mentioned… Nothing too taxing, a week at the most I'd say. Would you be able to help us out do you think?'

David waited a moment before saying, 'be happy to. When would you like me to come in?'

'Any time this week David.'

'Thursday morning?'

'Er… I'll get my secretary to confirm but how about 10.00? Don't want to be dragging you out of bed at the crack of dawn now you're retired.'

33

'Is there a standard form contract?'

'You mean How Much?'

'That amongst other things.'

'We'll have to sort that out with HR. Look I'll set wheels in motion. I'm sure we can get you the going rate.'

'That would be good Nigel. I'll see you on Thursday.'

'Great. Bye.'

David put the phone down, feeling, as he always did after a conversation with Nigel, as if he had somehow been sold short. Now what? He was free. Free to do anything, within reason, that he chose to do, but in reality it boiled down to three options; embarking on the pile of books he had been accumulating in anticipation of his retirement, making a trip to the bird reserve, or doing something to sort out the garden. All had their appeal and not one of them depended on, or affected, or even involved anyone else. He was free. He looked at the stack of books by the fireplace. Maybe eight crisp, new paperbacks all with their spines unbroken. All history, much but not all of it military. A biography of Oliver Cromwell, a history of the Arabs, something about prehistory, he couldn't remember what but the blurb on the back had been intriguing, something about genetics he seemed to remember. And sitting on top, calling to him almost, an account of Francis Walsingham's career as Queen Elizabeth I's chief of counter intelligence. He had had to restrain himself from making a start on it while he was still commuting. But now the moment had arrived. New life, new book… He put the kettle on and spooned the coffee into the cafetiere. Ten minutes later he was settled in an armchair, coffee and an unnecessary biscuit on the table beside him, retreating deeper and deeper into the murkier corners of 1570's England.

Maybe forty minutes later he was dragged away from Walsingham's battles with Elizabeth I for adequate funding by the sound of the phone. He wasn't expecting a call. He thought perhaps it would be the office with some additional details about his return. Or someone from India telling him they had detected a fault in his computer. But it was Gavin's voice that greeted him when he picked up the receiver. 'David, I've got some bad news I'm afraid. Eric died yesterday morning. Heart attack.'

'God. Was this unexpected?'

'He was on medication for high blood pressure, but no, nothing to suggest he was at serious risk.'

'In his sleep?'

'No, he was out walking the dog apparently, first thing. His wife, Nora, got worried when he hadn't come back for breakfast. So she called a neighbour. Apparently he always took the same route in the morning and they found him lying by the path. The doctor said it looked as if it was pretty much instantaneous. He didn't suffer much.'

'That's something I suppose.' That warmth and conviviality had been how many days ago? Four? Five? And now... Then David remembered how he had interrupted that curious spat between Eric and Terry.

'Eric...,' But David didn't want to speak ill of the dead. 'Looked... a bit tense perhaps the other night. But not as if he was on the verge of ....' Where was he going with this? 'What about his wife? She's been ill for a long time hasn't she?'

'I'm going down there this afternoon to see how she is. I'll let you know. And I'll be in touch about the funeral too.'

'Thanks. I'll want to come. By the way, I'm going back to work for a few days... no really... just tidying up some loose ends they apparently don't have time to deal with right now, but obviously I'll take a day off for the funeral.' They were both silent for a moment. 'Give Nora my … best wishes when you see her.' He'd only met her… maybe three times in his life, "love" seemed too much.'

'Will do,' said Gavin. 'Sorry to be the bringer of such bad news. And especially after such an enjoyable evening. We should do that again. Go out for a decent meal somewhere.'

'Yes, definitely.' Though he feared these days Gavin's idea of a decent meal might stretch his own budget.

'All right. Be in touch.'

David put the receiver down and reached for his coffee, but it had gone cold.

Thursday morning started as farce.

After many years of working in the building David was initially amused to find himself having to wait in reception to be escorted up to the 4th floor. Before he was allowed to proceed beyond reception a security guard, who had known David for many years, explained in deliberately unnecessary detail the precise limits on his movements within the building. The man was ex-army and still maintained a self-consciously military bearing despite greying hair and an increasing girth. He wore a South Atlantic medal every November 11th. The joke went on a little too long but David was happy to indulge the man, whose current job involved little enough in the way of entertainment.

Ten minutes later Nigel came to collect him. David appreciated the fact that he had come down in person rather than sending someone more junior.

'Good to have you back David, however briefly. This is a bit of an odd one. You'll be reporting to me but cc'ing Will Anderson on anything substantial you send me because it ties in to his... his area of responsibility.'

David followed Nigel into the lift. As the doors closed behind them Nigel began with an embarrassed tone, 'I'm afraid there's a bit of a problem with your employment David. Because you technically took early retirement Treasury rules mean we can't re-employ you as a consultant within eighteen months.'

'You asked me if I'd take early retirement. I did that as a favour for the department so you could take on a Middle East expert before the end of the accounting year. And I only left two months early.'

'David I know. And we're very grateful. And Ishmael is proving an enormous help. But the fact is we can't take you on as a consultant. However, HR think they have a solution. If you were to be employed by one of our existing consultancy companies the problem doesn't arise.'

'That can't be right?'

Ridiculously Nigel lowered his voice. 'It's not. But it means your national insurance number doesn't show up on our pay roll system so the Treasury don't find out. Probably. And if they do we say we're terribly sorry, it was an unfortunate oversight. And by then you should be gone.'

'Well so long as I get the same amount of money.'

The lift came to a gentle halt, the doors shuddered a little in their frame before sliding open. Nigel managed to avoid eye contact as he shepherded David out of the lift.

'Er... The company through whom we will be sourcing your services will take 20 percent.'

'Well pay me 20 percent more.'

'If only we could. But we don't have the budget. I had to fight hard enough just to get you this much.'

He'd only been back in the building twenty minutes and already David was itching to punch people. He placed his mobile into one of the lockers on the landing and turned the key.

'Do you think the union would be able to help here?'

'David, you're a consultant now. You're not allowed to join the union.'

David stood there for a moment, in silent exasperation, before following Nigel through the doors and down a corridor to one of the meeting rooms. There, greeting David with an outstretched hand, was Will Anderson, a former policeman off a graduate entry scheme. David knew him by sight but had never worked for him, had never, so far as he could recall, even spoken to him. He took in the neatly brushed brown hair, worn longer than most people's in the office, noted the care which seemed to have been taken over the choice of shirt, suit and tie, but decided to suspend judgement.

'So glad you can help us out on this one David.' The over friendly tone of voice immediately jarred. 'It's a slightly left field inquiry that is going to need a bit of tactful handling.'

David looked at Nigel and raised an eyebrow.

'Hear us out,' said Nigel.

'You know Lord Frampton,' Will continued.

'Not personally,' David replied.

'My understanding was that you worked quite closely with him in Northern Ireland.'

'Our paths crossed.'

'During the strike in '75 I gather?'

'Yes. That's right.' God. What a time. Protestant power station workers holding the peace negotiations to ransom. Unionist barricades going up all across Belfast while the army hung back, the province grinding to a halt and nobody knowing quite who was in control. Strange, strange days. And Frampton had left Northern Ireland shortly afterwards as he recalled. He was intrigued now.

'You haven't followed his career since?' Will asked.

'Not closely. I think he was a junior minister at the Ministry of Defence for a while?'

'No. There was talk of him becoming shadow defence secretary under Ian Duncan Smith but then there was that unfortunate comment about civilian casualties during the invasion of Afghanistan.' David looked blank.

'Anyway, after he retired from politics he ended up on the board of a security company called Four Square Security, with contracts in Iraq. And he also tried his luck in the oil industry. And now we've had a request from the CIA to check out some payments they say he made to various Iraqis. They are concerned he may have been paying bribes that have funded pro-Iranian insurgent groups.'

David nearly laughed. 'You mean as opposed to contributing to the Republican Party funds to ensure his company got a shot at the juicier contracts? I don't mean to be rude, but this is a wind up.'

'It does look a bit like that,' said Will, somewhat to David's surprise. 'We don't really know what's going on here. Nigel's guess is they had to hit some internal target for corruption investigations and this way they get to tick that box but we have to do the work. Makes as much sense as anything else. All we need you to do is to go through the motions, make sure he hasn't been too stupid, and write it up.'

'Don't find anything will you David,' Nigel added. 'We haven't got the budget.'

'So what's with the "tactful handling" idea?' David asked. 'I have many skills but…'

Will explained. 'I don't know what he was like when you knew him, but everything we hear is that he is… "difficult". Has an exaggeratedly high opinion of himself and won't take kindly to people like us quizzing him about his finances. We are rather hoping that someone with your pedigree… that he will take it better coming from someone who… has paid their dues if you like, has some history in common.'

'And I'm available.'

Will at least had the decency to acknowledge the point.

'OK,' David continued. 'What's the evidence against… Frampton? Sorry… I still think of him as Edwards.'

'I think he's pretty keen to be known as Lord Frampton now. The evidence?' Will glanced over at Nigel who raised his eyebrows in a gesture of exasperation. 'The details are all in the file. But in a nutshell the story is this. There's a chancer called Ali Al Jamail. He's a tribal bigwig of some sort. And after the liberation of Iraq he inveigled his way into the Al Dawa party. You can imagine how it goes. He can deliver votes so he gets a seat at the table. But he's complete a phoney. Al Dawa were solidly opposed to Saddam. Their leaders, the ones who weren't executed or imprisoned and tortured, had spent years in exile in Iran. Our friend Al Jamail doesn't join until that's all over. But he gets his feet under the table and he winds up in charge of issuing security contracts for Iraqi oil installations. You can probably guess where this is going.'

David nodded.

'There's a hundred different ways you can hide payments like this. Secret bank transfers. Paying commissions or consultancy fees to close friends or family members. But what Four Square security did was they invested in an oil field services company operated by Jamail's brother and uncle. A company called Dhi-Qar services. You'll find references to it in the papers. Which might have been a clever way of doing it, except for the fact that Dhi-Qar services has never traded. I think it's got a rubbish website and a post box address. Maybe the original plan was to build a real business. We don't know. But because there is no real business we're left with Four Square Security paying... Jamail's family essentially... what was it? $150,000? for essentially nothing and then getting a seriously lucrative contract from Jamail. And Frampton's fingerprints are all over the deal. He authorised the payment. He signed the contract. He's reported as being very tight with Jamail. It all looks really bad.'

'I can see that. What do you want me to do about it.'

'The best you can,' said Nigel. 'Establish... how deep a hole he's in. Explore the opportunities for presenting the situation in the best possible light. One option we were thinking of was Four Square Security bringing legal proceedings in Iraq to recover the money. They could be entirely for show, but even Frampton telling us the company's contemplating the step would help us fob off the Americans.'

"Explore opportunities for presenting the situation in the best possible light.' David could imagine what that would mean. Hours of work producing back dated electronic documents to support whatever story they eventually concocted. Forging documents wasn't easier in the digital age, just different.

But David's immediate question was, 'Why us? Why not the Foreign Office? Isn't Iraq their territory?'

'We tried that argument but they persuaded the Minister that Frampton's conduct is a domestic issue. But they've sent over, I'd hardly call it a file, but... a bundle of documents... notes really, they say they put together because of his business interests in Iraq. And one of their people is happy to talk to you. We got that much out of them. What I suggest is that you take a day or two to familiarise yourself with the papers, work out what you need to ask and fix up a meeting. There's government guidance on ... these sorts of payments... there's a copy in your folder. Just... tell the story in a way which is consistent with the guidance... and we can all get on with our lives.' He paused as if expecting a response from David but David's mind was partly elsewhere.

Will spelled it out. 'If necessary help him... help him with the details of the narrative.'

David nodded. His instructions could not have been clearer.

'OK.' Will stood up. The meeting was over. 'We've got a desk for you in a room down the corridor. We'll get you fixed up with a computer this afternoon. I'm afraid you'll have to go through all the security briefings again. Keep Nigel informed and cc me on anything substantial.' Will pushed the folder towards David. 'There'll be electronic copies of all these on the computer files but these will keep you going until you've got access. And until we sort you out with a safe we've agreed you can leave the hard copies with Nigel's secretary. And thanks for agreeing to come back for this. It's one more thing we didn't need at a time like this so it's really helpful to have someone take it off our hands so to speak.'

'What do I do about contacting Lord Frampton? I don't imagine he's going to be pleased to hear from us.'

'That's being taken care of,' said Will. 'Someone from my office has already been in touch with him. He's away at the moment so it will be a few days. Probably late next week apparently.'

'OK,' said David. 'I'll go and start reading in.'

'I can show him to his desk if you like Will,' said Nigel. 'It's on my way.'

'Thanks,' said Will. 'You'll be sharing the room with two other people but they're away for a couple of days. I'll introduce you when they get back.'

As they left the meeting David was tempted to ask Nigel how Will had known about his contact with Edwards in Ulster. Instead he asked, 'Who suggested me for this job?'

'I think you were just the obvious choice,' Nigel replied. 'We needed someone, you had just... become available and, as Will said, if you can restrain your natural bullishness for the limited time necessary, then ... because of your history you are eminently suitable. I can't honestly remember whether they asked for you or I made the suggestion.'

David didn't believe him. Someone, someone whose memory went back to 1975, had asked for him to be given this job. Asked for him but left it understood that he was not to be involved. That was worth knowing.

'What's keeping you all so busy right now? If I'm allowed to know.'

Nigel sighed. 'The Americans picked up a Somali, coming into Greece. Someone on one of their lists. He plainly knew a number of unsavoury characters but his story was that he was just involved in trafficking refugees. But, one way or another, they persuaded him to change his story and now he's claiming there's a plan for some sort of attack on a night club or something in London in the near future. And maybe there is and maybe he just said what he thought they wanted to hear to get them to stop... We've asked to see him but they're being a bit coy. We think they're probably holding him somewhere Congress wouldn't approve of and they're having to be more careful about that sort of thing at the moment. Either that or he's dead. Anyway the long and the short of it is we've got too much to ignore but not enough to go on. And this is manna from heaven for Steve Scott, as you can imagine.'

By now they had arrived at David's new office but Nigel continued talking.

'It's not like we've completely ignored the Somali community. But if there's not a hint of anything brewing I've been arguing we need to treat this, pretty sketchy, intelligence with caution. Poke around a bit more but don't panic. Of course Steve is saying we've never put enough resources into this area and just because we can't see it doesn't mean it's not there, specially if we haven't been looking very hard and what will the comeback be if we don't treat this as a priority and then something does happen. Sometimes I think he'd be happy to see a bomb go off if it got him five extra staff.' He paused for breath. 'Sorry David. This isn't your problem any more, but I've just spent an hour this morning fighting to keep Steve's hands off half my budget. This is your desk. Your two room-mates are working out of a police station in Bow for the time being, chasing up some of Steve's "leads". God knows when they'll be allowed to come home. The IT people are booked to take you through the security procedures at 12.00. I'd say let's have lunch but there really isn't time at the moment. By the time this nonsense is over it'll probably be time for another farewell drink.'

David laughed. 'Yes.'

'Oh yes, I almost forgot.' Nigel searched his pockets. 'Somewhere I've got the details of the person at the Foreign Office who can give you a heads up on the background to Lord Frampton's deal in Iraq. Seems like a nice enough chap. Edwin somebody. Yes, it's been a long time since I met an Edwin.' He found a piece of paper in his jacket pocket. 'Here we are. Edwin Birch. Not sure what his qualifications are exactly but they assured me he was the man you need to talk to. There's his phone number and email. And David, do please bear in mind. Lord Frampton may have been a Captain when you knew him but he is a member of the House of Lords now and … he's entitled to an appropriate level of respect.'

David decided to ignore this last remark. Instead he asked, 'Is Ginny going to open a file for me?'

'We're not formally opening a file on this one David.'

And at that moment a voice in the back of David's head, quiet but clear, told him to walk away. Turn round. Walk out of the building and go back to his books and his birdwatching and his garden. Told him this was not going to end well.

Instead he said, 'OK. Say hello to Manjit. Tell him I'll drop by at some point.'

'Will do. In the meantime I'm just hoping that if we do by some miracle find some misbegotten Somali with a bathtub full of acetone he doesn't turn out to be working for the Swindon office.'

'Or us,' David added with something between a laugh and a snort.

'Or us. Indeed. Unless it was someone on Steve's payroll... No. That's an unworthy thought.' Nigel shook his head. 'I had so much to do this week.' And with that he departed.

When Nigel had left David unpacked his teabags, his milk and his mug, hung his coat up and took stock. The window looked out onto the other side of the building from his previous office. No panoramic view of the Thames, just a large brown office block occupied by a fashion company whose name he could never remember. His two absent room-mates had left no clues as to their identity, no photographs on their desks, just the usual selection of biros and so on. And there was nothing on the walls except an A1 sized year planner which seemed only to be used for recording annual leave. "FRANCE" had been written in triumphant block capitals across a fortnight in August and "Italy" less dramatically over a week in September. Otherwise nothing but near silence. For a moment David's mind too wandered southwards. Maybe when this was over he'd treat himself to a trip to France or Spain. Maybe.

Then, with an effort, he pushed aside thoughts of a cold beer in the sunlit piazza of some historic Mediterranean town and turned his attention to the papers enclosed in the folder Will had handed him. Because it was this that kept him from walking away. The job. The involvement. The lure of the unknown. The prospect of some meaningful engagement above and beyond the mundane existence of his neighbours.

As Will had said, it was a curiously haphazard collection of papers, as if the FCO had started to put together a file then lost interest or, more probably, just got overwhelmed with other tasks. Whatever, it was a useful start. He skipped through the details of Frampton's military career. Frampton had played on his background first in the parachute regiment and later in the SAS and that had certainly boosted his profile but it was his time in politics that David assumed had got him the connections he had leveraged into a business career and so it was with the politics that he began. Frampton's time as a backbencher had been unremarkable. He had been a member of the far-right Monday Club and achieved brief notoriety for a speech he had made at one of the club's gatherings attacking Robert Mugabe over the brutal conduct of the Zimbabwean army's 5th brigade in Matabeleland. His exact words were disputed but the clear implication, that African people were too primitive to be allowed to run their own affairs, resulted in student protests disrupting a couple of his subsequent speaking engagements at universities.

Nonetheless, the tabloids had always liked him, for a while he made no further obvious gaffs and he had worked closely with a couple of Shadow Defence Ministers under Ian Duncan Smith. He had even been tipped for the job itself, at least by his supporters at the Daily Mail, who unfailingly referred to him as "SAS hero Captain Edwards". However, a couple of cuttings from the more specialist press attached to the chronology in David's file alluded to poor relations with some of the senior officers he dealt with and it looked as though, even without the unsympathetic remarks about the deaths of Afghan civilians Will had alluded to earlier, he might well have been passed over for the shadow cabinet. Once it was clear that his political career would progress no further he had stood down at the following election and within six months found himself on the board of Four Square Security. The folder included a few loose pages printed out from Four Square's website. The first two or three were what one would expect; glossy photographs of 4 wheel drives in presumably hostile locations juxtaposed with pictures of serious looking men with guns and a reassuring text about experience, training and professionalism. A final page in the little bundle, headed 'Corporate Responsibility' described a charity the company had established supporting projects in 'post-conflict environments' but gave no details of the organisation's size or budget.

Frampton may have been recruited for his Westminster contacts but he had apparently taken a serious interest in the company and made a number of trips to Iraq to observe operations on the ground. As a result he had been assigned a formal role 'Assistant Director: Training.' A typed note recorded. "It is not clear exactly how much time Lord Frampton devoted to this role but he appears to have taken it seriously and to have received additional remuneration. What is clear is that it was in the course of these duties that he first encountered Ali Al Jamail."

The next few pages spelled out the story Will had told about payments to Dhi-Qar services but included in the paperwork was a print out of an article from an on-line magazine *The Iraqi Reconstruction Review*, drawing attention to the deal. It quoted a spokesman from another, Texas based, security company, ProSecure claiming that the deal risked bringing the security industry and the Iraqi oil ministry into disrepute. The article stated that the *Review* had been unable to speak to anyone from Four Square Security but the company had issued a statement. "Four Square Security is pleased to announce its involvement with Dhi-Qar Services. The company is already involved in logistics and security in the Iraqi oil industry and looks forward to developing its business in these areas. As part of its commitment to building an Iraq that delivers for all its citizens Four Square Security is committed to the highest standards of business ethics and all its contracts are subject to well-established, industry-wide standards of due diligence." However, this claim was rather undercut by the article's report that the author had been unable to trace any evidence of economic activity on the part of Dhi-Qar Services beyond the construction of a rudimentary website. A final paragraph explained that ProSecure was itself owned by the Sonderberg Group, which had extensive interests in subcontracting for the military, both in Iraq and across the globe, and gave details of other projects the Group had recently made successful bids for.

There was a knock on the door and, without waiting for an answer, a young man walked in carrying a computer.

'Mr Nixon?' he asked without any obvious enthusiasm.

'That's me.'

'Great.' Also said without enthusiasm. 'My name's Simon. From IT. Can I see your ID please?'

David produced his pass.

'That's a temporary pass isn't it.' A look of concern came over the man's face and, for the first time, David paid him proper attention. He had untidy, fair hair and a put-upon air. The dark green fleece he was wearing seemed an odd choice for the office and his boots too looked like they belonged on the fells rather than institutional carpet.

'Yes, I'm just here for a few days.'

'Ah. That may be a problem. We'll have to see. Can I ask you to read and sign this while I set you up.'

David took the papers and pushed back his chair to allow Simon room to place the laptop on his desk and connect it to the various sockets. Once the computer was plugged in and turned on David watched as Simon typed away for a couple of minutes, performing whatever mysterious tasks the system demanded.

'OK,' Simon said. 'Have you signed both the forms?'

'I have to sign two forms?'

'Yes, there's a second form on the back of that page there. They both say more or less the same thing.'

David signed twice. There was no point in asking why.

'That page has your user name and your initial password on. You'll need to change the password once you've logged on. Now can you type in your username and password for me.'

David wheeled his chair back to his desk and typed. There was brief delay. Then, instead of the opening page with which he was so familiar, there appeared the word "Error" followed by a string of letters and numbers.

'That's rather what I expected,' said Simon. 'We have you down as a permanent member of staff.'

'I retired ten days ago,' said David. 'Might that have something to do with it?'

'Possibly. I'll have to go and see how you've been registered. I may have to get your line manager to approve an amendment to your registration.'

'How long will that take?'

Simon looked at his watch. 'It'll probably be some time tomorrow now. I'll… I'll see what I can do.'

Then, rather to David's surprise, Simon began to disconnect the computer.

'You're not going to leave that there?' he asked.

'I can't. Security. There's a terminal you can use in the library. If you get authorisation from your line manager.'

Once Simon had gone David looked through the rest of the file. Alongside the print out of from *The Iraqi Reconstruction*

Review there were cuttings from *The Daily Telegraph* and *The Daily Mail* recording the award of the security contract in glowing terms, while making no reference to Dhi-Qar Services. Both mentioned Lord Frampton by name and both suggested, in terms so similar they might have been paraphrasing the same press release, that the deal was a testament to the superior qualities of the British armed forces.

The last document in the batch was rather different; a photocopy of a recent report, no more than half a side of A4, of the police being called out to Lord Frampton's house to deal with a number of demonstrators who had turned up for some sort of a protest. The name of the officer was just about legible, Sergeant A. Henderson he reckoned, along with the name, and phone number of the police station. More out of curiosity than in the expectation that it would lead anywhere David called the number. He got through to a bored receptionist who in turn put him through to a hard-pressed colleague of Sergeant Henderson who was initially reluctant to give David the time of day. It took a heavy-handed reference to the fact he was calling from MI5 to persuade him to take David's number and pass it on.

He pushed his chair away from his desk and leaned back wondering what he should do next when Ginny popped her head round the door.

'Hello Ginny. You thought you'd got rid of me.'

'We did. But you're like a bad penny. You just keep turning up.' She giggled then turned serious once more. 'Can you phone this number? It came through to Nigel. It's a Mr Eldridge Baker. The third. He's American.'

'I rather thought he might be.'

'He's from the CIA. I hope you haven't been doing anything you shouldn't have.'

51

'Nothing they'll shoot me for.'

'Are you sure? He is American.'

'I think I'll be all right Ginny. Did Nigel say what it was about?'

'He said it's about your current project. That's all he told me.'

'Thanks Ginny, I'll get onto it.'

When she had left he dialled the number. Silence for a while then an unfamiliar dialling tone. After a couple of seconds a voice answered, 'Eldridge T Baker.'

'The third?'

'Speaking.'

'Good afternoon. This is David Nixon. I gather you just spoke to my colleague Nigel Richards. How can I help?'

'David, Nigel tells me you're heading the team that's investigating Lord Frampton.'

'Yes. That's me.' Team? What had Nigel told these people?

'I'm calling because I'll be passing through London next week. I'd really like to meet with you and explain the full extent of our ongoing concerns.'

'Certainly. My diary's pretty empty at the moment.'

'That's... fine. So David, how would ... let me think... how about Friday? Next week. I can maybe buy you lunch and update you on the latest information we have received from Iraq. Some of our sources there are proving... how shall we say... very forthcoming. It seems there's real concern in the oil ministry about this contract.'

'Can you send me any further details, copies of statements perhaps, before the meeting? It would be very helpful to have some advance notice of what's troubling you.'

'I'll see what I can do David.'

'If you would, that would be very kind. Eldridge.' Eldridge. Jesus. And please stop using my name in every fucking sentence. It's just pissing me off. Eldridge.

Eldridge then quizzed David about secure email servers at length in a manner that suggested he was looking for an excuse not to forward any supporting paperwork. There were apparently protocols Stateside that complicated matters more than David thought probable given the longstanding relationship between US and UK intelligence agencies. But maybe he was being unfair. Maybe a week was just not long enough to establish a link between two "fellow caseworkers" as Eldridge put it.

After the phone call he popped in to see Nigel and tell him about the meeting.

'That should be fine,' Nigel said.

I wasn't asking your permission.

'But best to see if you can meet that bod from the FCO beforehand. Edwin. You'll want to know what he's got to say before you meet the Americans.'

'I'll give him a call now. In the meantime can you authorise a request for his bank statements and his military record?'

'I should think so. I'll need some justification for the requests though.'

'He's the one who signed off the investment. We need to be able to say we've looked. And I was thinking, if this is a security contract, there might be something in there we can use to make the case that he's particularly qualified to run this sort of show. Just a thought.'

Nigel looked a little sceptical.

'The more we basically want to fob the CIA off, the more we need to make it look like we've done a thorough job don't we?'

'I suppose you're right. Yes, you're right. I'll put a request in.'

'And can you ask Ginny to get me all the company reports and accounts for Four Square Security too.'

'Will do'

'One other thing.'

'Yes?'

'They can't organise a computer for me. Because I'm a returning member of staff or something. They'll be in touch with you about authorisation. But in the meantime apparently you can get me permission to use a terminal in the library. For now is it OK if I go and do some background research at home and charge for the hours?'

'That's fine David. And I'll get Ginny to look into the organising permission for you to use the library.'

CHAPTER THREE

Monday was the day of Erics' funeral. David still had to go into London to get the train down to Woking which, because of the timing of the funeral, still meant traveling in the rush hour. He spent the first leg of his journey, into St Pancras, squeezed up against a young man in a startlingly blue suit with hair into which it would have been difficult to squeeze any more gel. Opposite him, her knees brushing his every time the carriage jolted over a set of points, sat a middle-aged woman whose expression could have indicated stoicism, or complete detachment from her surroundings. Despite the cramped conditions he nonetheless made efforts to read his paper. Martin Meehan had died. Talk about a blast from the past. He could remember Meehan being released from internment not long after he had arrived in Northern Ireland; they had held onto him till the end because he was so dangerous. And now, two lengthy prison sentences later, here he was being lauded as a statesman, someone who had sold the peace process to the knuckleheads and even sought some sort of reconciliation with the Unionists. David didn't doubt the die-hards would carry on, or that more people would be killed and maimed, widowed or orphaned over the coming years. This was

Ireland after all. But in substance it really did look like it was over. He closed the paper and leant back in his seat for several minutes. Faces, names, voices even, drifted back to him across the years, a whole enterprise which had been part of his life for so long was slipping into history. Perhaps he really did deserve the credit Nigel had given him at his leaving do.

The second leg of his journey, from Waterloo to Woking, was far calmer. Travelling against the tide of commuters he had an entire bay of four seats to himself. He was still working his way through the biography of Francis Walsingham but it was making grisly reading. There was no doubt Elizabethan protestants could have taught Al Quaeda a thing or two about the grotesque execution of religious opponents. And despite the distance in time David could not help but feel sympathy for the succession of hapless Catholics who fell into the clutches of the Tudor state. They too had been real people once and their agonies just as real as the agonies of the past few decades. From time to time his mind returned to the purpose of his trip and he tried to give some thought to Eric's life. But despite his best efforts his mind would soon return to the far more enthralling lives of men and women dead for so much longer.

The taxi to the church took no more than fifteen minutes, down indistinguishable suburban streets. One day, before too long, David thought, people would be making a similar journey for him. He wondered who would be there. If anyone.

There were more people than David had expected assembling outside the church. He spotted Gavin's substantial form standing to one side, talking to a couple of people he did not recognise and walked over. Gavin introduced him.

'David, this is Eileen and Stephen, they're neighbours of Nora's and they've been looking after her the last couple of days.'

'We've been helping Gavin really, he's been marvellous,' said Eileen. David guessed she was mid-seventies, thinning brown curly hair, an eager, bony face and a plain lilac coat.

'David is one of Eric's former colleagues.'

'Ah. One of the spooks,' said Stephen with glee. He was slightly stooped, with round glasses and enough hair left to form a respectable side parting.

'Long retired,' said David instinctively.

'Eric never let on what he did,' Stephen continued, 'not while he was working, but once he'd retired he let his guard down a little. But he always said it was much more boring than the television used to make out.'

'That's true,' said David. 'More filing and fewer car chases than advertised. Much more filing.'

'Filing's important,' said Gavin, smiling. 'We should probably go in.' The assembled crowd had slowly started making its way into the church and the four of them followed on.

Inside they found Terry and a couple of other faces he recognised, men of Eric's generation whom he had known only slightly. They arranged themselves along a single pew, aware from the glances in their direction that they had been identified as the men from MI5. At the front of the church, seated in a wheelchair and attended by a young woman, sat the sunken form of Eric's widow. At some point, thought David, I'm going to have to introduce myself and find something… appropriate to say.

The vicar was a cheerful, stocky woman in her forties, with, it seemed to David, a touching confidence in Eric's future

57

prospects. David had little doubt that when the end came, that was it and he had no idea whether Eric had believed in any sort of after-life. It wasn't the sort of thing you had talked about at work. So now, as he listened to the vicar welcoming them all to St Mary's church for a celebration of Eric's life and starting to talk of their faith in the resurrection he wondered who she was speaking for. Did anyone else in the church really believe that Eric was going to a better place? Did any of them hold out hope of joining him at some point? In most cases, by the looks of things, at some point in the not too distant future. Or were these just bromides to ease people through the initial shock of loss? His thoughts were interrupted by an invitation to stand and sing the first hymn, "Oh God Our Help in Ages Past" and the muffled rumble of forty or fifty people reaching for hymn books and stumbling to their feet overtook his musings.

The singing began hesitantly but the vicar and one or two other strong voices held the tune and gradually the congregation found a modest level of confidence.

Time, like an ever rolling stream,
Bears all its sons away;
They fly, forgotten, as a dream
Dies at the opening day

He could go with that.

After a few prayers the vicar climbed the steps to the pulpit and began an address that was plainly going to combine sermon and eulogy. She started with a few words about Eric's childhood, a father absent at sea for much of the time, and his own early career as a ship's radio operator before his transfer to the civil service. This was, it occurred to David, another speech at a leaving party, and he wondered how hers would compare to the one Nigel had made at his. He noted a couple of his colleagues exchanging glances, presumably wondering how she would handle his professional life. She continued, 'And we are very pleased to welcome a number of his colleagues from those days who have stepped out of the shadows for a few hours to join us.' There was laughter from a congregation given permission to relax for a moment despite the solemnity of the occasion and a few heads turned to look at David and his colleagues. David kept his eyes on the vicar and sensed an air of quiet triumph on her part. Having won her audience over she began to detail Eric's involvement in the sort of life the elderly live in the suburbs of the home counties. He had volunteered at the charity shop run by a local hospice. He had belonged to a book group where, if the vicar was to be believed, by drawing on his particular experience, he had brought a fresh and unconventional insight to the discussions. He and, until her illness had seriously limited her mobility, his wife Norma, had played an active part in the social life centred on the local branch of the Conservative Party where Norma's famous apple pies had graced many a bring and buy event. 'Eric's faith,' the vicar continued, 'was a tentative faith. With the passing years he had begun to think more deeply about the questions which concern us all. What is the purpose of our being here? Is there any deeper meaning to our existence? And do we have any continued existence beyond the world we know? In recent years Eric and I discussed these questions. I won't say that I fully convinced him, but he certainly came to believe in the possibility of a higher purpose and the possibility that our participation in that higher purpose does not end with our time on earth. The church believes in a loving God. A God who understands that life is difficult and confusing. Above all a God who is willing to forgive. Willing to forgive anything if we genuinely repent and willing to accept anyone who comes to him with an open heart and a desire to do right. Eric has left us now but I believe that he has gone to a better place, to be met by a loving Lord who has seen into Eric's heart, who knows him to be a man of principle, who has seen the love and tenderness he has shown to Norma throughout their lives but most obviously in these recent years and I believe we can all take comfort from that.'

Despite himself David was moved, perhaps because of his own intimations of mortality but perhaps, in part, because of the genuineness of the vicar; her evident willingness to engage with Eric's doubts and her eagerness now to offer some form of comfort to those he had left behind. He looked across at Terry for his reaction but Terry gave the impression of being somewhere else entirely.

The sermon was followed by more prayers and a reading of a Thomas Hardy poem that had apparently been a favourite of Eric's. The final hymn was Jerusalem. An obvious choice in many ways. A good tune. Something everyone would know. And the congregation duly rose to the occasion. The final verse rang out with confidence,

I will not cease from mental fight,
Nor shall my sword sleep in my hand,
Till we have built Jerusalem
*In England's green and pleasant l*and.

Building Jerusalem. Was that what Eric had thought he had been doing for all those years?

On the way out he found himself shaking hands with the vicar. 'A good sermon. Not that I'm much of a judge.'

'You're very kind. I do one most Sundays if you'd like to hear more.' Her smile was also a challenge.

'Thanks, but I live north of London. It would be a little far.' She didn't press the point.

Outside the church he found Gavin and his colleagues discussing a trip to the pub.

'There isn't any sort of wake,' Gavin explained. 'With Norma's condition it wasn't really practical but there's a decent enough place up the road. Back to the main road, turn left. The White Hart. I'll see you up there. I've just got to make sure Norma is being taken care of.'

Four of them set off. David cast a backwards glance at Norma but, with all the fuss surrounding her, it wasn't the moment to try and speak. A wheelchair friendly taxi was backing up and far too many people were trying to be helpful as it was. Terry introduced David to their two companions. The first was a large man called Edward Hanson, red in face and now supporting himself on a stick, but still recognisable as the man David had known in the early seventies. One of the Sudan Souls who had never quite adjusted to the relative banality of domestic policing, notorious for his long and largely liquid lunches, nominally liaising with sources in various African embassies, but no fool for all that. The second figure was more familiar, Daniel Howard, only a few years older than David and plainly thriving in retirement. Slim but obviously fit for his age, he retained the same eagerness David remembered from their shared time trying to keep tabs on the ever-fragmenting Left of the early 1970s. David asked after Daniel's family and found to his embarrassment that he had entirely forgotten about Daniel's

61

severely handicapped son, a man who, now in his forties, and despite plainly feeling much, had never spoken a word.

'We battle on,' said Daniel. 'The council were threatening to cut his funding, which would have meant him essentially living with us full time. We'd have coped but it would have been a completely different life. But fortunately, after months of arguments and letter writing. And endless form filling; his medication, his bowel movements, the number of bathrooms in our house, over and over again. Eventually they accepted they would continue to provide residential care for him rather than just respite care. But Anna's doing really well. Had a great time at Newcastle. She's working for Ford now. It seems to be going well and she's enjoying it. We're secretly hoping she doesn't marry the current boyfriend but otherwise it's all fine. How about you?'

David felt the same sense of perceived failure he always experienced when asked about his life by people whose own lives centred so much on their children.

'I've just retired actually. Finally reached the magic sixty, give or take, and now my life is my own. In theory.'

'In practice?'

'In practice they've dragged me back for a couple of weeks to do some… background checks they're too busy to finish off themselves. But after that I am finally free. It's been quite a ride though hasn't it. Who'd have thought it. Gerry Adams and Ian Paisley in the same room. At the same time. And they both emerged alive.'

When they reached the pub the slot machine by the door made David's heart sink but they found an area of tables beyond the bar, stretching round a corner that shielded them from the worst of the machine's distracting flashes and beeps.

There they removed their coats and organised the first round of drinks.

'Are you OK Terry?' asked Daniel.

Terry nodded but barely spoke.

'You and Eric were close weren't you,' said Daniel. 'This must be hitting you harder than the rest of us. I'm sorry. He was a dedicated officer. We all learnt a lot from him.' Daniel waited a moment for some response then asked, 'What will you have.'

'A pint of … what've they got. Green King,' said Terry. 'And a whisky if that's alright. A double if you don't mind.'

'Of course,' said Daniel. 'It's that sort of day. David? Edward?'

Daniel was still at the bar when Gavin arrived, fuming.

'What the bloody hell was that sermon all about. Calling us out like that then going on about how God will forgive anything, like we've all got cupboards jammed full of skeletons.'

'We've all got one or two, old boy,' said Edward, thankfully taking charge of a pint of Guinness from Daniel.

'I don't doubt you do Edward but Eric? He was a communications wallah. Radios and bugging and stuff. The worst he ever did was tap a phone or two that wasn't expressly covered by the warrant. God botherers! And I'm probably showing my age here but women God botherers. In the pulpit. It doesn't feel right to me. Anyway, let's drink to Eric. And to all the fallen. God rest their souls.'

David had no intention of drinking heavily. He had a long journey home and the days when he would travel that far after a serious session were long gone. Edward by contrast was a hardened drinker and steamed through pint after pint without obvious ill effect. And Gavin was a practiced drinker too. But there was an air of desperation about their efforts, so different from their previous meeting. The conversation failed to flow. In an effort to raise people's spirits David started to tell the story of a bugging expedition he had been on with Eric shortly after he had joined.

'Do you remember. 1972. People were really jumpy. The miners had come out for the first time since 1926 and there'd been power cuts and that picket was killed. Run over by a lorry.'

'Oh God yes,' said Gavin. 'And that idiot MP, what was his name?... came out and threatened to respond with violence...'

'So when the building workers came out...,' David went on, 'I'd just arrived in the office, but it seemed to me that... it wasn't panic... but it was...'

'The buggers were on the march,' Edward suggested.

'Exactly,' said David. 'So Eric and I went to place a listening device in one of the union offices. It was routine for him, but for me it was my first taste of this sort of thing and I thought I was James Bond or something.' In truth he'd been excited, but very conscious of being the new boy and more concerned with not making a fool of himself than with getting the job done.

'Eric knew exactly what he was doing and we got in through a back door in a matter of moments. Up the stairs. Far door on the right. Eric picks the lock in seconds. Up on the desk. Microphone in the light fitting and we're back out the door in a couple of minutes. Got in late the next morning and Jerry, who was running that team then, handed me an A4 envelope. Said, completely straight faced, "They've typed up the initial recordings for you. Let me know what you think."' He paused for effect. 'We'd bugged an office used by the

Cooperative Undertakers. All I'd got in my hands was one half of a handful of telephone conversations about coffin fittings. We had to go back the next night and bug the room on the other side of the corridor.'

It wasn't the funniest of stories but the fact was that Eric had never been much of a laugh and the tale fell flat. A silence settled on the party, broken only by a rattle of coins as someone scored a modest win on the slot machine.

'You worked with Eric pretty closely Terry. You knew him better than most,' said Gavin. 'You must have some fond memories. You were thick as thieves back in the seventies.'

Terry looked uncomfortable in the spotlight. He seemed to take a moment to collect his thoughts. 'I know a lot of people didn't like him. No, that's not right.' He was labouring over his sentences. 'People didn't warm to him. He wasn't what you'd call a warm person. Not a people person. But he took care of you when you joined, didn't he David. Made sure you were… that the public school boys didn't freeze you out.'

'He did,' said David, more to fill the gap in Terry's rambling than out of conviction.

'He had a bit of a chip on his shoulder about all that,' said Gavin. 'It could be a bit gentlemen and players at times though. With some of those old colonials.'

David was conscious of making an effort not to look at Edward. Terry appeared oblivious. 'Eric was a grafter, and he was very good at what he did,' he continued. 'And he was loyal. He knew how important what we were doing was. Which makes all this so unfair. With Norma. And she'll only get two thirds of his pension. And how's she going to manage on that?'

'We'll see what we can do,' said Gavin. Then, changing the subject, 'So what is it they've brought you back to work on David?'

David hesitated, but after two beers his caution was not what it might have been and, in any event it wasn't as if all these people hadn't been positively vetted.

'Lord Frampton? Tory peer? Gone into business in Iraq.'

People nodded. Even Terry seemed to be taking an interest.

'The yanks have made some bullshit complaint about him making corrupt payments in Iraq.'

'I rather assumed everyone makes corrupt payments in Iraq,' said Edward.

'That's what I mean,' said David. 'Why complain about him doing what everybody's doing? It makes no sense. Anyway, I've got to go through the motions and put in a report saying he's been a good boy. Two or three weeks work. Easy money. What's up Terry?'

All the colour seemed to have drained from Terry's face. 'Ask Eric,' he said finally.

'Eric's dead Terry,' said Daniel.

Terry didn't respond immediately. He finished his whisky, perhaps the third he had had along with the pints. 'Anyone like another drink?' he asked. 'May as well.' He spoke slowly in an effort to mask how slurred his words had become.

'No thanks Terry,' said Daniel, 'I think I'm ready to go home.'

'Me too old boy,' said Edward.

'You coming to the station Terry,' David asked. He didn't fancy babying Terry back to London but he was reluctant to leave him to make his own way home.

'No. I'll stay here. Thanks. I'm in no hurry.'

There was plainly no point trying to shift him so, rather awkwardly, the three of them made their way out, past the still bleeping slot machine, and onto the pavement.

'What's got into him?' asked Daniel. 'I know they were close but...'

'I'll give him a ring tomorrow,' said Gavin. 'Probably that bloody vicar going on about...'

David took a taxi back to the station. He sobered up slowly on the train to London and made several attempts to get back into his book. But somehow his mind kept returning to the hopeless, or was it desperate, look on Terry's face.

CHAPTER FOUR

David was still wondering about Terry when he returned to the office the following morning. Perhaps he would give him a ring. But before he had taken his coat off Ginny appeared at his door with a collection of papers.

'How was the funeral?' she asked.

'Good I suppose. A good turn-out. The singing was OK. It was terrible to see Norma though, his wife. Did you ever meet her?'

'I don't think so. She's in a wheelchair isn't she?'

'Yes. Has been for several years now. I didn't get to talk to her. There were too many people … you know…'

'Yes.' There was a silence as if they both felt they ought to have something more to say about an event as momentous as the ending of a human life.

'Here are the papers you asked for. The company documents don't have a security marking of course so… if you can leave them on your desk… I know we're not supposed to but Nigel's safe is a bit full at the moment. And we got a message from Lord Frampton. He says he is back in the country and he can see you tomorrow. But not till half past six. Nigel told him you could do that so I hope it's all right. I did ask Nigel if it might be better to wait till the day after but ...'

'That's fine Ginny. Thank you.'

'And we had a phone call from the Foreign Office. Edwin somebody. He said he knows it's short notice but he's free this afternoon if that's OK for you. I knew you were keen to see him so I said yes.'

'That's great Ginny, thanks.'

'Oh. And someone from IT came round yesterday. No peace for the wicked. About your computer. They left you a login for the computer in the Library.' She handed him a slip of paper with a string of numbers on it.

'Thanks. Did you get a name?'

'He said he'd call back. I can try and find out if you like?'

'Don't worry Ginny. I've got a reference number. I'm sure I can track someone down. Thanks for these,' he said, indicating the stack of papers.

'I'm afraid it looks like they've only sent half his army records over. I've asked for the rest. But the person I spoke to wasn't very keen to help I didn't think.'

'Never mind. Thanks for trying. I'll start with what I've got.'

He spent the first hour of the morning in the library ploughing through company records noting the various changes of directors and searching the internet for biographical information. The directors fell very clearly into two types, money men, and military men. With the exception of Lord Frampton, the military men were no older than fifty. There was no obvious pattern beyond reasonably rapid promotion but David guessed at a network of personal connections. The money men had generally worked for

69

smaller investment houses and merchant banks and several had overlapped at particular institutions but regular movements between employers were par for the course in the City these days and they had all moved sufficiently frequently that again David could detect no pattern. He wasn't even sure what he hoped to find.

Then he turned to the army file. It contained the usual details of recruitment, training, marks and reports from Frampton's time at Sandhurst and so on. None of it told him anything remotely useful. Turning through the pages of ageing forms, some probably unread since the day they had been placed on the file thirty years or more before, David formed the impression of a man who had been sufficiently committed to pass the selection for the Parachute Regiment, but not otherwise noticeably different from any other junior officer. It was only when he reached the very end of the file that he found something out of the ordinary. A typed A4 sheet of paper with nothing more on it than "The report on the incident in the Ardoyne on 3 April 1972 compiled by Major M Watson can be obtained from the central registry under the following reference."

He went and looked for Ginny.

'Can you see if you can get hold of this report for me?'

'From 1972? I can try. But you know what they're like with documents at the MOD.'

'Do you think we can try and trace this Major Watson?'

'I can ask Research.'

'We can probably do it on Google. How many Major M Watsons do you think the army had in 1972?'

'Let's see what we can find.'

And it took no more than ten minutes to identify a Major Watson from the period who had retired as a Brigadier in the late nineties.

'Brilliant. Shall we see if he's in the phone book?'

'What do you think the chances are of someone like him being in the phone book?'

'I don't know. People of that generation don't think not to be.'

And he was.

'Thanks Ginny. But can you try getting hold of the file as well?'

At that moment his phone rang. It was Sergeant Henderson.

'You wanted to know about the incident at Lord Frampton's house?'

'Yes. Thanks for calling back. Can you tell me roughly how many people were there, what they were protesting about, that sort of thing?'

'I can tell you what Lady Frampton told me.'

'You never saw them?'

'No. Obviously, he's a former MP, he's on our list, so when the call came in it should have received a priority response. But the cuts mean we're thin on the ground during quieter periods, like week day evenings. And there'd been a smash on the A 40. They sent me over but I was twenty miles away and by the time I got there it was all over. So, I know the response time was outside the target period but under the circumstances...'

David wondered whether to let him know this was not an issue about response times but reckoned that he would get more out of the man if he was anxious to make amends.

71

'But do you have no idea of who was there. These must be pretty dedicated campaigners to make it all the way out to his house in the country?'

'That's the curious thing. We've got cameras on both lanes of the M40 either side of the exit for his house so you can work out who's got off at that exit. Apparently they were complaining about the way his company had treated trade unions in Iraq. That's what Lord Frampton told us anyway. And we have a pretty good database of activists, particularly the hard-core trade unionists. Well... you must know more about this than me... and none of the car registrations matched anyone on the database. I can send you the list if you like?'

'Thanks. That would be helpful. Did you contact any of the people who have been campaigning on the issue?' There had been material on the file about this but he had only skim read it. He would need to go back to it.

'I made a couple of phone calls. More for form's sake than anything. Got some pretty hostile responses as you can imagine. They're not our biggest fans. But no one would even admit to having been there. We do try to stop people turning up at private houses. We're quite happy to facilitate their right to protest but we try to persuade them to do it at the company headquarters or something. It's not right to scare somebody's wife like that.'

'Lady Frampton was really alarmed was she?'

'It was hard to tell. Lord Frampton had got back by then. He was really giving out about how slow we'd been to get there. And to be honest, he did almost all the talking. Every time I tried to talk to her about it he interrupted. I wasn't too bothered because at the end of the day the only criminal issue was some graffiti and once I'd established that she wouldn't be able to identify who was responsible for that I lost interest. I didn't warm to Lord Frampton. Does that answer all your questions?'

'It does yes. That's very helpful. But if you could send me the list of cars which left the M40 at the relevant exit that would be great.'

'Sure thing.'

'Just out of interest…'

'Yes?'

'What exactly was the graffiti?'

'It said "Are you ready for anything?"'

'Did that mean anything to Lord Frampton?'

'Not a thing. Not something I've ever seen before either.'

'Oh well. Thanks.'

It was only a ten minute walk to the Foreign Office. At reception he gave his name and took a seat opposite three Asian men in suits talking in a language he didn't know, the two on the outside leaning in eagerly to the animated conversation. Businessmen or diplomats? He reckoned their ties were too garish for diplomats but what did he know. Five minutes later a young man arrived to collect him. Jacket but no tie and a bounce in his step.

'I'm Spencer.' He held out his hand. 'I'll take you up now. Have you come far?' Somehow there was energy injected into even this most banal of questions.

David did his best to maintain the civilities until he was shown into a nondescript office and Edwin Birch got up to greet him.

'Good afternoon Mr Nixon.' This man too was younger than he'd expected from their brief chat on the phone. And he had the easy confidence of a man who, despite his relative youth, entirely believed in his own fitness for his job. David knew it shouldn't irritate him but it did.

'Good afternoon, Mr Nicholson.'

'Edwin please.'

You started it.

David sat down and expected Edwin to do the same. But instead Edwin remained standing, looking down at the papers on his desk. And after a few seconds silence said, 'What the fuck'. Another moment or two of silent head shaking then, again, 'What the fuck.'

'It doesn't look good does it.'

'I'm not talking about Frampton. He's plainly guilty as sin. But...' Edwin started pacing the short distance between his chair and the door. 'I don't suppose you follow this stuff closely do you?'

'Just what I read in the papers.'

'Last year Pentagon auditors found Halliburton had probably overcharged for services in Iraq by, I think it was $250 million. No, it was a little bit more than that, but thereabouts. How much of that do you think the Pentagon paid?'

'$250 million?' David guessed. It wouldn't surprise him.

'Near enough. Not much less than $240 million.'

'Because of Cheney?'

'Because of Cheney, and all the senior officers who fancied cushy jobs with the company when they retired. And...'

'If the US tax payer is willing to swallow it...'

'It's not the US tax payer. Huge amounts of this comes out of Iraqi funds the UN have entrusted to the US government. Almost literally out of the mouths of starving children. And they come after us for this?' He shook his head in despair.

'How did this come about, this inquiry?' To David's relief Edwin stopped pacing and sat down.

'The CIA complained. And I've had a call from an interested party at the CIA. So anything you can do to put me in the picture would really help. He's coming over to London and he rather implied it was principally to talk to me.'

'You're honoured.' Edwin smiled.

'Honoured? Really?'

'Absolutely. Most CIA employees never leave the U.S. Half of them don't even have passports.'

'How come?' David had anticipated being fobbed off or patronised at this meeting but he had not expected to be baffled.

'The vast majority of their staff work in Langley, or at one of their many, many regional offices inside the U.S.'

'Doing what exactly?'

'That's a very good question. There's a lot of management going on but we do often wonder what exactly all these people are managing. Anyway. What are we going to do about Lord Frampton?'

And it seemed to David there was a twinkle in the man's eyes, an acknowledgment perhaps that Lord Frampton was something of a liability, and he relaxed a little.

'You've looked at the papers?'

'I have. Yes. But only just now as you were coming up the stairs. Sorry. We're somewhat under the cosh here at the moment. What can I say. If the service company had made even some effort to trade it might have helped make the deal look at least vaguely plausible.' Edwin's attitude now seemed to sit somewhere between amusement and despair.

'It does look pretty open and shut doesn't it,' David agreed. 'Though the fact the Americans haven't produced anything

75

damning does suggest that maybe Frampton and Al Jamail were sensible enough not to write anything too stupid down in an email or the NSA would have managed to pull it out of the ether.'

'That is grounds for hope, yes. But I'm still not entirely sure how I can help you.'

'The way my boss explained it to me the deal was that MI5 would deal with this, reluctantly, but you would help out with background. And your department provided us with some papers. He must have been on your radar.' David was feeling more and more like the meeting was a waste of time.

'I've seen a copy of what we sent you,' Edwin said. 'Obviously if we had been taking a serious interest in him we'd have put something more professional than that together. No. He was just someone in Iraq... someone important enough that we needed to have some sort of handle on what he was up to. In case anything went wrong and we were suddenly being asked all sorts of questions.'

Then Edwin leant forward and put his chin in his hands. He looked past David for a moment or two then he said, in a more business-like tone, 'You're being asked to respond to an American complaint about what a British subject has been getting up to in Iraq. I think the best thing I can do for you is give you some sort of sense of US-UK relations in Iraq.' He smiled. 'Which may or may not prove helpful to you. The reason you have been sent to see me is that I worked for the Coalition Provisional Authority, albeit only during the final months of its existence, working for Paul Bremer trying to get Iraq back on its feet again, so that's why I'm sometimes used as an Iraq reconstruction expert, and let's just say it was... not a happy experience. Relations between Bremer and the British had broken down pretty badly by then.'

'What went wrong?' David wondered where this was going but he was content to listen.

Edwin continued. 'Bremer was ... Paul Bremer headed the Coalition Provisional Authority, and ... he was a nightmare in many ways, but the specific problem that did for us was that he was telling Washington next to nothing about what was actually going on in Iraq. That is to say he was significantly exaggerating the scale of his achievements and seriously underplaying the problems and some of what he was telling them was.... essentially untrue. It was stunning to watch sometimes. But the British staff were obviously briefing the UK government about the situation and at some point Condoleezza Rice worked out that the British ambassador in Washington knew more about what was going on over there than she did. So she started relying on him for briefings. It was a ridiculous situation and it all came to a head, and this was before my time, it all came out when the US launched its assault on Fallujah after those Blackwater employees were killed. Bremer was telling her it was all under control. And it wasn't. The mood of the Iraqi people... they could see pictures of what was happening in Fallujah on Al Jazeera, it was... Everything was on the verge of falling apart, it was on an absolute knife edge, people I knew who were there were really, really... worried... and Bremer was just straight out lying about it to Washington and telling Condoleezza Rice that everything was under control and she said, "That's not what the British are saying." And he never forgave us for that. So by the time I was there we were cut out of most of the important decisions... we were treated with contempt by several members of his staff. So there may well be some residual bad blood behind their interest in Lord Frampton's activities.'

'Sounds possible. Or might the Americans just be sore about a UK company getting such a big contract?'

'I don't think so. And I doubt even the contract with the Iraq National Oil Company has a long term future. We're certainly hoping it doesn't. We're hoping Iraq is going to pass an oil law before too long which will open up the Iraqi oil industry to foreign investment. BP's got their eye on the Rumalia field and they have their own security systems.'

'I'm sure they do, but not for war zones surely?'

'BP operate in Columbia. You don't do that without serious back up. No, they'll bring their own people in, they'll probably train up the local police and so on and they won't have any need for Lord Frampton's people. If BP play their cards right they may even get the Iraqis to pay for it. They've got this sort of thing down to a fine art. So Four Square are on a time limited contract here. If all goes according to plan.'

'Whose plan?'

'HMG's plan. The Americans can afford to be relaxed about whether or not their companies get to develop the Iraqi oil fields but we can't. Shell is in a massive hole after booking all those non-existent reserves and BP's one of the country's biggest blue chip companies. A major component of many of our pension funds. And the tax revenue that's going to pay your pension. UK PLC needs this.'

The expression on David's face plainly made Edwin uncomfortable.

'Look, we freed them from Saddam and along the way we get access to some of their oil. Which we'll pay for. It's not the opium wars.'

David looked down at his notes to check what else he had to cover. 'What do you make of the complaints that Lord

Frampton was helping to suppress the unions in the oil industry?'

'To start with you have to remember that unions remain illegal in the oil industry, so although there is some evidence that Four Square Security were involved in removing union activists from the oil field...'

'What I've read isn't pretty. The campaigners say union leaders were deliberately sent to really dangerous places no one expected them to come back from alive. I mean...'

'I don't know about that. And in any event we wouldn't have a problem with that side of his activities.'

'The TUC seem to have been making quite a fuss about this.'

'No. As I say, the unions remained illegal. And from our point of view the unions are a problem because they're campaigning for the Iraqis to retain day to day control of their oil industry. Which obviously isn't what we're looking for.'

David didn't really know what to say to that.

'Have you considered the possibility that this might in some way be personal?' Edwin asked.

'How do you mean?'

'I saw him at a reception hosted by BP not long after the invasion and my impression was he saw a golden opportunity to leverage some influence and get rich. Like one or two others. And he homed in on Sir Richard Burke... like a heat seeking missile. He'd known Sir Richard slightly when Sir Richard was at the FCO and Frampton was involved on the defence side, though not as well as he made out I don't think. And of course Sir Richard then moved over to BP, as people from the FCO tend to do...'

'Is that your plan? David asked.

'It'll all be wind farms and solar panels by the time I retire. I'm going to have to make do with my gold-plated pension. No, but Frampton really put a few backs up at that meeting. And I hear on the Whitehall grapevine that he annoyed a lot of people at Defence. What I'm thinking is that somewhere along the line he may well just have annoyed someone on the American side, someone with the clout to bring the wrath of the CIA down on his head. Just a thought.'

'I can believe that. Yes. That's entirely possible.' He checked his notes again. 'What about this suggestion that payments were going to factions aligned with Iran?'

'Probably nonsense. Look the Americans have traditionally supported Iraq to counter-balance the power of Iran, certainly since the fall of the Shah. And what they've done by weakening Iraq so much with their invasion is to completely undermine that policy. There are really strong religious connections between Iraq and Iran so what they've ended up with, as a result of the power vacuum they created, is Iraqi politicians who are very close to Iran, and they're a bit miffed. But it's entirely their own fault. They probably just want someone else to share the blame.' He shrugged. 'Look. That's probably as much as I can usefully tell you. If you've got any further questions, if anything comes up by all means give me a call.'

'Thanks Edwin. You've been a great help. I think that sets me up for my meeting. It should be interesting.' He got to his feet.

'I'm glad to have been of some assistance,' said Edwin, but his mind was clearly already moving on. 'Spencer will show you out. I'd come down with you but I've got another meeting in 15 minutes.' Edwin had already found what were presumably the papers for his meeting and was flicking through them, occasionally comparing documents with a page that was formatted like a contents list. But he did eventually rise to his feet and shake David's hand.

'Must keep you pretty busy, this whole Middle East thing?' David asked, for want of anything better to say.

Edwin rolled his eyes. 'Mostly trying to stop them bombing things.'

'Good luck with that.'

And it was as he walked down the stairs, accompanied by Spencer that it came to him? 'Of course.'

'What?' Spencer asked.

David realised had spoken out loud.

'Sorry. I've just worked something out that has been nagging at me.'

'It's weird when that happens isn't it.'

"Ready for Anything" was the motto of the Parachute Regiment. It wasn't demonstrators demanding union rights for Iraqi oil workers who had scrawled that graffiti at Frampton's house. It was Paras. That missing report on the "incident" in the Ardoyne took on a new significance.

CHAPTER FIVE

As soon as he got back to the office he retrieved his papers from Nigel's safe and dialled Brigadier Watson.

'Good afternoon. This is David Nixon from the Security Service.' That usually got people's attention.

'Good afternoon.' The Brigadier was alert but unfazed.

'We're conducting an inquiry into matters relating to Lord Frampton but when your paths crossed he would have been Lieutenant Edwards.'

'That's going back a way.' Thank God. He'd got the right Watson.

'You will appreciate we can't explain the nature of our investigation but... the problem we have is that our files contain a reference to an investigation you carried out but, inevitably, the investigation report itself isn't with our papers.'

'You surprise me.' The Brigadier's tone was one of world-weary amusement rather than sarcasm.

'I was wondering, would it be possible to come and discuss your investigation?'

'I don't see why not. I'll need to check your credentials. David Nixon you say?'

'Yes. I formally retied a couple of weeks ago but I'm back as a consultant.'

'OK. And are you calling from a landline the powers that be would recognise as belonging to MI5?'

'Yes I am.'

'Good. Give me half an hour. If this all checks out I'd be happy to talk to you. Are you free tomorrow morning? I live in Oxfordshire, about half an hour beyond Oxford itself. Just short of Stowe on the Water. Do you have a car?'

'I do. I'll see you tomorrow. Mid-morning if that's convenient.'

'Look forward to it Mr Nixon.'

Only when he had put the phone down did David acknowledge to himself that there was precious little connection between the job he had been assigned and the lead he was now pursuing. With any luck Nigel was too busy with the Somali investigation to notice what he was up to. If he was challenged he would just have to say he had got carried away. But if it was Paras behind the graffiti then Frampton had lied about the protestors. He considered that fact for a moment or two but, without any further information there was nothing he could do with it. His thoughts turned to Terry's strange comments at the funeral. He decided to give him a call.

'Terry, hello, it's David here.'

'Hello.' The voice was guarded.

'I wondered how you were doing?' No response. 'You seemed a bit out of sorts at the funeral.'

'I'd had rather a lot to drink.' Then silence.

'Are you feeling any better now.' There was an indistinct response

'Terry. There was something else I wanted to ask you about. When I mentioned Lord Frampton's name at Eric's funeral your face went white. What was that about?'

'Must have been feeling a bit under the weather I suppose.' He sounded bored. As if he felt obliged to lie but not in any way obliged to make the lie convincing. Then he seemed to pull himself together and make a bit more of an effort to convince. 'I'd had quite a lot to drink.'

'There was something more than that going on. Don't mess me around like this.'

David was pretty sure now that Terry was drunk.

'I can't help you.' Then silence again.

David tried another tack. 'Do you need me to help you?'

There was nothing but silence. 'Terry?' Still nothing. 'Terry. If you're in trouble…' How could Terry possibly be in trouble?

'How about I come down and see you?'

'That's not going to do any good.'

David was about to ask why he shouldn't come down when Terry spoke again.

'If you weren't just doing a whitewash on the bastard you could ask him about his time up North.'

'Up North? What happened?' A clue, at long bloody last.

'You're doing the investigation. You ask him.'

'At least give me a hint Terry.'

After what seemed like an age Terry spoke again. 'You heard they got burgled? During the funeral.'

'Who? Eric? Nora?'

'Eric's house, yes.'

And David's mind went back to the strange scene he had walked into in the toilets at the Marquis of Granby. 'What were you and Eric arguing about at my leaving do? Terry...?'

The phone went dead.

David stared ahead at the wall for a minute or two. What a mess. He could hardly ask Lord Frampton about trips to the north of England when he was supposed to be investigating payments in Iraq. And he had no idea what he might be looking for anyway.

Half an hour later the Brigadier rang. He confirmed he would be happy to talk and gave David detailed instructions on how to find his house.

The next morning started bright. Even the few clouds were a brilliant white against the blue sky. It would, David thought, be a lovely day to wander round the bird reserve. Maybe in a week or two.

Beyond Oxford the A 37 was full of traffic bound for Cheltenham and points West. Was it just nostalgia or had the roads really been clearer, and driving freer twenty years ago? But the five miles from the turn off to the Brigadier's house were almost empty of cars and he relaxed. Between the pale stone walls which divided the fields there was nothing now but stubble, bleached by the autumn sun and bisected at regular intervals by the tram lines marking the path the sprayers had taken during the course of the year. The few trees in this landscape were beginning to turn to autumn colours and their leaves appeared to ripple and even shimmer under the erratic impact of the breezes. At the top of a rise on the approach to a village, exactly as detailed in his directions, a narrow lane, Drayton Road, contoured round to the left in the direction of a group of ash trees and thirty yards down the lane on the right a hornbeam-flanked drive led off to "Stowe Manor". David turned in and pulled up moments later in front of a substantial, old farmhouse of golden Cotswold stone. He felt the car sink inches into the gravel as he braked. When he turned off the engine its sound was replaced by the constant noise of the wind tossing and churning the yellowing leaves of the hornbeams.

The front door of the house opened almost before he had got out of the car and a tall figure strode out to greet him.

'How do you do David. Michael Watson.' Brigadier Michael Watson stood at least six foot two, and his seventy-eight years hadn't caused his frame to stoop or shrink one bit. He had a full head of wavy, greying hair, cut probably a little longer than in his soldiering days, and immensely bushy eyebrows. His eyes had sunk a little, and creased in the corners. There were still further creases around his lips and nostrils and his cheeks hung a little slackly off his jaw. But for all that, his manner was that of someone still fully and efficiently engaged in the business of life. 'Come on in.'

As he followed the Brigadier into the house David took in the subdued checked shirt and tie, the khaki moleskin trousers and the polished brogues, practically the uniform of a retired army officer. In the sitting room Michael indicated the sofa. 'Have a seat. Would you like a tea or some coffee?'

'Tea please,' said David. 'Milk, no sugar thanks.'

With the Brigadier gone David looked round the room. Opposite him was a fireplace, and to his right a bay window that looked out onto the garden; rose beds and an improbably healthy lawn. The room itself was surprisingly dark. Another window behind him let in little light and the sallow, greenish walls seemed to soak up most of that. A floor to ceiling bookcase in one corner appeared to contain mainly hardbacks, some at least plainly historical. David barely registered the paintings, but he did take in the photographs arranged on a table just inside the door. One of the Brigadier shaking hands with the Queen somewhere, a couple of a woman he assumed must be, or have been, the Brigadier's wife, more military photographs including a couple of recent colour pictures of a younger man in desert camouflage, and one of the same man, fresher faced, at what was, he guessed, his passing out parade at Sandhurst. He wondered what it would be like to meet the Queen. He had heard somewhere she was adept at putting people at their ease but he doubted he could ever shake her hand with the confidence the Brigadier seemed to project in the photograph.

The Brigadier returned with a tray on which were two mugs of tea, one with a teaspoon in, and a plate of milk chocolate hobnobs.

'Ah, hobnobs,' said David, trying to forget about his waistline.

Michael smiled. 'Nothing but the best.'

'Is that your son?'

'Yes. Simon. He's a captain now. Out there on his second tour. Due back next month. Now, what exactly do you want from me?' The brigadier sat down in an upright armchair to the right of the fireplace, deliberately or not leaving himself silhouetted against the bay window, making his face that much harder to read.

'I'm conducting an investigation into aspects of Lord Frampton's activities.' This was true as far as it went. But the implication that what followed related to his official investigation was false and despite himself David felt suddenly nervous. He took a moment to focus his attention and continued. 'There was some sort of disturbance at his home a few months ago and it's been suggested that this related to his activities in Iraq, specifically that it was a protest against his involvement in the clamping down on trade unions in the oil industry.'

'Yes.' The brigadier's tone indicated that he was following the thread but was yet to be convinced that it had anything to do with him.

'However, there isn't any firm evidence that this is what the disturbance related to.'

'When you say disturbance, what exactly are we talking about?'

'That's a very good question. There appear to have been a number of people present and some of them sprayed the words "Are you ready for anything," without a question mark, on an exterior wall. And, apart from Frampton's word, there's no evidence there were any protestors at all. And all the usual suspects deny ever being there. That's really all I know. But that slogan doesn't seem to bear any relation to trade union issues but it could relate to the parachute regiment. You conducted some sort of inquiry into his conduct shortly before he left the regiment and I'm wondering whether you could tell me a bit more about what that was about. In case it sheds any light on what went on.'

The brigadier raised his substantial eyebrows. 'Seems a bit of a long shot to me.'

David feared that was it. The Brigadier was dismissing the whole idea and was about to ask him to leave. Maybe even phone MI5 and complain about his time being wasted, which would be awkward. But the Brigadier had merely been organising his thoughts.

'No one ever questioned Alex's commitment. In a way he was perfect for the Paras. Aggressive, unreflective. And no shortage of physical courage. And you have to remember what Belfast was like in 1972. There was contact pretty much every day, and the wrecked houses... all those burnt out houses meant the place looked more like Stalingrad than somewhere in Great Britain.' He paused, as if he too was, for a moment, walking those streets again. 'And when there's an invisible enemy shooting at you from two sides, and you're taking casualties, that's when you find out who's got the stomach for the fight. And there's no doubt Alex did. Most of his men thought he was fantastic, or at least that was the reputation he had, but I was talking to, I think it was a company sergeant major, from his battalion, and he told me Alex got out of the regiment just in time.'

'What do you mean?'

'Alex's platoon had got into a fire fight on the edge of the Ardoyne... do you know Belfast?'

'Yes. I was there in the late 70's.'

'And two of his men were hit. And at that point they should have backed off. One of them was badly hurt. But Alex took his men forward. And the Sergeant wasn't there. He'd only heard what other people had told him. But the story was they ended up in a pretty confused half hour gun battle. Used up an absurd amount of ammunition blasting away at shadows. And in frustration... you might remember how these events used to attract groups of spectators.'

David nodded. He'd more or less forgotten but he could picture the scene now. Young, frightened men crouched in doorways shouting instructions as bullets ricocheted off the walls around them while, thirty yards away, housewives and children screamed abuse at the soldiers or shouted encouragement to the unseen gunmen.

'Well it seemed that as the platoon were finally pulling back one of these people shouted something at them and his guys grabbed two lads out of the crowd and beat them pretty badly.'

'And Alex didn't try to stop it.'

The Brigadier paused a moment before answering. 'The story was Alex ordered them to do it.'

'And what about the casualties?'

'They both lived. But one of them was in hospital for months. Invalided out in the end. Lost half his leg. And the suggestion was it could have been saved if he'd been treated quicker.'

'And how did you get to meet this sergeant?'

The Brigadier paused again. 'During my inquiry. The locals had complained bitterly. And there was a sense that... The Parashave never been the most disciplined of regiments, and this wasn't the only incident. This was well before Bloody Sunday but even then... there was a recognition in certain circles that this sort of behaviour wasn't helping so I was asked by General Tuzo to look into it. I'd done a two-year secondment with the regiment from '63 to '65 and the idea was that might encourage people to talk to me.'

'And what was the result.'

The Brigadier laughed but didn't smile. 'The shutters came down. I spoke to everyone on that patrol. Our focus was on the beating of the spectators. Our intelligence wasn't great at the time but we knew enough to be pretty confident there was some substance to the complaint. But they all denied everything pretty much. With varying degrees of borderline insolence.'

'Yes.' That tedious sense of superiority from sections of the military had been one of the minor irritations of active duty in the Province. 'So what about this sergeant?'

'He hadn't been on the patrol. He was an older man. Not that far short of retirement I think, and he'd seen action in Aden, and Cyprus I think, yes, because we'd both served in Cyprus, so we chatted about that for a bit and then I made some comment about Alex and he let rip. It wasn't the beatings so much as the carelessness about his own men that angered him. That was the first I heard of it but I mentioned it afterwards in the mess and it was clear there was quite a bit of ill feeling.'

'And what did Alex have to say about it?' David knew better than to lean forward at this point, make his interest clear and interrupt the flow, but this was what he wanted to hear.

'I never got to speak to him. He'd already applied to join the SAS and as soon as the investigation started he was packed straight off to Hereford. I heard there wasn't even a selection scheduled and he just hung around there for a month or so, just keeping out of the way. But I've no idea if that was true. Whatever, he was out of the province, out of General Tuzo's command and there was nothing we could do about it.'

'So there could be some disgruntled former soldiers out there.'

'Who've waited thirty years to do this. It seems unlikely.'

'So that was the end of it?'

'Yes.'

'And your paths didn't cross again?'

'No.' The Brigadier was silent but David could sense he was considering whether to say anything more. He waited.

The silence was only emphasised by the distant churning of the leaves in the grip of wind. Then the Brigadier asked, 'Does the name Sean O'Donnell mean anything to you?'

'Yes, it caused a bit of a stir.'

'We had something of an understanding with the Gardai when it came to crossing the border. If it had just been O'Donnell that had been killed there wouldn't have been too much fuss. Everyone knew who he was. But you may remember, it wasn't just him who was shot. There was another man. James O'Malley, a local taxi driver. No IRA connections at all. That cost us a lot of goodwill.'

'And that was Lord Frampton?'

'I have no hard evidence. They were something of a law unto themselves at Castle Dillon. A colleague of mine told me they had a draw full of spare barrels and so on for Browning pistols to use in actions which they didn't want traced back to them. So you wouldn't be able to prove anything. But Alex had passed the SAS selection and was back in the Province by then. The word was that it was Alex who'd killed them.'

'Was that widely known?'

'Not widely, no. I've never seen it suggested in print. But in principle anyone might have heard.'

There seemed nothing more to discuss. 'Well. Thank you very much for your time.'

'I don't know that I've been much use really. I hope it was some use.'

Driving back home David tried to make some sense of what he had heard. The conversation had reawakened his own memories of Ulster, stories he had long since pushed to the back of his mind and few of which he wished to revisit. So, with an effort, he brought his mind back to the matter in hand.

Ideally he would try to track down at least the soldier who had lost his leg but that was going to be hard to explain to Nigel. And nothing he had heard was going to make tomorrow's interview with Lord Frampton any easier.

CHAPTER SIX

That afternoon David looked once more through the papers that the FCO had provided on Frampton. And this time he paid attention to the pages dealing with Frampton's family background. Anything that might give him an insight into Frampton as a person would make the evening's task a little easier. The notes on these early years were scrappy, not even full sentences at times, and David sensed that whoever had complied the document had not had his heart in the work, but none the less the page and a half of disjointed commentary gave him something of a fuller picture. Frampton had been born in 1952, Alexander George Edwards. His father, Major Malcolm Edwards had been called up in time to see action in Northern Germany in the final months of World War 2 and then transferred to the regular army. His mother Elizabeth had been born in Southern Rhodesia, where her family had been tobacco farmers. One of her brothers had been a member of the Southern Rhodesian parliament at the time of UDI and a cousin of Frampton's, serving in the Rhodesian African Rifles, had been killed in the long bush war with ZANU and

ZAPU guerrillas; about the time, David noted, that Frampton himself had been on active service in Northern Ireland. Apparently there was a suspicion the cousin had been shot deliberately by one of his own, African, men, but an inquiry found no evidence to support this suggestion. Frampton's father's military career had clearly never taken off, he had retired as a Major in 1975, but he had won the George Medal in Kenya in 1954, 'displaying enormous coolness of mind', according to the citation, when a group of prisoners armed with stakes and rudimentary knives fashioned from corrugated iron had attempted to overwhelm their captors at the prison camp he commanded. Frampton had gone to Wellington College and then directly to Sandhurst from where he had been commissioned into the Parachute Regiment in late 1970. Taking command of a Para platoon at nineteen, twenty at the most, must have taken some balls. David imagined the young man's nervous first morning; the new boy eager to prove himself to two dozen hard-bitten, sceptical veterans and all too aware of the possibility of making a fool of himself. But he survived the experience and after two tours of Northern Ireland he had transferred to the SAS then returned almost immediately to the province.

He pictured the greyness, the seemingly endless rain and the grand but shabby Victorian buildings that spoke of a distant and long lost prosperity. And with those pictures came the memory of a wife back home he missed, missed maybe more than he let her know, a wife who seemed to blame him for the fact the Department had given him no choice in the posting to Ulster. But... Edwards. Back to Edwards. David topped up his glass as he recalled their first meeting. He had been walking down a corridor on one of his infrequent trips from Londonderry to Army HQ at Lisburn, two or three

95

weeks before the power workers' strike, when a Captain Jenkins he knew slightly from the Information Policy team, had come out of a meeting room ahead of him, accompanied by another, younger officer.

'This is Captain Edwards, he's on our side.'

David had been aware of being critically assessed by this man, ridiculously tanned by Ulster standards after his weeks of jungle training in Belize, before Captain Jenkins added.

'David's one of the good guys.'

They had shaken hands briefly and continued on their separate ways. What did he remember of that meeting now? His immediate recognition of the man as Special Forces, the sense of Edwards' instinctive distrust of anyone not in uniform and a feeling that, even after Captain Jenkins' recommendation, Edwards' attitude was one of grudging tolerance rather than acceptance. God, those had been the strangest of days. An economy that seemed to be teetering on the brink, unions that seemed to know no boundaries to their political ambitions and a fear that only some sort of radical action could bring the country back from the brink. Isolated in Londonderry he had been on the fringes of it all but he was well aware that colleagues were getting ready for something, and it seemed that Edwards was part of it. But there had been so many rumours then, rumours of unacknowledged operations, rumours of unacknowledged negotiations and deals. Who knew even then what the truth was, let alone after all these years.

David read on. Edwards had returned to the UK in 1975 and been promoted to Major in 1977. But he never went back to Northern Ireland and he was not amongst the soldiers selected for service in the Falklands. He had left the army in 1984 having advanced no further up the promotional ladder than his father. David knew Edwards had moved fairly swiftly from a military career to a conservative safe seat but it was news to him that Edwards had worked for a brief spell for the property developer David Hart, whose conservative party connections no doubt helped Edwards find his safe Lincolnshire seat.

There were a few other odds and ends. Dates of his applications for a shotgun licence. A short list of recent speaking engagements and the contact details for his agent along with a print out of his profile.

"Lord Frampton has led a varied and at times exciting life. Born into a military family he was commissioned into the Parachute regiment at the age of 20 and later successfully completed the arduous selection process for the SAS. In both regiments he served with distinction in Northern Ireland during the 1970s when the troubles were at their peak. He subsequently embarked on a political career, where his reputation for outspoken comment has won him both friends and critics. Since leaving politics he has pursued various business interests focussed largely in the Middle East. Lord Frampton's experience in the military, political and business spheres enables him to talk with authority to audiences around the world on the subjects of leadership, defence and Britain's role in a changing world."

It seemed that, like so many former politicians, he hoped that somewhere out there was an audience willing to pay for his words of accumulated wisdom. And he had spoken once at the Royal United Services Institute but otherwise the events he had attended seemed fairly low key. A couple of appearances for the British Legion, a cadet force parade or two and some local Conservative party gatherings. David guessed that few had attracted any sort of fee at all.

He read on through the accounts of Frampton's political career and refreshed his mind on the details of his business dealings. He made a few notes but the whole story seemed depressingly simple. On the drive up in the fading light it was Ulster not Iraq that occupied his mind.

The name, Denton House, was picked out in black lettering on one of the two stone gate pillars set back from the road. David turned in up the gravelled drive past the trees which hid the house from the road and parked beside the front door. Steps led up to the imposing, black painted wooden door sheltered by a stone porch supported on two pillars. And to the right of the house, on a brick wall which formed the rear of some long, low outbuilding were inexpertly sprayed the words "Are you ready for anything." David sat and stared at them, willing them to offer up some further clue.

But the lopsided letters offered up no more information so David climbed the steps and knocked. As he waited he tried to imagine a group of demonstrators assembled below him. But it was hard to picture angry trade unionists, armed with placards and loudhailers assembled in such a setting. Disgruntled soldiers didn't fit any more easily, but what else could those words refer to? 'Remember,' he said to himself. 'Remember to call him Lord Frampton. Not Edwards.'

The door was opened by a woman David immediately identified as Lord Frampton's wife. She was a slight figure with a nervous air. Aside from the pearls he couldn't have described what she was wearing but he knew it was the uniform of a woman who was or wanted to be seen as upper class.

'Mr Nixon?' The accent sounded contrived. It grated on him immediately.

'Good evening. Lady Frampton?'

'Yes. Do come in.'

It sounded as if she felt she was doing him a favour. 'Is this the work of the demonstrators?' He was looking over at the graffiti.

'The demonstrators... yes.' What was it in her voice? Nervousness?

'Is that Mr Nixon?' A voice from somewhere beyond.

'Yes dear.' Then she stepped back more or less concealing herself behind the door, as Lord Frampton himself appeared.

David took stock of the man who now stood in front of him. Maybe six foot tall. Tanned, presumably from recent visits to Iraq. Like his wife he had dressed from the cliched wardrobe of the country land owner, tan corduroy trousers and a shooting sweater with leather shoulder patches. David couldn't really see but he was willing to bet the tie that was just visible underneath would inform the initiated that the wearer belonged to some exclusive body. And the face? He wouldn't have recognised him from Northern Ireland if he'd met him in the street. But the hardness in the eyes was familiar.

'David Nixon. Good to see you again.' The warmth seemed to David the warmth of a professional politician. 'Seems an age ago. Come in.'

'I was just looking at the handiwork of those demonstrators.' He turned to Lady Frampton. 'It must have been horrible to have all those people turning up on your doorstep.'

But Lady Frampton just recoiled, stepping further back into the hallway.

'Bloody disgraceful turning up like that,' said Lord Frampton. 'Well come in.'

David could see no way to press him further on the subject.

99

'Let's get this over with. Come on through.' And without a further word to his wife he led the way down a corridor and into a large room which plainly served as his office. Straight ahead was a substantial wooden desk of a traditional design. Dark polished wood, with a column of drawers on either side supporting a leather covered desktop. The surface was reasonably neat; a couple of small piles of papers and, to one side a computer screen angled towards the chair into which Lord Frampton now settled himself. To the left a sash window gave out onto the garden, with a dark red curtain drawn back on one side. Shelves covered the walls on both sides of the desk, packed with a mixture of books, box files and more loose papers. The wall behind Lord Frampton was dominated by a competent if uninspired oil painting depicting a modern infantry engagement in the jungle. The soldiers in the foreground, pouring fire towards the middle distance, were European but their foes, placed further back in the landscape, appeared darker skinned, more oriental, less manly. From where he sat, in a padded leather chair facing Lord Frampton, David was unable to read the title but he guessed the picture represented an incident in the Borneo campaign, or perhaps Malaya. On the mantlepiece below the painting were a few photographs, a couple of family pictures and one of an infantry platoon, maybe twenty five young men in neat maroon berets holding their weighty rifles and gazing, some smiling, some stoney-faced, towards the unseen photographer.

'Are they your first platoon?' David asked, nodding towards the picture. Perhaps some of these men had been present at this "incident" in the Ardoyne.

Lord Frampton looked over his shoulder. 'Yes. My lads. I was so proud.'

'Are you still in touch with any of them?' But Lord Frampton was bending down to turn on his computer and the question went unanswered. Again, there was no way he could press the point any further.

To the far right-hand side of the mantelpiece David fixed on another picture, of a smiling man in his twenties in a military uniform David did not immediately recognise as British.

'Who's the young man on the end?'

The computer had begun to whirr through its start-up procedure and Lord Frampton, upright now, looked not at the photograph but away into the darker corner of the room over David's shoulder. 'That's Stephen, my cousin. Rhodesian African Rifles. Killed on the Mozambique border in seventy-four.'

'I'm sorry.' David sensed an opening. 'Were you close?'

'He was one of the best. His father was my uncle, my mother's brother. Took over the family farm, south of Bulawayo, where my mother was born. It was a beautiful place.'

David waited.

'He and I... We didn't see each other that often obviously, but in some ways... I used to love going out to stay with them.' He looked at David now. 'They had a neighbour, Sammy, who'd fought in Malaya, in the SAS. Used to come over sometimes and in the evenings we'd get him to tell us his stories about chasing terrorists through the jungle. Stephen and I used to spend hours in the scrub behind the curing sheds playing at hunting down the communists, laying ambushes and fighting desperate battles. Like boys do. But after UDI Stephen had to do it for real. We both did. But he was really in the front line. He sent me over a bottle of plum brandy with his sister when she came for a visit, shortly before he died… the Yugoslav pilots used to bring it in with them by the crate load… with a note saying he was hoping to come over on leave and maybe we could finish it together and swap stories about killing reds. But he never made it. I was going to open it the day they buried him but in the end I was out on ops. I've still got it in the drinks cabinet. Never opened it.'

David looked back to the photograph of this open-faced young man and waited for Lord Frampton to continue. 'They murdered Sammy too. Just walked into the yard and shot him down in cold blood, not long before it was all over. And then that bastard Carrington sold them out and now look at the country. A cousin of mine … another cousin who still lives there… says he drove past the old place a couple of years ago and the whole place had fallen apart. The government had handed it over to a bunch of,' Lord Frampton sighed heavily, '… idle "veterans" who could barely get it together to plant enough maize to see them through the year. And when he tried to take a photograph a thirty-year-old thug who wasn't even born during the war, came out and shouted at him, "It's ours now. Don't you ever come back." Made him want to weep. And to think what it used to be. Handed it over to the communists and the …' He was silent for a moment. 'But you can't say things like that now or they'll call you a racist.'

'I know what you mean. Anyway, shall we get down to business?'

'I suppose so. Get this nonsense sorted out.'

At that moment Lady Frampton arrived with the tea, and a plate of biscuits on a tray.

'Just put it down there will you,' Lord Frampton said.

'Would you like me to pour…'

'No. Thank you. I'll deal with it.' Lady Frampton left without a further word.

David decided to try his luck. 'I've been reading up on your background. You worked for David Hart for a while. What were you doing for him?'

'God, that takes me back. Milk? Sugar?'

Just milk thanks.'

'I was just out of the army. And Hart was working pretty much directly for Margaret Thatcher on the miners' strike. Making trouble for the NUM every way he could, funding legal cases against them and all that sort of thing. And he was providing practical support for working miners, those of them brave enough to stand up to Arthur Scargill and his bully boys. And someone suggested to him that I might be able to help out on that front.' He handed David a cup of tea.

'I was working on the miners' strike too,' said David, sensing an opening. 'How did you get involved?'

'I can't remember.' David didn't believe that. 'But it was a fabulous opportunity,' Frampton continued.

'Yes?' Lord Frampton now seemed positively eager to talk. David just had to lead him on.

'Some of the work was straight forward, just delivering cash to miners who's said they would go back to work. But some of the leaders of the back to work campaign were scared stiff of what the NUM thugs would do to them so my job was to provide protection.'

'Personally?'

'Some of the time yes, I'd stay at their houses, act as a body guard at meetings and so on. But, more importantly, I also recruited people. People with the right skills. Former soldiers. Mainly from the regiment.'

David remembered a rumour he had heard that serving soldiers had been deployed to bolster the police on the picket line. There was no way any significant number of troops would have kept their mouths shut for all these years but a handful of SAS troopers might have done.

Frampton continued. 'There was a group of us who saw Scargill and, what was the fella's name, Scotsman…'

'Mick McGahey.'

'That's the one. We understood what they represented and we … we helped defeat them. It's something I'm very proud of.'

'You don't make a big thing of it in your public statements.'

'No. Some of these things… they're best not… If you were there you'll remember. It wasn't all pretty. But sometimes that's the way it has to be done.'

David's mind was racing now. How did he pursue this point?

'I remember,' he tried. 'We had to bend a lot of rules to get what we wanted.' But Lord Frampton didn't take the bait.

'Yes. You know what I mean. Anyway that's how I ended up being selected for parliament.'

There was nothing more David felt he could do with this line of inquiry. The best he could come up with was to ask, 'How come?'

'I hadn't particularly thought about a parliamentary career at that point but David Hart said you're just the sort of person we need. I'll see if I can find you a seat. And he was as good as his word. And as it turned out I had a bit of a knack for it. Anyway, shall we get down to business?'

David had never conducted an interview like this before, one where the whole purpose was to conceal what had evidently gone on rather than to tease out the truth. But if they both wanted the same result how hard could it be?

'First off, I'm not cautioning you Lord Frampton. Nothing you say this evening can be used against you. The purpose of our discussion is to put together an account of Four Square Security's dealings in Iraq, particularly in relation to the Rumalia oil field which we can... confidently... share with the Americans, to lay their fears to rest. So to speak.'

'Got you.' David didn't sense any enthusiasm on Lord Frampton's part but he didn't need enthusiasm, just cooperation.

'The company was started by Brigadier Johnson and Lieutenant Colonel Saunders. Did you know these people before you joined the company?'

'I don't see how that has any relevance.'

'Lord Frampton I need to show that we have done a thorough job. So it's important that...'

'I'm sorry David. You're absolutely right.'

It was almost, thought David, as if someone had told him to be on his best behaviour.

Lord Frampton continued. 'Johnson had been in the Foot Guards so our paths weren't likely to cross.'

'Crap hats?' David tried a joke.

'That's not a term officers use but...' Frampton smiled indulgently, though it plainly cost him an effort. 'But yes, a different type of soldiering.'

He kept smiling but the phoniness was too much for David and he resolved to keep the rest of the meeting as business-like as possible. Frampton appeared to have reached the same conclusion and they rattled through the rest of the background. According to the papers Four Square Security was fronted by the two former soldiers David had mentioned but the real money had come from two closely related venture capital funds based in the City, funds which had in turn been set up largely under the direction of a Nathan Woodward, himself a former army officer who had left the service after only five years without ever seeing action. Frampton claimed some awareness of Nathan Woodward as a mover and shaker in the city but David suspected an element of hindsight.

David then quizzed Frampton on his involvement in the training of his staff.

'There was a lot of money being thrown around in Iraq so of course you got a lot of cowboys. Sometimes literally. The Iraqis are talking of banning anyone who's ever worked for Blackwater as soon as they get back control. Can't happen soon enough as far as we're concerned. So you either joined in the race to the bottom or you did what we did and made a point of doing it properly. Nathan even tried to introduce the term "boutique" security agency but it didn't stick.' Frampton laughed at the recollection. 'I didn't do the actual training myself. I'm far too far over the hill. But I knew what was needed and I could find the people to deliver it.'

'And the Rumalia contract?'

'We had developed a good reputation. We put in a bid and we got the contract.' Dead straight. No suggestion of anything out of the ordinary, anything untoward.

'This was a rolling contract rather than a fixed term contract,' said David. 'What was the reason for that?'

'I'll be honest, it was a real stretch for us. The company. Geographically, it was a new area and it meant increasing our staffing levels by fifty per cent. Obviously our competitors wanted the work so they made a big deal of this. We were confident we could do it, and we did, very successfully, but at the outset Jamail took the view it was an easier sell from his point of view if he could say that, you know, if we didn't deliver on the contract they could give us the boot without any fuss. Jamail stuck his neck out for us a bit. But we justified his trust.'

'Did you have some sort of connection with Jamail?'

David sensed hesitation of Lord Frampton's part.

'Some of our people had looked after him. Took care of him during the Sadrist uprising in 2004 so he'd seen our work up close and he'd been impressed.'

'And the contract really has been a great step forward for the company?'

'Oh yes. Early days. But the impact on our overheads has been limited. We've really kept those costs under control. And the outlook for our profits is... very favourable... We got a lot of good coverage in the press too. Some great stuff about how we were demonstrating the quality of British military skills. And some good stuff about the business side of things which has been great for the share price too.'

'You did well out of it?'

'Well...' The tone of false modesty made David want to retch.

The Frampton's patience snapped. 'This whole business is idiotic. Why should I be wasting my time ... Everybody knows Iraq is totally corrupt.'

'That's hardly in dispute Lord Frampton. But what we have to do I think is put the best gloss we can on your investment in Dhi-Qar Services. There's precious little... what would be very helpful is anything that supports the view that the company was, or was likely to become, a viable business.'

'Well...' It seemed to David that Lord Frampton had not prepared for the meeting.

'Are there any documents that show any business planning?'

'Of course there's…' Lord Frampton stopped himself just in time.

'Could you… perhaps… get some?' This is absurd, thought David. 'Some costings that show how you concluded that there might be a viable business?'

'I see,' said Lord Frampton, finally cottoning on. Jesus, David thought, this is like pulling teeth.

'They wouldn't have to be a complete business case. I suppose… documents can get destroyed in an environment like that.'

'I get your drift. I'll get in touch with my people in Iraq and see what we can… find.' Then, in a moment, his mood switched from resigned acceptance to frustration. 'God this is all so bloody stupid… Compared to what we did... Have you any idea what it was like out there. All those no bid, cost plus contracts to Dick Cheney's friends at Halliburton. For jobs they ballsed up completely without any comeback. When we got to Rumelia nobody had any idea how much oil was being pumped because Halliburton hadn't installed the meters they had been paid to put in. So the oil was just getting stolen. Across the country it was billions of dollars of oil. It was an utter disgrace. And they're coming after us for… what?'

'I know. It makes no sense. There's another, small, detail we need your help on. You took £20,000 out of your account in cash a bit over six weeks ago, 2nd September. Can you tell me what that was for?'

'Where did you get that from?'

David had already decided to lie about this. 'The Americans provided us with the information. We need to give them some sort of explanation.' Lord Frampton was suddenly flustered.

'They've got no business poking through my private bank details.'

'No. But they have done. So we really need to give them some sort of answer.'

'Very well. I'm having some building work done. And… you know what builders are like… only cash will do.'

'Yes. I do.' Twenty thousand in cash to pay a builder sounded unlikely. 'Can you help me on another issue?' Another lie. 'The Americans are concerned that your company may have overstepped the mark in dealing with trade unionists.'

'For God's sake. What is this all about? They torture people to death in Abu Ghraib and then they come after me for running a few communists off the oil field. This is a fucking joke. What exactly are they saying?'

'There's an allegation of threats of violence.'

'The individuals involved were simply told, very firmly, that they were being redeployed to the refinery at Daura. And if they didn't like it they could go and get another job somewhere else.'

'Daura was pretty dangerous wasn't it?'

'Not our problem. Those were the orders from the Iraqi ministry,' said Frampton

'Were you able to get that message across to the demonstrators last month?'

'Demonstrators!'

'Were there many of them?'

'A dozen I think. My wife was here alone. I'd have seen them off pretty sharpish. Listen. Do we need to talk about this anymore? I can get our people in Iraq to see what they can come up with. Pass it on to you.'

'That seems like a sensible way forward. It would probably be helpful if we could meet again so that you can talk me through the documents and how they lead you to believe that the company was going to operate effectively. I assume there's no company activity on the ground at the moment?'

'No.' Lord Frampton actually smiled at this. 'But I understand where you are coming from. I'll see what I can do.'

It was clear that Lord Frampton had nothing more to offer and David had nothing more to ask at this point.

There was no sign of Lady Frampton as they walked back to the front door. David would have liked an opportunity to ask her about the demonstrators. If only because it would have served to distract Lord Frampton from their recent conversation. Instead he asked him if he was planning on returning to Iraq any time soon.

'No. We've got a good team down there. I'd only get in the way. I'll go back in a few months. Touch base with Jamail and so on. But no. I'll be here for the foreseeable future.' He smiled. 'Are you worried I'll flee the country?'

'Not for Iraq. No.'

As he opened his car door David turned back to Lord Frampton who was standing on the steps looking down at him and asked, as casually as he could, 'How's the building work going?'

Lord Frampton didn't react for a moment. He clearly had no recollection of any building work. Then the penny dropped. 'Don't you dare get smart with me Mr Nixon.'

David had always felt himself to be a thick skinned individual but he had to acknowledge that he was shocked by the cold power of Lord Frampton's rage.

'We may have been allies in the past Mr Nixon. But you were only ever a bit player. Step out of line and I can, and will, crush you.'

CHAPTER SEVEN

1975

The train was dirty. And nearly fifteen minutes late now. It was presumably going to depart at some point but no one was in any hurry to say when, or to offer any explanation for the delay. Captain Edwards glanced at his paper but found he was too consumed with impatience to read anything. Through the windows, uncleaned since who knew when, he could see some of the station staff milling about, apparently without purpose, which hardly improved his mood. He tried his paper again but still couldn't focus. With his last month's pay almost untouched he had been tempted to go first class, it had seemed the proper way to travel to the estate of a peer of the realm. But there were too many other calls on his limited funds and he had settled for second class instead. He looked around regretfully at the shabby, in part thread bare, seating, the scuffed, grubby floor. Perhaps things were a little smarter in first. These days you wouldn't bet on it though.

The invitation had come as a surprise. He knew of the Duke's connections with Rhodesia but he'd never met him, or any of his family, on his own visits to the country. The letter had suggested some connection with his uncle and made a reference to "shared interests." And when he had asked his CO for the necessary leave to make the trip the Colonel had seemed to have some foreknowledge of the event. Something was up.

Eventually, and without any warning, the train jolted its way out of Liverpool station. An older man sitting opposite him said 'About bloody time,' and looked across at him in the expectation of some sort of response but he couldn't be bothered to engage. A few minutes later, undeterred by Edwards' silence, the man looked out of the window at the derelict buildings they were passing and said. 'This used to be one of the great cities in the world. One of the great ports of the empire. Now look at it.' Captain Edwards paid him a little more attention now. A civilian, old enough to have fought in the war but, if he had done, the military life had left no obvious impression on him. A reserved occupation? Some trivial medical condition?

'Have you lived here all that time?' he asked.

'All my life,' the man replied with a hint of self-importance. Under a pale brown Macintosh he wore a jacket and tie. His thinning, brownish hair was oiled and neatly brushed. 'I worked for the port authority from 1932 until I retired in '72, when it all changed. Containers and everything. When I started it was one of the hubs of the empire. Cotton from America, sugar from the West Indies... And you should have seen this place in the war. All the ships from America came in here. The convoys, the troopships, everything. And when the Americans started to arrive...' He looked Edwards

113

over. 'You're too young to remember all that. The shortages, the bombing… People always forget that Liverpool was bombed too.'

Edwards started to bridle. 'I'm on leave from Northern Ireland. I think I know a bit about bombing.' The man's response surprised him. In a lowered voice he said, 'You don't want to make too much noise about that round here. A lot of Irish. Many of them have got more sympathy for the IRA than they do for people like you. It's their history. And it's easy for them to come over here too. Just hop on the boat, like I imagine you did, and they're amongst friends.'

'So were you still working at the docks when they came out on strike?'

'What? The last time? Yes.'

'Disgraceful the way they let them …' he was going to say "piss all over the law" but he checked himself '… get away with it. Less than a week in jail. It was disgraceful.'

'What could the government do? They had to let them go or most likely there'd have been a general strike. And we can't afford that in the current circumstances. What would you have done? It's not the army. You can't just order them back to work. What can you do?'

Edwards couldn't be bothered to carry on with the discussion. Without attempting to hide his disdain he picked up his paper again and tried once more to focus on something. He couldn't bring himself to read any more about the Cambridge rapist or the violence in Lebanon but towards the middle of the paper he found an article about the fallout from the Baader Meinhof gang's attack on the German embassy in Stockholm. Someone was standing up to the communists and winning.

The other man got off a few stops later. He made as if to say good bye but Edwards gave him only the faintest of acknowledgements.

By the time he reached his stop he'd managed to read everything in the paper he had even a passing interest in. Against his better judgement, he'd even read the article about the Cambridge rapist. The country was sick.

He had been told to expect a car but he had no idea who he was looking for. To his delight a woman in her early twenties accosted him as soon as he emerged from the station.

'Captain Edwards?' She asked. Given that he was the only person to have got off the train she seemed to surprisingly pleased with her powers of detection.

'Alex. Sorry to be so late.' He put out a hand, then worried that perhaps this was an overly formal gesture and almost withdrew it before she reached out and took it in hers. She was several inches shorter than him and had a wide, pale face framed by short dark brown hair. She wasn't classically beautiful but he had hardly spoken to a woman in the last month and his mind started racing ahead with the possibilities.

'I'm Melissa. My father's hosting this gathering and he's terribly excited about all this James Bond stuff.' Her tone suggested she was rather enjoying it too. 'Just put your suitcase on the back seat.'

'So your father's the Duke?' he asked as she opened her door. The car was a red Austin that had seen better days.

'Yes, but don't take any notice of that. He was in Italy in the war. I think he's just really looking forward to a chance to talk to some real soldiers who might be interested in his war stories. We've all heard them far too many times.'

When they were both settled in the car she asked, 'Was the journey awful?'

115

'Just delayed for some reason. We left Liverpool about twenty minutes late. They never said why.'

'They never do, do they. You're just supposed to sit there and take it. Sorry about all the clutter.'

The car was indeed something of a mess, with an old newspaper in the footwell, a blanket and various bags in the back and a strong smell of dog. 'Don't worry about it,' he said. 'It feels homely,' he added, not entirely sure that was the word he was looking for.

'It's just there always seems to be so much going on there's never time to sit back and sort a few things out. Do you know what I mean?'

'If your father's a Duke what does that make you?'

'Don't pay any attention to that nonsense. But I'm the honourable Melissa.'

'Are you?' he asked in a teasing tone.

'If I had a pound for every time... But what exactly do you do in Northern Ireland?'

'Reconnaissance. Observation. That sort of thing.'

'Have you ever killed anyone?'

Just three days ago and another, alien world. A sudden tensing of the muscles in his stomach, a drying of the mouth. The voices of two men coming up the path. After two nights and a day, half buried in the damp earth beside a thorn hedge the time had come. When he heard the cottage door open then close he got to his feet, pistol in hand. He had already plotted a noiseless path towards the building. Through the window he could see both men, the target and a second man whose face he did not recognise from any list of known players. There was a bottle of whiskey and a single pistol lying on the table. Next to it was a plastic bag he guessed contained their groceries. He pushed the safety catch forward and waited until both men were in plain view then put two rounds in each through the chest, the gun jolting powerfully in his clenched hands between each shot. He ran round, kicked open the door and rushed in, his ears still ringing from the sound of the shots. One of the figures was face down, immobile, the other lay face up, groaning. He bent down and met the man's baffled gaze. 'Bye bye Danny Boy,' he whispered as he placed the pistol inches in front of the man's face, judged the angel for possible ricochets and pulled the trigger. In the confines of the cottage the blast was even louder, and the smell of the discharge that much stronger. Without getting up he turned to the second figure and, just as carefully, put a bullet through his head too. The blood from the chest wounds was spreading across the floor now and soaking, warm and sticky, into the knee of his trousers. As he rose to his feet he listened for any sound, any suggestion that someone else might be outside, but he heard nothing. He rummaged inside the plastic bag and found an apple. When his teeth punctured the skin a blissful, tangy flood swept through his mouth. He turned the single light off and pushed open the door. His two companions rose up from their positions and together they headed back North for the border. The Gardai had promised the area would be frozen till dawn so there was no hurry, just the satisfaction of a job well done and the promise of the first hot meal in two days and a comfortable bed.

'Just one or two,' he said. He meant to sound light-hearted but he could tell from the nervousness in her eyes that he had misjudged it.

'Gordon my brother's in the cavalry,' she said after a moment or two. 'Hussars. 7th something... I can never remember what the numbers are. Seems to spend most of his time in Germany getting drunk at regimental dinners. He spent a few months in Belfast last year though. Said it was absolutely ghastly.'

'He's right there. It's not a pretty spot. And the people... half of them are barely civilised. The houses some of them live in, they're more or less hovels. Bogwogs we call them. The first time I flew into Belfast the stewardess told us to put our watches back 300 years.' She hadn't, but it was a story he had heard more than once and it bore repeating.

Melissa laughed and from then on he was content to listen to her talking inconsequentially about her family and her life in London. He enjoyed the sound of her voice and she seemed happy enough with his occasional comments. After a journey of no more than twenty minutes they turned off the road down a drive that curved through a narrow belt of beech wood then straightened up along a broad avenue of substantial lime trees. However, the house, which came into view at the far end of the drive was a bit of a disappointment. He didn't know exactly what he had been expecting, but something more prepossessing than this admittedly large Victorian brick pile. They proceeded at a slower pace now down the pitted drive before pulling up on the gravel by the front door, alongside a number of other cars, some significantly smarter than Melissa's.

'If you grab your bag someone will show you to your room,' she said. 'I've got to go and collect someone else now and I'm a bit behind. Sorry.'

He retrieved his suitcase, and waved her good bye. Then he turned to face the house and savoured for a moment the fact that he was here as an invited guest, not some sort of tourist.

There was no one to greet him in the hall but he followed the sound of hoovering and found a middle-aged woman in a grubby pinafore pushing an ancient vacuum cleaner across an expanse of faded oriental rug. She looked up when he came in but carried on hoovering.

'I'm Captain Edwards,' he said. 'I'm staying for two nights.' He waited for a response. 'Do you know where my room is?'

'Ah yes. I'll show you, and, leaving the vacuum cleaner in the middle of the carpet as if to mark her place, she led him back into the hall and up the stairs without a further word. She was slightly more communicative once they reached his room, explained some of the foibles of the aged plumbing and told him where to find the other guests when he had unpacked.

Downstairs again it seemed to Edwards the drawing room had a grandeur lacking in what he had seen of the rest of the house. It was maybe a hundred feet in length and the windows, which stretched almost the whole height of the room, looked out over a large area of immaculate lawn bounded at the far end by a stone balustrade, beyond which the ground dipped out of sight. Mature oaks visible in the distance suggested an expanse of parkland stretching as far as a ring of low, wooded hills maybe half a mile away.

To his left, alone in an arm chair sat a man reading the Times, the same edition he had been reading on the train. But in the centre of the room stood three figures engaged in soft but animated conversation. Their faces turned towards him as he approached and the conversation died.

'Good afternoon,' said one of them, not quite quickly enough to disguise the sudden silence. Edwards guessed he was in his early forties, fit and determined looking, dark, oiled hair with an immaculate parting and, most strikingly of all, an American accent. 'Terry Jennings,' he announced. 'You are...?' Manners on the surface, a steely demand underneath.

'Captain Edwards.'

The man on his right, tall and slightly stooped, reacted. 'Ah, the man from the Emerald Isle. How do you do. I'm Stewart Nicholson. Very pleased to meet you.' About sixty Edwards guessed. And from the quality of his suit and the condescension of his manner probably the owner of one of the more expensive cars parked outside. 'We were just discussing the lamentable state of the stock market. Dicky here says that if it drops any lower he'll have to cut down to just the two gardeners, which is quite unrealistic for an establishment of this size. We were talking about the need to take matters in hand.'

The third, shorter, almost stocky figure, plainly Dicky, laughed. 'Very good to have you here Captain Edwards. You've found your room all right I take it? Got everything you need?'

'Yes thank you sir.'

'No need for the 'Sir' young man. I was never more than a Major, and that was thirty years ago now. It's a little early for a gin. But we can find you some tea or some coffee if you would like.'

'No thank you, I'm fine for the time being. It's a wonderful place you have here.'

'Wonderful. But bloody cold in the winter. Especially since the wogs jacked up the price of oil. But never mind all that. We're all anxious to hear what you've been up to in Ireland. Sounds terribly exciting.'

'Dicky I think the reason Captain Edwards is here is precisely because the sort of things he gets up to in Ireland are not for public discussion,' said Stewart.

'You're absolutely right,' said Dicky. 'I will restrain my curiosity. You're Michael Robertson's nephew aren't you.

My cousins, the Davidsons, farm in the same valley. We should ... But look, here we are, our very own, in-house general.'

A man Edwards recognised instantly had entered the room. He was largely bald and his remaining hair almost completely grey, but his deep-set, dark and intense eyes and the latent energy in his every step instantly betrayed a powerful level of determination. He had plainly met the assembled company already and made straight for Edwards.

'Captain Edwards, delighted to meet you. And very glad you were able to come. Have you got a moment for a chat?' He asked the question as if he would happily defer the discussion should the timing be inconvenient but Edwards was not fooled. This, whatever it was, was what he had been brought here for. And the time was now.

'Come into the study,' said the General. Edwards followed him out of the drawing room and down the hallway. Here was a man, he sensed, who knew what it was to command.

'You've got family in Rhodesia I understand.'

'Yes sir, an uncle and aunt and two cousins.'

'Whereabouts?'

'South of Bulawayo, before you get to the Matopos hills.'

'Beautiful country down there. Awful business right now, but they seem to be holding on. Maybe we can do something about all that when we've sorted out this mess.' The general opened the door to a dingy, book lined room and ushered Edwards inside.

'That would be good sir. It's such a tragedy. And now the Portuguese have given up, the Mozambique border's wide open. Sometimes I wonder if I'm fighting the right war.'

'There's a number of our people down there. If you wanted to go... But not yet. Have a seat.' The general gestured to one

121

of two arm chairs that faced a desk and settled himself into the other. 'Right now I need you here. We've heard good things about you. You've got the stomach to … get things done. And you're willing to take risks for your country? When the hour is right?'

'Yes sir.'

'How much do you know of what this… this meeting is about?'

'Domestic subversion?'

'You've hit the nail on the head. Domestic subversion. You read the papers, you hear about the strikes, maybe you think you have an idea of how bad it is. But I'm afraid it's worse. Significantly worse. The Soviets have penetrated the absolute centre of power. I can't tell you the details but they've compromised at least one central figure and the Labour back benches are packed with fellow travellers, or worse. And that means that, if the balloon goes up, we can't necessarily rely on the government to act.'

The general leant forward. 'The railway employees, the miners and the dockworkers could bring this country to its knees in weeks. We've already seen what the miners are capable of. The extent of the communist penetration of that union is shameful. Too many people have been asleep at the wheel for far too long.' He paused for a moment or two.

'I know,' said Edwards. 'That picture of that Soviet sub off the coast of Ireland… Surely people can see the Communists…' The general interrupted. He was smiling with pleasure. 'That was one of our little propaganda coups. That photo was probably taken off the North coast of Norway or somewhere. But the fact is that there is Soviet support of the IRA. They want to destabilise the country, and the communists and their fellow travellers will help them do it if we fail to act. Alexander.' It was the first time the general had used his christian name. 'What we fear is that there will be strikes on a greater scale than we have seen before and the ordinary civil authorities just won't be able to cope... there will be a risk of anarchy and the army will be obliged to step in.'

Edwards must have looked skeptical.

'Don't worry,' the General continued. 'We're not talking about a military coup. Legally, it's very straightforward. The army can be deployed on the authority of the Defence Council. No need to go to Parliament, just a couple of signatures, and all the indications are they won't be too hard to get, and that's it. On our way. It wouldn't be a permanent thing. Just long enough to get the situation under control.'

'When do we start sir?' He felt embarrassed at his own enthusiasm but the General nodded approvingly.

'When the time comes. Whatever some of the hotheads might tell you we can't just charge in, so for now,' the general smiled almost indulgently, 'it's simply preparation. The majority of the people in this country are decent, law-abiding people. They don't want a communist revolution any more than we do. Hundreds of them are writing in every week to offer their services. Ordinary people just wanting to do their bit for Queen and country. It's wonderful. But we have to be ready. And we have to be organised.'

'What about the power workers?'

The General acknowledged the point. 'Yes, in that sense the Ulster strike was a little too successful. The way they were able to bring the province to a complete standstill within days. We got rid of all that power sharing nonsense and the army can now get on and do its job but yes... we are now aware... and the unions are aware, of the difficulties of running power stations. And without power, as you know, everything grinds to a complete halt. But we have got contingency plans. That's all in hand. Don't you worry about that. That's not your problem. You will be assigned to the Resistance and Psychological Operations Committee.'

'I'm not really much of a committee man sir.'

'Don't worry Alexander, it isn't really a committee. In fact you might even recognise a couple of faces from Castle Dillon.' The general paused to allow this to sink in. 'I thought that'd cheer you up. They'll talk you through the details of your assignment, but I wanted to meet you before you went. See what sort of a specimen we've landed ourselves. And let you know how important what you are doing is. This country needs people like you. God knows it's a painful prospect but it may have to be done. There's some structures already in place that we can build on but your role will be crucial. You and your colleagues will target the most disruptive union leaders, the hard-core activists. We'll need to get those people off the streets as soon as possible. We're thinking of flying them all up to Shetland for as long as it takes for things to calm down. We're not expecting any shooting, though we'll have to be prepared obviously, but firmness and speed of action, that'll be the key. Does that sound like the sort of work you would be willing to undertake?'

'Absolutely sir. God. It's... it's exactly what the country needs.'

'Excellent. I'll introduce you to Colonel Spears tomorrow. He'll talk you through your deployment in more detail. And you'll see one or two faces this evening that you'll recognise... from the papers, the television...'

'Don't worry sir. Not a word.'

The General nodded in approval.

124

'We envisage your redeployment in a couple of weeks, initially to the Territorial Squadron in Birmingham where you'll receive some specialist training. That needs to be cleared with Northern Ireland but I don't foresee any problems. Actionable intelligence is a bit hard to come by at the moment because obviously we can't start asking Special Branch for their files without arousing suspicion. And there's a bit of a tussle going on with Whitehall at the moment about funding in this area. We can work around it but things may be a bit rough and ready at times. But I'm sure you'll bear with us.

'Pen-pushing...'

'We're not sure it's the civil servants actually. Plenty of them are on side. No. We think it's maybe the government itself that is driving the scrutiny. They're not stupid. Some of our people in the House of Commons say the Reds are looking a little nervous these days. Well, it's great to have you on board. As you can imagine, I've got a lot of people to talk to ...'

The General had stood up and Captain Edwards took his cue. 'It's good to know there are still young men like you, ready to do the right thing. I'll see you at dinner.'

'Thank you sir.' He hesitated a moment. 'If you don't mind my asking, why do we have an American here? Is he CIA?'

The General hesitated. 'He isn't officially anything. But the Americans have got the same serious concerns that we have about the integrity of this government. And their support for any action we take will be vital.'

'We need their permission to take back our country?'

'If the balloon goes up we're going to need to establish economic stability pretty fast. And that's going to mean commitments from American banks. Plus. We can hardly ring

125

them up the morning afterwards and say, 'By the way…'. Don't forget they've got several thousand servicemen stationed here. Just take Jennings' presence here as an indication of how serious we are. But there will be no US troops on the streets of Great Britain. I'm confident that won't be necessary. So be nice to Jennings. We have to keep them on side. I was planning to introduce you to him in fact. Part of the reason you are here is so that I can show you off to Jennings. Make sure he doesn't get the impression that this is just some sort of pensioners outing. And he's been very helpful in recruiting Americans to fight in Rhodesia. People with a lot of useful experience fighting the communists in Vietnam. He's on our side.'

Edwards left the room feeling elated. All the tiredness of the previous days had lifted off his shoulders. Here at last was someone with not only a grasp of what needed doing but also a plan. And a plan in which he could put his skills to use, help turn the country back into what it had once been. The drawing room was empty now except for the solitary figure still reading the paper, who again paid him no attention. There was no indication of where his host or his fellow guests had retreated to, and disappointingly no sign of Melissa, so he changed into his boots and went out for a walk. The sun shone down occasionally between the passing clouds and life felt good. He found that beyond the stone balustrade the garden sloped down to a small lake. There were flower borders around its shore but even to his untutored eye it was apparent that they were suffering from neglect. Plainly even the current complement of gardeners were struggling to keep up. He carried on walking and, just as the sun emerged from behind another cloud, the grounds opened up into parkland. The grass was reaching that tired end of summer phase but the canopies of the oaks were filled with summer life, the buzzing of innumerable insects and the passage of half seen birds, feasting on the season's abundance. A movement caught his eye. A single deer feeding at the base of a distant tree. He turned towards it and four more became apparent a little further off. In an instant he was transported to the bush beyond his uncle's farm, with a Kudu in view and the feel of a rifle in his arms. And the general's words came back to him. "Maybe we can do something about all that when we've sorted out this mess." Please God.

The company assembled for drinks around 7.00. Edwards had brought his mess kit but that now seemed excessive and he settled instead for the same suit he had travelled in. As he entered the drawing room once more he felt a sense of satisfaction at being included in this world. He had no idea if the pictures on the wall were any good but he knew they were the sort of pictures that belonged on the walls of houses such as this. And these were the sort of people who belonged in this sort of house and he was part of this. He stood for a moment, gin in hand, savouring the moment.

Wives, who had not been in evidence earlier in the day, had now made their appearance and the man who seemed to have been reading the newspaper all afternoon was introduced to him as Clive. Edwards asked him what he did and sensed immediately that he had committed a minor faux pas. 'Whitehall. Terribly dull,' was the answer given but he had already reached the conclusion that no one invited for this weekend did anything terribly dull. Then he found himself in conversation with Stewart's wife who talked to him about their children at unforgivable length; a son who had left the Foreign Office to work at Kleinwort Benson and a daughter married, with three allegedly delightful children, to someone working at the Baltic Exchange. Over her shoulder he caught sight of Melissa talking animatedly to another new arrival and he made his excuses, cutting the older woman off in mid flow.

He found Melissa talking with obvious enthusiasm about a horse she had been riding at a friend's farm.

'Alex, this is Malcolm. I was just telling him about a wonderful three year old that my friend Sally is going to lend me for a few months. Malcolm, this is Alex. He does something frightfully hush-hush in Northern Ireland.'

Malcolm looked at him with raised eyebrows and a smile that Edwards found hard to read.

'Hush-hush, but not that exciting,' Edwards said with calculated self-deprecation. 'It's much more boring than people imagine. You hardly ever get to shoot anyone.' To his satisfaction he saw Malcolm flinch slightly, but then Melissa backed away too.

Shortly before dinner was announced a stir passed through the assembled company. No one stared exactly as two men in their late fifties, accompanied by their wives, entered the room. Edwards too affected indifference. But Christ, even the general's warning had not prepared him for the arrival of two such familiar figures from the political world. This was for real.

The dinner itself was largely uneventful. Melissa was seated on the other side of the table and too far away to talk to, and Jennings had been placed beside her. Melissa appeared to be working hard to charm the American. Edwards found himself trapped between Stewart's wife, who made it clear she had not forgotten being abandoned so abruptly, and a woman who introduced herself as Maggie and turned out to be the wife of Clive, the man with the terribly dull job in Whitehall. She also turned out to be very well informed about Northern Ireland, to the extent that as he attempted to explain to her the twists of nationalist politics he found that she was, very gently, correcting him on points of detail. He shifted the conversation to the details of the weaponry available to the various parties and she made fewer interventions. Further down the table he was aware of conversations about finance, the price of oil and how the Jews at Warburg's were somehow going to facilitate a communist take-over. He didn't pay too much attention until Tony Benn's name was mentioned. The vitriol this name provoked was expressed so forcefully that he and Maggie were more or less compelled to discontinue their discussion and listen, until one of the politicians said, very calmly but with complete certainty, 'I guarantee that under no circumstances will Tony Benn ever become Prime Minister.' The room went quiet for a moment or two before conversation returned to its normal level.

Later, when the women had withdrawn, the men, softened by wine and brandy, reassembled at one end of the table. It seemed the serious business of the day was done and the Duke was at last free to indulge in his reminiscences. He had spent the final year of the war with a Gurkha battalion in the mountains of Italy. 'Marvellous chaps. Incredibly cheerful, and bloody good soldiers. Very correct, but stand-offish at first. Then one day, it's as if they've had a meeting and decided you've passed some sort of a test, and then it's all smiles and you're welcomed into the family. Didn't like us officers going out on patrol with them though. Said we made too much noise. But the only time I went out with them we captured twenty-three Germans. I say Germans, half of them were Hungarian or something and didn't want to be there at all. It was January, up in the mountains, bloody cold, and we caught them all taking shelter in a barn. They'd left just one poor devil outside keeping guard. Poor bugger never stood a chance against a Gurkha. Then we just burst in. One of their NCOs thought he'd put up a fight... One of my chaps skewered him with a bayonet pretty promptly and that was that. The rest of them were terrified we were going to give them all the chop... Some of the Indian regiments had a bad reputation for not taking prisoners... But once they realised we weren't going to kill them they followed us back to our lines as meek as lambs. The company commander thought I might get a gong but the colonel said no one in his regiment was getting decorated just for bringing in a collection of demoralised waifs and strays.'

His own tales, Edwards realised with a tinge of regret, would never form the basis of dinner party anecdotes.

'How was your recent trip to Rhodesia General?' asked Terry Jennings.

'Very good thank you. Had a good chat with Peter Walls. Who's doing an astonishing job with very limited resources. There's no doubt the pressure's increasing but they're extending the draft, and their special forces are superb. There's no suggestion yet it's anything they can't handle. And there's one big advantage to the departure of the Portuguese. Some of the Kaffirs may resent white rule, but when they see the state of Mozambique and Angola they realise they don't want communism. All in all I'd say it was looking pretty stable for the time being.'

'No problems with the oil supply?' There was a hint of mischief in Terry's voice.

The General smiled. 'None at all it would seem. It's almost as if the sanctions were designed to fail.'

'That's good to hear. Did you get a chance to relax, any R n R?' asked Terry, his accent still grating on Edwards' ear.

'Had a lovely few days with the Grahams. They've got a place just outside Umtali, mainly tobacco but some cattle. Almost like the old days.' There were one or two sighs. Edwards, relaxed now and happy to find himself in like-minded company, was on the point of speaking when the General continued.

'Had one bad day though. Not long after the war I'd spent a few weeks with someone from my regiment whose family had a farm further East, almost on the Mozambique border, in the Burma Valley. Really lovely place. He had a sister I rather fell for at the time. They've moved away now but I wanted to go and have a look, for old time's sake. People said 'Don't, it's too close to the border, the terrorists come through that way all the time, it's not safe and so on'. But I wouldn't listen so they got some of their neighbours together, they're mostly in the reserves anyway, and the local commander at Umtali sent a section along with us. From the moment we turned into the drive I knew I'd made a mistake. The place had been unoccupied for … I don't know, maybe five years by now. Maybe longer… The lawns were reverting to bush. I could see straight away that the whole place was in a state of decay. I'd have turned back right then if I could but all these people had made the journey out there just for me so I had to go on. The veranda which looked out over the valley, where Peter and Jessica and I had sat in the evenings when they brought us our gin and tonics, was almost overgrown with thorns. The view was just as stunning but… And half the windows had been smashed. I couldn't bring myself to go inside but you could see the mould on the walls, bat shit everywhere. And some *muntu* had made a point of crapping in the middle of the drawing room floor. I tell you... We mustn't let that happen here.'

CHAPTER EIGHT

O n the train into work the next morning David gave up trying to read after about ten minutes. Each time he opened his book he managed no more than a sentence or two before his mind abandoned Walsingham and his acolytes and returned to the equally uncertain present. On one analysis, his mission was more or less complete. Frampton had agreed to go along with a vaguely plausible account of the deal in Iraq. All David needed to do now was wait for Frampton to produce the documents from Iraq then write up an appropriate report and leave it to his superiors to try and persuade the Americans to swallow it. Not his finest hour perhaps but not something he would lose any sleep over. Except.

Except Terry was badly spooked. Except Frampton had made a cash payment of £20,000 and lied to him about its purpose. And no one, except apparently Lady Frampton, had seen these demonstrators, and why would trade union activists spray "Are you ready for anything" across the side of his house? The phrase made no sense in relation to trade union campaigning. But "Ready for Anything" was the motto of the parachute regiment. But then again why would anyone from the parachute regiment want to have a go at Frampton?

When he got to the office he dropped his things off and went over to see Nigel. There was no sign of him in his office and Ginny was nowhere to be seen either. For want of anything better to do he went looking for Manjit. He found him at his desk staring at some hand written notes.

'Hi David, I heard you were back.'

'Have you not got caught up in this Somali panic?'

'But I have. In fact that's exactly what I'm panicking about right now. Can't you tell?'

'Is there anything in it?'

'My guess is not really. Did you hear the Americans have confirmed that the original source is dead?'

'No.'

'They're now saying he wasn't in their custody. They may be lying of course but if he was being tortured by, say, the Syrians at their request that just introduces another layer of potential miscommunication. Nigel's in a meeting at the moment trying to persuade them to scale back the investigation until we know a bit more. Meanwhile Steve's people have raided half a dozen Hawaladors, which many of the Somalis use to send money back home, and they want me to look through all their records for evidence they've been moving funds for terrorists. Which I wouldn't mind doing if they had any real grounds for suspicion. But they haven't. There's a couple of these people whose records are, it has to be admitted, shit. They've taken money off individuals without taking copies of their passports and so on. And I don't doubt that's because many of these people are illegal and don't want to be flashing their passports around, even supposing they've got one. But basically they're just little people, trying to send a bit of cash back home to their poor families. Like my grandparents did. The sums are utterly trivial and there's not a sniff of terrorism. Is your day going any better?'

'Better than yours. How long is Nigel going to be tied up in this meeting?'

'Who knows. It's at the Home Office. I guess he'll be gone till lunch.'

'We should have a beer before too long.'

'That would be nice. But I don't think it's going to be today.'

'David!' It was clear Nigel's meeting with the Home Office had finished. It was also abundantly clear that Nigel was in a foul mood.

'David we need to see Will. Now.' He marched off in the direction of Will's office without waiting for David's response. Frampton, David guessed as he followed behind, had complained.

Indeed he had.

'Sit down.' Will's tone was glacial, tinged with disbelief. He enunciated slowly and precisely.'

'You had one simple task. You were brought in to help Lord Frampton deal with allegations of corruption. In Iraq. You were not brought in to conduct your own investigation into other entirely irrelevant... and private aspects of Lord Frampton's affairs. What on earth did you think you were doing?'

David could feel, rising up from his stomach, a wave of overwhelming contempt for Will. He struggled to contain it. It was a few moments before he could speak.

'We need to make sure all the angles are covered. The Americans are asking some very hard questions about all this.

We need to know what is going on if we're going to come up with a story that will stick. He took £20,000 out of his bank account in cash and he lied to me about why he did that. What do we tell the Americans about that?'

'Our brief is counter-terrorism, domestic subversion and large-scale drug smuggling.' Will's tone was still measured, still icy. 'Do you have any reason to believe Lord Frampton wanted his money in cash for any of those reasons?'

'No.'

Will raised his voice. 'Then keep out of it.' But there was a look on his face that showed he knew that by nearly shouting he had compromised his dignity, given away the fact that he was scared about how this would rebound on him. And that unnerved David because it suggested more powerful interests were in play.

'From now on you take absolutely no steps in this matter without clearing them with Nigel and myself. I understand Lord Frampton is going to produce paperwork to substantiate his account of events and we will take it from there. In fact, I don't see any need for you to do anything more until we receive those documents.'

David glanced at Nigel but he plainly did not want to speak if he could avoid it.

'I am booked to have lunch with our CIA contact today,' David said.

'Jesus.' Will paused. 'Do you think you can handle that without screwing it up?'

'I'm sure it will be fine,' said David.

'What do you think Nigel? Do we trust him not to balls it up?'

'I'm sure it will be fine,' said Nigel. 'It's just a case of listening to what they have to say.'

'Very well then.'

As they got up to go Will's phone started to ring. The door didn't close fully behind them and the words "Yes. He's been told" followed them down the corridor.

'David, in there you implied we got the information about the £20,000 in cash from the Americans. I chose not to mention it in front of Will but we didn't did we.'

'It still needed following up.'

Nigel shook his head in a gesture of despair. 'David. I won't cover for you again. You understand? Now go and enjoy your lunch with the CIA. And for God's sake, stick to the brief.'

Lunch with the CIA. Lunch at the expense of the CIA. The prospect had a glamorous ring to it. He googled the restaurant for directions, but also, he had to admit to himself, to gauge how up market the establishment was. And the prices were higher than he would ever have contemplated paying himself outside a major celebration. Despite Will's best efforts he left the office in a good mood.

And it was a sunny day. Above his head the translucent foliage of the plane trees shifted in the sunlight. He could sense the extra animation in the movements of the people on the street around him, energised by what might prove to be one of the last warm days of the year. Already the first few wilted autumn leaves were littering the pavement around their feet. It took him a moment or two to realise that his mobile was ringing.

'Hello David, it's Tim Evans, Rachel's friend.'

Ah yes. he remembered Tim. Always hovering round Rachel, never quite daring to make a move. At one point he'd wondered if the two of them had had an affair before he and Rachel had divorced. He'd even asked Rachel once when things had calmed down between them, but she'd just laughed.

'I'm afraid I've got some bad news David, Tim continued. 'Rachel's been diagnosed with cancer. Very late in the day.'

'Did she ask you to call me?'

'No. But I thought you ought to know. She's in the Royal Marsden in Sutton. The doctors say she's got maybe four weeks. But it's hard to tell. Someone with her spirit...'

'Thanks for letting me know Tim.'

'Do you think you'll go and see her?'

He had no idea.

'I'll need to think. But thanks for letting me know.'

If anyone had asked him a week ago he'd have said he and Rachel were still in touch but the fact was he knew nothing of her life now. They'd last spoken more than a year ago when she'd finally sold the house and needed to check something about the planning consent for the kitchen extension. Afterwards he'd looked up how much she'd sold it for and winced. And he knew where she'd moved to. She'd even sent him a change of address card. But he didn't know who most of her friends were, whether she'd patched things up with her sister, how she spent her time.

A crowd of Chinese tourists blocked the pavement outside the Houses of Parliament, taking pictures of Big Ben and of each other standing next to, by comparison, an impossibly tall policeman. David stared at the spectacle until a couple of them moved aside and he was able to walk on up Whitehall towards Soho.

He started to wonder what he should do about Rachel. She didn't know he knew. Did he owe it to her to make contact?

What would he say? His marriage was a part of his life he didn't think about too much. It ended, what was it, twenty-five years ago, and to the best of his ability he had shut off the pain and not looked back. There had been moments though, when he had looked back and wondered what might have happened. If he had given up his job, found something that had allowed more space for the two of them. His recollection was that it had been about more than that but, as he had learned during the rows of their final year together, everyone remembers everything differently, even the most recent, fundamental events lodge themselves differently in different minds. He made his way round Trafalgar Square, past Canada House, trying to push these thoughts aside and focus on his meeting. It was a chance to learn how much the Americans had on Frampton and what scope there might be for rewriting the story. That was the task at hand. The fact his world had changed was something to be dealt with later.

He was a little irritated that he failed to pick out Eldridge T Baker the moment he stepped into the restaurant. He had expected him to stand out somehow. Perhaps not a Stetson but something to mark him out as alien. In fact it was Eldridge, maybe ten years younger than David, and dressed in a pale grey suit and a tie that rendered him indistinguishable from any of the other diners, who spotted David looking round the room and waved to him discretely. He was sitting at a table in the corner of the room, a relatively secluded spot where, David told himself, he should have expected to find his contact.

They exchanged pleasantries then turned to the menus.

'This is on the company, so indulge yourself,' said Eldridge.

'Thanks.' David wondered if this was some sort of test. What judgement would be passed on him if he ordered the most expensive item? In the end pride prevented him ordering the sirloin steak and he settled instead for sea bass.

'An excellent choice,' said Eldrige. 'Shall we have a bottle of wine?'

'Yes. That sounds good.'

'What do you fancy?' Eldridge asked, passing David the wine list.

David opened up the large leather-bound volume and stared at the expansive list of wines, each described in terms that left him no better placed to make a choice. It felt like a dream in which he was faced with an exam in a subject he had never studied. Fuck it. He picked a mid-priced white and waited for Eldridge to tell him it was an excellent choice.

Instead Eldridge caught the attention of a waiter and placed their order. Eldridge was having a vegetarian dish, involving a number of ingredients David had never heard of, and what seemed to David an unnecessarily complex salad.

David expected the conversation to turn immediately to Lord Frampton but instead Eldridge began, 'Nigel tells me you've recently retired. I'm looking forward to that myself. My wife and I have got our hearts set on a small ranch in western Montana. 400 acres or so. Another two years in this game and we should be able to afford the sort of place we're looking for. What's your dream? What are you working for?'

What indeed. 'Beer money. Nothing more.' He didn't particularly want to discuss his hopes, such as they were, with Eldridge. Not just because he was almost embarrassed by their modesty, but because they were, to his mind, none of

Eldridge's business. And the American appeared to take the hint. For the next ten minutes he did little more than reminisce about the apparently simpler, more binary days of the Cold War. 'These days there's Muslim extremists and Muslim moderates and we're supposed to somehow work out the difference. We never had to worry about moderate communists.'

It was only once the food had arrived that Eldridge asked, 'So tell me. How is the investigation progressing?'

'We're just working on the background at the moment.' "We," he thought to himself. Best to toe the line but he hoped Eldridge didn't ask how many "we" were.

'Do you have any sense of where it's heading?'

'Too early to tell with any certainty. In my experience it's always best not to get ahead of yourself. We're waiting for further documentation. Until then I'm making no assumptions.'

'I admire your professionalism.'

Fuck off.

'Our concern,' Eldridge continued, 'isn't just the fact that he paid off Ali Al Jamail to get the contract, and I appreciate your... professionalism... but we both know that is what happened. If it was just the corruption we might not be so concerned. What really concerns us is the Al Dawa party connection. You know Al Jamail is a key figure in the party, and you know that the party is in effect a proxy for the Iranians. Until we got rid of Saddam they were actually based in Iran.'

'I'm... we're aware of the connection, yes, but I can't see it being a real issue in relation to Lord Frampton. I don't think his security team are ever going to function as an Iranian fifth column.'

141

'Not directly, no. But you'll be aware that there has been some controversy about Four Square Security removing employees from the sites they are guarding. For political reasons.'

'Union activists is our understanding.'

'Some of them certainly. And obviously we have no problem with that. But you can see how the same power could be used for other ends. And all Al Jamail has to do is label any opponent of Iranian interests as a Trade Unionist and Lord Frampton will have him removed. Potentially removed... with extreme prejudice.'

'He hasn't killed anyone as far as I know.'

'As far as we know. Not yet.'

'This all sounds a bit theoretical to me.'

It sounded more than theoretical. It sounded absurd.

Eldridge continued. 'We have a couple of reports from our people on the ground. Obviously I didn't bring them with me this morning but I'll get them sent over from London station.' And then Eldridge let the subject drop. Instead he moved onto British politics.

'What do you think of Gordon Brown? I know it's too early to tell for sure but do you think he's going to be any different from Tony Blair as prime minister?'

David had views on Tony Blair that were not fit to be shared in a public place, and he knew no more about Gordon Brown than anyone else who had read the papers. He did his best but he couldn't help but be irritated by the weight Eldridge seemed to attach to his views. Maybe it was just the way Americans were, he thought, but it felt uncomfortably like artful flattery.

Then Eldridge started to quiz him on the investigation into the Police killing of Charles de Menezes at Stockwell tube station.

'You people take this stuff so much more seriously. I guess maybe you're right to do so. Back home it's more like, "There's a war on. Some times the wrong people get hurt. That's just how it is."'

'There's people who think like that here too.'

'And half the time it's just journalists trying to make a story out of nothing.'

David couldn't be bothered to disagree.

It was over coffee that the conversation took the turn that David by now half anticipated.

'David you have a very good reputation. I looked up your record. Very professional. And discreet, if you know where I'm coming from.' That unnerved David a little. What acts of discretion might they be aware of? Or was this just more flattery? But Eldridge continued. 'If this relationship works out we'd be able to offer you some interesting opportunities. And we'd pay more than beer money.'

Eldridge's manner was calm. There was nothing to suggest the significance of what he had just done. In effect to try and recruit a still-just-about-serving member of a friendly intelligence organisation.

'Let's see how this matter plays out shall we?' Jesus. What was he going to do about this.

'That seems a very sensible approach. What do you think the future holds for the Liberal Democrats?'

143

Back at the office David knocked on Nigel's door. There was no way he could not report this approach, but if he did Will was almost certain to take him off the case.

'Come in.' There was irritation in the voice.

'Nigel there's something we need to discuss.'

'David this is not a good moment.'

'What's happened?'

'Does the name Maryam Aadan ring any bells?'

'Vaguely.'

'East End Labour MP. First Somali woman to be elected to the House of Commons. A bit of a firebrand. Very striking too. So many East African women are, though I suppose we can't say that sort of thing any more can we. You know who I mean? Gets in all the papers.'

'I know the one. Didn't the Daily Mail accuse her of showing a lack of respect for the Queen because she was wearing... something. Let me guess...'

'If you're going to guess that she's making a big fuss about our investigations amongst the Somali Muslim community...'

'You read my mind,' said David.

'She's made a rabble-rousing speech this afternoon in the House of Commons about how our heavy-handed raids and mass arrests of law-abiding citizens...' Nigel consulted one of the pieces of paper on his desk. 'Yes... "law abiding citizens who came to these shores trusting in the traditions of civil liberties this country was once renowned for throughout the world, are now likely to be recruited for the terrorist causes all right-minded citizens abhor by the heavy-handed actions of the very institutions whose role it is to..." etc etc.'

'She's not wrong there.'

'Do you want to write the ministerial statement David?'

'Why isn't that Steve Scott's job? He's Mr Somali Terrorism.'

'It should be, yes. But his first draft was … the phrase used, by the Permanent Secretary I think, was "insensitive to the point of being inflammatory". So I've ended up with the job. And the Secretary of State wants to make this statement before the House rises tonight. So unless your problems with the IT department risk causing sectarian riots in the capital within the next twenty-four hours, they will just have to take their place in the queue. In the mean time you can send me an email.'

The moment to speak up, to correct Nigel's misunderstanding and report Eldridge's attempt to recruit him, simply passed. David watched it go by.

And five minutes later Ginny came into his office with a note to contact the research team. They had finally pulled the details of all the cars leaving the motorway either side of Lord Frampton's house. Without a computer he had to go and physically retrieve the product of their efforts.

Downstairs he was greeted by a brisk woman in her thirties, in a tight pencil skirt and with a manner that invited no small talk.

'There's a hundred and forty-seven vehicles on the list the police gave us. We're assuming they picked the relevant period.' Her tone suggested she had no confidence that this had been done properly. 'There's only three we've got any data on so we've just printed those out for the time being.'

'Thanks.' He had an instinct to say something warmer and more appreciative but he sensed it would have been wasted breath.

As he walked back upstairs he flipped through the pages. Two were of no interest. The first was an environmental campaigner, with no criminal record and no obvious connection with Iraqi issues. The second was a union organiser in Unite who was also a member of the Socialist Party but had somehow failed to make it onto the police database. There were lists of campaigns he had worked on and demonstrations he had attended but none of them related to Iraqi oil workers. The third individual was a very different matter. Colin Stuart. An ex-para who had gone to work for Four Square Security, Lord Frampton's company, before being severely wounded and returning to the UK. Now living in Leeds. This was too much of a coincidence. The research team had even supplied a phone number.

There was no way Will was going to allow David to follow this up. And there was no way David was letting this go.

'Colin Stuart?'

'Yeah.' The voice was unwelcoming.

'My name's David Nixon. I work for the Security Service.' He paused for a moment, waiting for some sort of response but there was only silence. 'MI5?'

'I know what the Security Service is.'

'Can you tell me where you were on the afternoon of 4 September this year?'

'I'll have to check my diary. But nowhere special that's for sure.'

'Mr Stuart I've got a pretty good idea of where you were.'

'Good for you.'

'Mr Stuart, there's two ways we can do this. I can get the local police to bring you in, we can have a formal interview, take some pictures and show them to Lady Frampton, who I am sure will have no trouble identifying you, and take it from there. Or I can come round and we can have an informal chat about what went on and why, I get the information I need and you get no more hassle. That's how I'd like to do it. Would you be OK with that?'

'You can come if you want.'

'Are you free on Monday?'

'I'm at the hospital Monday. That'll be most of the day. But any time after that.'

'OK. I'll see you Tuesday. Late morning.'

David took the battery out of the phone. The handset and the Sim card couldn't be traced to him. The call location, the stairway of a public building with which he had no association, wouldn't link the call to him. Of course if anyone got the actual recording from GCHQ he was bang to rights but... there's only so much you can do.

CHAPTER NINE

Four days later David started early. The morning was bright and the roads were clear. He had his phone with him but the battery was safely tucked away in his pocket. He wasn't paranoid, just careful. Careful and engaged. Usually, when questioning someone, you had some idea of the sort of information they held, whether it was names or dates or details of particular events. Here he could not begin to imagine what he was seeking to uncover. He would just have to play it by ear. After the bright start the cloud soon thickened and by the time he joined the M1 the sky was as grey as the miles of tarmac stretching out ahead of him. He eased off the slip road behind a removals lorry and let a Mercedes doing at least 85 go past before pulling out into the middle lane and accelerating. The traffic was flowing but unevenly, choked from time to time by the bunching of HGVs or the closing off of a lane which left everyone doing 50, or thereabouts, while nothing happened behind a miles long barrier of orange and white cones. He turned on the radio and surrendered to the soothing embrace of Classic FM.

Beyond the windscreen the junctions drifted by, slowly counting up his progress northwards. Around Nottingham the weather closed in. It began to drizzle just enough to justify putting on the wipers and when he passed a wind farm he could see the tips of the slowly revolving blades disappear into the cloud layer towards the top of their cycle. An hour later he reached the junction with the M18. Here the M1 veered off to the left and he was in familiar territory. For nearly two years in the early 70s he'd been undercover here and the place names on the exit signs were laden with memories. Demonstrations. Strikes. And meeting after meeting. Miners, steel workers. And teachers. God, the bloody teachers. And a lot of beer. A lot of laughs too. And, despite the beer, and the often shambolic organisation, still that sense that maybe, just maybe, these people would build enough momentum to drag the whole country off on some doomed quest for the promised land. The miners in particular had been on a roll after their victory in '72 and there even been power cuts as their overtime ban began to bite. They had been bought off in the end but the bosses back in London had been jumpy ever since. Then a couple of people with connections to the Angry Brigade had joined the scene and suddenly the pressure was really on so they'd taken a load of the ring leaders out on drugs charges. Not his proudest moment. Planting bags of pills on people he'd been drinking with for a good while, but it had done the job. The sign said Leeds 8 Miles and he switched the SatNav on.

As soon as he got off the motorway it was clear the town had changed. In forty-five years that was to be expected but even so. Again and again the landmarks he expected to see along the way failed to emerge. Was it his memory or had the place really been remodelled that much? The Black Horse was still there though. Lock-ins and plotting. It passed out of

149

sight in seconds but for a minute or two he was back there. Arguing about the tactics, who to vote on and off committees and drinking so much great Yorkshire beer. For a moment even the smell came back to him. The landlord had been a Special Branch informant too but he hadn't known who David was. One of the things that used to piss Special Branch off. Sometimes, for light relief, his handler would let him see the reports on David submitted by the landlord. They were encouraging. "Not a mover and shaker." "Reliable." "Just another foot soldier." 'Excellent', his handler had said. 'Just what we want to hear.'

Now the SatNav was telling him to turn left, off the main road and into territory he didn't know. The road climbed past rows of terraced Victorian villas and as he headed out of town the amount of rubbish increased. An old bed. Ripped bin bags the council had refused to handle. Some forlorn looking To Let signs and, at the furthest end, windows sealed with Sitex, their blank aluminium surfaces the very antithesis of home.

But the 1970s estate that spread out at the end of this road was in relatively good shape. The areas of grass between the low-rise blocks of flats had been mown in living memory, the cars were in a better state of repair than many of the vehicles he had passed on the way up. He guessed that on a fine day the view across the valley to the open hills beyond would have been uplifting but today, with a damp wind blowing in, it gave the place a bleak, exposed feel. He allowed the monotonous tones of his electronic guide to lead him on and two minutes later he pulled up outside Windermere House; journey's end.

When he rang the bell he had to wait at least a minute before a voice on the intercom said, 'Yes.'

'Morning. Colin? It's David Nixon. We spoke on Friday.'

The front door buzzed and he pushed it open. Flat 10 was on the first floor, up an echoing concrete stairway. On the landing another door led down a corridor off which doors led to four flats. The first one on the right was ajar and David pushed it open. 'Hello?'

'Come in. This way.' There was a small hallway and the voice came from beyond another open door. David walked through into what was the living room, with a large window looking south across to the hills he had seen from the car park. Seated in an armchair to the left of the window was a slight, wiry man with short reddish hair wearing a dark green Helly Hansen fleece. Lent against the side of the chair were two crutches. The foot protruding from the man's left trouser leg was false. The television was on, some programme about properties it seemed, but the sound was muted.

'Cup of tea? 'Fraid you'll have to make it yourself. Moving about is really bad today.'

'Thanks. I will. Do you want one?'

'Milk. Two sugars. Thanks. The kitchen's across the hall.'

The kitchen was small, but tidy, the washing up was stacked neatly on the draining board beneath a window looking out at the neighbouring blocks. When he opened the fridge to get the milk he found a neat stack of ready meals and not much else.

He carried two mugs back through to the sitting room and handed one to Colin.

'How did it go at the hospital?'

'Fuck knows. The physio's good but I don't think the doctor's got a fucking clue. They keep changing my medication. I'm on that many pain killers and anti-depressants and they've all got side effects and they can't seem to find a combination that doesn't leave me feeling completely fucked most of the time. But you're lucky. This is a good day. By my standards.'

As he sat down in an armchair opposite Colin he looked around the room. There were a couple of photos on a single shelf, one of a parachute regiment platoon and one of Colin alone in a shemarg. Otherwise the walls were bare.

'Is that you in Iraq?' David asked.

'Yeah. Not long after I arrived. Still got the scarf. Not that I wear it much these days.'

'Did many of the others... in your platoon go into the security business?'

'Yeah. That or armed robbery. See that big bastard in the back row?' Colin pointed to the group photo. 'Him and another lad from C company are doing eight years for a fucked-up bank job in Sheffield. Fucking idiot. He was a good plumber. Could have made a lot of money. Mind you I can't really point the finger can I? Not the way my career choices worked out. Anyway. What is it you want to know? No scrub that. Tell me who you are again.'

'I'm David Nixon. I work for the Security Service.'

'That's MI5?'

'Yes. Do you want to see some ID?'

'Yeah.'

David pulled the plastic badge out of his breast pocket and passed it over. Colin looked at it closely while David tried not to stare at the prosthetic foot a couple of feet in front of him.

'I've no idea if this is real,' said Colin. 'But go on.' He wrapped the lanyard round the badge and tossed it back. 'What do you want.'

'I want to know what you were doing down at Lord Frampton's place on 4 September.'

'Who says I was there?'

'Your car didn't drive itself Colin.'

'I didn't fucking drive it either.' He waggled his prosthetic leg to emphasise the point.

'It didn't drive itself. You must at least know who took the car.'

'No idea mate. My keys are still here. Anyone with a bit of nouse could have hot-wired it.' Colin was starting to sound insolent. David needed to find a new approach before Colin shut him out completely.

'Colin. I'm from the Security Service. We don't investigate criminal damage. Which is all that whoever sprayed the walls of Lord Frampton's house would have been guilty of. I can't tell you the basis of my investigation. What I can tell you is that you're not the focus. Don't take this the wrong way but … I'm not interested in you. In what you've done. I don't want to waste my time filling in all the forms and writing up the witness statements and everything that I would have to do just to get you convicted of criminal damage.' He paused again to let the message sink in. 'My interest is in Lord Frampton, and issues related to Lord Frampton that have nothing to do with you or any message you may or may not have sprayed on his walls.' David was lying now but he had had years of practice.

'So why are you here?' The tone was still hostile but David sensed a wary, tentative willingness to engage.

'I'm trying to build a picture of what has been going on in his life recently, and some of what I need to know about relates to his involvement in Iraq.' Colin nodded slightly. An invitation to David to proceed. On sufferance.

'You did a couple of tours of Iraq didn't you, before …'

'Transferring to 5 Para. That's what we called it. So many of the lads jacked in the army and went freelance it was like

153

home from home. You kept running into old mates you knew from the battalion. All the time. It was ridiculous. Got so bad the army started running out of regulars. But why would you do the job for £12,000 a year if you could get 60?'

'So you went to work for Four Square?'

'Yeah.' Colin's tone was bitter.'

'What was the company like to work for?'

'Day to day, not bad. They were a good lot of lads. Mostly. Couple of German tossers from the Foreign Legion. Played shit heavy metal everywhere they went. But I mostly worked with English guys. We were allocated to teams and stuck with them. The OC was a really cool guy. SAS. No bullshit. Just really sensible. And it was all Greyman style. Beat up old Mercs. Underneath you had souped up engines, armour, the works but you looked like the locals.' Colin was heading off at a tangent but for now David was happy just to let him talk. 'The Iraqi mechanics were amazing. Cos of the sanctions they'd been keeping old vehicles on the road that would have been scrapped years ago back here. The chief mechanic was REME and he couldn't believe what they could do. He said there were ten-year-old Iraqi kids could do things in ten minutes with an adjustable spanner and an oil can it'd take one of his guys back home half an hour to fix. And they all supported English football teams. Couldn't understand why we all hated Man U.' Colin smiled at the memory. 'We didn't drive big shiny 4X4s and go round waving 50 cal machine guns at all the locals. None of that bollocks.'

'And that worked did it?'

'Most of the time. The real risk was the septics. They'd see the cars and the guns and they'd think we were the bad guys. And they didn't always ask for ID before opening up. Had a couple of real scares. Those cunts from Blackwater were the worst.'

'Was that how this happened?' David looked down at his leg.

'No. That was an RPG. We'd taken a client to an electricity sub-station. He was supposed to certify some work had been done. Some shit like that. Half the time you'd get there and there was no sign anyone had done any work at all. But sods law, this time the contractors had made the effort so we had to hang around. Somebody clocked us. Suddenly there's nobody on the street and you know something's up. Ben was yelling at the client to get a move on, we had to go. But he was too fucking slow. Halfway from the door of the building to the car and an RPG explodes against the wall behind us. Client ended up dragging me into the car. That was me done.'

'Didn't you get some sort of pay out?'

Colin's face darkened. 'Turned out they fucked us all over on the insurance. I checked them out. Before I signed. Glossy brochures. A couple of ex Tory ministers on the board. Including Lord Frampton. It all looked Kosher. But turned out we'd all signed a contract with some other outfit with almost the same name but these cunts were based in Jersey. They'd promised us insurance but when I tried to get some money off them, after this,' he tapped his leg, which was plainly false all the way up to the top of his thigh, 'I just got some bullshit letter. Took it to a lawyer who charged me five hundred quid for telling me it would cost thousands of pounds I didn't have to try and sue them in Jersey. So now I'm stuck here on ESA fighting the fucking council for a fucking ground floor flat.' Colin's face was turned towards the window now, his lips pressed close together.

'Jesus.' David wasn't easily shocked. 'There's no way you're going to get anything?'

'Could have been a bit more sensible with the money when I was earning. Thrown a bit less cash around on those trips to Thailand.'

'Did you ever meet Lord Frampton? In Iraq? Or in the UK?'

'Twice. In Iraq.'

'Can you tell me about that?'

'Sure.' Colin seemed more relaxed now, happy to talk even, now the pressure was off. He pulled himself into a more upright position and winced slightly but without making any sound. 'The first time was... I'd been there about a month. Obviously there was a bit of fuss. The boss and all that. We had a bit of a tidy up. But he seemed fine. He definitely wanted us to know he'd been in the regiment but ... he was no trouble. He got a bit impatient during the security briefing apparently ... sort of, 'Don't waste my time with this. I wrote all this' ... which was bollocks ... but he did what he was told. Seemed quite taken with the whole shemagh and dark glasses look.'

'So where did you pick him up.'

'He got a chopper out of the Green Zone to a US base outside Tikrit where we picked him up. Then we drove to an oil facility at a place called Chitril. This was late 2006 so it was starting to get a bit hairy. The militias had been getting stronger and you never knew what you were going to run into. We had three vehicles. The leading car had a driver and three men. Frampton was in the second car with a driver and two others. And some more firepower in the rear vehicle.'

'And you were in the second vehicle?'

'Yeah. Back seat. Next to the client.'

'How did it go?'

'Started fine. He told us there was a bit of an issue at an oil pumping station. But he was going to sort it out. Made it sound like an admin problem. Truth was an American oil crew, and two of our guys who were their security were all being held hostage by the workforce. And somehow we were going to go and spring them. The first problem was a checkpoint, about 40 miles from Chitril. They looked like Iraqi army but the front car radioed back that it looked wrong.'

'In what way?'

'You get a feel for it. Maybe there's too many hajjis hanging around who don't seem to be in uniform. Wrong weapons. Sometimes just from the way they stand you can tell they've never been through any sort of training. Anyway the lead car said, 'we're going to run this one.' So we all cocked our weapons and got ready to rock and roll.' Then he laughed a dry laugh. 'And Sammy looked round... Oh God, Sammy...'

'Who was Sammy?'

'Sammy was one of the South African guys. Had a great big black hole where one of his front teeth used to be. He looked fucking horrible but he was a great guy to work with... but sometimes he'd act a bit cracked and sometimes you weren't sure it was all an act. They'd seen some pretty brutal shit in Angola.' Done some brutal shit more likely, thought David, and the demons had pursued him all the way to Baghdad. 'So Sammy turns round as he's cocking his weapon and grinned, with this horrible black hole in his front teeth and said, it was sort of his catch phrase, 'Another day, another dollar...'

'And how did Frampton react?'

157

'He said, 'Give me a gun. Against all the rules but he was the boss. I waited for Ben to say something, he was our team leader, but he didn't. So in the end I just gave him my Glock.'

'Then what?'

'We started to slow down, make them think we were going to play nice then at fifty meters... pedal to the metal.'

'And?'

'They dived for cover. We never knew if they were for real or what. We radioed in to the US but they had no record of any official check point in the area, not that that meant much. Liaison was never their strong point.'

'The Iraqis or the US?'

'Neither really. Christ what shambles. It was the same when I was out there with the Paras. No fucking communication. Sammy was killed about a month later. An IED took out the vehicle he was traveling in on the road to Mosul.'

'OK. But what happened when you got to the pumping station.'

'Chaos. I don't know exactly what Frampton thought was going to happen. There was a crowd at the gates blocking the entrance. They'd built some sort of barricade. There were no guns or anything. No physical threat but they were shouting at us and waving placards and they definitely weren't letting us in. We stopped about 50 meters from the entrance. Ben got out of the car and this guy, respectable looking, wearing a suit, came walking over to meet us. He had a chat with Ben. All perfectly fine and Ben came back to tell us the score. The guys demonstrating at the gate were all union members and they weren't having any foreigners coming in and taking over their oil fields. The guys Frampton was supposed to be meeting were all inside. Being looked after but ... basically prisoners. And could we take them home with us and never darken their door again.'

'And how did Frampton react?'

'Badly. To put it mildly. Gave it all this... what fucking right did these people have to tell him what he could and couldn't do. It wasn't even legal to belong to a union in the oil industry. Saddam had had the right idea about unions. And all this crap. Which seemed a bit rich given that we were supposed to have liberated the poor bastards. But he took it personally. Felt he'd been shown up in front of us. I don't think he liked that at all. For a moment I thought he was going to ask us to shoot our way in.'

'How do you mean?'

'He sort of looked us over, very deliberately, as if he was assessing our firepower. It wasn't going to happen.'

'So how did it all end up?'

'Ben went back over to the guy in the suit, said OK, and about ten minutes later they let this 4X4 through the barricade with our guys in and we all drove back to the base. Turned out the idiot contractors had fitted the wrong size pump to some part of the system. It delivered way too much pressure and it had blown up a whole section of pipe. So the Iraqis had just told 'em to fuck off.'

'And that was it? Nothing else? No more checkpoints or anything?'

'No. The Yanks went down the road with a chopper but whoever had mounted the checkpoint was long gone and we had a clear run back. No. The only incident was...'

'What?'

'Frampton still had my Glock. And about 20 minutes after we'd headed back he asked if we could stop. I thought he needed a piss. But no. He got out of the car with the gun, said something like, 'It's been a long time' or something, took up a firing position and emptied the entire magazine at a rock. It was good shooting, for someone who hadn't handled a gun for a long time, but it was fucking weird. Then he got back in the car, tossed the empty gun onto my lap, and didn't say another word the whole way back.'

'You said there was a second time?'

'That was a couple of months later. Everything had really started to kick off after those dickheads from Blackwater got themselves killed in Fallujah. I was based down in Kut by then. The company had got a new contract with some contractors, Polish mainly, who were based there. A real cushy billet. Bloody cold though. And really wet, all winter. The Poles missed their home comforts. Spent a lot of their time trying to blag vodka and pork sausages off the Ukrainians who were stationed there. Vodka's quite hard to find in downtown Kut. And pork sausages. But it was quiet. No trouble anywhere we went. Some dirty looks. That sort of thing, but no real trouble. Easy money. Did you know there's a First World War British military cemetery in the middle of Kut?'

'Yes.'

'What's all that about?'

'Oil.'

'Jesus.' Colin laughed a mirthless laugh.

'What were these contractors doing?' David asked.

'Basically, they had a huge budget for sorting the place out and they were looking for ways to spend it. And people back at HQ would be boasting about some great project they'd just completed and you'd think. "We drove past there the other day and I didn't see any new class rooms." They'd got all the paperwork, the receipts, inspection reports and everything.

Just no fucker had actually gone and done the fucking work.'
Colin laughed. 'The look on their faces when you told them
there was nothing there... But it was starting to get uglier.'

'How?' David asked.

'Little things to start with. People just that much more
wary. Less keen to talk to you. And we started to see these
guys in black. Armed. Not looking for a fight but, you know,
not bothered that you'd seen them. Our interpreter, Abdul, a
lovely guy, started to get nervous. They knew who he was,
where he lived and everything, but he needed the money to
feed his kids so he kept coming. And then one day it all
kicked off.'

'What happened?'

'There was a massive demonstration at the governor's
headquarters down by the river. So we just grabbed our guys
and legged it to Delta, the Ukrainian base. Thought we'd just
sit it out out there. Then Lord Frampton turned up.'

'Out of the blue?'

'Not exactly. He'd said he was coming to meet some
people but everyone assumed he'd abort. What with
everything going tits up and half the province in the hands of
the Sadrists. But no. Late morning. Just as everyone's starting
to think about lunch he shows up. Three big armoured four by
fours. They'd belted all the way down Highway 6 from
Baghdad that morning. He knew things were rocky but I
don't think he'd got how bad they were. And he jumps out of
the vehicle and he asks, 'Where are they?' And of course no
one's got a fucking clue what he's talking about because it's
always times like this that comms get fucked up. So we had
no idea that there's a team of our lads heading into Kut with
the nob Lord Frampton's so keen to meet, and no one knows

161

where they are or whether they know what's going on. Situation Normal.'

'All Fucked Up?'

'Exactly.'

'So what did Lord Frampton do?'

'Started shouting mostly. Adam calmed him down. Well, waited for him to stop shouting really, then just started talking sense. Turned out there was a problem with the radios. So we managed to get in touch with the guys who were coming in. Warn them everything was kicking off and tell them to head for Delta. Ten minutes later they're radioing in to say they don't like the look of what they can see up the road and then ... Bam. One of the cars was a write-off. One of our guys was dead.' Colin furrowed his brow for a moment. 'No one I knew... The rest of them... and two of them were my mates, Eddie Smith and Kevin Barratt... and they'd holed up in a petrol station. So Frampton demanded that the Ukrainians sent out a rescue party. But the Ukes weren't having any of it. Don't think they were too impressed with Frampton. Bit too up himself. Too high and mighty. So he went and had a big argument with the guy in charge. Which achieved fuck all. Then Etherington turned up. The British Governor in Kut. He was trying to persuade the Ukrainians to go back into town and rescue his guys, who were trapped in the CPA HQ. But the Ukrainians weren't having any of that either. So Frampton said, 'Looks like it's down to us lads. And he snapped straight into operations mode. Stopped all his shouting. Listened to everything Adam had to say. Basically agreed with everything he said but turned it into an order. Like officers do.'

'So what was the plan?' David asked.

'We knew the location. It was a village, just a few houses really about three miles out of town. The guys knew we were coming for them so their job was just to hang on. Conserve ammunition. Wait for the cavalry. Our problem was they'd see us coming so the plan was pretty basic. Get in close with the armoured vehicles. Get out. And kill the fuckers. The plan was to drive all the way up to the village then get off the road either side and exit the vehicles under cover if possible. Then advance up both sides of the road. In the open you're vulnerable getting out of the vehicle but as soon as you can get into some cover, put down some covering fire we'd have the edge.'

'How?'

'We were professionals. Aimed shots. Coordinated fire and movement. They could get lucky but there was only ever about twenty of them, according to the guys, and they'd taken care of a couple already. And the hajjis didn't like a stand-up fight. So, with the ten guys who'd come down with Frampton it looked doable. Adam managed to blag a few grenades from the Ukrainians. They were a bit sheepish about just sitting on their arses while everything was kicking off. And then we loaded up. Another day, another dollar.'

'And how did it pan out.'

'Tough. Tougher than expected, yeah.'

'What happened?' David asked.

'They got lucky.' David didn't say anything, just waited.

'They saw us coming. No way round that but one of the vehicles Frampton had brought down from Bagdhad had a top mounted machine gun. So they pulled off the road as we approached to cover us. The insurgents got some rounds off at us but nothing that was going to seriously dent the armour. A couple of guys appeared with an RPG but the covering fire from the machine gun pretty much persuaded them to keep their heads down. They got one rocket off but they'd no time to aim it and it went wide. We found one of those guys soon after we got off the bus, still alive just, but with most of his arm taken off. Which sort of concentrates the mind. So we got to the edge of the village OK. It was a bit hairy exiting the vehicles 'cos there were still bad guys right up close but we scared them off basically. They weren't up for close combat. Adam slotted two of them almost immediately and they pulled back. Then we started to move up the street. That's when you need eyes in the back of your head 'cos the bastards could be anywhere.'

'Where was Lord Frampton?'

'He stayed with the vehicles. Somebody had to or there was a risk these guys would get round behind us, destroy the vehicles and then we'd all be trapped. And the other mad thing was, everyone was still in their houses. I kicked a door open round the back of the first house and there was about eight of them, terrified. Kids and everything. Just told them to lie down, and moved on. But it doesn't help. Knowing that one fuck up… A grenade in the wrong window, and you've taken out a whole family. Anyway, it was going according to plan. We were moving up the street. Five or six of us on each side. The lads at the petrol station were on the same radio net now. They were reporting that the guys they were facing were starting to act worried. Firing dropping off and so on. And we were pushing them back. They'd pop up, spray a lot of rounds in our general direction, but just comfort fire, nothing aimed properly, then run back to the next wall, the next building. We'd killed two on our side of the street. One of them jumped over a wall then stuck his head back up, in exactly the same spot where he'd gone over. Easy. And I got one of them

164

at point blank range. I came round a corner and there he was. Just about on the end of my weapon. Messy, but quick. And you're thinking 'we're in control. It's all going according to plan.' Then they got Mark. He was working his way up the other side of the street and he got hit and he was down in the road. And this great shout went up of "Allah Akbar" and they stopped running. Mark had managed to crawl into a ditch, a gutter really, by the side of the road but he was badly hurt and you could see the rounds striking the ground all round him. Adam tried to get us organised to put down enough covering fire so he could drag Mark back into some sort of cover but it looked horrible. Their blood was up now and I didn't rate Adam's chances. Then we heard the sound of one of our vehicles coming up the street and it was Lord Frampton. He'd been listening on the radio. He overshot, then reversed back so he'd parked between Mark and the insurgents. He got out and tried to lift Mark into the vehicle but it was too much of a struggle so Adam got in there and dragged him in and Frampton was shooting over bonnet, cos they were well pissed now, really didn't like the idea of the rescue squad spoiling it for them and for a few minutes there was a lot of incoming. And, fair play to him, once Mark was safely loaded into the vehicle Lord Frampton kept shooting. He didn't just get back in the car and wait for us to sort it out. But, after that it didn't take long…. they'd no training. They made themselves obvious targets and we killed I don't know, four or five more before they got the message and fucked off.'

'Out of the village?'

'Yeah. The shooting stopped and two or three minutes later we heard an engine start and the next thing we knew there were two pickups heading off up the road.'

'Did you shoot at them?'

'Outside the rules of engagement. Another day we might have done but not with the boss watching. And we still had to get back to Delta. Didn't want to waste any more ammunition.'

'So what happened then?'

'We got over to the garage. Careful like. Cos you don't want to do all the hard work then have a blue on blue at the last minute. But it was fine. They'd had another lad wounded but he was going to live. And Lord Frampton walked into the garage where they'd been holed up like he was Lawrence of fucking Arabia. Walked straight over to sheikh what's his name, hand out and saying, what was it?' Colin affected an upper class drawl. "Sorry we took so long. Bit of a hold up on the way." And I thought, "You fucking wanker." But that sheikh lapped it up. Fair play to him I suppose. He risked his life. But who he risked it for... We got a company email a few weeks later saying, "we are looking to expand our operations substantially" and the future looked bright for everyone. Then I got my P45 a few weeks after that and didn't think about it again. It was only when the deal was announced six months later and I opened the paper and there's a picture of the bastard grinning away like the cat that's got the cream shaking hands with the bloke I recognise from the garage. And I thought it's thanks to matey boy, and the rest of us, and what we did that day in Kut that he's now fucking minted.'

'And you felt he owed you?'

'Too fucking right.' But then he smiled. 'Of course I didn't do anything about it. And I've got no idea how my car came to be seen on the CCTV down there.'

'I interviewed Lord Frampton and he never mentioned his part in this. Why would that be?'

166

'He wasn't licensed. If that had got out the other companies would have made all sorts of trouble for him.'

'There's one thing that troubles me Colin.'

'Just the one? You're a lucky man.'

'It's this. Not long after your visit Lord Frampton took £20,000 out of his bank account in cash.' David looked at Colin for a reaction, but there was none so he continued. 'Which is what you'd do if you were paying someone off.'

Colin gestured at his surroundings with a movement that said as clearly as one could wish, 'If I had £20,000 would I live like this?' And David had not a moment's doubt that Colin was telling the truth. Then Colin's face lit up. 'If he pays out like that maybe another trip would... not that...'

David cut him off. 'Listen. Like I said, I'm not interested in a trivial act of criminal damage. If you think of anything more let me know.' He handed Colin a card, one of his old ones, with the new telephone number written in in biro.

'Like what?'

'I don't know. Anything that sheds light on what Lord Frampton was playing at.'

'I only met the guy those two times. And anyway, I'm done with all that shit. This is what I have to deal with now.' He was right, thought David. There was nothing more he had to offer.

'There was a ground floor flat came vacant in that block over there. Do you know who they gave it to?'

'No,' said David, but he could guess.

'A family of fucking hajjis. Fucking hajjis in my flat. I see her down at the shops sometimes, all wrapped up in...' He couldn't be bothered to finish the sentence.

'Well thanks for your time. And good luck. With the council and everything...'

167

'Civi cunts.' But his tone was one of despair as much as anger.

'I'll let myself out.'

There was nothing more he could say. No practical help, no consolation he could offer. With something approaching relief he shut the door of the flat behind him.

It was still not midday. He had picked somewhere from the Good Pub Guide the night before and now he was looking forward to "a traditional pub with views over the surrounding countryside and a reasonable selection of local beers." But this dream was eclipsed by the image of Colin in his neat, soulless flat, with the remains of his right leg propped up in front of him, gazing impassively out of his window. Used, chewed up and spat out.

After forty minutes driving David pulled over at a pleasant looking stone built pub called The Royal Oak with a blackboard outside promising "Home Cooked Fayre". The car park, which separated the pub from the small village it served, was empty and inside he found just two older men leaning silently against the bar, each with a freshly poured pint, and a barman in his mid twenties drying glasses. A Kinks song he couldn't immediately put a name to was playing very softly in the background.

'Afternoon,' the barman said and the two drinkers turned to face him. 'Afternoon,' they both mumbled in a not unfriendly fashion before returning their gaze to the ranks of bottles arrayed in front of them beyond the bar.

David returned their greeting and asked for a menu.

'Sure.' The barman handed him a laminated cream sheet which offered the predictable range of sandwiches and mains and, without any great enthusiasm, he plumped for moussaka and chips. He eyed the range of bitters, most of which he did not recognise, and asked for a pint of Theakstons. 'Should have had the salad,' he thought to himself as he made his way over to a table by the window. There he spread out his newspaper and started to read a story about parliament's inquiry into the tax arrangements of one of the larger pharmaceutical companies, while at the same time eavesdropping on the conversation which was now unfolding at the bar. A local builder had fallen out with one of the farmers in the area, there had been an altercation at the builder's yard and conflicting accounts of the episode were now circulating in the village. Then the conversation drifted off into the technicalities of three phase electrical wiring which were apparently at the heart of the problem, and David lost interest. But the company tax issues were not much more engaging. The parliamentary committee seemed divided between Tories who thought Britain should be "open for business", which apparently implied being extremely relaxed about the use of tax havens, Labour members who wanted to "work with businesses to create a society that was fair for all" and a lone Lib Dem who described the arrangements as "scandalous" but was essentially ignored.

David wondered if he should check his phone. Perhaps, it occurred to him, going incommunicado was more of a risk than leaving a trail. They would have to go out of their way to look for that information but they could stumble across his absence. He was a good distance from Colin's flat now. It was probably safest to check for messages.

There were no messages. But there were three missed calls from Nigel. He went out into the car park and rang back.

'I've been trying to get hold of you all morning.'

'Sorry, I had my phone on silent for some reason.'

'Where are you now?'

'I'm in the pub.'

'OK. Now listen. It's essential that you take no further steps in this case. Is that absolutely clear?'

'Clear as a bell.'

'Good. Do nothing at all to take this matter forward. We're not taking it any further. Can you get into the office tomorrow morning?'

'Yes.'

'Good. I'll speak to you then. Bye.'

The phone went dead. David looked out across the rooftops of the village to the bare hills beyond. After the warmth of the pub it suddenly seemed very chilly out here. He looked up and down the road for no reason, then walked back inside.

The moussaka arrived with an injunction from the barman to 'Enjoy.' It was fine. The beer was fine. But inside he felt numb. What had just happened?

His immediate feeling was one of disappointment. The thought of returning to his ideas for a vegetable garden filled him with no real enthusiasm. The pile of unread books beside his armchair held slightly more appeal. But his plans for bird watching, for boning up on the minute differences between a hundred different species of warbler, for training his ear to distinguish one bird call from another, filled him with nothing more now than a dry sense of duty.

But that wasn't the real problem. The real problem was Eric. The diligent, dutiful operator, the stoic, caring husband who cared no more. The problem was Eric's crippled wife, deprived now of what must have been, he guessed, the one remaining source of light in her life. The problem was Terry, Eric's closest colleague, drunk and disturbed at the funeral by

170

something he would not name. The problem was the broken, bitter man he had just left, and, more than anything, the problem was the memory of Lord Frampton, standing on his porch, puffed up with arrogance and entitlement, threatening, "I will crush you."

The real problem was he couldn't walk away.

When he finished his meal David ordered a coffee and sat for half an hour weighing up all the arguments against what his instincts told him, ever more insistently, that he would do. When he got back into his car he removed the battery from his phone again.

CHAPTER TEN

An hour later he had parked in Bradford. His first port of call was a market stall, run by a courteous Sikh with a blue turban and a greying beard, where he picked up a basic second-hand smart phone, and a pay as you go SIM card. At two further stalls he bought additional phones and pay as you go SIM cards. Then he took £250 out of a cashpoint. Back at the car he plotted a route to Huddersfield running as far as possible on minor roads where the chances of CCTV were less. After four years sitting in an office staring at spreadsheets a part of him felt energised by this turn of events. But at the same time he realised that, to a greater extent than ever before, he simply did not know who or what he was up against. And he had never before worked without back up. Interesting times. But he was getting ahead of himself. If he fell at the next hurdle it was over before it had started. As he threaded his way through the backroads of a succession of small towns he started to plan how best to handle what was going to be, by any standards, an awkward conversation. He checked his rear-view mirror regularly and at one point pulled over for five minutes but there was no hint of a tail and no real likelihood of one yet. As he sat in his car, carefully watching the vehicles that went past he thought about the possibility that, like Eric, he too would be dead in a week or two. A gap appeared between in the flow traffic and he pulled out.

When he got to Huddersfield he parked half a mile from the house. He made a careful note of how his possessions, the plastic bag with the remains of some fruit in and an old newspaper, were laid out before taking an indirect route, watching all the time. The address he had dated back to when he had had to sign off a file review ten years before. It has been a strange moment, a reminder of such a different time. When he reached the street he walked past the house, one in an anonymous row of terraced two up two downs, looking for the obvious signs, but there were no people sitting in parked cars, no one loitering nearby for no apparent reason, nothing. It seemed unlikely, to say the least, there would be anyone but these habits were hardwired into him. He walked back to the front door and knocked. He wasn't nervous exactly. You didn't last in this job if you got nervous about this sort of thing, but he knew this meeting was a serious test. As he stood there waiting for someone to answer the thought crossed his mind, ridiculously, that perhaps he should have brought some flowers. He was still smiling when he heard footsteps inside and as the latch turned he quickly reverted to a neutral expression. And it wouldn't necessarily be Mike.

But it was. Greyer now and the moustache had gone, but the same stocky muscular figure, the same energetic grey eyes.

He gave Mike a moment to take in the situation. It had been a long time but there was no doubt Mike knew who he was. 'Hello Mike. It's David. There's a reason for this.'

Mike just looked at him. There was no suggestion he was going to lash out but David could still sense the coiled reserves of energy that had fuelled so much of their campaigning efforts in the seventies. Then, ever so slightly, Mike nodded.

'Something happened here, hereabouts, during the miners' strike. Something serious enough that some very senior people are willing to go to enormous lengths to cover it up.'

'Serious like planting drugs on people and getting them banged up for two years?' The same voice too.

'Serious like killing people. At least that's what it looks like.' But he'd saved the best till last. Now he rolled the dice. 'Mike, I've jumped ship. They've ordered me off the case. I'm ... freelance.'

A long silence. A soft 'Fuck.' Another long silence, then, 'Come in.' David knew he wasn't home yet, not by a long way, it could still go horribly wrong but he had got himself a hearing. He followed Mike into the sitting room. The place was neat and clean. More china on the shelves than he would have expected. A few books, but just novels and local history and guide books, no hint of the radical David had known.

'This is the wife's room,' Mike said. 'Sit down.'

David sat on the sofa, feeling encumbered by his overcoat but this wasn't the moment to take it off; he'd been invited in on sufferance, not welcomed. Mike now sat opposite him in an armchair and waited. Unexpectedly David got a sense of how a suspect felt just before they lurched into a confession. He was almost tempted to apologise for framing Mike all those years ago but that wasn't the way forward right now.

'Does the name Lord Frampton mean anything to you?'

'Yeah. Tory peer I think. Right wing. Even for a Tory.'

174

'He was in the army before that. Parachute Regiment then SAS. Came out in 1984. He went into parliament soon afterwards but his first job was working for David Hart.'

Mike leant forward ever so slightly.

'You'll remember David Hart provided protection for a number of miners, especially in Nottingham, who were defying the strike …'

'Scabbing.' The interruption was matter of fact.

'Challenging the NUM. Lord Frampton, or Alexander Edwards, as he was then, recruited men to protect these people, he recruited them principally, as far as I can tell, from the SAS. There's a possibility some of them were even serving members who were given time off for this work. If that's true that's not something they'd want to come out but I don't think they'd kill to keep it secret. I don't know what happened, but something occurred… during that period… that someone very powerful wants buried.'

'And you say they've killed someone to keep it quiet?'

David was silent a moment. 'It's not clear. Somebody died the other day. I don't know they were murdered but … there is a suggestion it was murder and a suggestion that it was related to what Lord Frampton was doing during the strike. I was brought in then … during the strike… because of my background, they threw everything at it … and I was given your file so I know you were very involved in organising picketing and so on. Lord Frampton can be a bit of an unguided missile, he's a man with a short fuse. They got up to something, something that would be career terminating for Lord Frampton if it came out now.' David waited for a response. The seconds ticked by.

Mike spoke quietly, calmly even, but every word was weighted with contempt. 'You've got a nerve.' This was where it got tricky. 'You spend eighteen months spying on us, we treat you like you're one of us, you eat with us, you drink with us, you stay in our homes, then you frame four of us for drug offences, three of us do time... my son was four when I went in and nearly six when I came out. They kept moving me from prison to prison, mainly down south, deliberately, so visiting was hard.' He was silent for a while. 'He didn't even like having me in the house when I first got out.'

'This won't make up for any of that.' David said. It was worth acknowledging that unpleasant truth. 'But if we can find out what they are hiding it will mean justice for someone. With any luck. You can't immediately think of anything? Anyone going missing or something like that.'

'Woah, woah, woah. You don't just rock up after forty years, tell us you're one of the good guys now and ...'

David knew he had to wait.

Then Mike's tone changed, colder rather than angry, and more business-like. 'I'm not talking to you on my own. I'm not going to decide whether to trust you.' A few moments more passed in silence. 'You say you've gone freelance. Do they know that?'

'Not yet. Depending on what we find, or don't find, they may never know. But if anyone's keeping tabs on me they might even know now.'

'How come?'

'The moment I took the battery out of my mobile. When that signal died anyone watching would have guessed something was up.'

'And why would anyone be watching you?'

David thought of his stunt with Lord Frampton's building work, but he wasn't going to share that information yet. 'Who knows. If I really am investigating something that leads somewhere they don't want me to go they'd have every reason to try.'

'Who's they?'

'Lord Frampton, and anyone with an interest in covering for him.'

'And you think "they"'ve already killed?'

'Possibly.'

'Jesus, if they did Orgreave in plain sight what would they kill to cover up? I'm going to call...' Mike paused, plainly running a list of possible names through his mind. 'Brian Hebblethwaite,' A dry laugh. 'He'll be pleased to see you. Dennis Holby and Guy Lansley. You can tell them the whole story and we'll decide what to do about it together'

'Not Dennis,' said David.

'God. You got to him?' Mike's voice was somewhere between despair and incredulity.

'They got him for breach of his bail conditions. Told him with the fines he wouldn't be able to pay and everything he'd end up going to jail for a good long while. Like you he had a young boy.' Until the magistrates got wise to it it had been a useful trick for getting the trouble-makers put away. Take some thug who should never have been bailed and drop him off so far from home he couldn't possibly get back in time to make his curfew then drag him back in front of the magistrates for breaching the terms of his bail. Or threaten to if he didn't start informing.

'Jesus, is this how you've lived your entire life?'

David ignored the question. 'Don't be too harsh on him. It wasn't down to him that you lost.'

David watched Mike gently shaking his head, perhaps thinking through all the meetings Dennis had attended, all the

177

hours of planning that must have been reported straight back to the authorities.

'Anyone else I need to know about?'

'Nobody's bothered with you lot anymore. It's drug dealers and Islamists. That's all that counts now. This is ancient history for them.'

'So why are you so bothered all of a sudden.'

David started to wonder if he had miscalculated. 'I'm going to have to explain myself to the other two when they get here. Let's go through it all then. All right?'

Mike nodded. 'I'll call them.'

'Keep it low key. And don't mention my name. As low key as possible.'

Mike left the room and David was unable to hear what he was saying to either of them. When he returned he explained they'd be coming round together about half past six.

'Do you know them two as well?'

'I think I recognise the name Hebblethwaite.'

'You should do. He's another one that goes back to Leeds. Used to drink in the Black Horse. He was a social worker then. Got involved in a lot of the support work during the strike. You wouldn't know Guy unless you came across him during the strike. He was a miner. Had a lot to do with organising picketing in Nottingham.'

David shook his head. 'What did you tell them?' he asked.

'Just that something had come up in the constituency party we needed to talk about. Our M.P. looks about twelve and doesn't really know how to talk to ... the old guard. He's always pissing somebody off about something. My wife might be back by then. She won't know who you are. Best not to tell her. She won't be impressed.' Mike seemed to

178

laugh at the thought. 'I'll just say you're here to talk about local party stuff. Do you have a name we ought to use?'

'Just David. David'll do. But David Charlton if anyone asks.'

Six thirty, thought David. That was an hour and a half away.

'I'll put the news channel on if you like,' said Mike

'Yeah.' It'd fill the time.

'Do you want a cup of tea?'

'Please.'

'Milk, one sugar?'

'You're good, but no. Just milk now.'

When he returned with the tea and sat down again David had a good idea what was coming. He decided it was best to take the initiative.

'Mike, this isn't going to be easy.'

'David, you might be out the door in an hour and a half. Real easy.'

The silence dragged on until, without any hint of bitterness or aggression Mike asked, 'How did it feel? Lying. On oath. About people who'd trusted you. Who'd opened their homes to you.'

'At the time... We thought the revolution was coming.' Quite literally. He remembered the atmosphere of paranoia in F section when he had joined. And he remembered too the whispered conversations, the half secret discussions about what, in the last resort, they were going to have to do to face this threat, discussions that he, as the new boy, was not party to. It had been a different world.

'We did too,' said Mike with something of a sigh. 'When the miners brought Heath down, then the IMF had to come in and rescue us... We thought it was just a matter of time.'

David continued, 'You knew those guys...Andy Moore and Richard...'

'Long.'

'... Richard Long were from the Angry Brigade?'

'We knew they'd been around some of those people, but the Angry Brigade were just a joke. You were there when Andy was talking about them. You knew. You knew he didn't take them seriously. You knew we weren't going to start planting bombs.'

'They had the connections.' But he knew that Mike's points were fair. And with thirty years of hindsight the paranoia of the times seemed ludicrous. The best he could come up with was, 'You can't go hanging around with people like that and calling yourselves revolutionary socialists and expect the authorities to do nothing...'

'I understand that,' said Mike, almost sarcastically. 'I just want to know what was going on in your head.'

'Maybe we should go through all this when the others get here,' said David. 'Because it all boils down to the same thing. After what I've done are you going to trust me. Or not.'

Mike nodded. Which was a relief for David. Because the details of the operation were coming back to him. In his first reports David hadn't described Andy and Richard as real threats. It was head office who had panicked and put the pressure on and, in the event, supplied the drugs. And it was his boss Richard who had persuaded, or ordered, David to go into the witness box and say that he had witnessed drugs being moved by Mike and his colleagues. "These people are going to instigate strikes and wreck our industries David. They are going to destroy people's faith in the ability of the government to manage this society so they can take over and run things their way. They're quite open about that and we know what that looks like in practice. Do you want to stand by and watch them do that?" He didn't, but it had not been a comfortable experience. His cross examination had been brutal. He and the defence barrister had taken an instant dislike to each other but that had somehow made it easier. The judge had made him feel more uncomfortable because David had sensed that the judge knew exactly what was going on. And the accused, all people he had known well, some of whom he had liked and had had good times with, their venom was hard to take. But what had left by far the worst taste in his mouth was the jury. No matter how hard he reminded himself that he was doing this to protect them. From anarchy, from commissars perhaps and collectivisation, lying to them and seeing his lies believed by this collection of ordinary, trusting, well-meaning people had been the hardest part.

'I've got a few things to sort out,' said Mike. 'I'll leave you to watch the news. See how they're getting on in Iraq.' When Mike closed the door behind him David felt an emptiness. He had stepped out of his old world but had not been accepted in to this new one. He was in limbo. And as his mind started to wander something began to nag at him. The fact that when Will and Nigel had first briefed him Will had known of his connection with Frampton in Northern Ireland. If there was someone above them all, pulling the strings, perhaps it wasn't anything Frampton had done, or at least nothing he had initiated, which people were seeking to conceal. Perhaps it was something Frampton, and presumably Eric, had been privy to. Perhaps he should try Terry again. See what Eric had been doing during the strike.

Maybe an hour later the door bell went. David heard Mike walk down the hall and open the front door. It seemed Brian had given Guy a lift and they were arriving together. Through the door he heard Mike saying, 'It's a bit different from what I said on the phone' and he brought the two of them into the sitting room. David had stood up, still wearing his coat.

Brian looked at David first with a look of puzzlement and then with a mixture of disbelief and disdain. 'What the fuck is he doing here?'

'Guy,' said Mike, 'This is the... rat who planted the drugs on me and Brian and the others. Back in '73.'

'And he's here because?' Guy asked.

'Why don't we let him explain. Take a seat.'

Guy and Brian sat in the two empty armchairs. Mike remained standing, leaning against the wall, his stance suggesting he was going to take a lot of convincing. David sensed the challenge. Now the moment had arrived he was more excited than daunted. But before he could start Mike added, 'I was going to ask Denis too, but it turns out David and his friends blackmailed him into becoming an informer. During the strike.'

'You came back for that did you?' said Brian. 'Christ alive.'

'You've got a lot of reasons not to like me,' David began. 'So I wouldn't be here without a reason. I'm just asking you to listen to what I've got to say and if you hear what I've got to say and you tell me to fuck off I'll go. But listen first.' He let the message sink in then began to tell his story in a more conversational tone. 'A few weeks ago a colleague of mine died. Apparently of a heart attack. He was in his seventies. It's possible. But there was no autopsy and heart attacks are easy enough to induce if you inject the right drugs. And he had a close friend, another colleague, they were... they were close... and that colleague is now terrified. Meanwhile I get asked to investigate a Tory peer, Lord Frampton.' He looked

182

at his audience for a reaction but he detected none. 'Before he became Lord Frampton he was a Tory MP, Alexander Edwards.'

'I remember that bastard,' said Guy. 'Said we'd never have had the poll tax riots if we'd still had the death penalty.'

'That's him,' said David. 'I'm retired now, just a few weeks ago and they brought me back to do this "little job". Apparently he... he got into the security business in Iraq, he's ex-military, and he got a big contract and the Americans think he paid people off to get it. But that's by the by. The point is I mentioned this to... let's call him John, at the funeral, and when I mentioned Frampton's name John went white. And I rang him up a few days later. And I think he was drinking... he didn't make complete sense, and I don't think he wanted to. But he implied he was involved in my colleague's death.'

'Who was involved?' asked Guy. "John", he did the digital inverted commas, 'or Lord Frampton.'

'Lord Frampton,' said David. 'Sorry. And he said "Ask him" that's Frampton, "ask him what he got up to up North."'

'And what did he get up to "up North"?', Brian asked, his voice still dripping with hostility.

'He worked for David Hart,' said David. And he saw this name hit home. 'Frampton was ex SAS. And he seems to have recruited a number of his former colleagues to act as body guards or security for the working miners' movement.'

'And you want us to help you find out what exactly he was up to?' Guy asked.

'It gets better,' says Mike.

David allowed a moment's silence before he delivered the punch line.

'This afternoon I was pulled off the investigation. It's being closed down. They know there's something else going on. Not just the payments in Iraq. But he was a Tory MP. He's connected. Whatever it is that's going on, nobody wants to know.'

'So how come you're still here?' Brian asked, still hostile but curious too now.

'Because I'm not planning to let this go. I didn't go into this job to…' why was he struggling for the words? '…let someone like Lord Frampton get away with something like this.'

'My arse,' said Brian. 'You spent your whole life helping people like Lord Frampton get away with things like this. Then all of a sudden it's someone you know who gets hurt and…'

'And what do you want from us?' asked Guy. His voice was calm but the note of contempt was inescapable.

'Help finding out what it was that happened during the strike that he's so anxious to cover up. It's got to be something serious or it wouldn't have cost Eric his life.'

Guy nodded. 'And we should trust you because…?'

'Because if I'm not telling the truth what am I doing here? What possible motive could I have for coming round here with this story if it wasn't true? I don't mean to be rude,' he smiled and hoped he would manage to lighten the atmosphere, 'but I'd be very surprised if any of you were up to anything these days that we'd be interested in infiltrating. And if you were there'd be much easier ways to go about it than this. All I'm asking is…'

'All you're asking?' Brian's voice was thick with sarcasm. He hesitated for a moment, as if casting around for the best line of attack. 'You spend your whole life working to keep us down and you think you can walk in here and tell us a little story and we'll just fall into line.' His tone was turning to cold anger now. 'The Tories crushed people in that strike. Some people came out of that strike hating the police. Me, it's the DSS I'll never forgive. Stopping benefits for no reason. Taking the food out of the mouths of children. I had a woman... I had a woman come in once, she had no food in the house, her child benefit was late, and she came in to see me, they'd sent her a Giro for 70p. No explanation. She put it on the desk in front of me and when she tried to speak she just began to sob. You crushed people. Just crushed them. Good... good people. Just fighting for a decent life. And you crushed them.'

David could almost touch the hatred. He looked over at Mike, who was watching Brian's performance without any apparent emotion. He waited a moment for the intensity of feeling to dissipate.

'That's done Brian,' said David, 'and it can't be undone. And I entirely... I understand that you don't like the idea of me as an ally. But my enemy's enemy... I was a foot soldier. I don't expect you to like me or forgive me. I thought what I was doing was right but... That was then. This is a chance to get back at someone far more significant than me.'

Brian stared at David without comment. David continued. 'All I'm asking... What I'm asking, is that you make some inquiries about what this man was up to. Anything you find out you'll know about before I do. Any time you think it's not worth the effort or... or I'm not someone you want to keep working with... you stop.' He turned to Mike and Guy. 'What do you two think?' He fixed his gaze on them, hoping their silence didn't hide further reserves of hostility.

But Brian got in first. 'I think we tell him to fuck off.'

'Me too,' said Guy. 'Lie down with dogs. Get up with fleas.'

'That's the way I'm thinking too,' said Mike. 'But tell me this David. There were people that suspected you were a phoney. Smarter people than me. They reckoned your politics didn't add up. You knew the slogans but you hadn't done the thinking.'

'That was true of a lot of people,' said David.

Despite himself Mike laughed. 'But I stood up for you. And when people asked me why, I said because you'd punched that copper when he tried to arrest Nick for decking that guy from the National Front. Was that all for show?'

'No. But you got the story wrong. I never punched anyone. I stood my ground and after a few beers the story changed. I didn't change it. Somebody else started saying I'd punched a policeman and I never said I didn't.' He laughed. 'It got me into trouble with my handler because he heard it as gospel from some other informant.' It was the landlord at the Black Horse but he wasn't going to tell them that. 'And he wouldn't believe me when I said I hadn't done it. Told me I was losing my objectivity.'

There was silence in the room. David felt he'd lost but he couldn't think how else to make his case.

'Fuck it,' said Mike. 'What have we got to lose. Like you say David, we don't have to like you. Can you live with that Brian? Guy? Like he says, we can stop it any time we want.'

Grudgingly Guy said, 'I can live with that. If that's what you want to do.'

'Brian?'

Along pause then, 'OK. But it's your baby.'

'Good,' said David, and he pressed on before Brian could say anything more. 'But right now no names spring to mind? No obvious, unexplained disappearances?

Mike sucked his breath in and said, 'Lots of people went missing. There was no money, people tried to find work. People scabbed and moved house. A lot of the older blokes died. Well before their time. Just gave up.'

The other two looked at each other.

'There were loads,' said Brian. 'A lot of people went south to look for work. There's people I haven't seen for years. I'll have to think.'

'It's most likely someone who was heavily involved in the strike,' said David. 'There'd be no reason for him to have gone after a bit player.'

'There were those brothers who went to Australia,' said Guy. 'The Nesbitts. They'd been committed on the picket line. Said their cousin had got them jobs in Broken Hill paying a fortune, Said they were going to be out there three years, make a fortune then come home and buy a pub. But they never came back. Maybe they never went?'

Guy frowned a moment and asked, 'What about that fat bastard... what's his name? The one who ran off with all the money?'

'Oh God...' Mike looked at the ceiling for a moment. 'Chris... Chris Meadows. No that was ages before. The seventies sometime. And there was nothing unexplained about that. He fucked off with all the money.'

Brian leaned forward into the conversation. 'We should check the obituaries in The Miner. If it was anyone politically active, they might get a mention.'

'Yeah. Who'd have the back copies?' Mike asked.

'We can track them down easily enough,' said Brian. 'I'll get onto it.'

'OK,' said David. 'This is what I suggest. I go back to London. Sign off with the department and all that, I assume

187

they'll want some sort of report but that's by the by. Meanwhile you ask around. Nottinghamshire is the obvious place. I don't suppose you're on speaking terms with anyone who kept working?'

There was a general shaking of heads.

'Pity, because those would be the people you'd really want to talk to. Was there someone, someone on your side, trying to keep tabs on Silver Birch and his people?'

'Dutch Elm? What was his name...?' Mike looked at the others for help.

'Chris Butcher,' said Brian.

'That's it. Chris Butcher. Yes, there are people in Nottingham we can ask. And it wasn't all civil war. And time's healed some wounds. Maybe someone we know down there still talks to someone on the other side.'

'I doubt it,' said Brian. 'You remember going picketing down there. After a couple of weeks it was bloody.'

'We can see,' said Mike. 'How do we stay in touch?'

'Mobiles,' said David as he reached down into his bag. 'This one's for you,' he said handing one across to Mike, 'and this one's for me. Don't use it for anything else. Don't switch it on in the house. Charge it without the SIM card in. When you need to contact me get a couple of miles away from your house first. I'll check the phone for messages a couple of times a day. If you come up with something send me a text to say when you will call. Let me write this all down.' Mike found him a piece of paper and he started putting down the details. 'Never say "Frampton". GCHQ will pick that up in an instant, if they've been asked. We'll use... pick a really popular name.'

'Mohammed,' suggested Guy.

'Ideal'. And they worked through terms for information, dates, times and so on. After ten minutes they had a vocabulary worked out which would provide no clue to anyone about the true sense of any text message.

'If we get to speak it will get harder.' As he copied out the list of agreed codewords David ran through his mind the problems which could arise. 'If you get to the point where you want to talk to me then unless it's urgent for some reason, the best plan is to meet face to face. Let's agree somewhere now, then all we need is a code word for meet and a coded time. And here's my number for another mobile if you need to contact me urgently. I'll keep it on all the time, but only use it in emergencies. Its pay as you go so it's not linked to me now but if you ever do use it it would be too easy to trace it back to me. Is this all clear?'

'What if we want to meet you in Nottingham?' Brian asked. 'No point in you coming all the way up here if we are just going to take you back south to meet someone down there.' So they agreed a rendezvous in Nottinghamshire too.

'Now who's had least contact with the police?'

'Me I suppose,' said Guy, looking round for confirmation. The others nodded their consent.

'Right, give me your address. I'll post you some good quality pictures of what he looked like then. Don't flash them about. I don't want them pinned up on notice boards with a note saying "If you remember seeing this man round and about during the strike call this number" OK?' Even Brian managed a smile. 'Just ask if anyone remembers seeing him or hearing his name being mentioned, or if they picked up anything, any rumours, no matter how ridiculous, particularly about protection for working miners, because we're trying to put our finger on something really out of the ordinary. Best thing is show them a number of photographs, not just Frampton, other people too. And another thing. Keep an eye out for anyone who seems to be taking an interest in you. Anyone following you. People hanging around outside the houses of anyone you go and see. And like I say, don't ever mention his name over the phone, do all that stuff face to face.' David looked round at the three of them to make sure they were taking this in. 'If I'm right about my friend's death then there's a pretty serious team looking after Lord Frampton and you need to be careful.'

Mike straightened up against the wall. 'And what do we tell people about why we're asking?''

'Yeah. You need to have a cover story don't you. Could you be doing some research?'

Brian chipped in. 'But we're also going to tell them not to talk about this aren't we. How does that fit?'

'We'll work something out,' said Mike. 'The people we know know how to keep their mouths shut.'

'Good.' David wished he could go round with them, ask the questions, watch their backs, but that was out of the question. He would just have to trust them, hope they didn't screw it up.

'I've brought some cash, to cover petrol and so on. If I give you £250 that should cover petrol and a couple of nights in a B & B if necessary.'

'So are we working for you now?' Brian asked.

'You're putting the hours in, I'm just sitting at home waiting. As you like.'

'We can take our petrol money out of it,' said Mike, 'but nothing more. Let's keep it simple. Anything else?'

'One other thing. There's an outside chance I'll want to meet you. If I text... I don't know... "See you Sunday" we

190

need a rendezvous for the next day. A car park somewhere where there's no CCTV so somewhere out of town. Somewhere walkers go. That sort of place. 8.00 a.m. and 4 p.m. say. You got a map?'

Mike produced a 1:25,000 scale OS map from amongst the guide books on the shelves behind him. It was double sided and unwieldy but eventually they got it spread out, the right way up, on the sitting room floor.

'Somewhere not too popular,' David said. He scanned the map for parking spots amongst the hills. 'This looks fine.' He pointed to a blue "P" on a ridge a few miles south west of Sheffield.

'Looks good. Can I use your toilet before I go.'

'It's the door on the right at the far end of the hall.'

The toilet was bare. David didn't know what he had been expecting. A framed picture of Arthur Scargill? But the room was as impersonal as the toilet in a hotel room, just the scent of cleaning products and a chill breeze blowing in from the half open, frosted window. It was a long drive home and he would be getting back far later than he had anticipated when he set out that morning. The best laid plans…'

Back in the front room he asked about the easiest way of getting to the M1. No one who heard the banal, level headed discussion which followed would have guessed for a moment the tensions which existed in the room.

'I'll wait to hear from you,' David said, with a confidence he did not feel.

Brian and Guy nodded. Nothing more. Mike showed him to the front door. David wanted to say something, he didn't know what, something that acknowledged or claimed some sort of relationship beyond a reluctant alliance born of necessity, but no words came. As he waited a moment for inspiration he thought perhaps Mike was going to laugh at the absurdity of where they found themselves but all he got was a curt, 'be in touch,' before the door was closed, not quite in his face.

The light was fading now. He looked up and down the street but saw nothing to trouble him. In the circumstances he could see no point in taking a different route back to where he had parked. He found the car as he had left it, with no sign of anything having been moved. He settled down into the driver's seat, pulled the door closed and focussed on the directions he had been given. In the event, as soon as he got himself onto a main road the motorway was signed and he could stop trying to recall Brian's precise list of turns and landmarks, which was something of a relief. He did not want that man's voice echoing around his mind any longer than necessary. The traffic was light and within thirty minutes he was pulling off a roundabout and down a slip road marked "South". What a day.

For the first ten or maybe twenty miles David concentrated on nothing more than driving, watching the speedometer, judging the distances of the surrounding vehicles and keeping half an eye out for a tail. He varied his speed to see if anyone tried to stay with him but, as he expected, he saw nothing to arouse suspicion. He turned the radio on but found he did not want the distraction and turned it off again after a few moments. It wasn't until some way past Nottingham that he really began to think about what he had done.

Plainly he was in breach of everything that mattered in his contract. He had bent the rules before, both with and without the approval of his superiors, but always with a view to achieving something in line with the organisation's aims.

192

This, however, was unexplored territory and it felt... he felt exposed. Not the least of his problems was that he was working with amateurs. One lapse of phone discipline, one incautious conversation and he would find himself in the frame.

Seemingly out of nowhere a car cut in in front of him. He braked and checked behind him but there was no one close. Had his mind been wandering? His speed was fine. Just an idiot trying to get past one more car before their exit. But his train of thought was disrupted now. He noticed more cars had their headlights on and he switched his on too. All the dashboard controls lit up and the vehicle felt more like a cocoon, a vessel more isolated from its surroundings.

Despite the risks he was running it had been, he told himself, a successful operation; sources recruited in testing circumstances. He wanted to congratulate himself on a job well done. But other thoughts intruded. There had been a time when he and Mike had been close. He had genuinely liked the man and he knew Mike had liked him. It didn't surprise him that it was Mike who had persuaded the others to go along with his plan. In the seventies he and David had both thrived on a bit of risk, both felt enormous frustration with the more procedural minded members of their group. It wasn't just the fictitious punching of a policeman that had started to trouble his handler. He had started to live the role a little. But that was then. Was there any way back when you've lied on oath to get someone two years behind bars? He realised he had half hoped that Mike would have been impressed by the sheer front of his knocking on Mike's door and laying everything out so openly. But it hadn't worked out that way.

The traffic seemed to be getting denser. And the tail lights of the vehicles ahead glowed brighter as the evening darkness thickened. He tried the radio again and this time he was soothed by what he heard. Nothing he could place. Beethoven maybe, but whatever it was it had a timelessness to his ears that he found reassuring.

CHAPTER ELEVEN

On the train into work the next morning David thought hard about how to play his meeting with Nigel. Unless Nigel was lying to him, and that seemed unlikely, he wasn't being taken off the case so that it could be passed on to someone who could be trusted to take a more tactful approach. And if it wasn't his lack of tact it must be the fact that he brought up the cash withdrawal. But that seemed to make no sense at all either. If Lord Frampton was still operationally active in some way, which seemed unlikely in itself, he would hardly have been funding operational work by taking cash out of his own bank account. And if he wasn't operational then why would senior management be interfering in this way. And was there any way he could use his final day in the office, if that was what it was, to pursue what had now effectively become his own, independent investigation? By the time his train passed through Watford Junction he concluded that he had hit a brick wall and so, to the annoyance of the passenger immediately to his left, who was huddled over the computer on his lap and typing with an intensity that suggested whatever he was working on needed to be completed before he arrived at his office, David stood up and fetched his book down from the pocket of his coat in the luggage rack and instead immersed himself in the homicidal efficiency of Francis Walsingham. He reached the office a bit after 9.00 to find that Nigel was in a budget meeting for the next hour or so.

'He should be back around 10.30,' Ginny said brightly. 'But I'd give him time to make himself a coffee before you speak to him. He's not always in the best of moods after these meetings.'

David thanked her for the advice. He wanted to ask her how she was getting on with finding a home for her mother but his time was short so instead he headed down to the library to use his temporary login. Who knew what he might be able to glean in his final hour and a half of access.

But when he switched on the terminal and typed in his login details the machine responded with a simple 'Access denied. Invalid Login.' He tried two more times with the same result. Wearily he dialled the IT help desk. He no longer even needed to look up the number.

This early the help desk was apparently under-employed and someone answered almost immediately. David explained his problem. He heard the patter of fingers on an unseen keyboard, followed by silence as his unseen interlocutor assimilated whatever had now appeared on his screen.

'Your access has been revoked Mr Nixon. You need to speak to your line manager.'

'Can you tell me when it was revoked?' David asked.

No further typing, just a simple, 'You'll need to speak to your line manager sir.'

There was no sense in pressing the point.

'Thank you very much.'

'Er… We are conducting a customer care survey Mr Nixon. Would you be happy to take part?''

'Is this an on-line survey?'

Back upstairs there was still no sign of his elusive room-mates. To fill the time David went to make himself a cup of tea and there he bumped into Manjit.

'Morning Manjit. Are you winning?'

'It's hard to tell.'

'Looks like this is going to be my last day. Have you heard?'

Manjit looked a little sheepish. 'Nigel did say something.'

'Am I in deep water?'

'Not exactly. I don't think.'

'That's hardly reassuring.'

'I'm sorry David.' Manjit paused, obviously wondering how much more he could say.

'Is it so bad we can't have that beer.'

Manjit smiled. 'No. No. It's not that bad.'

'Thank God for that.'

'No. It's just a bit embarrassing. But Nigel had better explain.'

'If it's my last day shall we do the beer this evening?'

'Don't see why not. No, that'd be good.'

'Great.' And somewhat awkwardly David took his leave, not entirely certain this trip to the pub would ever take place. Then, for want of anything better to do he settled down in his office and carried on reading his book. An hour later Ginny knocked on the door.

'Nigel's back.'

'Has he had a cup of coffee.'

'He has.' She took in the fact that David was doing nothing that looked like work. 'Is everything all right?'

'Looks like this is my last day Ginny.'

'Has something gone wrong?'

'That's what I'm about to find out.'

'Oh dear. I do hope not.'

'What's the worst that can happen.'

'I suppose.'

He followed her down the corridor and knocked on Nigel's door.

'Come.'

As he opened the door David looked back to see Ginny giving him a smile that said "Good luck".

'What's happened?' he asked Nigel.

'Sit down David. I'm afraid it seems we've sent you on a bit of a fool's errand.'

'How so?'

'Your friend from the CIA.'

'Yes?'

'Turns out he's not actually from the CIA.'

'What? So who is he?' David managed to hide it but he felt a wave of near panic sweeping over him. How on earth had he allowed himself to be taken in? And more importantly, by who?

'He's a CIA contractor.' Just as quickly David felt an enormous sense of relief. His failure, if any, had at least been less than total.

'Yes,' Nigel, continued. 'It seems most of the people at Langley these days are contractors. And half of those are ex-CIA who left the agency to set up consultancies doing exactly what they were doing before but for twice the money. 9/11 has been an absolute bonanza for the U.S. intelligence community.'

'OK. But why does that mean I'm off the job? They're presumably still doing work for the CIA.'

'Not in this case David. Or at least, we strongly suspect that's not what's going on. Yes, they are contracted to the CIA and that's why the approach came through the proper channels and we took their request at face value. But the company itself, Williamsburgh Associates is owned by The Sonderberg Group, who also own...'

'Jesus,' David interrupted. 'Prosecure.'

'Got it. So what we are trying to establish is whether Williamsburgh Associates are taking an interest in Lord Frampton because the CIA have an interest in his activities, or whether they are merely trying to make mischief on behalf of Prosecure because Frampton's company beat them to the security contract at Rumelia. And as you've probably guessed, the reason why we were so keen that you stopped your investigations immediately was that the less you have uncovered the easier it is for us to say to the Americans that so far we have uncovered no evidence of wrongdoing. Not that you'd have thought an inquiry into who's bribing who to get contracts in Iraq is something the American government would want an investigation into either.'

'How did this come to light,' David asked.

Nigel laughed a little uncomfortably. 'Your friend Manjit I'm afraid. I fear he is understandably a little bored with pouring through all those bank records. You'd left that man's business card on the desk and he did some googling. Said it took him five minutes, but whether that's true or whether he just didn't want to admit how much time he's spent off the job so to speak...'

'That would explain why he looked a bit embarrassed this morning. Do you want me to write up a report on where I have got to so far? It's probably easiest for me to make sense of my notes.'

'That won't be necessary,' said Nigel a little brusquely. 'Besides you don't have access to our computer system any more. We'll be in touch if we need anything. I'll make sure you get paid for a full day for today.'

Nigel seemed to think that was the end of the matter but David was keen to see if he could glean something more.

'Sorry about all the grief you got on my account from Lord Frampton.'

Nigel took the bait. 'What exactly did you do to upset him so badly?'

It did not cross David's mind to give an honest answer. 'With hindsight I'd say I treated it as more of an interrogation than a ... cosy fireside chat. Old habits I'm afraid.'

'It'll blow over. But I'm surprised by how much clout he turned out to have.'

This was more interesting. 'He is a former MP.'

'I mean how much clout he has in our world. But, as I say, it'll blow over. You haven't entirely ruined my career I don't suppose.'

'I'm glad about that,' David laughed

'Were you never ambitious David?'

'Given where I started from I haven't done too badly.'

But Nigel plainly had no appetite for a discussion of class and opportunity and there the conversation ended.

When David shut the door behind him Manjit was eyeing him nervously.

'You owe me a beer.'

'I'm sorry David.'

'No. Good work. I've taught you too well. Listen, I've got some errands to run. You've got my mobile, give me a ring when you know what time you'll be finished. Now Ginny.

200

Can I take you for an early lunch? Celebrate my new-found freedom.'

Manjit covered his eyes in mock shame.

Same pub. Ten days later. A world of difference. David would make his pitch but he would make it in the most general terms. He wanted to give Manjit as little hard information as possible to protect both of them.

Manjit bought the first round.

'Nigel thought you might just have been bored,' said David.

'I was just curious. Well, curious and bored. It's not the most exciting work. As you know. And some of the people you have to deal with too. Obviously when people hear my name they can tell I'm British Asian but I don't have an Asian accent and over the phone they can't see me and sometimes they forget. Some of the crap I have to listen to. And sometimes they remember half way through and they say things like "obviously I don't mean people like you."' He shook his head in frustration. 'The other day I was on the phone to a policeman in Merseyside. By the time I got off the phone I was thinking of joining ISIS. And I'm a Sikh.'

'You may not believe it but things have got better over the years. Looking back on it now, the things I used to hear when I joined. The things I used to say probably. Any news of a move yet?'

Manjit had been placed in David's team rather abruptly when the end of operation CREVICE meant that large numbers of people had to be re-deployed at the same time. He had been told it was only a temporary measure but three years on he was still there.

'Nigel keeps telling me he's keeping his ear to the ground. He says he wants to find me a decent posting. And I think he means it. But he's got a hundred and one other things on his plate. And if I don't get something more high-profile I'm worried that I'll get side-lined. Pigeonholed as the quiet backroom sort. I didn't join MI5 to be an accountant. I want a bit of drama. By the time CREVICE was over I thought I'd rather die than set foot in Luton ever again but now I'd go anywhere for some action. Even Luton.'

'Didn't they offer you a move to one of the regional offices?'

'Yes. Newcastle. When I said anywhere...'

'You'll be OK. But don't be embarrassed about pushing him. He's got a responsibility for you. Not that I'm necessarily the best person to look to for careers advice.'

'What happened? Nigel looked really panicked when the calls started coming in?'

'Panicked?'

'Maybe not panicked. Spooked? He implied that you'd gone in there like a bull in a china shop, but ... I don't know.'

'Manjit, the other day you said you still have your principles.'

Manjit took a deep breath. 'Why do I suddenly have a bad feeling about this?'

'Because you're a smart lad.'

'Oh dear.'

'Hear me out.' It was a fact of the business that you needed to get people to like you if you wanted to use them and in reality that often meant you ended up liking them too. And that could sometimes make it harder to put pressure on them. But recruiting someone you already liked was a new one on David and it felt just a little dirty.

'Your instincts are right. It wasn't my lack of tact that caused the problem with Lord Frampton. It was something else.'

'Do I get to hear what?'

'No. Best not. Let's just say, and you'd work this out for yourself if I don't tell you, let's just say that, in the course of the interview, I brought something up that spooked Lord Frampton. And I don't know what the significance of "this thing" might be. But it looks a lot like my bringing up 'this thing' caused Lord Frampton to bring pressure to bear on Nigel through contacts he had with high-ups in the intelligence world there's no obvious reason to expect him to have. Are you following me?'

'I wish I wasn't.'

'I haven't got to the good bit yet.'

'I'm sort of hoping you don't.'

'Manjit something happened during the miners' strike that some well-placed people are desperate to cover up.'

'A conservative government shut down a perfectly viable coal industry in order to score an ideological victory over organised labour?'

'You don't believe that bollocks do you?'

'You look at the numbers David. Half of what they claimed were operating costs were one off redundancy payments and stuff. There was over-capacity but nothing worth making that much fuss about.'

'And since when did you become an expert on the economics of the coal industry in the 1980s?'

'Since I went to University David? And studied politics and economics? But... you were saying...' Manjit's laughter was just on the right side of kindness not to rattle David and he wasn't entirely sure if Manjit was being serious or just winding him up. More beer would make this easier.

'I think I need another pint. Kronenbourg?'

'Thanks David. I could use another one too. And can you get some crisps? Salt and vinegar if they've got them.'

With two more full pints in front of them the discussion continued.

'What you've no doubt worked out by now Manjit, is that I'm not letting this go.'

'Go on.' There was a coldness in Manjit's expression David could not recall ever seeing before.

'In that bag,' said David, indicating the carrier bag on the seat beside him, 'is a pay as you go mobile phone with fifty pounds in credit on it and one number in the contacts list. What I would like you to do is keep your ear to the ground and send any information that sounds relevant to the number in the contacts list. I would also like you to check the phone at intervals to see if you have heard from me. Now, speaking as your careers adviser, my advice to you is that you take this phone away with you and throw it in the river on your way to the station. However, you said you wanted some more drama in your life.'

'I think I said I wanted some more drama in my job.' Manjit's voice lacked any emotion.

'There's more purpose in what I'm asking you to do than in what the office is asking you to do right now.'

He watched Manjit's face, half hoping he would refuse. Instead Manjit stared ahead without speaking. He took a few crisps from the packet, ate them deliberately, then took a long draught of lager.

'I'm thinking aloud here,' he said eventually, still without making eye contact. 'And I'm wondering why you would want to go to these lengths to investigate something that took place so long ago. I'm assuming you wouldn't try to involve me if you didn't think it was serious. And I'm assuming you wouldn't want to put me in jeopardy just for some piece of personal score settling. Because my impression is you don't like this Lord Frampton.' He picked up the now half empty crisp packet and extracted another few crisps.

'No,' said David. 'I wouldn't do that.'

Manjit still didn't speak.

'I've thought hard about how much to tell you Manjit. There is more, obviously. But, for both our sakes, I'll leave it at that. But there is one more thing I should tell you. This is not risk free. And I don't mean you might lose your job.' He didn't need to spell it out any more clearly than that.

Manjit finally made eye contact. 'It's that serious is it?'

'It is.'

'You know, there was something I didn't like about Nigel's reaction to the phone calls he was getting, or the way these people made Nigel feel.'

'Even Mr Ambitious could sense there was something wrong?'

'He's not that bad David. But yes. Hmm. And if even Nigel has a bad feeling about what's going on I'll keep my ear to the ground. But I'm making no promises.'

'Thanks Manjit. That's all I'm asking.'

Manjit took the phone from David's carrier bag and transferred it to his little rucksack. 'So how's the bird watching going?' he asked.

But they didn't linger over their second pint. There was an unaccustomed awkwardness between them now. And when they parted outside the pub David felt an emptiness. He knew

205

there were trains to Sutton from Victoria. He decided to go and see Rachel.

It was rush hour and he had to stand the whole way, squeezed between a stocky, dark haired man he guessed was from Latin America and a girl with dyed blonde hair and a personal stereo turned up to maximum volume. He tried to work out what he was going to say but nothing came.

As he approached the entrance to the hospital David passed two elderly, hollow-cheeked men in their pyjamas sitting in wheelchairs, each attached to a drip hooked over a wheeled stand, smoking and passing the occasional throaty comment.

'My daughter-in-law... says she wants to take the kids to Disneyland next year. Asked me if I could lend her £500.'

'That's a lot of money... to see an out of work actor dressed up as a mouse.'

'Yeah... Fireworks are supposed to be good though.'

David walked by wondering how much longer they were of this world. Ahead of him a young woman in a pink tracksuit struggled to negotiate the hospital's revolving doors on her crutches. He gave her an arm to steady her and together they squeezed through into the brightly lit reception. There a bored looking West African woman at the information desk gave him directions to Rachel's ward and he headed down a long corridor which stretched away past a crowded Costa Coffee, increasingly uncertain whether this visit was a good idea.

Half way down the corridor a queue had formed outside the pharmacy and he had to squeeze past more people in wheelchairs. The mood was livelier and less depressing than he had anticipated. At the end of the corridor was a lift but the display indicated that it had now reached the fourth floor and was heading on up so he took the stairs. He found Rachel's ward down another corridor on the third floor. On the left-hand side of the ward a row of windows looked out over the back of a line of terraced houses and beyond them, more roofs and a couple of church spires standing proud of their surroundings. The ward itself was divided into individual rooms lining the right-hand side and, rather than peer into each one, he asked a nurse where to find Rachel. She pointed, without speaking, to a door just a little further down the corridor. He took a long, slow breath and walked through.

It was a shock, more so than he had expected, to see her, after so many years, looking tired, exhausted even, and with hair that had lost any hint of sheen. To think that once, the two them, half a lifetime ago, had meant so, so much to each other.

She looked round as she heard him enter.

After a moment staring at him intently she said, 'Ever since Tim said he'd told you, I was wondering if you'd come and rather hoping you wouldn't. But now you're here. I'm glad you came, I think.' She spoke slowly and her voice was a little deeper now but instantly recognisable.

'I'm sorry it's come to this Rachel,' said David looking helplessly round the room. He was equally uncertain whether his visit was a good idea. 'I understand it's … a matter of weeks.'

'Certainly concentrates the mind. But I don't know why I'm glad you came.' Her gaze shifted down to her lap. 'It still hurts, and I don't like you for it. That place changed you David. For the worse.' She looked him straight in the eyes. 'You were a different man when you came back from Ireland. Look I don't believe in kissing and making up for the sake of it. You hurt me too badly for that. But I'm glad you came.'

He was seized by an entirely unexpected drive to kiss her, but he didn't and the moment passed. Then, awkwardly, he stepped forward and took her hand. She didn't resist and he squeezed it very gently.

'So am I.' Was he? He didn't know. He sat down in the chair beside her, still holding her hand. Without thinking he continued.

'Do you remember when we drove down to Cornwall,' he heard himself say. 'That summer. It was your idea we left at 5.00. The roads were empty. It was beautiful...' He looked across at her. She was looking back at him but her expression was impossible to read.

'We turned off the ....' But then he found he couldn't go on. And the tears streamed down his face. His hand was still in hers. He waited for some reaction but her fingers remained limp and his tears continued to flow. He didn't dare speak. In the silence he found he could remember almost nothing of that holiday. Just the picnic on the way down, on a grassy hillside somewhere off the main road, ... in the sunshine ... with the constant buzzing of insects ... and happiness. Rachel remained silent. Eventually he stood up and as her hand slipped out of his he felt the gentlest squeeze before her fingers fell, unresisting, from his grasp.

When he reached the door he turned to say good bye but she was facing away from him now, staring out of the window, no longer showing any interest in his presence. He waited and after a moment she looked back towards him.

'Good bye David.'

How long had that taken. Ten minutes? Fifteen? To wrap up the only real love of his life. And the greatest source of pain he had known. Or was that losing Jimmy Doyle? Him and Rachel. That was just broken hearts. Jimmy was a father of four, then, because of a promise David had made and couldn't keep, nothing more than a broken body dumped in a ditch. Had that scarred him more? Should it have done? Did it matter? He was half way down the stairs before a pair of nurses sharing their indignation at a last minute shift change passed him in the opposite direction and he became aware once more of his surroundings.

CHAPTER TWELVE

The first contact from Mike came much sooner than he expected, only four days after the meeting with Mike and his friends. The text read 'White 9 18'. The message was 'The Coach and Horses, 7.00 pm on the 16th.'

He guessed they'd been busy. Or just lucky. He left at 3.00, more than enough time but he didn't dare risk being late and missing them. He looked out for a tail but there was plainly no one following him and once he joined the motorway he relaxed.

Relaxed until he thought once again of Rachel, lying in that bed knowing she had only a couple of weeks to live and knowing that what she had done with her life up till then was all that she would ever amount to or be remembered for. And it weighed on his mind that he had wrecked, or perhaps his job had wrecked, the marriage that was, he imagined, her best hope of happiness. By contrast, her jobs in the planning departments of various London Boroughs had never seemed to provide her with much satisfaction. So far as he could judge she had been good at her work. But she had minded too much about the inefficiencies and the poor decisions and at the same time she had lacked the political skills necessary to rise far enough to change things for the better. She had fallen out with colleagues in Barnet and eventually moved to a similar job in Merton. 'Why does nobody have any balls anymore?' she had demanded one evening. Her willingness to speak unvarnished truth to power had been one of the qualities that attracted him to her. But the longer commute to Merton had taken its toll. And it hadn't taken long before her frustration at how her colleagues rolled over in the face of bullying by councillors led once more to rifts at work. He'd been in Northern Ireland by then, coming back only sporadically and with his own issues to deal with. If he had been around more... Who knew? And she had fallen out with her sister too, over the sale of their parents' house though the rift went deeper than that, and, when he had last been in close contact with her, her two nieces were still not speaking to her.

There was a silver Renault behind him which had appeared on and off in his rear-view mirror for he wasn't sure how long now. He slowly reduced his speed to nearer sixty and kept an eye out for any other car that seemed to stay with him. The Renault came up behind him but soon went past and eventually disappeared out of sight some way ahead. He switched on the radio to blank out any further maudlin thoughts.

He arrived in Nottingham with more than an hour to spare. He drove past the pub to make sure he knew where he was going then found a chip shop and parked up. The place was busy, which was encouraging, and the man ahead of him in the queue was plainly a regular.

'You all right Dan?' the woman behind the counter asked. She wore a white coat with the name of the shop printed on the breast pocket above an embroidered dolphin, which seemed inappropriate. There were splashes of fat down the front.

'Aye.'

'Sheila?' And the bright lights reflected on her lipstick as she mouthed the word.

'She's doing fine.'

Someone behind him chipped in. 'Your turn to do the cooking eh Dan?'

Dan turned round. 'At least I don't send my kids out in the rain when it's my turn.'

For whatever reason this provoked laughter from all three of them and David felt suddenly isolated by their warmth. Dan paid up and stepped aside to wait for his order to finish cooking.

'What'll you have pet?' the woman asked David

'Just a small chips thanks.'

'We've got a really nice bit of cod? Fresh today.'

'Chips'll be fine thanks.'

She scooped up a helping, laid it out on the paper and deftly wrapped it into a cone.

She took his one pound fifty. 'Salt and vinegar's up at the end of the counter.' And she was onto the next customer.

He ate the chips sitting in his car. It would smell of vinegar for days now. He wondered for a moment whether he should make another visit to Rachel. But no. That ship had sailed. And of course the vinegar had barely penetrated beyond the first two or three layers of chips so below that it was just potato, but he persevered. If he was going to allow himself two pints he needed to line his stomach.

He drove back to the pub and checked the time. He was still twenty minutes early. No matter. The pub itself was a good choice, almost cavernous with numbers of interior walls cut through with archways as if they were in a cellar. He guessed the place catered for the Sunday lunch crowd but early on a weekday evening it was dead. It took him a good minute to check the various, discrete sitting areas and establish he was the first to arrive. He got himself a pint and waited.

Five minutes later Mike and Guy arrived with a third man he did not recognise. On their way to the bar they passed out of his line of sight without spotting him but a couple of minutes later Guy poked his head round the corner.

'He's over here,' he called back then, without waiting for the other two, came over to David's table.

'Were you followed?' David asked.

'Don't think so,' said Guy.

'Did you check?'

'No. Not really. We just…'

'Next time. Every time. You slow down. You pull over. You take a circuitous route.'

'OK. OK.'

'And who is this person? How did you find them?'

Guy looked over his shoulder but the other still hadn't appeared. 'We've got a contact down here. Barry Jones. He was an NUM activist. Stayed out the whole strike. Nearly cost him his house. We got him to ask around. Tell people there was a journalist wanting to do a piece about how the police suppressed the strike in Nottingham. And anyone who said they had a story to tell he went and asked them questions and… along the way you know… showed him a picture of your man. Along with… other things. And Malcolm said he'd seen him, said…'

'Let him tell me the story. But what can you tell me about Malcolm?' At this moment Mike and Malcolm appeared in the archway behind Guy. David held up his hand, asking them to wait a moment.

'Don't know him, said Guy. 'Barry says he's OK. Came out at the beginning but like a lot of people, once he realised the strike was never going to take hold down here, he went back. There's no reason not to trust him. He did better than most of them down here but when you hear what he's got to say…'

'Yeah. Great.' David beckoned Mike over and the pair joined them at the table.

'David. This is Malcolm,' said Mike.

David was struck most of all by the belly, a pendulous excrescence over which was stretched a beige zip-up cardigan. Somehow a belt encircled the lower regions of this bulge and held in place a pair of neatly ironed brown trousers. But, if his cheeks were a little plump, Malcolm's gaze was firm and he shook David's hand in a no-nonsense manner.

'I've seen this bastard you're looking for,' he said, sitting himself down opposite David. There was a fussiness about the way he sat down, something that suggested he was looking forward to being the star of the show. Mike and Guy took their seats alongside him.

'That's what you're interested in isn't it?'

'That's right,' said David encouragingly.

'Yes. I saw him in our village one night, he was out with one of the patrols. They were sending patrols out into all the mining villages to try and intimidate the strikers and all. And there were some pickets down from Yorkshire staying in a house over the road from me. A young lad, Ray Ledburn, his parents had died but he still had the house so he'd plenty of room and the police had got wind that four or five pickets were staying at his house.'

'How did they find out?' David asked.

Malcolm paused for effect. Looked round at his audience and continued. 'More than half the men were still working. And they didn't like having to walk past those pickets every morning. Anyone could have found out. Anyone could have passed the word on. The village was split down the middle. At the social club there was a line... strikers on one side, working miners on the other. And fights in the car park. Even today... Anyhow, two van loads of coppers turned up late one evening. First I knew of it was the sound of them banging on his front door, yelling at him to open up. I didn't see it but Ray told me that as soon as he opened the door they just barged straight in. When I got out there they were dragging the pickets out. And they were handling them really roughly. One of them tried to make some sort of... I don't know... some sort of a stand and they beat him to the ground. Then they just threw him into the back of the van. Literally threw him. It was disgusting. And it was all, 'Fucking commies' and "You're going to fuck off back to Yorkshire and don't even think of coming back" and I remember, clear as day, thinking "What country am I living in?" After they'd gone I went into the house with Ray, and they'd trashed it. Doors smashed, things just thrown onto the living room floor, like lamps and stuff. The poor lad was in shock. He'd been born in that house. His mum and dad had just died, both of them in the last year and now this. He just sat down on the sofa and cried his eyes out. He moved away after the strike. I don't know what happened to him.'

'And how was Lord Frampton involved in all this?'

'What's a bastard like him doing getting made a Lord?' Malcolm raised his glass to his mouth and when he placed it back on the table David noticed the level of beer had dropped at least three inches. 'He was there. I don't know how he got there. Don't remember whether he went back with the police or what. But when I came out of my house, which was directly over the road, he was standing, with another couple of men, fit looking bastards, they didn't look like police, just watching, but watching like they liked what was happening. And he saw me looking at them and he called over to the police sergeant who was in charge and the sergeant shouted at me to get back in the house.'

'And what did you do?'

'Just stood there. I wasn't moving for those bastards. Well not unless they'd threatened to do me like they did those pickets. I'd've moved then.'

'Did you see him issue any instructions? Did you get the impression he was actually in charge?'

'Not exactly. I don't remember him saying anything else. And I was more worried... more thinking about Ray, because I didn't know if he was still inside you see or if they'd already grabbed him and put him in one of the vans. He was a really good-hearted soul.'

'And these men who were with him? Did you notice anything more about them. How they reacted to him? Or to what was going on?'

'Not really.' Malcolm looked a little put out that he had done his best and David still didn't seem to be satisfied. 'It was dark so there was just the light of the street lamps. I remember... like... wondering who they were. Because they weren't police. And I thought, if they're not police, you know, who are they? What are they doing here?'

'Well, that's really helpful Malcolm. Thank you. That really helps fill in the picture.' Malcolm's beer was as good as finished. 'Would you like another pint?' David asked. The man deserved that much at least.

'I wouldn't say no.'

'Mike, Guy?' They were both fine. Neither of them had drunk even half of theirs. David was only just ahead of them but he got himself another one anyway. When he got back to the table the conversation had turned to football, a subject in which he had no interest at all and nothing to contribute. And with its talk of unjustified penalties and outrageous wage packets it sounded to him exactly like every other football conversation he had ever listened to. Except that it soon became clear it wasn't so much a conversation as a monologue on the part of Malcolm, to which Guy, and to a lesser extent Mike, were paying just enough attention not to appear rude.

When Malcolm got to the end of his second pint he offered to get a round but Guy explained that they all had a long way to go.

'David, you'll stay for another won't you?' Malcolm asked.

'I've got even further to go.'

'Do you want to give me your number? In case I think of anything else?'

'If you think of anything else let Barry know. But this has been really helpful. But please, for the time being keep it to yourself that I've been asking about this. If he gets wind of the fact that I'm interested that might make it harder to get information.'

'Mum's the word.'

'Brilliant.'

Then, as they left the table Malcolm asked, 'Who are you writing this for?'

'I'm freelance,' said David. 'I've got a couple of publications in mind but I haven't approached anyone yet so if you could keep this to yourself for now...'

In the car park Mike dropped back to allow Guy and Malcolm to get ahead a little. 'Was that any use?' he asked.

'It confirms the sort of thing he was doing. But apart from that…'

'We need to keep digging?'

'Yeah.'

The invitation had been unexpected. Over the years their paths had crossed from time to time and he had twice invited Peter to dinner. On both occasions Peter had declined. The excuses had been plausible and delivered with regret but Frampton had got the message. So any other time the suggestion of a drink at Peter's club would have delighted him but coming so soon after their previous conversation it left him feeling just a little wary.

When he announced himself to the doorman he was admitted with a deference just the right side of obsequiousness and directed towards the Connaught Room. He had never joined a club himself. However appealing, the annual fees had always been a stretch too far. But all that had changed now. The Rumelia deal had lifted him into a different league. The club's website had merely said that membership fees would be disclosed on application but Frampton didn't doubt he could pay them several times over now. Maybe it was time. As his heels smacked on the polished tiles of the hallway he wondered if perhaps he might ask Peter to put him forward.

The room to which he had been directed further whetted his appetite. Leather sofas and armchairs. Portraits of worthies, past members he assumed, on the walls, a gentle murmur of conversation and, discrete but alert, a waiter, if that was what they called them here, keeping an eye on the needs of all those present.

Peter was seated half way across the room on the right-hand side, occupying one of three armchairs arranged around a small circular table. He spotted Lord Frampton the moment he crossed the threshold and rose to greet him.

'Good evening Alex. Good of you to come, particularly at such short notice. What can I get you?' Frampton shook the

219

proffered hand and asked for a whiskey. The waiter appeared at their table unsummoned and within moments a tumbler of single malt was in his hand.

'Your investors are a happy bunch right now,'' Peter began. 'I'm told the Times might be running a piece on the company's achievements.'

That was true. Frampton had spent much of the afternoon briefing the PR company they worked with following an approach from a freelancer who had regularly placed pieces in the paper. But how did Peter know?

'It's nice to get some recognition for what we've done. UK plc needs to make a bit more noise about our successes.'

'Absolutely Alex. You and your colleagues have done sterling work. It hasn't gone unnoticed.'

The warmth of the whiskey burned its way across his tongue and down into his chest. Lord Frampton began to wonder whether he was here to discuss some business proposal. The nervousness he had felt about the meeting was starting to melt away.

'This is all really good news', Peter continued. 'But we may have run into a problem.'

'How so? I was told the investigation was closed.'

'It is Alex. It is.'

Go on, Frampton thought. Spit it out.

Silence. Save the background chat in the room.

Don't play that game with me, Frampton thought. If you've got something to say, say it.

'There are some people asking questions about you.' Peter's tone remained urbane but there was an edge to it now.

'Journalists?'

'No. Retired miners it seems. They're asking questions about what you got up to during the miners' strike.'

"I was working for David Hart. That's not a secret. And my name... has been in the papers recently..."

'Alex, your name has always been in the papers. Why now?'

'You tell me.' Frampton wasn't bothering to keep the irritation out of his voice now.

'David Nixon went North a few days ago. It's not entirely clear why, or where exactly he went. He took the battery out of his phone before he set off. He stopped off for lunch on the way back, called in to the office and he was told that the investigation was over. Half an hour later he took the battery out of his phone again and disappeared who knows where. A few days later people from that part of the world start digging into your past.'

'You know more than me Peter.'

'There is a channel of communication Alex.'

Frampton waited for something else but Peter said nothing.

'Perhaps his phone ran out of charge,' Frampton suggested eventually.

'No Alex. They can tell. It was over half full. He took the battery out.'

'And is there any link between him and the people asking for me.'

'Yes. There is.'

And Frampton remembered David's final question, about the £20,000, and suddenly the world felt a colder, less welcoming place. He waited for the next blow.

'Tell me about Eric Hanley.' said Peter.

221

CHAPTER THIRTEEN

In the days that followed David was unable to settle to anything. No operation in his career had left him as uneasy, as distracted as this. He had imagined that in retirement he would be devoting time to his garden. There was no doubt it needed attention. But the designs that he had formed in previous months now seemed half baked. He bought more books and visited garden centres for advice but he was unable to turn any of this vast amount of information into a satisfactory plan of action. He took the mobile for which Manjit had the number on every trip, along with the mobile for which Mike had the number, and the moments between turning them on and seeing every time that nothing had come in were the only moments he felt any sense of purpose. He withdrew cash in modest amounts on each trip but spent only on his card. He left a tell-tale on the back and front doors each time he went out and checked them every time he returned but never found them disturbed.

The evenings were the hardest. None of the DVDs he had acquired with such care seemed to draw him in. Not one of the several series on ancient history he had been so looking forward to had any spark. 'And who,' he thought to himself, 'finds David Attenborough annoying?' He switched from one to another in frustration, and he drank. Four or five whiskeys every night. And they were not pub measures.

One afternoon the phone went. As soon as he heard Tim's voice he knew.

'In the end she went peacefully. The palliative care there was superb. She felt no pain.'

'When's the funeral?'

'Next week.'

'When?'

'It's family only David.' There was silence. 'Close family.' Another long pause. 'I know she was very pleased you came to see her.'

'Did she say so.'

'Yes. It meant a lot to her.'

'Thanks for calling Tim'

'Are you all right David?'

'Yes thanks.' Silence. Tim started, 'We should get together...' He tailed off.

'Thanks for letting me know Tim.'

That night he drank two thirds of a bottle of whiskey. He didn't cry. He didn't get drunk. At dawn he stumbled into bed with even his shoes on.

The next day he forced himself to get a grip and just take a decision about where to place his vegetable patch. Once that was done the digging provided him with some relief. But he dug too vigorously for a man of his age and, despite a long hot bath, he retired to bed that night feeling like a wreck of a human being.

The next morning he woke up stiff but better rested than he had been for days. In the afternoon he dug again in moderation and in the evening he made a list of seeds to buy on his next trip to the garden centre; perpetual spinach, broad beans and some onions. He drank a single whiskey.

Two days later he straightened his back and admired two neat rows of onion sets with their tips poking out of the soil. The broad beans and perpetual spinach too were in, though there was nothing but the smooth raked surface to show for his work. The only fly in the ointment was the message he had received from Manjit that morning, sitting in the car park at the garden centre where he had bought the seeds and the onion sets. "Nigel asking if I had been in touch with you. I asked why. He said no reason. Not completely sure I believe him." He had immediately texted Mike to warn him that perhaps their activities had come to someone's attention, but there was nothing else he could do. Nothing except wait.

Another intended strand of his retirement life had been proper cooking. Up till now that plan too had gone by the wayside but tonight he made a start. And with surprising ease, in forty minutes he found he had knocked up his first ever vegetable stir fry. Admittedly the dish owed most of its flavour to a Thai green curry sauce that came straight out of a jar from M & S but there was no harm in that. The carrots could have done with a minute or two longer but essentially he had cooked a healthy, meat free and thoroughly tasty supper. He had two whiskeys to celebrate but he felt no need for a third and he went to bed, if not content, then at least less troubled by the lack of progress than he had been up till now.

The following morning he headed out in the car shortly after breakfast. He could not resist the desire to check his phone again. What did he really have to go on? Manjit's gut feeling that a quite possibly innocent inquiry from Nigel might indicate suspicion of his activities on the part of MI5. It was a slight pretext for the sense of engagement he was experiencing and he knew that. But after days without any news he was lifted by the possibility of action. So when a dark blue Astra seemed to dog his moves through the outskirts of Milton Keynes he put his concerns down to an exaggerated sensitivity.

He could only find a parking space at some distance from his favourite cafe, an unremarkable but friendly place run by a Portuguese family who knew him by sight if not by name. He was looking forward to a smile from the owner's dark-haired daughter but not, he found, as much as he was looking forward to checking his messages which was why he ended up queuing for his latte just round the corner from where he parked, in a bright, noisy establishment surrounded by earnest looking young men and women with Apple laptops. He didn't mind the breezy fake-friendliness of the barista, but the coffee came with some sort of a leaf design in the foam, which he could have done without, and cost him at least a pound more than he would have paid at his usual place. He found a space at a counter which ran the length of the window and turned on the phones. Nothing from Mike. Nothing from Manjit. He stared at the blank screens, willing something to appear. He had worked on slow cases, and cases which never led anywhere, but there was always something, however hopeless, that one could do, if only to provide the relief of activity. Here, now, he could only wait, and hope. And he contemplated the real possibility that nothing would ever happen. That his friends in the north would never turn anything up, and that this was what he had left to him in life. A bit of bird watching, a bit of gardening, a bit of cooking. And the occasional trip into Milton Keynes.

Heading out of town there was a beige hatchback, a Peugeot, which seemed to be keeping pace with him. To lose it would be easy. Anyone can pull away from the lights as they turn red, or drive round a block. To establish whether you are being tailed without giving away your suspicion is a bigger ask. It takes a bit of apparently innocent confusion over which lane to get in, subtle variations in speed. David tried them all and with each exercise he became more convinced this was a tail. And the driver might have been worried that he was starting to look too obvious because, as they were leaving town he turned off. To be replaced by the blue Astra. David was alive again.

When David turned off down the road he lived on the Astra carried on down the main road. Did they have his home under observation by another team? He checked the tell-tales on the front and back doors, but both seemed undisturbed.

But there was a message on the answer machine. David pressed play and Nigel's voice broke the stillness. 'David, I was wondering if you could come in tomorrow. Something's come up. Nothing major. Give me a call when you get this message. Speak soon.'

This phone call coming on the same day he first noticed a tail and so soon after Manjit's message seemed too much of a coincidence. He stood in the centre of his sitting room, thinking. Who was following him? Should he ring Nigel back? Should he go down to London tomorrow? Step one. Ring Nigel. Deny anything but see what he might add.

He dialled, and got Ginny.

'Shouldn't you be out with your telescope instead of bothering us?'

'Nigel left me a message. Asked me to call him back.' Any other time he would have been happy to chat.

'I'll put you through.'

'Ah David. Thank you for ringing back. Yes. It's not a big deal but there's a couple of points we'd like to clear up.'

'I thought the whole thing was buried now.'

'So did I, but Will Anderson's got a couple of questions about ... I'm honestly not sure what he's concerned about. But it's another day's money.'

'Fair enough. What sort of time?'

'He and I are both free all morning so ... say 11.00?'

'That's fine. How is it going with the Somali investigation?'

'Don't. I'll see you tomorrow.'

'11.00 o'clock.'

Where was he now? Nigel appeared to think little of the issue. Which made it hard to make sense of the cars. Maybe Will Anderson was more troubled than he had let Nigel know, and he had put the tail on him. Or it wasn't Will either, it was the people who had killed Eric. If they existed.

He went to the loo. And froze. The positions of the bottle of bleach and the bottle of general purpose cleaner, which both lived on the window sill, had been reversed. The sill itself seemed to have been wiped. He was sure he hadn't left it that clean. Someone must have left some sort of marking on it as they came or went and cleaned it off. And replaced the bottles in the wrong order.

Plan B.

He had a case packed and a route planned but he wasn't going to make a move just yet. Give them time to perhaps stand some people down. Make his second trip of the day look less surprising. In the meantime he made himself a thermos of coffee and enough sandwiches to cover supper and breakfast. He heated up the remains of the stir fry in the microwave and was impressed all over again.

His car was parked in the garage and he could load up his suitcase without being observed. They'd have no reason to expect that he was making a run for it so no reason to try stop him as he drove away. If they followed him he had to try to lose them without making it look deliberate but if he could only do it in an obvious manner then so be it.

So far so good. All this was meat and drink to David. What he didn't like was not knowing for sure who was tailing him. When he placed his suitcase in the car, along with the bag of all the cash he had been withdrawing and a spare can of petrol, he taped a kitchen knife to the underside of the dashboard. What he also didn't like was having no back up.

The beige Peugeot picked him up within five minutes of him leaving and seemed to be changing places with a pale Fiesta. David slowed a little to try and get a proper look. He only managed to pick out the first three letters of the registration plate but that, combined with the make and colour, was enough to make him confident he could identify the car if he saw it on his tail again. His plan was Milton Keynes in the rush hour. If he couldn't lose them there he deserved whatever he had coming.

And it proved easier than he had expected. Chance delivered him at a junction just as the lights were changing. He ran them leaving the Peugeot two cars behind and helpless. He turned off immediately after the junction and had the enormous satisfaction of passing the Fiesta heading down the same street in the opposite direction, presumably on its way to intercepting him. He pushed the car as much as he judged possible without attracting unwanted attention. If they were serious there would be a third car somewhere he hadn't spotted yet. With any luck they still thought he was making a second trip to town and would concentrate their search in the town centre. From where he was starting the quickest route out of town was up the A5. Traffic was slower than he would have liked but the number of cars would make it more or less impossible for his tails to find him. Unless they had a motorbike on the team as well. But twenty minutes of careful observation gave him no cause for concern. He was on his way.

And if there was no motorbike it probably wasn't MI5.

Once he had put some distance between himself and Milton Keynes he turned off the main road. At the first opportunity he pulled over and texted Mike to let him know he was on his way. 'Be extra careful. If it's your investigations that alerted them you may be in the frame. Batteries out of phones whenever you travel.' Then he sent a message to Manjit. 'Called in by Nigel. Will knows I'm up to something. Tailed and visited at home. Now tail free and going north. Keep me posted.'

He had worked out a tortuous route North avoiding main roads and towns which might be covered by CCTV. In a spiral bound note pad he had listed the succession of turnings, with likely sign postings, and the distances between each junction. He had plotted the route from his house, not Milton Keynes so it took him ten minutes to get onto his planned course but from then on it was, in theory, simply a matter of reading off the next turn on the list then resetting the mileage on the odometer to zero every time he turned. Slow but steady progress. Of course it wasn't as simple as that. The distances were approximate and the signage erratic. Once it got dark he switched on a clip-on LED light angled to illuminate his note pad. He crossed the turnings off one by one. He knew it would be slow. But he didn't mind. It was good to be taking action.

After four hours and several wrong turnings he was only half way. He pulled over for a break and a cup of coffee. He turned off the engine and killed the headlights. Then he poured a cup of coffee from the thermos and got out of the car. To the south west the low clouds glowed orange with the reflected glare of Birmingham's street lights. To the east it was Leicester that stained the night sky. He could hear the low, continuous rumble of traffic from distant main roads overlain with the sound of a single car making its way along the B road he had just crossed. He could see its headlights picking out in turn the individual silhouettes of a row of oak trees as it turned through a sweeping corner. He wondered idly who was in that car and where they were bound.

He soaked up the smell of the coffee as he raised the cup to his mouth; coffee in the darkness with an uncertain, possibly dangerous, future bearing down. He smiled to himself. Retirement was turning out to be more engaging than the last few, desk bound, years in the office. The rendezvous was 8.00 a.m. and he would be in plenty of time. It would be tedious if Mike had not yet picked up his message, but David guessed he would have done and would be there on time, as eager as David to grapple with this new set of circumstances. Mike, he was reasonably confident, would have checked his phone every day.

David drove for another two hours, working his way slowly through the pages of his notebook. Over time the roads emptied until he found himself driving for twenty, thirty minutes at a stretch without seeing another car. Inevitably he missed a couple more turnings but around 4.00 a.m. he turned the next page of his notebook and found only three more turnings listed. After the third his notes read "1.3 m Carpark on left." The road started to climb across the face of a steep hill, first through a pine plantation then as the gradient lessened, across open moorland. He drove until the odometer started to turn to 1.5 and there it was. Not much more than an open patch of ground bounded by large rocks, with a metal goal post like structure at the entrance to prevent tall vehicles gaining access. He turned in and parked as far from the road as possible. It was twenty past four. And he was knackered.

It took a good couple of minutes for his eyes to adjust to the darkness. He poured himself another coffee and got out a sandwich, suddenly aware of his hunger. The first mouthful seemed to contain as much pickle as cheese and the sweetness took him by surprise. He chewed slowly, savouring the completion of his journey as much as the satisfaction of his hunger, listening to the wind blowing gently round the contours of his car.

When he had finished eating he got out and stretched. Broken clouds were moving across the sky allowing glimpses of constellations too brief to enable him to identify them. He could spot the Plough if he could see it all at once but he wasn't going to pick it out now. The hilltop seemed to form an extensive, heather clad plateau with the dark mass of a gentle summit rising up half a mile to his left. The valley behind him was largely hidden by the lip of the ridge but he could see lights on the far hillside, a hamlet just large enough to justify a couple of street lamps. The orange glow visible on the horizon North East of him was Sheffield. He shivered. The wind was fresh and unfeeling. It reminded him of his isolation. He stood there for maybe twenty minutes.

Back inside he had another cup of coffee and a sandwich. It was going to be a long wait. He tipped the seat back and tried to sleep. It seemed an impossible task, with all the uncertainties flowing through his mind, but he must have managed because he found himself fumbling into wakefulness sometime after dawn, stiff and chilled and in need of a piss. He looked at his watch. It was just gone 6.00. Only two more hours with any luck. Outside the sky was an unbroken grey. The top of the peak he had seen when he arrived was now lost in low cloud and wisps of cloud occasionally blew across the car park. He found a ham sandwich in his bag and chewed it slowly. His mouth was dry and he had to wash the doughy mouthfuls down with sips of tepid coffee. Time dragged.

He heard the sound of a car climbing the hill and looked at his watch. 6.55. Probably too early for Mike. The car, a Range Rover, pulled off the road and parked about thirty yards away from David. He didn't know what sort of car Mike drove but he doubted it was a Range Rover. He turned the rear-view mirror and watched a man, so well wrapped up against the weather it was impossible to judge his age, get out of the driver's door and walk to the back of the vehicle. When he opened up the back two rangy looking dogs jumped out, barking excitedly. The man slammed the door back down again and the three of them headed off in the direction of the cloud-bound summit. Over the next half hour two more dog walkers arrived. None of them would necessarily think twice about a man sitting in a car when they arrived. But if he was still just sitting there when they returned that might stick in their minds. He willed Mike to arrive.

Then a Golf that had seen better days turned into the car park. This looked more promising, he thought. The vehicle came to a halt the far side of one of the other parked cars. When a head appeared above the roof of the intervening vehicle it was Mike's. David got out and walked over to meet him.

There was an awkward moment when David thought they were going to shake hands but Mike just asked, 'What's up?'

'Someone's put a tail on me. Two cars at least but there was probably a third I never saw. And they broke into my house while I was away. And my boss asked me to come in. They had some questions about what I'd done round here. After what happened to Eric I decided to clear out.'

'Makes sense.'

David had hoped for a little more. 'Is there anywhere we can hide my car?'

Mike thought for a moment or two. 'Yes, I know someone with a garage they don't use. We can call round there.'

'And what about somewhere to stay?'

'Just for tonight you can stay with my son. Steve. He's got a spare bed. We'll sort something out properly after that.'

'Shall I follow you then.'

'Yeah. Do.'

'Can we get there just on the back roads? If they pick up my licence plates on the cameras they'll know I'm here.'

'Yeah. We can do that.'

'And your phone's not on is it.'

'No.'

Without more they both got into their cars. David followed Mike out of the car park and along a series of lanes that lead eventually into what he assumed was a suburb of Sheffield. They briefly joined a main road and crossed a junction with signs mounted on gantries but he couldn't spot any cameras. Shortly afterwards they turned into a 1960s estate consisting of rows of more or less identical pale brick houses, each with a garage attached. Mike soon pulled up outside one and

David tucked in behind him. Before he could get out of the car Mike came over to his door.

'Best you don't meet him. Just wait here.'

Mike was inside the house for so long David began to wonder whether there was a problem but after ten minutes the garage door swung up and open and Mike stood inside beckoning him in.

'We had to clear a bit of junk first. How much stuff have you got?'

'Just a suitcase.' He leant forward and untaped the kitchen knife from beneath the dashboard.

'Is that really necessary?'

'Better safe…'

CHAPTER FOURTEEN

They left the town on a road still lined with houses on the uphill side but as they continued to climb the buildings petered out and narrow, stonewall bounded fields stretched up to the ridge on their right as well as down to the small, rocky stream in the valley to their left. The road crossed over the hill in a gully lined with hawthorn, brambles and the odd rowan tree and then descended steeply into the next little town. The first couple of the houses were boarded up; metal grills bolted across windows and doors, and on one the remains of a poster claiming, improbably, that the premises were patrolled by guard dogs. Further on there were a couple of shops before they turned left into the High Street. The first hundred yards looked normal; a Boots, a Tesco's, a couple of banks, a pleasant looking pub. But a set of traffic lights at the end of this stretch of shops seemed to mark some sort of boundary. Beyond the junction there were a number of charity shops. First, a spruce enough looking branch of Oxfam, its windows filled with colourful pictures of smiling Africans at work in their fields and Indian women in brilliant saris enjoying their newly installed water pump. But the shops supporting local charities showed no such style.

Their dusty windows displayed a mix of shabby furniture, old paperbacks and clothing many years past its sell by date. And the number of empty premises multiplied as they drove on, interspersed with kebab and chicken shops and the inevitable bookies. Outside another pub, under banners advertising Sky Sport and "Curry and a pint £3.50 every Thursday", a group of girls and boys in their late teens sat smoking and drinking, topping their pint glasses up from barely concealed plastic bottles of supermarket cider.

'God,' David sighed.

'You won,' said Mike. 'This is what your victory looks like.'

David wanted to say 'This isn't what I fought for' but instead he said, 'You think your lot would have done any better. All those dreaming teachers and manipulative trots and bolshie shop stewards.' They passed yet another William Hill framed by Marie Curie Cancer Care on one side and a boarded-up chicken shop on the other. 'And Tony Benn.'

'What have you got against Tony Benn.'

'That pipe-smoking fraud. He wouldn't have recognised the real world if it had punched him in the face.'

Mike turned sharply off the High Street and up into a maze of residential streets. 'We'd never have hung all these people out to dry. Never have told them it was their fault if they couldn't find a decent job. Never have sold the country's soul to the banks. Fuck, we'd never have invaded Iraq. Were you up for that?'

'Not that one, no. That one had 'Massive Fuck Up' written all over it. You can blame that on the idiots at MI6. And the Labour Prime Minister.'

'Labour!' he snorted. 'Were you on the march then?'

'No. Why? Do you think one more would have made all the difference?'

Mike turned the car down yet another street of red brick terraced houses and started to slow down, looking for somewhere to park. They passed a woman pushing a pram with some difficulty over the cracked surface of the pavement, followed by a small boy in a bright blue kagool clutching a plastic aeroplane, before Mike found a space and pulled in ahead of them. David made to open his door.

'Let her go by first,' said Mike.

'Do you know her?'

'By sight.'

They heard the rattle of the pram's tiny wheels banging against the asphalt ridges of the footpath and then the boy's voice. 'What are we having for tea today?'

'Sausages love'

The pair drew level.

'Sausages and beans?'

'If you like love.'

Mike gave them another few seconds and opened his door.

The air was damp and still. Apart from the receding couple the street was empty. David picked his case up from the back seat and followed Mike back up the street past a couple of houses to a green painted front door numbered 25. Mike knocked and ten seconds later the door was opened by a tall, well-built man in black jeans and a dark green T Shirt. His hair was close cropped, greying ever so slightly at the temples and he had rings in both ears.

'Steve, this is David.'

'How do,' said Steve, stepping back to allow them both to pass through into the narrow hallway. David looked up and down the street but saw no one and followed Mike through into the front room.

There was a scuffed brown leather sofa against one wall opposite a large TV with a gaming console and a rack of other devices plugged into it. In front of the sofa was a low table with an ashtray on it, a packet of Rizlas and a couple of ripped up cigarettes. There were another two, equally shabby armchairs and, either side of the window, shelves the height of the room overflowing with CD's.

'David needs to stay out of sight for a couple of days.'

'OK.' Steve remained standing as he processed the information. 'Tea?'

'That'd be a start son.'

'Milk, no sugar thanks,' said David. Steve nodded and went through to the kitchen at the back of the house.

Decades ago he'd heard that boy on the tapes, asking his daddy when he was coming home.

Mike looked at him and more or less guessed what he was thinking.

'You recognise him from the surveillance pictures?'

'Can't say I do. It's been a while. They grow up so fast these days.'

They both sat down in silence. David looked around the room. A Joy Division poster was the only art work. The few books mixed in with the CD's seemed to be mainly thrillers. The silence dragged on.

'He's not followed in his father's footsteps then?'

'I brought him up right but then came The Summer of Love. Things have never been the same since.'

Just then Steve came in carrying three mugs of tea and with an opened packet of biscuits clutched under his left arm. 'For me there's no such thing as a class enemy.' He placed the three mugs carefully on the table then turned to David and looked him over carefully, 'Just a capitalist lackey who hasn't done enough E's yet. And you look ever so slightly like a copper. If you don't mind me saying.'

'Worse,' said Mike. 'But he's on the side of the angels now. He says.'

'Do I get to hear the story?'

'Best not son.'

'But your dad's right, I'm on the side of the angels.' David laughed. 'Your side anyway.'

'That's good. Have a hobnob.' David took a biscuit. 'You can have the kid's bed. If you don't mind a Sponge Bob Squarepants duvet cover.'

'Thanks. That's fine.'

'How long will you be stopping?' Steve asked. David looked at Mike.

'I'll find somewhere else for him by tomorrow. Day after at the latest.'

'And these people who might want to find you David?'

'I won't lie. There's an outside chance it could get ugly. But it's me they want. They've got no quarrel with you.'

Mike leant forward in his chair, his forearms resting on his knees, 'Steve, I wouldn't bring you into this if I didn't need to. It could be important.'

'I thought you'd given all this up dad.'

'So did I. But then along comes Mr Plod here and brings it all up again.'

'Maggie's long gone, you know.'

'Yeah, but her spirit lives on.'

'So who the fuck are you? Ghostbusters?'

'Sort of,' said David. He took a careful sip of the near scalding tea.

'How's the lad doing?' Mike asked.

'Seems happy. They've got him playing chess at school. I let him beat me most of the time but he nearly had me for real the other day. I'll maybe bring him over at the weekend. See how you do.'

'That'd be good. Give us a call.'

No one spoke. A car went past and David realised how quiet the street was. Then Mike's comment from their first meeting came back to him. "He didn't even like having me in the house when I first got out." Was this unease between father and son on him too?

'Did you have a look at the computer courses they're running at the college?' Mike asked.

'Not yet,' said Steve. 'I've got the brochure somewhere.' And after another brief silence. 'I'll have a look. Later.'

Mike took a mouthful of tea and put his mug down.

'Listen. I've got some shopping to do for your Ma. I'd better be going.' He got up and Steve saw him to the door. On the doorstep they exchanged a few words David couldn't catch and then he heard the door close and Steve came back in.

'Don't mind me,' David said. 'In fact, if it's OK with you I'll get my head down for a few hours. I've been driving all night.'

'Sure. It's the bedroom at the back. It's a bit of a mess.' Steve made to get up.

'I'll find my way.' Mess was no disincentive. A mattress and a duvet was all he wanted.

It was late afternoon when he awoke, a dream slipping away from him as he regained consciousness. He'd been with some people, somewhere, they'd just come out of a large building and there had been some urgency about their situation. He struggled for a moment to remember more, but it had gone.

He got himself dressed and went downstairs to find Steve engrossed in a video game, chasing Germans through a succession of bunkers and trenches all the while expending an implausible amount of ammunition.

'You get some sleep?' Steve asked without looking up.

'Yes. Thanks. I feel a lot better.'

'The kettle's out the back if you need a cup of tea. Do you play?'

'No. I'll just make myself a tea thanks. Do you want one?'

'I'm fine thanks.'

Five minutes later David sat in one of the armchairs wondering how this would all play out. But staying up all night followed by an unaccustomed afternoon nap left him feeling a little dazed, helpless almost. He shut his eyes as if to sleep again and had nearly dozed off when he heard the characters in the video game talking about Falaise.

'My dad was there,' he said after a few moments following the action.

'Where?' Steve asked.

'Normandy. '44.'

Steve unleashed a final burst of automatic fire into a flaming building and pressed pause.

'That's something.'

'He didn't talk about it much. He died when I was in my twenties. Before I plucked up the courage to ask him I suppose. But I do remember one day an old mate of his from the army came round. Can't remember his name but he'd emigrated to Australia after the war and he'd come back to visit family and he came over for lunch. And it was all asking about the children and how's your job and so on. And then he and dad just started to talk about the war. My mum went out in the end, but I sat there listening to everything.'

'What were they saying?'

'A lot of it was just laughs to start with. Do you remember so and so? What a pillock somebody was, that sort of thing, and the sort of bravado you used to get in war comics... looking back on it now I think they were just skirting round the stuff they really wanted to talk about because my dad got up to make some tea and when he got back the two of them didn't say anything for a while then one of them said something like, 'Do you remember Billy?' And from that moment on they forgot all about me. There had been some awful night, when this bloke Billy had got killed and a bunch of their other mates, people they'd been with for a long time. I don't remember any of the details. I'm not sure they were entirely clear what had happened, not after that length of time and everything. But I do remember my dad's friend turning to me when he was getting up to leave and saying. 'It's nothing like the fucking movies son. Don't you ever forget that.' And my dad was always very strict about swearing, and there was an adult talking to me in our living room and swearing, and all my dad said was, "No. Nothing at all."'

Steve stared ahead at the screen for while. 'I can see why you never got into this then.'

And David remembered too how he had sat beside his father, who was dosed up on morphine in the hours before he died of cancer, as he relived the entire desperate episode in awful detail, sometimes shouting at David for help. It was a peculiar feeling to know that his father's last memory of him was of someone struggling franticly to clear a Bren gun stoppage as their friends died around them.

'Does your dad talk about the old days?' David asked.

'He used to. But I just couldn't take it. By the time I was… fifteen?… I'd had a belly full. I wasn't going down that road.'

David looked around him. Surely even working for the cause was a step up from living like this?

Steve sensed his disappointment. 'You can't imagine what it was like after the strike. It wasn't just the pits that went. Maggie managed to shut pretty much everything else down too. And the backbiting about the people who'd gone back to work early. It was mental. Two guys on our street, lived next door to each other, been best mates for ever. And one of them went back to work three weeks before the end of the strike. Three weeks. And they've never spoken to each other since. Walk past each other when they go in and out the house. Not a word. Mental. And dad drank too much so me mum fucked off for a while. The last thing I wanted in my life was politics. Then the Stone Roses came along. And ecstasy. And I was gone. Fuck school. Fuck work. After all that shit it was just magic. Just so beautiful. It was this massive release for everybody. Just amazing. Free festivals all over the country. I don't think I was straight for about two years.' He gave a wry look round the room. 'Still, all good things come to an end. Specially when you have a kid. You ever taken ecstasy?'

'No, I haven't.'

'You should give it a go mate.' Steve laughed. 'Cooped up in here for a couple of days, you might as well. I can find some, no trouble. I reckon it'd do you good.'

'I've got enough to be thinking about for the time being, but thanks.'

Steve returned to the fray but after a few minutes there was another series of explosions followed by silence and David looked up to see Steve staring at the ceiling mouthing 'fuck'.

243

A moment or two later he leant forward and asked, 'You want some supper?'

Thanks. Yes.'

'It's beans on toast,' he added, as if to offer David a chance to change his mind

'That's fine.'

'I could stick some cheese on top if you like.'

'Why not. You only live once.'

'I'm going to watch the football in a bit. Hope you don't mind. League Cup replay. After a disappointing home draw Huddersfield are now away to Wrexham. I'm sort of honour bound.'

'Might take my mind of things.'

While Steve was in the kitchen David mentally ran through what little he had established. But there simply wasn't enough information to make sense of everything. The essential connections were still hidden and, unless Mike found someone who could unlock the mystery, or Manjit overheard something, there was no obvious way for him to fill in the gaps. And what had happened to bring it all to the surface now? Maybe Lord Frampton's past had nothing to do with it. Why should some episode from the '80s, however murky or discreditable, come back to haunt him now? Given the unsavoury company he was keeping today why not assume the explanation lay entirely in the present? Then, in his mind, he saw once more the expression on Terry's face at Eric's funeral. Terry had been out of the game for 5 years now. If he was scared, this thing had its roots way back. That was one way into this puzzle, but short of door stepping Terry, which would be a high-risk approach right now, he couldn't see a way forward.

He was still wrestling with the apparent impossibility of progress when Steve came in with two plates of beans on toast. Garnished with grated cheese. Using an old newspaper Steve offered him as a mat he rested the plate on his knees. The shreds of cheese were starting to melt and little rivers of oily fat had begun to flow into the dips between the individual beans. Suddenly he was hungry.

While David started to eat Steve fiddled with the television controls and a rather grainy picture of a slowly filling stadium emerged on the screen.

'Reception's not very good here,' said David.

'It's not reception. It's file sharing. Over the internet. I'm not fucking paying for Sky. And this way, even if the football's crap, which is an occupational hazard when you follow Huddersfield, at least you get the satisfaction of stealing from Rupert Murdoch.'

'I thought you weren't political.'

Steve sat down on the sofa next to David and started to cut off a corner of bean-soaked toast.

'Not like my dad no. But you've got to have some principles.'

They ate in companionable silence for a few minutes as the spectators filtered into their seats.

'Do you follow football?' Steve asked.

'No.'

'I started just to annoy my dad. He used to quote Chomsky all the time about how sport is a distraction for the working classes promoted by the ruling elite,' he put a fork-full of beans into his mouth and his words became slightly mangled, 'to distract the working class from the political issues they ought to be looking at.' He swallowed and continued a little more clearly, 'And I thought if it's a way of ignoring politics

I'm having that. Drove him nuts. Bugger is now I'm stuck with a third-rate team, guaranteeing me a lifetime of footballing disappointment, and a government of corrupt neoliberal arseholes. Do you want ketchup or anything?'

'I'm fine thanks.'

At that moment the doorbell went.

'Are you expecting anyone?' David asked.

'Probably someone asking if I want to go and watch the football in the pub. Like I've got that sort of money.'

Steve got up to answer the door. David thought for a second of retreating to the kitchen but before he had moved Steve's cry came from the doorway, 'Fucking he...'

David sprang to his feet and his plate pitched across the room planting a mess of beans, toast and cheese in the doorway. A second later Steve was bundled into the room, skidded in the remains of David's supper and crashed to the floor. David was still heading forward and the fist he had no memory of forming crashed into the throat of the half-seen figure in the hall way. Two more blows and the figure slumped to the ground. One hard stamp to the head and. Silence. David pushed the front door shut then bent down to retrieve a pistol which had fallen from the man's hand and checked the safety catch before tucking it into his waistband.

Behind him Steve slowly got to his feet. David dragged the unconscious body into the living room and the two of them looked down at the masked, unconscious body. David pulled up the balaclava to reveal the face of a dark-haired man of perhaps thirty. A mobile earpiece in his right ear was fizzing with what sounded like frantic questioning.

'What the fuck?' asked Steve, still shaking.

David found himself in a strange place. The same, cool, clear place he'd found himself in twice before, long, long ago in Ulster. If he'd paused to think about it, which he didn't, he'd have realised he was almost happy. His mind started racing. 'Steve, how many people do you know on this street?'

'What?' It was a simple fucking question. David forced himself to remain calm.

'If you called up all your friends on this street and told them to get outside and look around, how many people could you get out there? It'll scare off the back up team.'

'Back up team?'

David's cool took a bit of a knock. 'You have no idea how much danger we are in right now.'

'I think I fucking do mate. Some ninja's just piled in through my front door and pointed a fucking gun at me. And I don't think he was playing cowboys and Indians.'

'Steve, people like this operate as a team. Somewhere, within a hundred yards of here, almost certainly with a visual on this house, there's a car with two more guys just like him in it. And they're not playing cowboys and Indians either. Now please, for the love of God, how many people do you know on this street?'

To his relief he saw a light go on behind Steve's eyes. 'Six or seven perhaps?'

'Start calling them. Get them out on the street. Offer them anything. Beer?' Steve smiled and began to dial.

'Phil? Mate. Earn a pint? Get out on the street now. Don't ask, just do it. And when you're out there bang on Neville's door and get him out. Yeah, he gets a pint too. Everyone gets a pint. And make all the fucking noise you can.'

He called another number. 'Darren. Earn yourself a pint. Get out on the street now. Fuck the football. Two pints. Anyone you can get out on the street gets a pint. But fucking

247

do it now.' A brief pause. 'Nothing. Sober. Straight. Just do it.'

Outside David heard a door open. Seconds later another and someone shouted something he didn't catch. Steve very cautiously peered out of the front doorway and shouted into the road, 'Look out in the street boys and girls, there's nudists everywhere!' One of his friends took up the cry, curtains were pulled back and two or three more people stepped out of their houses. Then an engine started, headlights came on and a car accelerated away from half way up the street. Steve grinned and looked across at David. 'Your round.'

David smiled and pulled a couple of twenties out of his wallet, paused then added a third. Steve took them eagerly, looked left and right out of the door once more then half ran over to one of the figures standing across the road. When he got back he found David looking down at the unconscious figure stretched out on his living room floor.

'Well, what are we going to do with Action Man?' Steve asked.

'The first thing we do is take his picture. Can you move his head so he's looking upwards.' Steve bent down and gingerly adjusted the intruder's head so that it gazed blankly up at the ceiling. 'Thanks.' David stood over the comatose figure and lined up his mobile to take a shot. 'Profile please now.' Steve giggled and turned the face through ninety degrees and David took a few more pictures.'

'You got a Find My Assassin app on your phone?'

'Not on my phone, no. But these might come in handy.'

'You're going to break into the cop shop aren't you, hack into their system and match those pictures to their database? And you're going to want me to keep a look out from a darkened alley opposite. It's going to be like The Bourne Identity. But in Huddersfield.'

David's mind went back to the aftermath of a brief firefight in West Belfast and a fresh faced private who'd blabbered on in much the same way till his sergeant had put him firmly back in his box. But as he stood up straight again he felt the barrel of the silenced pistol pushing against his left thigh and he focussed back on the present.

'Who are you texting?' Steve asked.

'A friend who does have a Find My Assassin app. See if he can help us.' God knows whether Manjit would be able to do anything with the pictures.

'We need to tie him up Steve. What have you got? Rope? Cable ties?'

'Phil will have loads of cable ties.'

'OK, can you get us a dozen? Just tell him you'll explain everything later. And we'll use one of your chairs… one of those chairs in the kitchen to tie him to.'

'Woah. How long are you going to keep him here?'

'Steve. He's going to come round in a while. Do you want to deal with him tied up or untied?'

There was a low groan the from the figure on the floor.

'Look I can't just keep hitting him till you decide you're ready. Get the fucking cable ties. Please. We'll secure him. Then we'll decide what to do next.'

Steve continued to stare at the prone figure. Then, ever so slightly, it moved. David gestured, exasperated, unable for the moment to think what else to say, and, finally, the penny dropped. Steve spun out of the door and returned two minutes later with enough ties to secure a small army of would-be assassins. David swiftly linked two of the ties and wrapped them round the figure's ankles, pulling them tight. Then he tied the man's wrists together crosswise.

'I've got a cellar,' said Steve. 'If that helps. What's the plan?'

'The plan is … The plan is to keep this guy secure. For long enough for me to get out of here and cover my tracks.'

'Great. What about me? I'm not so sure I want to be hanging around here waiting for his mates to come and rescue him.'

'You tell the police this guy came round, broke into your place. They'll pick him up and that will be you out of it.'

'And when they ask me why I've tied him up with all these cable ties?'

'Just say you're naturally cautious.'

'What about the gun?'

'What gun?'

'So you want me to lie about there having been a gun?'

'No, just don't mention it?'

'But what about this guy. He knows there was a gun. He's going to want it back.'

'Yes, but he's not going to bring that up with Mr Plod is he. Look they don't care about you. And they can get another gun. From your point of view this will blow over, but yeah, maybe go and stay with a friend for a few days. Now let's just shift this bastard somewhere we can tie him up properly.'

'There's some pipework in the hall. You could tie him to that maybe,' said Steve.

'Good idea. We're going to need a gag too. Have you got any gaffer tape.'

'Yeah. I think so. I'll have a look.' Steve went back into the kitchen and David waited, listening to the sound of drawers being opened and wondering what he could use if

Steve drew a blank. And what next? How had they found him? Where was he going to go now? Was there a secure way of getting back in touch with Mike?

'Got it,' Steve called from the next room and David's mind returned to the task in hand.

'Thanks.' David wound the roll of tape twice round the man's head. It was a strangely intimate feeling to hold its close-cropped contours in his hands and it occurred to him that this same man might have murdered Eric. As he ripped a strip of the tape from the roll there was a knock at the front door.

'Who is it?' Steve called out.

'Darren mate. What the fuck's going on?'

'Can you tell him to go away,' David asked, but he was too late.

'What the fuck are you doing? And who the fuck is he?' Darren was a bit over six foot tall, perhaps not as bulky as he looked in the confines of the narrow hallway but still a sizeable figure. And he was unfazed, David noticed, by what he saw.

'Who? The guy lying down or the guy tying him up?' Steve asked.

'I was thinking… what the fuck is going on?'

David stood up. 'Darren. This isn't a good moment. Can you maybe come back later.'

Darren gave David a look that said something like "who the fuck are you" and asked Steve, 'Are you OK?'

'I'm fine. This is a mate of my dad's. And this is someone who wants to kill my dad's mate. I have absolutely no fucking idea why. Listen, we're all a bit up tight… my benefit comes in on Thursday. You couldn't let us have an eighth on tick?'

'You can have this,' Darren said, pulling a plastic wrap out of his pocket. 'On the house. You look like you need it. Do you want me to skin up? You look a bit … tied up.'

'Thanks, yeah. David? Are we done with this bloke or do we have to do anything more, like tie his shoelaces together or something?'

David looked on helplessly as Darren sat himself down in the sitting room with a packet of cigarette papers and started pulling a cigarette apart. 'Steve, I've got to get away from here. I've got to meet up with Mike and find somewhere else to hide up. Let me think. Is there anyone, a friend of your dad's or anyone, who could drive me out of here?'

'Maybe… Darren, is your car fixed?'

'Yeah. Got it done last week.'

'Could you take David somewhere?'

'I'm your dealer, not a fucking taxi service.'

'Darren,' said David, 'I'll give you a hundred quid to take me… Steve is there anywhere you can describe to your dad in a way that someone listening to the call won't be able to identify? I don't know… like where your mum gets here hair done? And tell him to meet me there. Or a pub you can describe without naming? Somewhere that's not just round the corner.'

Steve nodded. 'Where's me fucking phone…'

'Here mate.' It was on the table in front of Darren. He took a break from heating the lump of resin in his fingers and passed it over.

Steve dialled. 'Dad. It's me. Look, it's all gone tits up here… David'll explain, but this bloke piled in with a gun… no… we're all OK… David says can you meet him at the pub where, I'm not allowed to say what it's called in case anyone is listening, but the pub we went for Owen's birthday... Darren's going to take him I think.'

'I ain't said I'm taking him anywhere,' said Darren, before licking the gum on the cigarette paper and folding it carefully down onto the body of the spliff. 'Like I said, I might be your dealer, but I'm not a fucking taxi service.'

David pulled the gun out. 'Darren, I had to take this off this guy down here. The sooner I'm out of here, the sooner Steve, and everyone else round here, is free of all the trouble that's looking for me. Where's this pub you're talking about Steve?'

'The Antelope, just across town. Twenty minutes at this time of night.'

'Twenty minutes for a hundred quid Darren. That's not a bad deal.'

'Yeah, but you've got blokes trying to shoot you. I'll do it for two hundred.'

'OK. Two hundred. But we need to be gone now.'

Darren didn't even look up. Instead he lit the spliff and took a long deep drag, held it down for ten seconds or so then exhaled for almost as long. 'You take this Steve. I'll be back in forty minutes. Let's go.'

'Darren, can you take another passenger?'

'Who?'

'Him,' said David pointing at the figure trussed up on the hall floor.

'Where does he want to go?'

'Anywhere we can drop him off where he won't be found till the morning.'

'Like where?'

'The street behind ASDA's quiet,' said Steve. 'There's just a load of bins there.'

'You've got to be fucking kidding.'

'Either that or we leave him here and call the police,' said David. 'I'll give you another £200.'

Darren looked at Steve. 'You owe me big time mate.' Then to David, 'You got the money?'

'Yes. Where's the car?'

Darren laughed. 'Man, you've got a gun. I'm not going to scam you.'

'I wouldn't shoot you for four hundred quid. Get me to the pub and I'll give you the money. And Steve. You should probably go and stay with a friend for a couple of days. No one's going to come looking for you but it's probably best to keep your head down. OK?' And he gave Steve what he hoped was a reassuring look.

CHAPTER FIFTEEN

David at the pub for nearly an hour before Mike arrived, with Guy..

'How the fuck did they find you so fast?' Mike asked.

David shrugged. 'GCHQ record everything. As soon as I went off the radar someone could have started trawling all the related phone calls. How long after you left me at Steve's did you switch your phone back on Mike?'

Five seconds' silence then, 'Fuck. As soon as I was stopped at the lights.'

'If it was you asking questions that alerted them in the first place that would mean they could be watching you. And Steve's on the system,' said David. 'Benefits. Electoral roll, council tax, whatever. You turn your phone on no distance from his house and they join the dots. OK. New phones everyone. Two each. One you can use from your house but just to let people know you want to make contact. And another that you never, ever, switch on, anywhere near your house, that you use to actually talk to people. And you label the phones. OK?'

There was mumbled assent. David fished a hundred pounds out of his wad and handed it to Mike.

'What happened exactly?' Mike asked

'They sent a team to get me. One guy came in through the front door, but I dealt with him. There was a car outside but Steve got his neighbours to come out and make a noise and the back-up team, however many they were, drove off.'

'And what have you done with the man you "dealt with"?'

'He's OK. We've left him tied up round the back of ASDA. Someone will find him in the morning.'

'So who put these people onto you?' Mike asked.

'People who want to look after Frampton, must be the most plausible explanation. MI5 would be pissed off with me if they knew what I'm doing but they wouldn't try and kill me.'

Then Mike spoke. 'Let's be blunt David. We don't owe you any favours. There was a time I'd happily have killed you myself. You nearly got Steve killed. And you expect us to carry on protecting you. For what? Just asking.'

No one leapt in to defend David.

'You have to take a view.' He looked each of them in the eye in turn. 'I'm onto something. At the very least there's no doubt about that now. And it relates to you, or the people around you, in some way. And it's serious enough for people to kill. Whatever else we've learnt tonight, it's pretty plain now my colleague was murdered and if the man who told me that was right about that we must assume he was right that it relates to something that happened here.' He let that sink in. 'You have to ask yourselves, do you want to take more risks to give me, us, a chance to get to the bottom of … whatever this is, or not? Your call.'

It was Mike's turn to look across at Guy.

'We've got nothing to lose,' said Guy, which seemed to David to misunderstand the seriousness of what had just happened.

'You think GCHQ could have tracked you,' Mike said, 'but you think the people who attacked you aren't official. How does that work?'

'The lines are blurred these days Mike. I had a meeting with the CIA about Frampton's dealings in Iraq. Only it turned out it wasn't the CIA, it was a CIA contractor who worked for a company that was owned by the company that had been competing for the same contract Frampton's people were awarded. News International have no problem persuading policemen to provide confidential information and the powers that be don't seem too troubled. Tail wags dog more and more these days. Let's go.'

'Who are we going to see?' David asked once they were moving.

'A woman called Diane,' said Mike. 'I picked her because she's not part of the...'

'The usual suspects?' David offered.

'Exactly. I only know her through the Palestine Solidarity Campaign. She wasn't involved in any of the... any of our past activities. I think she just votes Labour. But I've heard her talk about some of her trips to the West Bank. She's spent time there as an observer. Watching the Israelis demolish people's houses, that sort of thing. So she's got backbone. And if I tell her it's for a good cause, I think she'll be OK. If not we try somewhere else.'

257

No one had much more to say. David made a mental note of the turns they took and the names of the villages they passed through. It was twenty minutes before they turned off the main road but only a couple of minutes later that they pulled up outside a row of nineteenth century brick cottages in a cul-de-sac on the edge of another village. Mike got out and rang the doorbell of the furthest house. He had shut the car door behind him and David heard nothing more until Mike returned several minutes later and said, 'It's OK. I haven't told her the details but she knows the basic story and she knows there's a risk. Her name's Diane. Come on in and I'll introduce you.'

Old hippie was David's immediate reaction. A handsome woman, a full figure and an air of considered determination, but an old hippie none the less. Not so much from what she wore, a sweater, probably home knitted, and a dark skirt, more the decor of the living room, very obviously home-made book shelves, Indian looking throws over the two sofas and a framed print of what he took to be some eastern text hung on the wall above the fireplace. But, as Mike's stories of her time in Palestine suggested, there was some steel in there too. And a safe house was a safe house.

'David,' he offered. 'How do you do.'

'I'm Diane. You're welcome. Mike tells me you need somewhere for a couple of nights while he sorts out somewhere more permanent.'

'Yes. And Mike has told you that... putting me up isn't entirely risk free?'

'He has.' And he was struck by her calmness. 'I don't have a spare bed, but other people tell me the sofa's comfy enough. Come on in. Have you eaten?'

'I started on some beans and toast but...'

'I'll heat up some dhal. Are you all right with brown rice?'

'That would be great,' he said with as much enthusiasm as he could feign.

'How about a whiskey too?' And she smiled for the first time.

'You read my mind.' He hoped she hadn't.

'We'll leave you to it then,' said Mike. 'Someone will call tomorrow. It'll be a number you don't recognise. But whoever it is will talk about having finished the washing up. Then they'll tell you we're getting some more leaflets printed. If they say they've managed to get a good price that means we'll come over tomorrow to pick you up.' He smiled at David. 'We have some experience of working around people who tap our phones. We'll be in touch.'

David forbore to mention how amateurish much of their coding had been during the strike. 'Mike,' he said.

'Yeah.'

'You should probably take some precautions too.'

Then the door closed behind them and Diane turned to David.

'Have a seat,' she said. 'I'll pour you a whiskey, then I'll find you some supper.' As she bent down to pick the bottle from a shelf at the bottom of the bookcase his eye was drawn to her behind. He found his experiences that evening had re-ignited his longing for one last fuck before he died.

'It's very good of you to put me up... under the circumstances. How much did he tell you about what happened earlier?'

'He said a man with a gun came round to where you were staying but,' she stood up again and turned to face him, holding a bottle of Famous Grouse in her left hand, 'you managed to overpower him. He didn't say so, and I don't

259

need to know, but I assume you now have the gun.' It was a matter of fact statement not a question and once again he was impressed by her coolness. She found a glass and poured him a very generous measure. 'This will help take the edge off things.' He took the glass eagerly and relished the feel of the first warming sip burning its way down his throat. 'The amber nectar. That's perfect.' In a matter of moments the world seemed a better, more manageable place. 'Thank you.'

'I'll go and put some rice on.'

In her absence he got up and took his coat off. It still contained all his money. He would have to find some way of dividing it up. It was too easy to imagine losing everything otherwise. Then he began idly scanning the titles on her bookshelves, struck by the hotchpotch of sizes and different coloured spines. Plenty of novels, most of which he had never heard of, but it all looked pretty high-brow. Further along, towards the kitchen door the books became more political, with a strong feminist bent. Tonight was plainly not going to be the night.

'You're welcome to read any of those,' she said, reappearing from the kitchen. He was pretty sure she was teasing him.

'The rice'll be another ten minutes.' She sat down on the other sofa.

'Thanks. Maybe I will. Listen, do you have anything I could use to make a money belt?' He laughed. 'You're welcome to charge for B&B. But at the moment it's just stuffed in my coat pockets. It'd be good to secure it a bit more.' He held out the great wedge of cash he was carrying.

'I've got a money belt but it may not hold that much. I'll go and find it later.'

'Thanks.' There was a silence she plainly felt no pressing need to fill.

'Listen, if anything does happen tonight, stay upstairs. They won't be after you. Your best chance of surviving is keeping out of it. If you haven't witnessed anything they've got less reason to worry about you.'

'Thank you. I'm not sure if that's going to make it easier for me to sleep tonight or not.'

'Have a whiskey. That'll help.'

'I think I will. Then I'll check the rice.'

She remained in the kitchen with her whiskey until the food was ready. David was pleasantly surprised, the rice was nuttier than he was used to but the dhal, heavily flavoured with coconut, went down very easily.

'Not as bad as you expected?' she asked with the beginnings of a smile.

'Much better.' The sort of thing he ought to learn to cook himself, but probably never would.

She seemed content to allow him to eat in silence. No football, no Call of Duty. When he'd eaten maybe two thirds of the dhal and was slowing down he asked, 'How much did Mike tell you about... how I find myself in this situation?'

'He was a bit short on detail. Deliberately. He told me you were MI5... and that I wasn't to trust you an inch.' He enjoyed the mockery in her eyes. If they had more common ground he could easily be tempted. 'But that, for reasons he wasn't going to explain, you were now, in some way, "on the side of the angels" and, again for reasons he wasn't going to explain, in need of somewhere to hide for a while. Is that about right? To be honest I don't want to know too much.'

'That'll do.'

The tone of her voice changed. 'I was active in CND for many years … it was people like you who spied on the people I worked with.'

'Were you at Greenham Common?'

'No, but I knew women who were. Which makes it a bit odd for me… having you in my house.'

'Cathy Massiter wasn't the only one to have concerns about what we were doing.'

'She was the only one willing to blow the whistle.'

'That's true.' And in truth it wasn't something that had troubled him at the time, or given him pause for thought in later years. He'd seen them then as naive irritants undermining the defence of the realm and he'd had no cause to change his mind since then. 'I'll spare you the details,' he said, 'but that wasn't my line of work.'

She gave him a look that suggested she didn't regard that as absolving him of any responsibility.

'Were you living here then?' he asked.

'Why?'

'I'm wondering if this address would appear in their records.'

'I was just an ordinary member. Would they have been interested in me?'

'That doesn't mean… Like I say, it wasn't my area, but if you were talking to the people at Greenham they might well have opened a file on you.' "They," he thought. "We" would have been more accurate. Strange to think her details might once have passed across the desks of Terry or Eric.

'I suppose I shouldn't be surprised,' she said turning her gaze from him to the wall. 'But no. I was living in Sheffield at the time that was all going on. I moved here in '96 when my mum died and I inherited a bit of money. I'd had enough of the city by then and I was only teaching three days a week so the traveling was manageable.'

'I've just moved to the country. Well … yes. I haven't moved far but I'm a few miles outside the town I used to live in.'

'Just you? There's no one sitting by the phone wondering where you've got to?'

'Just me. I really wanted a bit of peace and quiet. I'd just retired. I only came back for a few weeks extra work to help them out on something.' He laughed somewhat bitterly.

'Really?'

'Yes. I was all set to spend my days birdwatching and reading... reading history books.' For a moment he pictured the volumes by his bedside, a history of the Wars of the Roses and another on Henry VII. Would he ever get to finish them? '… then my boss rang up and said can you come back for a week or two to … well, never mind what. But it wasn't meant to be a big deal. Just tidy up a few loose ends was the gist of it.'

'So, what…? No, it's best…'

'It is,' he agreed. For all his training he was surprised by how tempted he was to confide. But, with the possible exception of Manjit, he had no real allies now and sharing was a luxury he had turned his back on when he had driven away from home, God, just over 24 hours ago…

'You're a bird watcher are you,' she asked, in a softer, more conversational tone.

'A beginner. I've always wanted to know more and there's a really enthusiastic guide at the nearest RSPB reserve. Gave us an amazing talk about cuckoos the other week.' This wasn't the moment to mention how those hours in the hides took him back to his days on surveillance jobs. 'Are you a twitcher?' he asked.

'I think I'm a birder rather than a twitcher. I can't tell one warbler from another.'

'Nor me. I'm better on the bigger ones.'

'Me too. I struggle with the SBJs.'

Small Brown Jobs. He knew that one. He said, 'They got very excited at the reserve near me. There was a short eared owl there for a few days. I went down three times. Never saw it once.'

She didn't respond. He chased the remainder of his supper round the plate with a fork, succumbing in the end to temptation and pushing the final mouthful on with his finger.

She looked at her watch? 'Do you mind if I put the news on?'

'No. Might do me some good to be reminded I'm not the only one with problems.' She laughed, which took him by surprise, then reached forward for the remote and flicked on the television. But the set was angled to be watched from the sofa David was sitting on so she moved over to sit next to him. As she squeezed down beside him he shuffled over to make room.

'That's alright,' she said, smiling briefly in his direction before turning to face the television. But they remained in physical contact. Diane seemed entirely oblivious but David had to force himself to concentrate on current affairs rather than the vanishingly small chance of sex.

The news was as bad as ever. The Americans were trying to impose their will on yet another recalcitrant area of Iraq. Generals mouthed the usual platitudes about avoiding civilian casualties. And the journalists, embedded with the relevant units now for weeks, seemed to take these assurances at face value. But their credulousness was undermined by the accompanying footage showing detonation after detonation blasting columns of debris into the air above the city. And whenever combat troops were shown, the cityscape they were fighting their way through suggested they had taken no more care for civilian casualties than had the invaders at Stalingrad.

'I'm not sure why I watch this,' Diane said eventually. 'It never gets any better. I suppose I feel I owe it to the people who are there, but we rarely get to see anything of them. It's just more generals lying about how many people they're killing. And these useless journalists lapping up everything they're told. And it's even worse when they're reporting on the British troops.'

The News moved onto sport. 'Do you have any interest in this?' she asked.

'No.' As the words left his lips he realised he would have liked to hear how Huddersfield had fared against Wrexham but before he could say anything more Diane had silenced the television.

David wondered if she just wanted to be left in peace but he had another go. He liked the sound of her voice, and the way she moved as she turned her attention from the television to him stirred the thoughts he was trying so hard to suppress.

'Mike said you've worked as an observer in Palestine. How did you get into that?'

He was starting to fantasise about her body, about her body pressed against his, but the grizzled cold war warrior schtick he generally relied on in these circumstances wasn't likely to work here. Perhaps the sound of her voice, the taste of whiskey and his imagination would have to suffice.

'I was part of the Ecumenical Accompaniment Programme. In the UK it's run by the Quakers and I was brought up as a

Quaker. I'm not a believer any more but you... it's a bit like being Jewish ... it stays with you. Anyway, I went to a talk by someone who had been an observer. You have to do that when you've been out there. Go round and tell people about it. It was 2004. A bad time.' She looked directly at him now. 'We'd failed to stop the war and it was all starting to go wrong in Iraq, and I wanted to do something... something that... helped. And, despite everything, in many ways it was an amazing experience.' Her gaze drifted off again. 'You'd watch someone's house being bulldozed and the next morning they'd invite you round for coffee in the ruins, to thank you for having been there. The people were absolutely amazing. But some of it ... it was hard.'

'What did you have to do?'

'We would do things like accompany children to school, because of the abuse they would get from settlers, or stand at checkpoints and observe the behaviour of the soldiers. The idea is that just by being present you can influence behaviour. Some of them didn't care. Some of them made a point of not caring. For our benefit. You'd see some horrible things.'

'Like what?' David wanted to know, but most of all he wanted her to keep talking. If they hadn't ended up on different sides...

'Abuse really. Old men, and women, being treated with a complete lack of respect. And they're powerless, and that's what's... You can't intervene, you just have to note down what happens and report back to the UN.'

And he saw an opening. 'I was working on domestic terrorism before I retired. And Israel was one of our bugbears. It was the subject the radicals always brought up. US support for Israel and Britain's refusal to take any sort of stand. And we had no answer.'

266

She didn't respond immediately, so he continued, 'What was the worst thing that happened to you?'

She had turned towards him when he asked her but now she looked straight ahead of her which made it easier for him to admire her without appearing to stare.

'A lot of the time the Palestinians are scared to work their land when it's close to a settlement. The settlers will come out and attack them. And the army will just watch. They won't intervene. Because there's a law that says if Palestinians don't work their land for three years in a row they lose title to it. But sometimes we go out with them and it will be OK. There was a farmer, Yusef, who owned a piece of land across from one of the settlements. He hadn't dared graze his sheep there for over a year … the last time he tried a very threatening group of young men with guns had come over and shouted abuse at him… they've all got guns, it's horrible… had come out and told him to clear off. Anyway, a group of us, a couple of observers… and some Israeli peace campaigners too…. arranged to go out with them one morning. We got there really early. It was one of those magical moments. Dawn. It was a biblical landscape, I don't know if you remember those illustrated bibles we used to have, but it was just like that, the hills, the sheep, the clothes some of the older people still wear. Although the houses were the typical, jerry built …. shelters almost. In some ways these places have a sort of Mad Max feel. Improvised water cisterns… solar panels propped up all over the place and... And everyone was so pleased to see us… I remember sitting there with a small cup of … really hot coffee as the sun came up, thinking this is what I came here for. Eventually we set off with the sheep. Yusef and his brother were nervous, I can remember Yusef's wife holding his hand and talking to him very quietly before they left. And the children had a real sense that something was up. I didn't have more than a couple of words of Arabic but you could tell they were excited too. Anyway it took us about an hou to get to the field. And of course the sheep loved it, because it hadn't been grazed for months. And I think it had rained a few days before so everything was green, much greener than you generally see there. And for an hour or so everything was fine. Yusef had started to relax, we'd brought food and I was thinking about maybe having a bite and something to drink. Then I saw Yusef tense up. And I looked over to where he was looking and there was a jeep driving down from the settlement. It pulled up about fifty yards from us and four men got out and came walking towards us. They all had guns slung over their shoulders. My colleague Neal, he'd been out there longer than me, he walked over to them, really just to say hello and explain who we were and what we were doing. They just barged past Neal and so I walked forwards so that I was between them and Yusef and his family.' And he could picture her, making her stand, and he realised his longing was not simply physical. 'For a moment or two they were slightly fazed by the fact that I was a woman. But they went past me too and one of them walked over to Yusef, put his head about two inches from Yusef's face and spoke... so quietly I couldn't hear what he was saying but Yusef was clearly terrified. Then they turned round and went back to the jeep and drove off. You try to find love in your heart for everyone, no matter what but sometimes it's so hard. Yusef wanted to pack up there and then but Neal persuaded him to keep going for a bit longer. The Israeli activists took photographs to prove he'd been on the land. Then we all went back feeling … deflated.'

'Well you got him onto the land for a while. That was something.'

'That wasn't the worst of it. The worst of it was that two days later the Israeli army turned up at their village, gave them a minute to get out of their homes and destroyed everything. Palestinians never get planning permission so they build without it and hope. We went back to have a look the day after. It was the only time during the three months I actually broke down. There was just rubbish everywhere. Smashed solar panels, broken timber... Yusef was incredible. 'We endure,' he said. It's what they all say. And his little girl was sitting there... I had to take a couple of days off after that. My boss was really kind. Said, 'Go and spend a couple of days sightseeing in Jerusalem. Have a look round the churches in the old city. But what do I see? Teenage soldiers with guns and helmets pushing young Arab boys against the wall, demanding their ID.'

And then Diane began to sob, very slowly, very quietly. 'Oh David... Why do we keep doing this to each other.'

The look in her eyes melted everything inside him. She leant a little of her weight against him and he put his arm around her. He felt more nervous of her reaction than he had felt since his teenage years. But it was all right.

'You did everything you could for them.' He liked her smell.

'Sometimes, it's all too much...' and she moved against him again and he ran his hand down her arm and took her fingers in his. After he didn't know how long she looked up into his face and he kissed her very gently, first on the forehead, then as she nuzzled against his face, on the lips. They kissed for a long time, as if anxious to test each other's seriousness before making any irrevocable move. David was torn between pent up desire and a desperate anxiety not to mistake a yearning for some tenderness for something more and create yet more trouble for himself. Perhaps, he thought, this was as far as they would get.

'Come upstairs David, it will be far more comfortable in a bed.' David felt a wave of gratitude flowing through him. And a longing simply for intimacy that took him by surprise.

There was a moment, as he undressed, when the awareness that she was a stranger to him in so many ways almost stopped him in his tracks. But when she turned to him, naked except for her shirt and bra there was a mischief in her smile and that was all he needed.

Afterwards, they lay in each others arms with a degree of ease that surprised David. His longings were uncomplicated. Her physical needs and desires he understood but still, she was Greenham and he was MI5. How could it feel so right? He asked her.

'I don't suppose we could ever make a couple,' she replied, 'but deep down, you're a good man. You've taken a massive risk to do something you think is right. And if I'm going to throw myself on anyone when the going gets hard and I need a bit of tenderness, it's got to be a good man. Especially one who isn't bad looking for his age.' And she ran her free hand through his hair and kissed him again very deliberately. David felt as if much of the weight of the day was being lifted off him.

'I don't suppose today was the worst it's been for you,' Diane said.

'No.' God no. Nothing like.

'What's been the hardest.' And, God knows why, but he told her.

'Ireland. I'd not long arrived. We were taking over informants from… it doesn't matter, but there was a big hand over. And it wasn't going well. There was a leak in our system, or leaks. And several of our sources were murdered, just after we'd taken them over. There was a story one of our people lost ten informants. And shot himself. But I don't know if that was true. Anyway, I was responsible for a man called Jimmy Doyle. Late twenties but he already had four kids. A bit of a chancer I thought. He liked the money. But he thought the Provos were idiots too. Playing games that got too many people hurt. He was the person who told me how people who used to come up from the south for a few days stone throwing then go back home with a suitcase full of condoms and make a packet on the trip. Anyway, he was scared. Because the IRA made no secret of what they were doing. It was written on the walls. "Touts will be shot." He was really scared. Wanted me to get him and his family out. Off to London. But we really needed him. He was drinking regularly with a very gobby IRA member, a relative of his, not a senior figure but someone in the loop who couldn't keep his mouth shut. So I had to persuade him not to run. I told him we were tightening things up. That I would keep his name out of the reports I wrote. And he trusted me. A week later they fished his body out of a ditch. And he had been badly tortured. I had to go out there to identify him. When I got there his body was still in the ditch. They had to wait until it was light to remove it in case it had been booby-trapped. So we stood there in the cold, waiting for dawn. There were soldiers standing round, everyone a bit nervous in case the IRA had set up any little surprises, and I felt they were all looking at me and thinking, "this is your fault." I'll never forget the sound his body made as they finally dragged him

271

out of the water and rolled him onto the tarmac, face up, his dead eyes rolling back and a black, bloody hole where the final bullet had exited. It wasn't him anymore. It was…'

To his surprise she held him tighter. And she said more or less what he had said to her. 'You did everything you could for him. He knew he was running a risk.'

He knew he should have stopped there but he went on. 'A week or so later we found out who'd done it, or at least the name of one of the people involved. And one of my colleagues in the RUC who'd also worked with Jimmy, said, 'We can take care of this. We just need to know when the army are going to be around.' The guy was someone on our radar anyway. So I checked it out with our liaison people. Said I was trying to set up a meeting with an informant. Needed to know when the coast would be clear.'

'And the RUC killed him?'

'RUC, UDF, it was hard to tell the difference in those days. But they killed the three men they found in the house when they got there. The target, his brother and some other poor bastard who just happened to have called round. And they thought this was great. Made it look more like a random sectarian killing than something based on intelligence. That was my worst day.'

He heard her deep intake of breath.

'Did you ever say anything to anyone?'

'No.'

'And you've lived with it ever since?'

'Ever since. I tell myself there's people who've done worse. I wanted to see one bastard taken out of circulation. I was new. I didn't begin to understand the depth of some of these people's hatred. But it can't be undone.' He sensed her withdrawing. 'So much for your "good man" idea.'

272

'I suppose I shouldn't have asked.'

'If you'd seen Jimmy's body... if you'd felt the guilt and the anger... But you were brought up to turn the other cheek for real. I was C of E and not very much of that.'

He felt paralysed. He wanted her arms around him, he wanted to recreate their intimacy, but he didn't dare make the move which would force her to make her feelings known.

'I can see how it happened,' she said at last. Tentatively he stoked her shoulder. She responded with the gentlest rubbing of her foot against his leg, but when he kissed her she barely reacted. They lay there almost frozen for maybe fifteen minutes. Eventually she said, 'the plan was for you to sleep downstairs with the gun. I'd feel safer.'

He collected his clothes without a further word and went down to the sitting room. He made himself reasonably comfortable on the sofa, with the pistol stowed under the cushion he used as a pillow. He had got his longed-for moment of passion, but at what price? And what he had not told her, what he had never told anyone, was that he had driven the car. He had heard the three men's final shouts of panic overlapping with the blasts of the gunshots that had ended their young lives.

He slept fitfully that night, woken two or three times from dreams that, just like the day before, slipped away as he tried to remember them.

CHAPTER SIXTEEN

He was woken early by Diane leaving for work. She said something about having some preparation to do for a class that morning and told him to help himself to anything he could find in the kitchen for breakfast. He tried in vain to gauge her attitude towards him but her words were few and her manner, he sensed, studiedly neutral. 'See you later,' he tried but he got no response.

He dozed on for another half hour, warm and very comfortable beneath the blankets, but wary of slipping back into yet another anxious dream. In the end it was a growing need to relieve himself that forced him from his makeshift bed. He risked a dash to the toilet without carrying the gun but once he got dressed he wedged it into his belt. It dug uncomfortably into his back, particularly as he walked, but unless it was on his person it was as good as useless. He wanted to check his phone for messages but ideally not here, not where he was staying. With the gun in place he went round the house, methodically checking the doors and windows were shut as securely as possible. Only then was he ready to think about breakfast.

There was orange juice in the fridge and some upmarket looking museli in a jar. He eyed the soya milk with suspicion but it seemed to be almost indistinguishable from the real thing. When she got back he would have to ask her what the point of it was, he doubted it was cheaper. It was a curious feeling to be rummaging through what was, for all their brief intimacy the night before, a stranger's kitchen, searching her cupboards for a bowl and a spoon, opening her fridge and seeing the trivial, but none the less personal, details of her life.

He was half way through the cereal when the phone rang. He still had a mouthful of nuts and oats when he answered. A man's voice, but not one he was confident he could recognise, told him they'd got a good price on the leaflets. No reference to the fact that they were getting more printed which was the formula that had been agreed, but it was close enough. They were coming over today. Well, he supposed it saved them both from any further awkwardness. He would have welcomed another night with Diane, but he was far from certain she would have felt the same.

They came a bit after 8.00. And from the moment he opened the door David knew what had happened. It was written on their faces. In the way they stood there. He could not begrudge Mike the note of triumph in his voice. He owed Mike. But he could have done without the look of smug triumphalism on Brian's face.

It was Mike who spoke first. 'Accessory to the murders of Kevin O'Donoghue, Martin O'Donoghue and Steven O'Malley.' The power of Google. 'Get in the car. We've found somewhere else for you to stay.'

It took David only a minute to collect his belongings. As he walked out through the front door to the waiting car Brian said, slowly, quietly, venomously, 'We own you now.'

David made for the front passenger seat. He imagined this was not the arrangement they were anticipating. He also guessed, correctly, that in their surprise, they would not order him to get out and sit in the back. It was a small point but it was worth putting down a marker. But he opted not to engage with Brian's look of annoyance. That would have been pushing his luck.

They set off in silence, which suited David, he was thinking hard. There was no point in trying to justify himself. Diane would have told them everything so they had already heard anything he might have to say by way of a defence. Maybe later it would be worth at least talking through the whole episode but how did their knowledge of what he had done change things now? They all still wanted to bring Frampton down. Plainly he still needed them and they understood that. But if they threw him to the wolves now they might lose their chance of getting to the bottom of things. So for the time being the logic of their alliance held. But if working together had been a struggle before it was going to be even tougher now. And as for what would happen afterwards, right now that question seemed to him impossible to answer.

'Who's my host tonight?' He did not want to make it sound like a joke but he did not want to give them the impression he was cowed. Brian might think they owned him but he was not going to make it that easy for them.

'We've found a house for you,' said Mike. 'One of our people is off on holiday. Says we can have it for a week. He's

276

told the neighbours you're a cousin of his up from London visiting a sick aunt.'

'Guy's babysitting you,' Mike added. 'Obviously you're free to walk out the door any time you want.'

In other words, "We own you."

It was a bright, clear morning and the sun was still low enough in the sky to dazzle them from time to time as the road twisted left and right. Before long they turned off the main road down a lane David was sure they had not travelled on the previous evening. After a mile to two it led into a suburban housing estate, all neatly mown lawns and net curtains, and after a few minutes more they pulled over.

'Will this do you Brian?' Mike asked.

'Yeah. Catch you later.' Brian got out and, as he shut the car door, he eyeballed David, wringing one last drop of triumph out of the situation.

'Did you bring him along as back-up?' David asked.

'There was no need for back-up,' Mike said. 'He just really wanted to see your face.'

David decided to leave it at that. Another couple of turns and they were passing through the edge of the town. Roads led off on either side into industrial estates where David imagined people living out what passed for normal working lives. He did not, even now, want to join their number. Better even this than a lifetime of drudgery.

Before long they joined a dual carriageway leading out of town and Mike accelerated to a speed that David judged was some way over the limit. He looked across at the speedometer.

'This isn't the day to get pulled over Mike.'

Mike looked back at him and David sensed his irritation but a moment or two later he slowed back down.

'Mike, if there's a lay-by pull over. Give us a chance to see if my contact has got back to me. It's early days but we're a long way from anywhere so it'll be safe to turn the phone on.' Mike nodded. Five minutes later Mike pulled into a parking area screened from the road by some scrubby undergrowth and a few poplar trees. There were a couple of HGVs parked up and Mike made to pull in behind them but David told him to drive on to the far end. 'That way if they notice us at all they'll only be looking at the back of our heads.'

He pulled the phone out of his pocket and switched it on. He could see a phone mast poking over the tops of some trees across the road but who knew whether it belonged to his network. His phone lit up and he entered his access code. The phone immediately displayed three bars then beeped to indicate a message. It could only be Manjit. He clicked on the message icon and began to read aloud.

'You don't half pick them. Dennis Taylor. SAS regular.' David sighed. 'What is it about that bloody regiment.' He carried on reading. 'Sent to train the KLA in 1998.'

'Who are the KLA, asked Mike.

'Kosovo Liberation Army. They were fighting the Serbs.'

'When NATO started bombing?'

'Before.'

'Before? Why?'

'You'd have to ask the Swindon Office.'

'The Swindon Office?'

'MI6. I have no idea what they were doing there. Causing trouble no doubt. Or training people to cause trouble.'

'You're not a fan?'

'When they laid an ambush... this was in Ulster... they had a nasty habit of shooting any innocent passers-by too on the off chance they might be involved in whatever was going on too. Tended to upset the locals.'

David looked up from his phone and stared straight ahead of him. The verge was littered with drinks cans and bits of paper and plastic bags. Immediately to his left was a gap in the vegetation where countless travellers must have pushed their way through to find a bit of cover and take a piss. The silence inside the car was loaded with Mike's unspoken accusation. 'I thought I was setting up one IRA man. Who had tortured someone I knew, someone I was responsible for, and then murdered them. If I could have my time again I wouldn't do it. But you don't get your time again do you. There's no way I can put it right. So that's how it is. There weren't any others. None that were down to me anyway.'

'You mean there were others?'

'You read the papers. Anyway...' He had no sense of Mike's reaction to what he had said. And he realised he did not just want a working relationship with Mike. He wanted Mike to like him again. He was going soft. He continued reading Manjit's text message, 'Strongly suspected of becoming involved in KLA drug trafficking. Recalled to the UK but nothing proved. Left the army by mutual agreement March 2000. Ended up in Iraq. Employed for 6 months by Four Square Security. Now thought to work for Global Protection Ltd. Had to be pretty circumspect about accessing this info. Uploaded your photo into the system along with a batch of material supplied by the US. Didn't dare follow any of the links in case it drew attention to my search.'.

'So what does that tell us?' Mike asked.

'It's exactly what you would suspect. Known to Lord Frampton, and Four Square Security but not currently, officially on their payroll. Just the sort of person they'd send after me if it's him and his business partners trying to keep a lid on things. But this is interesting.' He carried on reading from Manjit's text. 'Two days ago Will Anderson... that's the man who was managing my investigation into Frampton... came over to see Nigel... my old boss, who's also involved... with an older man I haven't seen before. Looked like he had a visitor's pass. They went off together for half an hour maybe. When Nigel came back he asked me if I'd heard from you. Very casual. Wouldn't have thought anything of it apart from all this. Stay safe.'

'So what does that mean?' Mike asked.

'It means ... it suggests MI5 had concerns about me even before I went on the run.'

'But you're sure it wasn't them trying to kill you.'

'Yes. Quite sure. That's not how it works. However...'

'What?'

'Well there's two possibilities aren't there. Either MI5 and Lord Frampton's friends found out I'm up to something independently, or there is some communication between them. And if they are talking to each other it might suggest there's people in MI5, or people MI5 answer to, who wouldn't mind seeing me dead.'

'How come?'

'If they found me at Pete's because of your phone call that looks like GCHQ, and somehow that information finds its way to Frampton. Who's not going to use it to try and kill me unless he thinks he's got at least tacit permission.'

'And when you say "people MI5 answer to" who do you mean? Who are you thinking of?'

'Yeah...'

'No. I mean really.' Mike asked. David shook his head. He had no idea. 'Jesus,' Mike said in exasperation, 'The system looks after its own doesn't it.' He looked around the lay-by like he thought someone might be about to leap out at them from behind the bushes. 'We're in some deep shit aren't we?'

'Looks like it.'

'Thanks a bunch.'

'You want to go back?' David asked.

'I've been fighting this battle all my life. Just never thought I was likely to get killed before.'

'Welcome to my world.'

'When were you ever going to get killed?'

'Every day of my life. In Ulster.'

'That was different,' said Mike.

'Feels pretty much the same to me.'

'Yeah, but ...'

'But what?' Somehow David felt he had the upper hand now. Maybe it was just that he had been here before. 'We've got what we came for. Let's move on.'

Mike turned on the ignition, nosed up to the mouth of the lay-by and negotiated his way back onto the dual carriage-way. 'Of course you know the other possibility?' David said.

'What?'

'There's a leak at your end. How many people knew you'd parked me with your son?'

'Two. No three. But they're all solid.'

'You thought I was solid. Just think about it.'

They drove in silence for a couple of miles until they passed under a gantry laden with cameras and David's brain kicked into gear. 'Whose car is this?'

'No one you know. No one obviously connected with us.'

'Are you insured?'

'Is that a major concern right now?'

'If we get stopped.'

'They'll just tell me to show up at the station with the papers. I'll get fined for not turning up but they won't find you.'

'And you're sure the car isn't linked to you in any way.'

'A friend of the wife's. From one of her women's groups.' Mike laughed in mock irritation. 'That's another thing we've got to thank you for. They kept out of this sort of thing before the strike. Now they're up to all sorts. Even now.'

'They knew their place before?'

Mike laughed more openly. 'I didn't say that. What were you doing in Northern Ireland that was so dangerous?'

'Running agents. Some of it was straight forward, criminals you could turn in return for dropping charges… that sort of thing… but those sort of people are only going to pick up gossip. The people you really wanted to recruit were the ones who were really deeply involved. Approaching people like that, meeting up with them after you'd recruited them, sometimes you found yourself in places you didn't want to hang about.'

'And this guy who died, was he one of those?'

'Not a major player no. He just knew people who were part of that world. Childhood friends. Cousins some of them. That sort of thing.'

'So how did you get him to work for you?'

'Money partly. They were mostly poor as fuck in the areas where the IRA were strong. Even an extra fifteen quid a week could make a huge difference to their lives.'

'You'd give them that little?'

'Yes. But Jimmy wasn't just in it for the money. He was smart enough to see all the killing wasn't doing anyone any good in the long run. He had a wife and four kids. At twenty-eight. He didn't want them growing up in a world ruled by the gun. Sometimes he'd hassle me for more money but then he'd start to talk about peace and ending the violence as if it really mattered to him.'

'So how did he get caught?'

'We never found out. But there was a leak in our system. Somewhere. Someone informing on us to the IRA. I thought I'd kept his name out of circulation but maybe the information he was providing was traced back to him. Once you suspect someone you just feed them a story no one else will have, just make something up, and if that story turns up with the other side that's pretty strong evidence your suspect is an informer.'

'Diane said he'd been tortured.'

'He had.' David could still see the blackened spiral burns from where they had pushed Jimmy's face down on the glowing rings of an electric cooker. Curls of burnt, blistered flesh. 'Then they shot him in the head and dumped his body in a ditch.'

As he spoke David was not looking at Mike but he heard his sharp intake of breath.

They drove on in silence. Half an hour later they turned off the dual carriageway and as they climbed a gentle hill the sun once again shone directly in their faces. David pulled down the sun shade.

'Is this our destination?'

Just up on the right. It's a quiet estate. Police shouldn't be around. The fridge is stocked. Guy will show you around.'

'Is he going to be there all the time.'

'Can't see any need.'

'Where is this exactly?'

'Sheffield.'

'Just to be clear Mike, what is the deal? I help you get to the bottom of what Frampton got up to and you don't … take things any further?'

'Diane's the one with the information… your confession. We don't control her. But she came to us, not the Police. If you're straight with us and we find what we're looking for I don't think she'd go to the Police. Not if we said you'd been straight with us.'

'Was I set up?'

'Nobody asked her to go that far. Perhaps she liked you.'

'I don't think she does any more.'

'There is one more thing we are going to need,' said Mike.

'What's that?' David asked. Bloody hell. How stupid. How naive. He almost deserved this.

'Wait till we see Guy,' was all Mike told him

They were driving through the housing estate now. Brown pebble-dashed semis, front gardens separated by low, generally neat hedges. There were beds of roses laid out in front of some of the houses and vegetables growing in front of others. It reminded David of his childhood. Mike turned the car down a cul-de-sac and pulled over at the far end.

'That's us. Number 7.'

Guy was waiting for them and had the door open before they were half way up the path. His greeting to David was a brief, almost unintelligible version of 'hello.' They passed down the hallway, to the kitchen at the back of the house. It was a strikingly neat room, with polished granite surfaces, shiny, varnished pine units and a pine table in the middle. The window in the far wall looked out over a well-kept garden, a small patio and beyond that a trimmed lawn and a shed. Two narrow borders down each side and chestnut paling fences keeping the neighbours out of sight.

'Tea?' Guy asked.

'Yes, milk no sugar thanks,' said David.

'Mike?'

'I'll have a brew, yeah.'

Mike took a seat at the table. David sensed they were both waiting keenly for the moment when they would ask whatever it was they were going to ask him. The kettle was obviously recently boiled and within moments Guy had poured out and passed round three mugs of tea. The only sounds in the room were the occasional clink of a teaspoon on a mug and the subdued hum of the fridge. Guy seemed to consider joining them at the table before stepping back and resting his behind against one of the kitchen tops. The two of them looked at David. No one touched their tea.

'What we want,' said Mike, 'is the names of all your informants from the strike.'

David said nothing, but his mind was racing. How much leverage did he have? Did they have any idea of the scale of the operation? How many names could he hold back?

'Thank you for not bringing Brian,' he said eventually. 'That would have made it much harder.' He offered nothing more.

'Look,' said Guy. 'No one's going to get their legs broken. But we're going round with our hands tied behind our backs right now. We're trying to ask around about Frampton but all the time we have to keep asking ourselves, "Could he be a nark?" You know. "Is it safe to ask so and so." And if we're honest, yes... we just want to know.'

Then Mike spoke. 'Some of them obviously we know already. Like you said, people spending money they shouldn't have. Asking too many questions. But we need the full list.'

David had no idea if it was true they knew anyone's identity. 'Are you going to take any... sort of... action against these people?'

'David, you're in no position to impose conditions,' said Mike. 'And I don't think I owe you any favours.'

'Yes, but do you want to be working with someone who would sell out the people who trusted him just to save his own skin? It's like you said Mike, we're in some deep shit. What sort of person do you want to be working with at a time like this?' He took a breath. 'People are weak. People like me are trained to exploit those weaknesses. Your people weren't trained. No one just offered their services. We had to seek out people who were vulnerable in some way and we knew how to do that. And how to exploit their weakness. They shouldn't be judged too harshly.' It was the best pitch he could make but he knew Mike was right, he had no bargaining power. 'What I'm asking is that you don't tell the world. Just tell the people you have to tell. And there's no need to let them know you know.'

Mike looked over at Guy. David saw their eyes meet for a moment or two before Guy nodded, just enough to indicate agreement. To what exactly wasn't clear but there was nothing more David could do.

'OK.' said Mike. 'Here's a note pad. Give us the names. Where they were from, and anything else we need to know.' He pushed the note pad, and a biro across the table towards David.

David took the pen and paper with a cold, heavy heart, but there was nothing he could do beyond trying to conceal the depth of his defeat. The names came to him easily. Even after all these years. Tony Wilberforce. 45. Bearded and slow moving. Caught shoplifting in Rotherham. A hopeless thief the store detective had said. But two children to feed and a wife who believed too much of what she saw on the news and had little sympathy for the strike. A man who just wanted to do right by everybody and who couldn't bear the shame of a conviction. Richard Thwaites. 19. A pale face and a body not yet filled out into manhood. Played the trombone in the colliery band alongside his father. Arrested for obstruction, i.e. nothing, while picketing in Nottingham, bailed on condition he stayed out of the County and re-arrested down there three weeks later. Told he would be remanded in custody for several months if he didn't cooperate. Garry Edwards. Picked up in a raid on a pub. No great supporter of the strike and angry at the way the union officials allocated the few, paid days of essential maintenance work to their mates. He'd almost leapt at the chance to take the money. And so on. He dragged the process out as if that somehow made a difference, but within fifteen minutes he handed Mike a list of eleven names. Block capitals in the hope that it might disguise his hand writing. This was not a list he ever wanted pinned on him. Eleven of the twelve he had recruited or handled during that bitter autumn and winter more than twenty years ago. Together with their home towns or villages, the pits they had worked at and their level of involvement in the organisation of the strike. Even the approximate dates had come back to him with surprising ease.

'Is this all of them?' Mike asked in a tone just short of threatening. David was struck by the contrast between the bland domesticity of the setting and the predicament in which he found himself.

'It is. I did think of holding some back. But… I'm in too deep… Never mind what you've got on me. If we don't get Lord Frampton I'm in far more serious trouble from whoever's protecting him. No. That's all the names I know. Special Branch probably had some more. And there will have been people inside NUM headquarters but I wasn't involved in that side of the operation.' He took a mouthful of his cooling tea. He was done.

Jason Batterby was the only name he had held back. Jason had reported the harassment of his working neighbour, damage done to his car, abuse hurled at his children. David had got wind of his action and arranged to meet him. He was the only informant over whom David had had no hold. He had agreed to work for David only when David had given his word that his identity would never be revealed and he had refused to take any money. Beyond general gossip, almost all of what he had provided had related to acts of intimidation, things he said he would have reported to the police even had there been no strike. David baulked at handing his name over.

'Right,' said Mike. 'I'll get on it. I'll see you later Guy.' And without a word to David he left.

The front door banged shut and Guy said, 'Your room's upstairs at the back. I found some clean sheets. The couple next door, Jack and Sheila, they know you're here. Told them you were visiting this sick relative. You'd be working most of the day. On-line like, so they wouldn't see much of you. OK?'

'Sounds good.'

'But Mike said you'd need to be driven somewhere a good distance from here so you can call your mate without being traced?'

'Yes. But late this evening is probably best. Give him time. He won't have anything more before then. Got a message from him this morning.'

'What did he say?'

'He ID'd the man who attacked me at Steve's. But that didn't really help. Just another freelance thug with a murky past. But what's not so good is it seems that MI5 already know I'm in hiding.'

'Who told them that?'

'Exactly.'

'This tea's cold. Do you want another?'

'Why not.'

Guy took David's half-drunk mug and tipped the remains of the tea down the sink along with his own. He had his back to David as he rinsed out the cups with a scourer.

'What did you do it for?' he asked. 'You're not like them.' The sound of his voice was partly masked by the sound of running water and then the clatter of the mugs on the draining board.

'Like who?' David asked.

'Lord Frampton. And his lot. You can see why they'd want Mike locked up. See the unions trashed. But you're not ruling class.' He turned to face David. 'What was in it for you?'

'I was at Saltley Gates.'

'You? Were at Saltley Gates?' Guy looked around for a tea towel.

'As a copper. And whatever you lot say, it was mob rule. I saw people trying to go about their lawful business. Being stopped by a mob. Drivers having to keep pick axe handles in their cabs just to be able to do their jobs.' It was a long time since he had thought about that day. The terrific pushing and shoving, sometimes it had felt like he was riding a wave of bodies; the roar of the pickets every time the lorries tried to get through, moments of near panic when he thought he was going to trip and disappear beneath the feet of the crowds of miners and police. 'And with that tit Arthur Scargill, who was a known communist...' David sensed Guy's annoyance. 'He was. He was a member of the Young Communists, and nothing he ever said or did after that even hinted that he'd changed his views. And he'd organised the whole thing with the help of the local communists, and he was standing on top of whatever it was with his megaphone directing things like a ... military operation.'

'And what did you think,' asked Guy quietly, 'when all those trade unionists from across Birmingham, from all the engineering workshops and all the factories, came marching over the hill? Didn't you think, "Maybe this is the people. This is real democracy". Not the Sir Humphreys. Not Heath and all his rich friends in the city.'

David shook his head.

'No. When we had to... surrender... and lock the gates to the coking depot, I thought I'm getting out of uniform. Into Special Branch. Wherever. And I'm going to fight this.' It had been a bitter, bitter day. He remembered fighting back tears. Of shame, and frustration. The tears of failure. 'My father fought the Nazis. I wasn't going to watch everything he fought for destroyed by a bunch of thugs like Scargill.'

'You thought we were Nazis?'

'I thought you were fools. Lead by people... people who would ride all over the rights of anyone who disagreed with them. Just like they did in Russia, and Poland and...'

'And looking back now?'

'I still think I was right. And I'll be honest. I thought the same thing when I came here in '84. The same mobs trying to stop people who wanted to go to work. Like they were lawfully entitled to. And I've heard nothing to change my mind.'

290

David wondered if he should have held back. But he did not see any real need. And he didn't have any other story to tell anyway. He watched as Guy, who had forgotten about the tea now, pondered what he had said.

'These informers of yours,' he asked eventually, 'you must have talked things over with them. What did you think they were striking for? I mean, did you think they were revolutionaries? Or just sheep?'

More like sheep than revolutionaries.'

'You didn't think they believed in what they were striking for?'

'I think they believed. It was just a question of persuading them they'd been had.'

'And that's what you did? Or did you just threaten them?'

They had been grim meetings some of them. Some people didn't take too much persuading. Particularly later in the strike. But David remembered one man in his late twenties. Steven Ford. Married with two children. His wife was threatening to leave him. Move back south somewhere and take the children with her. Like so many others he had been arrested for picketing in breach of his bail conditions but David was threatening him with a charge of GBH too after he had broken a policeman's jaw in a scuffle. Two policemen were willing to swear it was Steven who had thrown the punch. David didn't believe them but that didn't matter. What mattered was the man was looking at maybe a year inside, probably losing his job after the strike and rarely seeing his children again. Even so, it had taken three interviews, over a couple of days, to bring him round. It seemed as if half his family were miners. He had a brother and a cousin on strike. He said his grandfather had been one of the last to go back to work after the 1926 strike. David had won him over in the end by focussing on Scargill's vanity and authoritarian style, presenting him as someone wholly at odds with the collectivist ethos Steven believed in so deeply. And it had hardly been worth the effort. Steven had provided him with limited intelligence and had done so grudgingly. He had missed meetings, failed to follow instructions. In the end David had given up making contact. And there had seemed no point in carrying through on the threats of prosecution he had made. Had he persuaded or threatened?

'A bit of both.'

'And when you saw all those police. Like Nottingham turned into a ... more or less a police state. Road blocks everywhere. People arrested if they set foot in the county. Thousands of coppers everywhere. Stopping everyone. Demanding to know where they were going. Great convoys of minibuses full of police coming up the M1. You never thought 'Maybe this is about a bit more than a few uneconomic pits.' You'd been in Northern Ireland. It didn't remind you of anything? I did two tours of Northern Ireland. It looked bloody familiar to me.'

'You were in the army?'

'Prince of Wales regiment 1972 to '77. I didn't fancy going straight down the pit at seventeen. And I'll tell you, when I came back... from the Emerald Toilet... nobody would believe me when I told them the things we got up to over there. They believed me right enough though after what they saw the police do in the strike. And the government didn't throw all that at us just to close down a few pits that weren't making enough money did they.' Guy was warming to his theme now. And David was trying to picture him, forty years younger, wearing the Queen's uniform and with a rifle in his hand, dishing out whatever it took to keep the peace. 'They were coming for the NUM,' Guy continued. 'We were the last line of defence against everything they stood for and they knew it. She said it herself. "The Enemy Within." They knew if they could beat us they could do anything they wanted to the working class. I'm proud to have been part of that. I knew what I were fighting for. And so did the thousands of the lads I fought alongside. Maybe some of them were sheep. There were plenty didn't pull their weight. But no. We knew what we were doing.'

David guessed the suggestion he had been fooled had stung Guy. There was a hint of anger in his voice. But David had been stung too. The way Guy had stressed the words 'we' in his final sentence had carried the clear implication it was David who was the sap, no more than a hired thug doing the dirty work for an unprincipled, ungrateful elite.

'I was here for … everyone who didn't want to be bullied into striking… by a union so scared of its own membership it never had a ballot… it had to rely on intimidation to bring people out. And I was here for all the people whose jobs depended on the coal. And for everyone who'd voted for a government that was going to stand up to people like Arthur Scargill. Guy, I was there on some of those picket lines. I saw the hatred, I saw people throwing bricks at the buses taking people into work. There's no way that's right.'

'I'll tell you what's not right. Scabbing.'

'People have a right to work.'

'People don't have a right to work. They need to work. To pay their bills. Feed their families. Nobody went in because they wanted to exercise their right to dig coal. They went in 'cos they were desperate. Hadn't paid the electric for six months. Everything on HP had been repossessed. They'd no food. But they still had no business going back.'

'What right do you have to tell a man he can't work if that's what he chooses to do.'

'You said your dad fought the Nazis. Did the government come round to his house back then and say "we seem to have a war on. Would you like to take part?" Did they fuck? No. They said "We're at war. Here's your orders." This was no different. We had the most right wing government in years fighting us with all the forces of the state. Those bastards were set on crushing everything generations of workers had fought for. You had the BBC, the newspapers, all lying through their teeth. Coppers by the tens of thousand. Everywhere. It was war. You didn't get to chose to take part.'

'That's not how I saw it,' said David.

'So why are you here David. Eh? You're here because Lord Frampton,' he stressed the word "Lord", 'Lord Frampton, or one of his cronies, had one of your mates killed. One of your mates who spent his life working for the establishment. And when you get too close to finding out what was going on MI5 pull you off the case. And now they're trying to kill you. And you still don't know which side you're on. You need to wake up son.' Guy got to his feet and stood over David in triumph, his anger apparently dissipated by the sense that he had made an unanswerable case. David looked back up at him, outwardly impassive.

'I was going to make us a cup of tea,' said Guy. 'I'll put the kettle back on.'

Where now? thought David.

'And the joke is,' he continued. 'Who's protecting you now? Us. The people you fought against all them years ago. My old team, my section I used to call them. The four lads I used to go flying with.'

'Flying?'

'Flying pickets. Danny had a car, an old Cortina, and we could fit us five in at a pinch. Used to go down to Nottingham week after week. Watched each other's backs. We had it all worked out. Ordnance Survey Map, compass, torches. Never used the M1. Not after the first week. We didn't always get through. But we were better than most. Used the side roads, farm tracks sometimes. One day, on the picket line, a snatch squad tried to grab one of us. We gave them such a battering they had to send another snatch squad in to rescue them.'

'And all for what?' David asked.

'We turned some back. Specially early on. And we were supporting the ones who'd had the courage to come out with us. And we were tying down the police too. It was costing the government a fortune. Piling on the pressure.'

'They loved you for that. The police. All that overtime. I knew one policeman. Made so much money from the strike he built himself an extension. Called it the Scargill Wing. They didn't want it to end.'

'Anyway, it's one of those lads from my squad. This is his son's house. That's how we got it. And they're all still solid. I've told them all. Something's come up. Might need you. They'll be right behind you… right behind me, if we need them. Not like your people. Here's your tea.'

'You've got a point there,' said David, despite himself. 'It's never really gone away has it.'

'What, the strike?'

'Yeah.'

'It never will. I got a phone call last week from my grand daughter. Really made up. She'd got a job. In a call centre. Minimum wage. Eight hours a day being screamed at down the phone by poor bastards who've been messed about by their privatised gas supplier or whoever. And the bosses

295

timing her toilet breaks. And she was happy. Happy to have got the job. That's what Thatcher did to us. The decent jobs. The respect. All gone.' He sat back in his chair. His tone was almost wistful now. 'We never thought they'd close down the whole industry like they have. We thought they were planning to shut down some pits then privatise the rest. And we knew what privatisation meant. Lower pay. Worse conditions. Cutting corners on pit safety. Union rights under attack. It would have been back to the old days. We weren't having that.' He looked round as if hoping to find something. 'I should have got some biscuits.'

'It all went anyway. It's all gas turbines and windmills now,' said David.

They finished their tea in silence.

'Look, what do you want to do?' Guy asked eventually. 'You need a lift out somewhere to check for messages tonight. What sort of time?'

'Ten maybe. Does that work for you?'

'That'll do. Do you need anything else?'

'I'm fine,' said David. 'It's OK to use the radio and TV and everything?'

'No problem. And the Wifi code is by the router in the front room. Well, I'm off. We can stop off at a shop tonight if you think of anything.'

'OK, and Guy?'

'Yeah.'

'Don't tell your section anything more will you. It's need to know in this game. All the time.'

'Right.'

When Guy had left David took his bag upstairs. The bedroom belonged to a boy, he guessed in his early teens. There was a single bed and a small desk in the corner laid out for homework, a large poster of the current Sheffield Wednesday team on one wall and another poster of Hermione from the Harry Potter films on the wall above the bed. Next to the bed was a small bookcase with a couple of Airfix models and maybe twenty paperbacks on its shelves. David spent a couple of minutes looking out of the window. From here he could see into the neighbouring gardens and he made a mental note of the layout. In the event of any excitement he wanted to have a clear idea of the possible exits. He checked out the other rooms both upstairs and downstairs then took up a position on a sofa in the front room, away from the window but with a view down the street. He placed the gun on the floor within easy reach but out of sight from anyone entering the room from the hall. Then he got out his laptop. It was brand new, bought for cash and never previously connected to the internet. When he had finished setting it up he typed in the wireless key and started googling. This aunt he was visiting needed to be as real as possible, and that meant a real disease, a real hospital and everything else that might come up in a casual conversation with a neighbour. Work, he hoped, would allow him, for a little while at least, to push to one side the sense of failure and defeat that was threatening to overwhelm him.

This time it felt more like a summons than an invitation. And a summons to a bench in Saint James Park at that. No more cosy chats in the club it would seem. It was mid-afternoon. Clouds pushed past the sun, blocking it out for minutes at a time, but even when it shone there was little heat in it now. And each gust of wind ripped a few more leaves off the plane trees lining the Mall. It took him back to a November day in 1974. Remembrance Sunday. He was back from Ireland on leave and his father had come up to London for the ceremony at the Cenotaph. He had felt proud to stand beside his father that day, and he had enjoyed the pride his father had so obviously felt at being accompanied by a son in uniform. On their slow walk back up The Mall towards Victoria station they had been acknowledged by ex-servicemen bearing medals awarded for service in all corners of an Empire whose memory had not yet gone cold and acknowledged too by younger men in uniform whose experience of combat was limited to the same wretched streets of Ulster he knew so well. His father never made it to the Cenotaph again. His mind had started to slip away soon afterwards but it took him another six years to die. And on occasions when it had pained Frampton too much to see the man he had known reduced to a shell of his former self he had thought back to that walk down the Mall and taken some comfort from it.

And he tried once more to take comfort from it as he awaited what was bound to be an uncomfortable conversation.

It didn't help that Peter was late. Or that he made no apology.

'Alex. You're to call your people off.'

'Peter, this could be the end for me.'

298

'I'm not here to negotiate. You have had your chance. But your credit is spent. After what happened our credit is substantially diminished too.'

'He won't talk.'

Peter's tone was one of icy exasperation 'Apparently half the street was involved. And your man was all over the place.'

'He's solid.'

'I've seen the transcript of his interview. He was a mess. In any event, if they track David Nixon down again they're not going to risk telling us where he is in case we tell you. It's over.'

'What if they find...'

'We'll cross that bridge if we ever come to it.'

'If I go down...'

'Alex, nobody's going down.'

Frampton hadn't intended to threaten, he had surprised himself. But he was glad he had because what he read into the dismissiveness of Peter's response was, 'If push comes to shove we'll hang you out to dry.'

Peter too seemed to have felt that he had let something slip. His tone became conciliatory.

'We still have clout. If ... it starts to look difficult we will be right behind you. We can fix things.' Then more breezily, 'But that's jumping the gun. We're up against one renegade MI5 employee...renegade retired MI5 employee... and a couple of northern agitators whose best days are far, far behind them. I don't think you've too much to worry about.'

"You". Not "We", Frampton thought. Out loud he said. 'Understood.'

'Good. I'll be in touch.' And with no more than that Peter left.

Frampton watched him walk away in the direction of Whitehall. No hint of concern in his demeanour. And a cold, consuming anger swelled across Frampton's chest. You have lived a life of privilege and ease, pushing money round the city, exerting influence in cabinets and boardrooms. While I've run the risks. Done the dirty work you don't want to acknowledge. And at the first hint of trouble you'll cut me loose. That's not how it works.

When Peter was out of sight he moved. He had learned his tradecraft thoroughly. He picked a circuitous route and he walked for forty minutes before he was satisfied there was no one on his tail. Then he found a phone box and dialled a number from memory. He spoke a few words into the receiver and replaced the handset. Exactly four hours later, after a similarly careful journey he called a different number from a different phone box. This time the phone was answered.

'It's been a long time.' God he hated that accent. If he never heard another Ulsterman in his life it would be too soon.

'I've got a job for you.'

'Pay well?'

'Well enough. Do you have anyone on the Mainland, ready to move at short notice.'

'There's one or two.'

CHAPTER SEVENTEEN

G uy came to pick him up around half past nine. He let himself in and placed a four pack of beer on the little table which stood in the hallway.

'Thought you might like…'

'Thanks. Yes. But let's get this call done first.' Were the beers a peace offering after their argument? A consolation for having been compelled to give up the names of his informants? Or just kindness?

'Thanks.'

There was a light drizzle, just enough to justify the windscreen wipers. There was something soothing about the sound of their rhythmic scrape and thump across the windscreen. Guy drove carefully, well within the speed limit, down streets lit up by orange neon and faced by buildings tinted orange in their glow. The few pedestrians they passed looked hunched and purposeful.

'Pull over and look for a tail?' said Guy.

'Very good,' said David.

'This man Eric,' Guy began when they were parked up. 'He must have been a good mate of yours for you to go this far out of your way for him.'

'No,' said David. 'He was... He was a bit touchy. A bit intense. Not everyone liked him. I got to know him better than most because I trained under him for a few months.'

'So it's just the principle?'

A good question. 'Murder's quite a big principle.'

'You could have gone to the Police.'

'They'd have gone to Terry, who would have told them he'd never said anything to me about Frampton. And that would have been the end of it.'

'You're taking a big chance chasing this up on your own.'

'I know that now.'

'What if we don't find anything?'

'That's a good question. No further news?'

'Not yet. Mike's going to see a couple more people tomorrow. And Brian might be on to something.'

'Yes?'

'There was a young activist, Shane Kemp, died in a car crash one night. He was coming back from Leeds. A band called The Mekons or something had been playing a benefit for us and he was bringing the takings back. But there was no other vehicle involved. Brian thinks it looks dodgy. He's looking into it.'

No other car had pulled over. There was nothing to suggest a tail. Guy looked at David, who smiled his approval and they pulled out into the traffic.

They drove on in silence for another fifteen minutes or so.

'How about here?' said David.

'Tesco's?'

'They should have a car park.'

'OK.'

The car park was largely empty by this time of night and the few cars there were were clustered round the entrance.

Guy drove towards the far end where the light from the full height windows of the shop front barely dented the darkness, and came to a halt.

'OK?'

'That's fine. Now let's see what he's got to say for himself.' If anything. He pressed the start button. He needed a boost now. The phone lit up. The clock face appeared then a bleep to indicate a text. He opened it.

'Call urgently,' he read aloud. He dialled and lifted the phone to his ear. Guy watched.

A dial tone. One ring. Two rings. Three rings. Then an answer.

'Hello David.'

'Nigel.' Fuck. Fuck. Fuck.

'You need to come in David.'

Fuck. A deep breath or two. David was struck dumb.

'David. Manjit is in Paddington Green Police Station at the moment. And this could all get very ugly very quickly. But if you come in now we can try and find a way through.'

'Who's trying to kill me Nigel?'

'No one's trying to kill you David. That was an error. And what did you give to that man? Come in now and we can sort this all out.'

'And if I don't come in?' There was a pause.

'David, I'm worried about you.'

'Drive!' David yelled. Guy looked at him in astonishment.

'Drive!' He started to pull the phone apart. For seconds his thumb nail refused to find the groove that would allow him to pull the back off the phone and extract the battery.

'Guy, they've got Manjit. They will have traced this phone. Get out of here…'

Guy drove. Skidded on the smooth wet tarmac as he turned into the exit then headed left up the hill towards a set of lights.

'Take it easy. They'll have someone heading this way in moments. They'll get all traffic stops for any sort of erratic driving...' His thumbnail finally slotted into the groove. He wrenched the back off the phone so hard the battery jumped out and clattered into the footwell. 'Just stay calm and get us away from here.'

'What did you give to that man?' Nigel had said? What was that about?

The lights turned red as they approached. 'No need to run them. We're almost certainly fine. They don't know what sort of car they are looking for. And they won't get anyone into the area...'

'Manjit's your man on the inside is he?' Guy asked.

'Yes.' He stared ahead without really seeing anything.

'He must have known what he was getting into,' Guy said as the lights turned green and they pulled forward.

'Yes. He did. But still... He's ...'

'Do we need to take a different route back?' Guy asked.

'No. No the way we came looked fine.'

'Was he a good mate?'

'Yes.' Fuck. 'Yes, he was a really good man. I liked him a lot more than I ever liked Eric.'

'So what do we do now.'

'Get me back home. Then we just hope that you or Brian come up with something.'

'And your mate?'

'Who knows.'

It was raining harder now. Between every sweep of the windscreen wipers the raindrops scattered more and more of the light from the street lamps before another pass briefly restored clarity. Fuck.

They heard the sound of a helicopter somewhere off to their left heading back in the direction they had come from.

'Do you think that's for us?' Guy asked.

'Who knows.'

Guy dropped David off outside the house.

'Let Mike know what's happened when you see him. But don't say anything over the phone.'

'Got it. Will you be OK?'

'Yeah.'

But he wasn't. He was far from OK. He hurried up the path to the front door and in the cold and wet struggled with the lock, listening to the sound of Guy's car fading into the background noise from the city. Alone now he opened the door into this house to which he did not belong and turned on the light. He looked at Guy's offering, still sitting on the hall table. Four cans of lager and a stolen Glock didn't have the same class as a revolver and a bottle of whiskey but they would do the job just as well.

CHAPTER EIGHTEEN

David woke up feeling awful. For just a moment he thought it was the beers. Then he heard once more the sound of Nigel's voice over the phone. "Manjit is in Paddington Green police station." He rolled over as if the world might be different on his other side but the pain and the anger and the regret were just as strong. Christ. Another life he'd ruined. He stared at the little book case beside the bed and tried to decipher the titles of the books. Half a dozen of them, plainly favourites, were so well read the creases down their spines completely obscured the lettering.

He wasn't normally given to self-pity but for just a moment he was tempted to keep lying there as if in hiding. He tried taking refuge in the memory of his hour or so of happiness with Diane but he couldn't fool himself about how that had ended. Finally, he took a deep breath then swung his legs out of bed and started to dress himself. Keep moving forwards. Just keep moving forwards. Once dressed he pulled one of the well-thumbed volumes from the shelf. "Harry Potter and the

Half-Blood Prince." He turned the volume over in his hand and started reading the blurb on the back.

"Harry has been burdened with a dark, dangerous and seemingly impossible task - that of locating and destroying Voldemort's remaining Horcruxes. Never has Harry felt so alone or faced a future so full of shadows. But Harry must somehow find within himself the strength to complete the task he has been given. He must leave the warmth, safety and companionship of the Burrow and follow without fear or hesitation the inexorable path laid out for him." Fucking hell.

He ate breakfast without tasting anything. Then he shaved, snagging his left upper lip on the razor and it took ten minutes for the blood to stop flowing. He wandered round the house, double checking windows were locked. He lay down on his bed, gazed at the ceiling and wondered how Manjit might have got caught. Or maybe Manjit had decided to give David up, had traded him in for a decent career move, and never set foot inside Paddington Green. He lay there for another hour or more, hardly thinking. For one blessed moment he almost fell asleep.

Around midday he dragged himself downstairs and boiled the kettle for some soup. He managed to get through the soup but the slice of bread he had buttered remained untouched. Outside, the sun was shining but a walk risked conversation with the neighbours and he didn't feel like doing anything anyway.

It was early evening when he heard a car coming down the cul-de-sac. It was Guy. David didn't get up. Just waited for Guy to let himself in.

'What are you reading?'

'Harry Potter.'

'Bloody hell. We could do with some of his magic right now. Look, Mike wants you to come over and meet someone. It's not exactly what we're looking for but he wants you to talk to the guy. See what you make of it.'

Another source, another pub.

'Evening David,' said Mike. 'This is Alan.'

Alan could have been sixty but easily ten years younger and maybe just as much older. What remained of his hair was shaved almost to his skull. And even without the leather jacket his face would have given a message of "Don't mess with me". They shook hands.

'What will you have?' David asked.

'A pint of Kronenbourg please,' and Alan smiled, revealing an unexpected warmth.

'Mike? Guy?'

They were on Kronenbourg too and David made his way to the bar. The barmaid looked up, then added the finishing touches to a text and came over to serve him.

'Cheers,' said Alan when David had sat down. Again that flash of warmth.

The nearest customers were several tables away. Only the occasional word of their conversation, work gossip of some sort, reached David's table and it seemed quite safe to talk.

'Let's hear it.'

Mike nodded at Alan.

'God. It's been a long time since I thought about any of this you know.' He looked around at his audience. 'After I got made redundant... I was a miner... I went to work on the building sites. They were always looking for sparks. But I could never keep me big mouth shut and I ended up getting blacklisted. Couldn't get work for months at a time. We didn't have a holiday for four years.' He made it all sound like a joke, an detail of ancient history. 'In the end the wife said, if you don't get your head down and earn some money we're going to have a pretty miserable old age. So I got a job with a small building firm. Family owned. Decent enough in their way. I kept my nose clean and just got on with the job. And once that Tony Blair came on the scene I didn't want anything more to do with the Labour Party anyway. So I've been out of this for a long time. But you want to know about Chris Meadowes?'

'It's Lord Frampton I'm really interested in,' said David.

'Well let me tell you how it was. I was an electrician at Thurcroft in the strike. Went picketing regular like. I got lifted one day. They gave us all a pretty savage battering. Then I was questioned in the nick. Not questioned exactly but they … they wanted me to inform. They knew my history.' He nodded towards Mike. David looked to both of them in turn hoping for an explanation.

'Alan was a member of International Socialist then,' Mike said. 'Got arrested for… assaulting a police officer?'

'It was at an anti-racism demonstration. It was all bollocks, and they did me for resisting arrest too, because they knew who I was, and I got six months suspended. But when they questioned me at the nick they had my file from back then and everything, like they knew I was going to be on that picket.'

Mike looked questioningly at David. The truth was, given the phone taps and the informers, the police might well have known Alan was coming but David wasn't going to comment on that. Instead he asked, 'And did you agree to inform?'

309

Mike looked shocked at the suggestion but all Alan said was, 'Did I, fuck.' David realised Alan had shown no curiosity about who he was. Afterwards he would have to ask Mike how much they had told Alan.

'But what... what Mike and Guy wanted me to tell you about,' Alan continued, 'was what happened afterwards.'

'Yeah?'

'He didn't!' shrieked one of the women sitting at the other table. Alan looked briefly over his shoulder then, as the laughter behind him subsided, carried on, but more quietly now, like he was aware of the possibility of being overheard.

'What it was, was ...'

'The dirty bastard!' Followed by more shrieks. Alan raised his eyebrows and continued. "... as they were taking me back to the cells a bunch of coppers came past me, two senior coppers and a couple of civilians. One of them was this short arse in a three-piece suit. Gabbing away like he was cock of the walk. But looking at the photos I reckon one of them, the other one, was your man.'

'Yeah?' So far so good but...

'The thing is, and I was so messed up, cos they'd been brutal that day... I was so messed up I just got this weird feeling I'd seen him somewhere before.'

Mike and Guy leaned in.

'You know how sometimes... And it wasn't exactly that I'd seen him before, it was like a feeling that he was in the wrong place. When Mike showed me the photos it was just... yeah, I've seen him. And then I remembered where I'd seen him before. I reckon I think it was in the Black Horse one night, years before. He was asking after Chris Meadowes...'

'I've heard that name,' said David. 'Who is he?'

'He's the fat bastard who went missing,' said Mike. 'In 1975.'

'And ran off with all the money?' David asked.

'The very one,' said Guy.

'How sure are you?' David asked Alan. 'That it was the same person.'

'I wouldn't want to bet my life on it. But why would I get that feeling, if it wasn't. You know, I had a lot of other things on my mind right then.'

'And what do you remember about meeting him at the Black Horse?'

'We chatted for a couple of minutes, maybe a bit longer. I can't remember why he said he was looking for Chris. And if Chris hadn't gone missing later on I wouldn't have thought anything more of it. But when we realised what had happened it just nagged at me a little.'

'This man went to a public school and then Sandhurst. He must have stuck out like a sore thumb in the Black Horse,' said David.

'There were all sorts involved in those days. Look at Vanessa Redgrave. Tam Dalyell's some bloody highland laird but he knows what's going on. Just because this man didn't have a flat cap and a whippet, didn't mean he wasn't on the level. And Chris knew all sorts. He was treasurer of the NALGO branch. He went to conferences and all that sort of stuff. He even tried to get adopted as a candidate once, for Parliament like, but there was no way he was ever going to be picked. He was far too left wing, even for those times. But he was one of those people who knew everyone so... But yeah, all the same I had this doubt.'

'Did you mention it to the police.'

'No. I think I mentioned it to a couple of people. Maybe even to you Mike? No? But you know, they just said, don't bother. It didn't amount to anything and we didn't want anything more to do with the police than we had to.'

'And how much money did he run off with?'

'It were about a hundred and fifty grand weren't it Mike?'

'About that, yeah.'

'And where did all this money come from? It was just a union branch. That sounds like a lot?'

'Yes,' said Mike. 'We'd started a campaign for the reinstatement of three of our branch members who'd been sacked for abuse of the council's facilities. It was stupid stuff. They'd been doing branch copying at work and they'd done a lot. They were taking the piss, no doubt, but they were sacked 'cos they were good, hard-working trade unionists.'

'There was a bit more to it than that,' said Guy. 'It was all to do with the internal politics in the Labour Party. They were on one side and most of the councillors were on the other, so they took the opportunity to get rid of them. Anyway we had an appeal for financial assistance and after he's disappeared it turned out we had had a couple of really big donations from foreign trade unions and Chris... just couldn't resist the temptation.'

And a chill ran through David's body. He got a cold, certain feeling in the pit of his stomach. His eyes glazed over and he only half heard Mike saying, 'David. What is it?' He didn't answer.

'David? What?'

'Alan. Thanks. I need to discuss this with Mike and Guy.'

'Alan's on the level,' said Guy.

'Does he know who I am?'

'Pretty much,' said Guy.

'That's not how it's supposed to work Guy. OK.' David looked round to reassure himself no one could overhear.

'Chris didn't run off with the money. Chris is dead. Lord Frampton killed him.' And another moment of clarity kicked in. 'Jesus. There's a tape.'

'Slow down David. What tape? How do you suddenly know all this?'

'The money. That's what MI5 do. They did it to John Hume in Northern Ireland, they did it to Scargill during the strike. Unexplained payments to make someone look dodgy. Lord Frampton must have killed Chris Meadowes then the money was moved in and out of the branch account to make it look like that was why he disappeared.'

'Why the fuck would anyone want to kill Chris?'

'I don't know,' said David. It was a fair question.

'What did you mean by "a tape"?' Guy asked, as if he thought David was deliberately changing the subject.

'Because that would explain why Eric was involved. Eric was a specialist in recording. Phones, meeting rooms, whatever. And his house was burgled during the funeral. It happens. There are people who do that. But it's too much of a coincidence here. Look, there was some really weird stuff going on in the mid 1970s. Spycatcher and all that? And it was ridiculed when the book came out. But it wasn't all nonsense. I missed out on most of it because I was in Northern Ireland but there were definitely people making preparations, putting out black propaganda, preparing the ground … look we were terrified of what you lot were going to do. That's why Mike… I did what I did and … it never came to anything, but people were making plans.'

'For what?' Alan asked.

313

'A coup. Well not exactly a coup, but people felt there was a real risk that everything would get completely out of hand, the unions would bring everything to a complete halt and the army would have to step in. And they were making preparations. You remember General Walker and GB75? His army of volunteers who were going to step in and come to the assistance of the ... well obviously it was going to be the army wasn't it? But that was just what was happening in the open. There was a lot more going on behind closed doors. I wasn't really involved. Like I say, I was in Northern Ireland. And I was a new boy but I had a sense of what was happening. And I met Lord Frampton a couple of times in Northern Ireland and he was close to the people who were... on that wavelength.'

'This tape,' said Guy.

'Eric and Terry, I'd always assumed they were in the know. They were part of that clique. And shortly before Eric was killed Lord Frampton took £20,000 out of his bank account in cash. Now I think that was to pay Eric off. Eric even told me he's come into some money just before he died. Eric must have been involved in the killing somehow and he must have recorded Lord Frampton making some sort of admission, and he must have... he must have read about the small fortune Lord Frampton was making, and thought... Eric's wife was sick. She needed constant care. It was expensive and there was Lord Frampton with all the money you could possibly want. Jesus.'

'Why pay him and then kill him?' Mike asked.

'Pay him to buy time. Then kill him because you know he will come back for more, or he did come back for more. I don't know.'

'So who's got the tape now?' asked Alan.

314

'An interesting question Alan.' David took a couple more deep breaths. 'Terry was frightened. Very frightened. So he must have known that Eric was killed for bringing this subject up with Lord Frampton. That must mean that Eric at least discussed with Terry what he was going to do. There's no other way he would have connected Eric's death with Lord Frampton.'

'Unless Lord Frampton threatened Terry after Eric started blackmailing him?' said Mike.

'Could be,' said David, 'but I doubt it. Eric and Terry were a team. I reckon Eric discussed what he was going to do with Terry. Maybe even suggested they both asked for something. I don't know.'

'So what do we do now?' Guy asked.

'I think we have a chat with Terry. They might have found the tape in Eric's house. But he wouldn't necessarily have wanted to keep it there. Or he might have kept a copy somewhere else. And if he let anyone else know, who else would he have told? There's a good chance Terry knows something more. In fact, I'll bet he's got a copy of the tape. If Eric had any sense he would have had a back-up copy as insurance.'

'Do we go and see him?' Guy asked.

'I think we do. But I'll make a call first.'

'Now?' asked Mike

'No. We need a new SIM card. And it's best to make the call at some distance from here. And what we should do is buy him a phone first thing tomorrow morning and courier it down to him. We can get some hooligan on a motorbike to get it to him before lunchtime. But if I can persuade him are you all up for a trip down to Warwickshire tomorrow evening?'

Everyone nodded their agreement.

'Here's the cash,' said David. Can I leave it to one of you to get the phone to him. I'll give you the address. And put in a note saying turn it on this afternoon.'

'No problem,' said Mike. 'Do you want another pint David?'

CHAPTER NINETEEN

Late the next morning Guy picked David up from the house to go shopping.

'You got a phone to Terry?' David asked.

'Yup. Courier texted us to say he'd signed for it about an hour ago.'

In town they picked up another pay as you go SIM card and another phone from a kiosk near the high street. The young man behind the counter was eager to help but David struggled with his combination of Yorkshire and Indian accents. After a couple of false starts he also bought an adaptor to charge the phone from the car's cigarette lighter.

'Why buy another phone,' Guy asked. 'Why not just swap the SIM card?'

'They can detect the type of phone you are using. Use a different type of phone and it's harder to connect the calls.'

'Sneaky buggers.'

'You don't know the half of it.'

'Where do you want to go to make the call?'

'Let's head West again. That way, if they do manage to connect the calls it will look like I'm making short trips from a base over that way. OK?'

'You're the boss.'

On their way back to the car they bumped into one of Guy's neighbours, a woman in her fifties with improbably blonde hair, pulling an empty tartan shopping trolley in the direction of the shops. Guy attempted to introduce David but had plainly forgotten his cover name.

'David Charlton,' he said, holding out his hand. 'I'm just up here for a few days. My aunt's in the Royal Hallamshire, recovering from a stroke.'

'They're very good in there,' the neighbour reassured him. 'They looked after my dad so well when he had his fall.' She placed her hand on David's forearm. 'She'll be getting the best care you could wish for.'

'She's in the Royal Hallamshire is she?' said Guy once they had parted.

'Yes, and her name is Dawn.'

'Surname?' Guy asked.

'Don't worry about that, just try to remember my name. I'm still David, but David Charlton. OK?'

'Sure. David Charlton,' Guy repeated more or less to himself.

'The Royal Hallamshire is where they took my wife,' he added. 'She had a stroke too.'

Oh fuck. 'I'm sorry.'

'You weren't to know. Three years ago. Not a day goes by...'

And out of nowhere a wave of grief descended on David.

'You all right?' Guy asked.

David found he couldn't speak. He took a deep breath or two. 'I lost someone. The other day.' He took another breath. 'But it's all right.'

Guy gently, briefly, put a hand on his shoulder.

'Just head west?' said Guy when they got back to the car. David nodded. 'It'll take the phone twenty minutes I guess to get up a decent charge. Then we can just pull over anywhere we get a signal.'

They turned out of the car park and almost immediately found themselves queuing at a red light.

'I've been thinking about Chris,' said Guy. 'All these years I've thought of him as a... low down... thieving bastard. He was a good man. Liked to be someone. Liked being on all the committees, knowing everybody. But his heart was in the right place. And for thirty years his name has been mud. Wonder where his body is. Probably out on the moors somewhere. Or dumped in a mineshaft. It'd be good to find it. Do something to make up for all the... the injustice of it all.'

'At least now you know.'

The light ahead turned to green and the cars in front started to move forward. They made it right to the front of the queue before the traffic lights turned red once more.

Guy continued. 'Then I was thinking, should I be happy that he wasn't a bastard after all, or sad that he's dead, not alive somewhere, enjoying his ill-gotten gains.'

'Both I suppose.'

'It's a fucked up world.'

After another set of lights or two the traffic moved more freely. 'Out towards Queensbury sound OK?' Guy looked across at David.

'Anywhere west will do.'

After a few minutes silence Guy asked, 'So how does it feel to have come over to the dark side?'

David laughed quietly. 'This is the dark side is it?'

'Took some balls to knock on Mike's door like that.'

'What was he going to do?'

'Clout you. For all you knew.'

'Maybe. I don't know.' David gazed at the shops they were passing, two estate agents, a phone shop, a queue of weary shoppers waiting for their bus to take them home. 'I thought there were rules… things we didn't do. Maybe there were. Maybe things have changed.'

'Things haven't changed. They've brought the army in before. Killed three miners at Featherstone and two more at LLanelli. Whenever things looked like they might really change. It's always been like this.'

David checked the phone to see how far it had charged.

'Any signal?' Guy asked.

'Haven't put the SIM in yet. No point in giving them any more data than we need to. I'll give it another ten minutes then we can see about finding somewhere to call from.'

'Right you are.'

And ten minutes later, with the battery at least a third charged, David inserted the SIM card. The phone blinked a couple of times then displayed a maximum strength signal. 'Pull over anywhere,' said David. A few moments later Guy drew in behind a parked lorry and David dialled.

'He probably won't answer the first time. Or the second. But he will pick up eventually.'

'Unless he's gone shopping.'

The phone rang and rang. Then it cut out. David dialled again. The phone rang until once more it cut out. David tried a third time. And a fourth. And just when David thought it was going to cut out again the dial tone ceased and a husky voice said, 'Yes?'

'Terry. It's David. We need to talk about the tape.' The outside world seemed to shut itself out. The only sounds he was aware of now were the laboured, hesitant breathing of Terry on the other end of the phone and the thumping of his own blood in his ears.

'What…'

'Terry, don't even bother. Don't bother about how I know. That's not important. What matters is that I know what happened to Chris Meadows and I know there is a tape and I know you have a copy. And now we just need to find a way out of this mess.'

He waited for a response. He could hear still Terry's breath. At least he hadn't hung up.

'Terry, I think there is a way out of this. Do you want to hear it?'

'Yes.' The voice was hesitant but at least it was contact.

'I can come down and collect the tape. That way you're no longer in the frame. Then I let Lord Frampton know that I and my friends have it and that we are going to the police. Eric wouldn't have tried to blackmail Lord Frampton with a tape that incriminated anyone except him so it won't make trouble for you. And once he knows we're the problem you've got nothing to worry about. How does that sound?'

'I can't. I can't do that.'

'What's the problem? I can come over, pick up the tape and you're off the hook. Terry, they ransacked Eric's house. They know it's out there. They know you were close.' That was a guess. 'It's only a matter of time.' Fake the authority David told himself. Fake the confidence. If you believe, he'll believe.

'What will you do with it?'

'Not your problem. But we'll make it clear that Eric recorded it. No one will know you had any involvement.'

There was a long silence. To push him harder or to wait? David decided it was best not to press.

Eventually Terry spoke. 'It's got to be just you.'

'Of course.' He could feel the weight lifting off his shoulders. 'Just me. No messing about. Matter of seconds and you're clear of the whole, messy business.'

'When would you want to come?'

'Tonight. The sooner it's done the better. OK?'

A hesitation, then, 'OK.'

'Right, I'll call when I'm about an hour away.'

He heard Terry mumble a soft 'All right.' David hung up.

'Poor bastard,' said David. He rested the phone in his lap and stared out of the window ahead of him. The wording on the back of the lorry in front promised "Total Logistic Solutions" whatever exactly they were.

'He took it all right?'

'He's absolutely terrified. I bet he's been cooped up in his house for the last couple of weeks doing nothing but panic. He didn't look too good at the funeral and it doesn't sound like he's doing any better now. Still it works for us.'

'How so?'

'If he was thinking clearly he might have called my bluff. I didn't know he had a copy of the tape. And he might have wondered why no one had burgled his house looking for a copy. For all we know they found the tape when they broke into Eric's house and they think they're in the clear on that.'

'You're a bit of a bastard aren't you.'

'Didn't Mike tell you?'

'Now you mention it…'

Guy executed a deft three-point turn, waved an apologetic acknowledgement to a van driver who had been forced to slow more or less to a halt, and headed back into town.

'You lot really thought there was going to be a revolution?' he asked.

'A lot of people did. Looking back on it I think a lot of it was down to half of MI5 and most of the army having spent most of their careers keeping the lid on dissent in the colonies. When I joined the office was full of them. They got back to Blighty and half of what they saw here was exactly the same stuff they'd been paid to clamp down on back in Bongo Bongo land. It seems another world now.' It really did. 'Did you ever hear of a Soviet defector called Golitsyn?'

'Can't say as I did.'

'It's a long, sorry story, some people say he was sent over by the Russians just to make mischief, but basically he persuaded a lot of people that Harold Wilson was a Soviet agent. Including half the CIA. And quite a few of my colleagues. Add that paranoia to the mix, student riots, strikes and everything, and if you're not careful you're going to see revolutionaries everywhere. Anyway, best let Mike and Alan know we're on.'

'I thought you said you were going alone.'

'That's another reason I don't believe he's thinking straight. If he was focussed he'd never have believed that. Let's go and see Mike.'

There were bolts on the door of the house Mike was staying in and an unfamiliar voice challenged them when they knocked but Guy was recognised by the gatekeeper and they were admitted. When the door was opened two substantial figures filled the hallway. David was ushered through into the kitchen without being introduced. They found Alan there too. David explained what had happened.

'You just bluffed him?' Mike said. 'What if he'd denied all knowledge of ... everything?'

'It was a risk. One more risk. But I've been playing this game long enough to trust my instinct.'

'And your instinct is that this is going to work?'

'It is.'

'Do you want to grab some food?' Mike asked. 'There's not much but there's some soup in a pan on the cooker and some bread and butter.'

'Thanks.'

Mike lit the gas under the soup and they talked through their options.

'Will four of us be enough?' Alan asked.

'The more the merrier,' said David. 'And two cars would be good. It's hardly likely to be an issue but if you've got a valuable cargo it's always good to confuse people about which vehicle it might be in.'

'What sort of people are you thinking of?' Alan looked a little perturbed now.

'It's just the percentages. I'm not expecting anyone to come after us, but if anyone does it gives us an edge.'

'What about Steve and Darren?' Mike suggested, his back to them as he reached into a cupboard for some bowls.

'Are you sure,' David said. 'Last time I saw Darren he wanted four hundred quid to drive me twenty minutes down the road.'

'I think he'll be all right. Steve says you made a good impression. And he's tough, and he's got a car. We can all look after ourselves, but let's be honest, no one here's going to be running a marathon any time soon are they?' He handed out bowls and spoons and started to serve out the soup. 'And he knows there's something up. It's not like we're bringing in someone new.'

'Do I know Darren?' Guy asked.

'I doubt it,' said Mike. 'Not unless you've developed a taste for the Class A's since I last saw you.'

'He's one of those is he?'

'I'll give Steve a call,' said Mike

'We need to speak to him, and Darren, face to face,' said David. 'Just check he's around.'

'Jesus,' said Mike. 'The idea that anything I say on the phone might be going straight to Big Brother is doing my head in. You spooks have got a lot to answer for.'

Mike dialled and they all waited in silence to see if Steve answered.

'Hi. You around?' Another pause. 'OK. I'm coming over. See you in half an hour.'

'Do we all go?' Alan asked.

'Yes,' said David. 'We pick up Darren if he's going to come and we get cracking.'

'When are we going to get some food?' asked Guy. 'I mean… proper food like.'

Mike scowled in mock indignation and David laughed. Sitting in a kitchen plotting and joking; it was almost like old times.

'We'll stop at a services somewhere,' said David. 'We've got to get down to Terry's before he has a chance to change his mind. Once we've got the tape we're in control. OK?'

The front door banged. David looked at Mike, whose expression changed in an instant.

'That'll be the wife.'

David braced himself.

The kitchen door opened. In walked a woman of about sixty. Five foot six perhaps. Black hair streaked with grey tied back in a bun and a pair of eyes that left no doubt as to the strength within.

'Afternoon Anna,' said Guy.

Anna looked round the table and fixed on David.

'Are you David?'

'I am.'

'I don't want you in the house.'

'I'll wait outside.'

'Finish your soup,' said Mike.

'How's that daughter of yours getting on Guy?' said Anna. 'She started that new job?'

'Not till next month.'

David drank his soup. He went as fast as he could without obviously rushing. It was almost comic. At one point he made eye contact with Mike. And he didn't imagine it. There was a fleeting, conspiratorial spark. As soon as he had finished he stood up and left the room. No one spoke exactly but Guy acknowledged his departure. Once outside David realised he didn't have the keys to the car. He couldn't bring himself to knock on the door again so he stood outside in the cold till the others had finished.

CHAPTER TWENTY

After the alarming events of the week before, Steve had taken refuge at a friend's house half a mile from where he lived. They scooped him up and, with three of them squeezed into the back seat, drove over to find Darren.

'What exactly is this all about?' Steve asked.

Mike explained. 'There's a bloke called Terry, lives somewhere near Birmingham. He's got a tape we want.'

'What's on the tape?'

'Somebody confessing to something. How much shall I tell him David?'

'Ideally, less than that.' David twisted his head back so that, from the passenger seat, he could just about make eye contact with Steve. 'Steve, this person we are going to see's got something we want. Something that... when we've got it... will put an end to all that nonsense the other night at your house.'

'That'd be good. Karen's asking why I'm staying at Jason's. She doesn't like me having Dean to stay there, which I can sort of understand. I've told her the cooker's bust but that can't go on for ever… yeah if we can sort this out, that'd be good.'

'Anyway,' David continued, 'this man we're going to see. He's really scared. I've given him a more or less sensible reason to give the tape to us. If everything goes according to plan we just have to show up. He hands it over and we come home.'

'No guns?'

'No guns. He's… he's someone I've known a long time. The worst that's going to happen is he's going to change his mind.'

'Yeah? And if he changes his mind?'

'If he changes his mind… he changes his mind. Well we might threaten to look through his place pretty thoroughly if you know what I mean. But we're not going to beat him up, or torture him or anything. But we turn up looking like we're not going to be happy if he doesn't cooperate, if you know what I mean.'

'Sure.'

Darren lived on the same street as Steve. He opened the door for Steve and looked irritated by the size of the deputation but allowed them all to pass. The house was another two up two down like Steve's, with a mountain bike in the hallway they all had to squeeze past. The front room contained two extremely shabby sofas at right angles to each other with a large, low table occupying the angle between them. This table was covered in the detritus of smoking; empty tobacco pouches, an Irving Welsh novel, with the back cover partly roached, at least three ashtrays, along with some broken CD covers, a couple of mugs, one half full of cold tea or coffee, and other less easily identifiable bits and pieces. A guitar with only four strings was propped against the wall.

Despite the fact that it was early afternoon a cloth covered most of the window and the light, such as it was, yellow and dim, came largely from two desk lamps placed on the floor. And on one of the sofas were seated two pale faced teenage boys, one with lank, dark shoulder length hair and acne, and the other with a crew cut of indeterminate colour and what looked like the remains of a black eye.

'Can we have a word with you alone,' David asked.

'Fuck off,' said Darren to the two youths.

The two rose silently to their feet and left.

'Have you got any plans for the evening?' David asked.

'I can't fit you all in my Fiesta.'

'What happened at Steve's the other night can be fixed. Tonight. We drive down to near Birmingham and we pick up a parcel from a colleague of mine and it's all over. We're not expecting any trouble but it would be good to have two cars. Two people under fifty. And two cars.' He decided it was best not to explain that the advantage of two cars was that it would help confuse any pursuers. 'Shock and awe.'

Darren looked up at them but said nothing.

Steve sat down on the unoccupied sofa. 'Darren mate, I can't stay at Jason's for ever. And Karen won't let Dean stay over at Jason's. And I can't pretend the cooker's fucked for ever. She's threatening to have her dad come round and have a look at it. And then I'm in a world of pain. Come on, it's a road trip. We'll get some tunes. It'll be a blast.'

'OK mate,' said Darren after another moment of two. 'But the old farts get to travel in their car. It's just you and me in the fiesta. No offence,' he said looking up at the others. 'I'll want me petrol money though,' he added.

'I saw you coming,' said David and handed him a hundred pounds in folded twenties.

'We off now?' Darren asked. David nodded.

'OK. I'll need a piss. And it'll take ten minutes to get my shit together. Make yourselves at home.'

'Any danger of a cup of tea?' Alan asked as Darren was leaving the room.

'Steve can sort you out,' said Darren. 'You know where everything is.' Then he was out the door.

They heard the sound of his footsteps on the bare wooden stairs followed by a door opening and closing somewhere above them.

'How many teas?' Steve asked.

'I'm not sure I'd risk it,' said Guy, looking round almost pityingly.

'I've never come to any harm,' said Steve. 'Does anyone else want a brew?'

'I'm with Guy,' said David. Mike shook his head too.

'Just you and me then Alan. Milk? No sugar.'

'Aye.'

And Steve went through to the kitchen. The others settled down a little awkwardly on the sofas, apart from Guy who followed Steve through. He returned a minute later, shaking his head. 'You're a braver man than I am Alan.'

'You really think we can knock this thing on the head this evening?' Mike asked.

'We'll need to make a copy of the tape,' said David. 'Or several copies, but yes, once we've got the tape and handed it over to the police we've done as much damage to Lord Frampton as we can. The people who are protecting Frampton won't be able to do anything more, so they'll stop coming after us. Who knows whether or not they'll then prosecute Lord Frampton. I bet there'll be pressure from certain quarters not to do anything. But we can send copies of

330

the tape to journalists. Put it up on the internet somehow. We can get the story out there. Will that do?'

'I suppose it'll have to. How do we handle it when we get there?'

'Let's talk that through when Darren gets back down here.'

Steve returned with two mugs of tea and handed one over to Alan. David watched the light that had managed to make its way through the window catch the steam rising from Alan's mug. Sitting in a small-time drug dealer's front room with a bunch of superannuated Trots and an unlicensed pistol in his coat was not quite how he had imagined his retirement.

'It's all right,' said Alan, after taking a sip.

'I told you you'd live,' said Steve. 'You don't want to change your mind Guy?'

'That's not a kitchen in there. That's a petri dish.'

Steve picked up the guitar and absent-mindedly plucked at the untuned strings.

'You still play at all?' Mike asked.

'Not for ages.'

'You were in a band weren't you?' Guy asked.

'Yeah. Half Tyke Half Biscuit.'

'What?'

'We were a Half Man Half Biscuit tribute band. More or less. Played at the Rose and Crown once. Weren't asked back.'

'Steve,' David said. 'I had a very brief contact with MI5 last night and they asked me what we gave the man at your house. We didn't give him anything. What...'

'Darren slipped him a couple of Es.'

'What?'

'When he was dragging him behind the bins he said. Pulled back the duck tape you'd stuck over his mouth, popped a

331

couple in and sealed him back up again. Said he thought it might do him some good. You know. Spread the love.'

David could think of nothing to say.

Upstairs a door banged again and they heard Darren's footsteps descending. He stuck his head round the door and gave Steve the thumbs up. 'Are we good to go everybody?'

'Come in a moment Darren,' said David. Darren stepped inside the room. 'Sit down. We need to talk this through.'

Reluctantly Darren squeezed onto the sofa next to David.

David looked around the room to make sure he had everyone's attention. All eyes were on him. 'We're going to see an old colleague of mine. He's scared and I've offered him a way out. But he's only expecting me. Maybe he'll have wised up by the time we get there but the fact is he may be surprised I'm not alone. Whatever he says, there's no negotiating. We all go in. I'll ask him for the tape. I know him well. I can probably talk him into giving it to us even if he fancies changing his mind. The most that's going to happen is that I'll suggest that if he doesn't hand it over we'll look for it ourselves. Go through his place. Thoroughly. But we're not going to beat him up if he gets difficult. If the worst comes to the worst we leave empty handed. Are you all happy with that?' He looked round at everyone. 'I want to hear you say "Yes".' There was a murmur which he took for consent.

'We'll head down the M1 and meet up at the Watford Gap services. We can get a bite to eat and then we head off in convoy. Darren, get Alan's number. But all phones off till we get to Watford Gap. I'll give you the address for where we're going Darren. Do you have a SatNav?'

'Yes.'

'OK. You don't put the address in the SatNav. There's a real risk that if you do that someone will pick it up, connect it to Terry and decide to come along too. Is that clear? You don't touch the SatNav unless, and I'm sure this won't happen, unless we get split up after we leave Watford Gap. Have you got a road atlas?'

'Yeah.'

'Bring that. Are everyone's phones fully charged?'

There were murmurs of assent.

'I can charge mine in the car,' said Steve.

'OK, but you take the SIM card out. Any questions?'

'Are we breaking any laws?' Darren asked.

'Like you'd care,' said Guy. Darren gave him a brief, angry glare. 'I'm on bail. For possession. I don't mind helping out but...'

'No,' said David. 'We're just going to see a friend of mine. It's fine.' Apart from the gun. If anything goes wrong and if the court doesn't believe you knew nothing about that then you're fucked. 'Let's go.'

It was a long two and a half hours down to Watford Gap. Guy drove. David sat beside him in the passenger seat. This time he had not claimed the position but Mike and Alan seemed to acknowledge that it was his operation now. Having been off the scene for so long Alan was enjoying the chance to catch up on news of old comrades. David recognised the odd name but had no desire to involve himself in the conversation. They started talking about an anti-racism march they'd taken part in, the one where Alan had been arrested.

'You were on that one too David,' said Mike. 'Do you remember?'

'Can't say I do.'

'You must do. You were there when Nick Thwaites decked that arsehole from the National Front, and it looked like it was all about to kick off.'

'Maybe. Vaguely.' He remembered it vividly. The chants of 'Nigger lovers,' the abuse turning to shoving and the odd bottle being thrown and how the police did nothing until one of the NF mob had taken a swing at Nick and Nick had felled him with a single punch to the stomach. And it was Nick the police had moved in on, until David had managed to usher him away. And most of all he remembered the seconds staring, face to face, with the first policeman who had gone for Nick, willing him to back off and wondering which side he himself was on.

As they crossed over into Nottinghamshire Guy started reminiscing about his days as a flying picket, pointing out where the police had set up road blocks on the exits in their efforts effectively to seal the county off.

'What they never tell you,' he said, 'is that before they brought masses more police in, we were winning. We were getting more and more of the lads to stop out. The strike was spreading in Notts.'

David remembered that all too well. And he remembered the sense of panic simmering beneath the surface in London, the fear that despite the stockpiles of coal, and for all their preparations, the conversion of coal fired plants to dual use, despite everything, the miners were going to win again. That was when he had been brought in. Nobody could face the thought of another defeat.

'That's when they starting just lifting people,' said Mike, 'for nothing. Just to get the numbers off the picket line. And that was just the start. By the end they'd do you for anything, stepping off the pavement, stepping on the pavement, walking on the grass, sitting on a wall. Some days nobody dared open their mouths. One week we were policed by plods from Wiltshire. Listening to that accent, all that West Country stuff, they sounded almost cuddly. Turned out the ones they'd sent us had cut their teeth beating the crap out of the convoy and they couldn't wait to get stuck into us. I never understood why they hated us so much.'

'Some amazing times though,' said Guy. 'So many good people. So much spirit. Some days the singing was...'

'Seems like ancient history to me,' said Alan. 'Another time anyway. Were you at Kiverton? Towards the end? That was grim.' His voice was different now. All the good humour David remembered from the night before had gone. 'The strike was crumbling. I remember one morning the lads being chased through the woods in the fog by those bastard coppers with the short shields and the truncheons and everyone who fell behind being given the beating of their lives. Mate of mine, Sandy, tripped and they were straight onto him. I could hear him screaming but I didn't dare go back for him. I just kept running.'

And there, to David's relief, the trip down memory lane came to a halt.

'Any sign of Darren and Steve?' Mike asked after a while.

'Not seen them since a few minutes after we joined the motorway,' said David. 'They're somewhere up ahead.'

They pulled into Watford Gap services a little before 7.00. The carpark was maybe half full. Guy nosed along a couple of rows looking for somewhere as close as possible to the

335

building before pulling up between a pristine white Range Rover with a personalised number plate and a dark blue Volvo with the back seats piled to the roof with duvets and packing cases. David got out, stretched and looked around but in the semi-darkness he could not immediately spot Darren's car. He took the road atlas from the shelf in front of the passenger seat and shut the car door. The evening was colder than he had expected. A couple returning to their car walked by with their coats wrapped firmly around them, their hands buried deep in their pockets and their heads hunched down.

'We'll find them inside easily enough,' said Guy, slamming his door shut. 'They're both big lads. They'll stand out right enough.'

'People hungry?' David asked.

The light and warmth inside the services was a welcome change from the claustrophobia of the car and the chill of the outside. But the noise took David by surprise. He counted three babies, all plainly disconcerted by their unfamiliar surroundings and making sure that everybody knew. A lengthy queue stretched back from the till at the cafeteria and, beyond the food counters, Steve and Darren had found themselves a table by the windows and were tucking into something that looked a lot like two Full Englishes.

'What kept you?' Darren asked.

'The speed limit,' said Guy. David noted the tension between the two of them but it hardly seemed mission critical. What they didn't need though was an unnecessary brush with the law.

'Darren?'

'Yeah?'

'Once we've done the job you can do what you like but for now… just take it easy.'

'OK.'

'Right, what's everyone having?' David asked in a brisker tone. 'Let's go and see what there is.'

'The fry-up's ace,' said Steve through a mouthful of sausage as they set off to join the queue.

Fifteen minutes later they were all back at the table.

'Cheers for this,' said Alan. He and Mike had followed Steve's advice. David and Guy were looking at two enormous pieces of cod and enough chips to keep them supplied in fats and carbohydrate for a very long time.

'My pleasure,' said David. 'Right. From now on we travel in convoy. We'll go in front because I've been there before. Once. If we lose you Darren we'll wait for five minutes then we'll press on. Only if we lose you will we try and call. Steve, for as long as you have us in sight don't switch your phone on. If we lose you at a set of lights we will pull over a hundred yards further on, somewhere where you can pull in behind us, and wait for you. If, and only if, we get separated and you can't find us again within five minutes or so put the SatNav on. If you've lost us we ought to be there before you. But in the unlikely event that you manage to get there first, don't stop. Drive past at least another hundred yards, far enough away so he won't hear you pulling up. Walk back to the house and wait for us. The one thing we don't want is him seeing a couple of strangers, particularly two big blokes, turning up on his doorstep unannounced. You got that?'

'Got it.'

David opened up the road atlas. 'See this village here? Terry lives just the other side, the road takes a sharp left-hand bend and his house is no more than twenty yards further on, on the left.'

'We've got the SatNav. We'll be fine.'

For the next little while they all ate in silence. David sensed his laying down of the law had killed the appetite for chat.

'This is different,' said Alan at last.

'What do you normally have for your tea?' Steve asked.

'I was thinking more of … I always fancied myself as a secret agent. All that excitement, foreign travel, man of mystery sort of thing.'

'You're living the dream now,' said Darren. 'Do you want that black pudding?'

'Have it. I think I've bitten off more than I can chew.'

'I'm just looking forward to being able to sleep in my own bed again,' said Steve. 'How about you dad?'

'I want to nail this bastard Frampton.' Mike put his knife and fork down. 'David, this mate of yours, Terry? He must be guilty of something too mustn't he?'

'Yes. But Eric will have been careful. There'll be nothing on the tape that'll incriminate him, or Terry. If Frampton ends up on trial maybe he'll try and take Terry down with him. But Terry's a pro. He's in a mess right now but he's unlikely to admit to anything under questioning.'

'You're not just sticking up for him because he's a mate?'

David looked up at the ceiling. He was aware that everyone else had stopped eating and was waiting for his answer. What was he doing?

'No. He can take whatever is coming his way. Me too, for that matter.' Nothing more had been said about his confession to Diane. He didn't want to spend the next few years in jail. But he felt just then … accepting somehow of whatever fate, or his companions, had in store for him.

'You got skeletons in your closet too?' Darren asked.

'Don't go there,' said Guy. 'Honestly…'

338

Darren raised his eyebrows but said nothing more.

Was Terry a mate anymore, David wondered? Right now what Terry was, first and foremost, was a route out of this… situation. He drained his tea and sat back to gather his thoughts.

'We should be going soon. It's about half an hour from here. Everybody clear what we're doing?'

Mike hoovered up the last of his beans. 'Yep. Let's go.'

Outside it seemed to David it was even colder still. 'Where are you parked Darren?'

'Somewhere over there, near that minibus.'

'OK. Wait for us by the fuel pumps and tuck in behind us when we come by.'

'Roger that.' Darren performed a mock salute.

'And remember. We're not at home to Mr Cock-Up.'

Darren laughed as he turned away.

The car park was noticeably emptier now. The Range Rover and the overladen Volvo had both moved on. As he got back into the car David felt a tightening of his stomach. This was it. Play his cards right and this mess would all soon be over.

He g dialled Terry's number. Terry answered almost immediately. 'Forty minutes… Yes, just me… OK.'

'You're a bastard,' said Guy, without malice.

'That's what got me where I am today.'

David looked over his shoulder at Mike.

'When this is over, if you like, I'll tell whoever I need to tell that I lied in court.'

After a moment or two Mike's face broke into a grin. 'You fucking would too.'

Darren fell in behind them as they passed the petrol station and together they headed South at a steady 70 miles an hour.

So many cars passed them at 80 or more that David started to worry they were making themselves conspicuous. At the next junction they turned off. Darren followed them round the roundabout, sticking a little too close in his eagerness not to lose them. Guy kept looking in his mirror, plainly worried that they were going to bump. Then the road straightened up ahead of them and Darren dropped back again. They fell into a rhythm. At each turning Guy would indicate well in advance and slow down, in truth more than necessary. Darren would move up uncomfortably close then back off once they had navigated the junction.

'I think he's taking the piss.' said Guy.

'Better that than get too relaxed and lose us,' said David, but it was starting to wind him up too.

'I think he just doesn't like being told what to do,' said Mike.

Ten minutes later they were passing through a sizeable village. Two pubs, an upmarket car dealership which seemed to specialise in second hand Land Rovers and, towards the end of the high street, road works which reduced the traffic to single file. As Guy went through the lights they changed to red. David twisted uncomfortably in his seat to try and see if Darren and Steve were following but before he could fully turn round Mike had managed to look back. 'They've stopped.'

'Fuck,' said Guy.

'Don't worry Guy,' said David, turning back to his front. 'Just pull over when we get to the other side and we'll wait for them. It'll be fine.' Probably.

There were a number of cars beyond the roadworks waiting at the lights for their turn to pass through but Guy found a space a bit after them and pulled over.

'Put your left indicator on Guy. Make sure they don't miss us.'

They waited for what seemed like an unnecessarily long time for the lights to change back again. At last they heard the sound of cars moving in their direction.

'Was that them?' Guy asked as the first car went by.

'I think it was,' said Alan, who was looking out on the right-hand side of the car.

'Bugger,' said David. 'Mike turn your phone on. See if you can get hold of Steve. Pull out Guy, we need to get on.'

'I can't, there's more traffic behind this lot.'

'Just pull out. Jesus. This is an operation. Not your driving test.' David took a deep breath or two. 'Sorry Guy. When it's clear. They're bound to work out they've missed us and then they'll pull over. It'll be fine.'

Eventually Guy pulled out. Round every corner David expected to see Darren's Fiesta parked up and waiting.

'Bugger. Mike can you call Steve.'

'I'm not getting any reception at the moment.'

'Turn right here Guy.'

'Do you think they'll have turned off here?'

'Fuck knows but that's the way. If they're paying attention to the map they'll be ahead of us. If not… I guess we're on our own. Just keep on. It's not far now. And keep trying your phone Mike. If we can still link up that'd be best.'

'I've got reception now. I'll call him.'

David could hear the dialling tone. He willed Steve to answer. But in vain. Then Mike got through to voicemail.

'What shall I say?'

'Tell him he probably missed the right turn a mile out of the village. Tell him to get back to us as soon as he gets the message. Guy, just keep driving. If we hear from them we'll try and link up. But unless he gets back to us we just press on. OK everybody?'

They drove on in silence. Mike dialled twice more but to no avail.

They arrived at another village, smaller than the last and boasting only a handful of streetlights.

'This is the village I was telling them about. Keep your eyes peeled. They might be here.'

They weren't.

'We should be about there now,' said David. 'Just round the next corner on the left.'

'Where's that useless son of yours got to Mike?' Guy asked, conversationally. 'And his cocky dealer mate.'

Mike looked at his phone. 'Nothing.'

They turned the corner.

The house was as described, a near perfect looking country cottage. White walls set in a black wooden timber frame, low eaves and dormer windows. There was even a climbing rose stretched over the porch that sheltered the front door. They pulled up on the opposite side of the road. Journey's end.

'Do we wait for Steve and Darren?'

'No. They might be five minutes away. They might have got lost and take an hour. Four of us should be enough. Remember what I said. Look mean. Say nothing more than necessary. We just want to get in and out as quickly as possible.' If Terry was as nervous as he seemed on the phone he would crumble. David led the way up the brick garden path to the front door and knocked loudly. Moments later he heard footsteps dragging on the hall carpet and the door was pulled open. Terry looked dreadful, unshaven, with eyes that looked like they hadn't seen sleep in days. It took Terry a moment to take in the figures lined up behind David and when he did he recoiled. 'You said you were coming alone.'

'I lied Terry. Of course I brought back up. Can we come in?' It wasn't a question.

Terry stepped back to allow the four of them to troop past him, his face a mask of fear and dejection.

'The sitting room's on the left, do you want to go in there.'

The room was low ceilinged with exposed beams and an open fireplace at the far end. heaped up with cold ash. The sofa and the armchairs looked comfy, if a little worn. Until a few weeks ago it must have felt like the perfect retirement bolthole. But the ceiling was so low Guy had to bend his head down uncomfortably so he sat down in one of the armchairs and the others, uncertain of what their next move was, followed suit. Only Terry and David remained standing.

'You want the tape,' Terry said.

'I want to know why Frampton killed Chris,' said Mike. 'Why the fuck did he do that?' David looked at Mike in frustration. This was not the plan. But there was nothing he could do now.

'He never meant to kill him,' said Terry. 'He was on... it was termed a counter-subversion deployment, in anticipation of a break down in law and order... They had limited intelligence. They told us they believed Chris was a central figure among left wing militants.'

'They?' David demanded. Not another bloody angle to this story.

'Frampton was working with someone else, obviously army but he never told us his name. So anyway they had kidnapped him. Completely outside their orders.' He looked helplessly at David as if hoping that David would put an end to his questioning, but David just looked on without pity.

343

Terry continued. 'So they had started questioning Chris.'

'You mean torturing,' said Mike.

'I wasn't there. All he told me afterwards was it was nothing they hadn't done in Northern Ireland. Stress positions, some... physicality, but nothing life threatening, that sort of thing, only he wasn't built for it and he had a heart attack.' Terry stopped as if hoping that was all he needed to say.

'So how did you and Eric get involved?' David asked. There was menace in his voice now. He could not help himself. He wanted answers too. Terry looked around, bewildered by the situation, a colleague, a former friend even, and three hostile strangers in the sanctuary of his living room and all offering no quarter.

'I was his MI5 contact for the operation. He rang me. Said he needed urgent help. He didn't spell it out but I had a good idea. So Eric and I were despatched...'

'By who?' David demanded.

'They're dead now. Howard Speakes if it makes any difference. David, everybody who was involved is dead or retired. Why couldn't you just leave it alone?' He looked imploringly at David. David just stared back. Terry wilted and carried on. 'So we drove up there to help sort things out. There wasn't much to do. Nothing they couldn't have done on their own really but I think they thought we were going to work some sort of magic. We wrapped the body, weighted it so there was no danger of it coming back up to the surface, punctured his stomach so the gases wouldn't get trapped in the body, then dumped it in a reservoir.'

'Which one?' Guy asked.

'Does it matter?' Terry asked almost in despair.

'It's his last resting place. It matters.'

'Fewston.'

344

'And the tape?' David asked.

'I didn't even know at the time, but Eric had rigged the van. It was only afterwards he told me about it. He thought it offered us some protection. He said that if they ever tried to hang us out to dry we could threaten to take him down with us. It seemed unlikely to me but... Eric was a suspicious character. You know what he was like.'

'What's on it?' David asked.

'Jesus, David. Why don't you just listen to it. It's out the back. Let me just hand it over and you can...' Terry seemed at the end of his tether. The pitch in his voice was rising, but David wanted the whole story and he knew now that if he pushed he would get it.

'What's on it.'

Wearily, Terry continued. 'On the drive to the reservoir Eric said we would need to make a full report when we got back. Frampton seemed to think it could all just be ... swept under the carpet. But Eric got him to tell the whole story. I think Eric must have made some cuts because it's only Frampton's voice you hear, but it's a really clear recording, for something done in a moving van, with the equipment we had in those days.'

'Eric was nothing if not professional,' said David. 'And did he tell you he was going to blackmail Lord Frampton?'

'Yes. He asked me if I wanted in. He had seen the reports of how much money he was making in Iraq. I didn't want anything to do with it. But then I didn't have Norma to worry about.'

'And did you know Lord Frampton paid him £20,000?'

'He told me. Not how much. Just that it had gone well. Then, two days after we all came up to London for your leaving do I got the tape, well a copy of it on a USB, in the post. That made me worried. Something must have made him think he needed a back-up copy somewhere. Then three days after that he was dead. Supposedly of a heart attack. There's nothing more I can tell you. Look. It's out the back. Cached in the barn wall. Come on, I'll show you. You can take it. Do whatever you want with it. Just…'

'Let's go and see,' said David. Everyone got to their feet and followed Terry through the kitchen to the back door. Terry was shaking like a leaf. Outside the gravel scrunched under their feet. After the lights inside they were now all pretty much blinded by the darkness, but in front of them the shape of the barn was clear enough against the night sky. It felt like there was going to be a frost. Just as David heard the last of the party close the kitchen door a security light flashed on. And there in front of them, conjured out of the darkness by this sudden brilliance, stood two jet black figures, each with a pistol clasped firmly in two hands, pointed forwards.

'Everybody down on the ground. Now.' The figure on the right shouted. The accent was unambiguously northern Irish.

Everyone froze. The light glinted on two pistols, shifting continually to cover every member of the party.

'Do as he says,' said David. The last thing he needed was people out of control.

'Face down. Now!' the same figure shouted,

Slowly, everyone got down, first on to their knees then reluctantly each stretching themselves out face down in the gravel. David's mind was racing. Who were these people?

'Terry,' said the one who seemed in charge. 'Which one's David?'

David could not see Terry's response, but he didn't need to.

'Right, put these cable ties round his wrist.'

'I'm not...' stammered Terry. David sensed the man was close to tears now.

'Do it. Now. Or you'll end up where he's going. Fuck's sake Terry. You said he was coming alone.'

That accent again. These people could only... Jesus... Frampton's contacts from the dirtier side of the Troubles. His bladder gave way. The warmth of his urine seeped down the inside of his thighs. Please God...

Mike's mobile rang. 'Leave it,' shouted the other figure. 'Don't move.'

Once the cable ties were on it would be game over. David just had to hope they would be sufficiently reluctant to shoot Terry to give him his chance. He would have to judge it just right. He looked over his shoulder to see how Terry was placed.

'Face down!'

'Terry,' David whispered. Terry leaned forward. His balance was that much less secure. 'David... there was nothing else...'

It was now or never. He grabbed Terry with his left arm and pulled him forwards. At the same time he rolled onto his front and pulled the pistol from his waistband. Thank God he'd slipped the safety as they had left the kitchen. Maybe, just maybe, his sixth sense had saved them. As Terry fell forwards David got two rounds off at the left-hand figure. At least one of them hit. But the other man was too quick for him. He sprang forward and kicked David savagely in the shoulder, and now stood over him, his left foot planted forcefully on David's right arm, preventing any further mishaps, his body braced for the final shots.

It was over. So much for bird watching David thought...

347

Four shots blasted out from the direction of the road. David picked up a pair of muzzle flashes out of the corner of his eye but what held his attention was the sight of the man who stood over him spinning round, jerking at least twice as rounds smashed through his upper body, then collapsing in a heap. The man's gun flew out into the shadows somewhere as he fell. The man himself continued to groan softly.

David turned to the two figures advancing from the gateway. Both clad in boots, black trousers and thick black jackets and still warily holding their guns out in front of them. The bulkier of the two he did not recognise. The other, more slender figure bringing up the rear was, without a shadow of a doubt, Nigel.

Slowly, everyone got to their feet. David could feel his trousers, warm and sticky with piss, clinging to his thighs. He wondered if the others could see.

'How the fuck did you get here?' He asked, wide eyed, his ears ringing from the noise of the shots.

'Magic,' said Nigel, in a voice still trembling with adrenalin.

It was amazing, thought David, that the man could be visibly shaken and at the same time unbearably smug.

'Don't give me that ... I'm not in the mood.'

The more distant of the two gunmen was trying to raise himself up. Nigel's companion fired two more rounds and the man collapsed. David winced. The ringing in his ears redoubled.

'Is there anyone else,' Nigel asked, still looking around him.

'No, that's it. As far as I know,' said David.

'Terry, is that it,' Nigel demanded.

'Yes, just the two of them.'

Nigel placed his gun in a holster on his belt. 'GCHQ picked up someone googling Terry's home address this morning. When they alerted us to that we got them to run through all the calls from this location. So we heard yours and came over.'

'Armed?'

'The ISP for the google search didn't seem to match up with where you were calling from. Your friend from IT security, Derek Stephens, said it didn't mean anything, but I wasn't going to take any chances. Just as well really.'

'But you didn't call for back up when you saw those people arrive?'

'They must have got here before us. We didn't have a clue they were here till just now. Not a bloody clue. Terry must have contacted Lord Frampton from somewhere else. And he sent these two goons.' He looked down briefly at the body by his feet. 'I've never shot anyone before.'

'Frampton sent these people?'

'Presumably. No one else is after you are they?'

Only then did it dawn of David. There ought to be more people. MI5 wouldn't send just two people out if there were firearms involved. He looked around. And Nigel read his mind.

'It's just me and ... Clive... David.'

At that moment they heard a car draw up outside. Nigel turned towards the noise and pulled his gun out from his holster again but at the sound of Steve's voice David motioned him to put his gun down. 'They're with us.' Nigel seemed only half convinced. He replaced the gun but kept his hand on the butt. The man whose name was almost certainly not Clive stood to one side, his pistol clasped in both hands but pointed downwards.

They heard two car doors slam and a few seconds later Steve emerged from the darkness of the road. He stared at the two figures facing him.

'Fucking hell David. You said "No guns."'

David shrugged, apologetically. Nigel and Clive relaxed.

'Can you check the bodies Clive,' said Nigel.

'The bodies?' said Steve. A spliff hung, forgotten, in his right hand, an elegant coil of smoke rising up and drifting, David couldn't help noticing, in the direction of Nigel. 'Jesus.' His gaze fixed on the two corpses, now both completely motionless.

Behind Steve a second figure emerged from the gloom. In his right hand was an open can of lager. 'Hi Mike.' Mike nodded in recognition.

'Those are bodies Darren,' said Steve. 'Shit. I'm glad we did those E's, I wouldn't want to be dealing with this shit straight.'

'Too right.' Darren too stared at the scene in disbelief, his eyes moving from Nigel's pistol to the inert figures Clive was now searching and back to Nigel. 'You want one Mike?' He pulled a small plastic bag out of his pocket and offered it to Mike.

'No thanks Darren. I don't do those.'

Darren looked again at the devastation laid out before him. 'This might be a good time to start mate.'

'I'm all right. I wouldn't mind a go on that spliff though son.'

Steve snapped out of his daze and passed the joint over. The look on his face suggested it was the first time in his life he had seen his father smoke a spliff.

'Mate?' said Darren offering the bag to David.

David shook his head. Darren looked Nigel up and down and put the bag back in his pocket.

'David,' said Nigel, 'do you know these people?'

'They were our back up.'

Nigel gave the pair a disbelieving look.

'If the SatNav hadn't fucked up,' said Darren, swaying slightly, 'we'd have been right on it.'

Clive pulled something from the pocket of one of the corpses and brought it over to Nigel. 'This looks like it,' he said.

'Yes. Thanks,' said Nigel quietly, then tucked the package away in his jacket.

'They're both dead,' Clive confirmed.

'Do you know what's on that memory stick, Nigel?' David asked.

'No David. And I wouldn't know even if you told me.'

'You don't care?'

David looked left and right. Darren and Steve were no good for anything. But nobody was going to shoot anyone and with Mike, Guy and Alan they had the numbers. He nodded to them encouragingly. Mike moved forward but Guy and Alan remained where they were.

'Nigel' he said with all the firmness he could command, 'that's what we came here for and…'

Clive stepped towards them. He said nothing, merely adjusted the grip on his gun. It was still pointed downwards but his stance made the message clear and in the stillness that followed David could feel, almost viscerally, the ebbing of his own power, the bile of his defeat rising up from his aching stomach. It was over.

Then Nigel indicated, by the merest inclination of his head, he wanted a word. David had to move close to Nigel to hear

351

his near whisper but even so the shadows cast by the security lights completely concealed Nigel's expression. It was as if his words came out of some very distant, unknowable place.

'David, I've got to sort this mess out now. So it would be very helpful if you... and your friends... could make yourselves scarce. And if you could discourage them from making a fuss about this... There will be no records. It will not be worth their while.'

The threat was no less real for being implied.

David stared down at the two bodies. Had all their efforts been for nothing more than this? He felt numb. Completely numb.

'And what about Manjit?'

'He will be fine.' Nigel's tone relaxed a little. 'Obviously he couldn't continue working with us but the way he almost succeeded in covering his tracks while ... working for you was impressive. We've emphasised that all this is covered by the Official Secrets Act and found him a job doing corporate security for an investment house. On something like double his current salary I believe. You could say you've done him a favour.'

'And the man who charged into Steve's place trying to kill me?'

'I don't think you'll see him again. I understand he's gone to Goa.'

David was still struggling to absorb what Nigel was telling him.

'David, don't think too harshly of me.' David looked back at the near blackness of Nigel's face. 'David, not everyone back in London is going to be overjoyed to hear that you survived tonight.'

A chill ran down David's spine. He made to speak but found he was lost for words. There was no point in asking how far the collusion went. Perhaps he really should be thanking Nigel for sticking his neck out and not allowing him to be murdered? Or maybe not. Clive had been in the lead. Perhaps, left to his own devices, Nigel would have waited till he was dead before intervening. Who knew? He realised Nigel was holding his hand out expectantly. He stared blankly at Nigel's face.

'The gun, David.'

He placed the weight of the pistol in Nigel's outstretched palm then turned away and walked back to the others.

'Darren, does your offer still stand?'

'What?'

'I'll have one of those pills if that's OK.'

'Sure,' said Darren matter-of-factly. 'They're normally a tenner, but under the circumstances...'

He pulled the plastic bag out of his pocket again and extracted a small orange tablet. 'You might want a swig of this,' he gestured with the can, 'to wash it down.'

'Thanks. David placed the pill in his mouth. It tasted so vile he twisted his tongue to avoid any contact. Then he raised the can, still moist from Darren's lips, to his mouth, took a swig of the sweet, frothy beer and swallowed.

He wondered where he was going.